About the Author

Stephen Bloy is a semi-retired, management, business and education consultant with a passion for English history, especially local history. Although originally a qualified engineer, he has a Doctorate degree in Education from the University of Lincoln and, an MBA degree from the University of Humberside. Since retiring he has found the time to indulge himself in what he now sees as his third career. Stephen has undertaken several history related projects and given many talks on the darker side of the social history of Grimsby, upon which the story is based.

Dedication

This story is dedicated to the memory of the many fishermen and fisher-lads of Victorian Grimsby, who gave up their lives as they harvested the bounty of the sea. Their undoubted courage, in the face of daily hardship, appalling conditions and brutality provided both the cause and inspiration to tell their story.

STEPHEN BLOY

HIDDEN TRUTH

A CIP catalogue record for this title is available from the British Library.

ISBN 978 184963 789 3

www.austinmacauley.com

First Published (2014)
Austin Macauley Publishers Ltd.
25 Canada Square
Canary Wharf
London
E14 5LB

Acknowledgments

I would like to thank my family and friends for their continuous support and encouragement as I researched and wrote this book, and especially all the strangers who shared with me the stories they knew or had been told.
I also offer very special thanks to my wonderful partner Sarah. Not only was she an invaluable audience and, sounding board as chapter by chapter the story progressed, her continued reassurance ensured that the book would be finished.

Contents

Part One

Chapter 1

A sombre and sad affair!

Unless it was absolutely necessary, it was not the weather for venturing outside. An icy north east wind, which chilled the body right through to the bone, thrust rapier-like throughout the streets. Bitterly cold driving rain and sleet beat heavily against the windows. The low rain clouds and the smoke from the chimneys of the houses created smog that swathed the town in a grey-brownish haze. Every now and then, the wind, which was raging harder than normal for November, would blow in violent gusts causing doors and windows to rattle, slates to come off the roof and chimney pots to come crashing to the ground. At times, the howling wind sounded like all the fiends of hell were trying to escape at once. It really was a foul day!

Safe and secure inside his home and appreciating the warmth of the fire burning in the grate sat Jacob Rawlings. The welcoming flames of the fire, flickering and dancing, made an ever changing kaleidoscope of shadows and patterns on the walls of the room. Not that he really noticed. Staring out of the window and deep in thought, he was remembering the many times, long ago, when the weather had been like this and far worse. In those days, Jacob and fishermen like him had no choice but to be outside in the gale-force winds and rain. That was how they made their living. As he dwelt on those thoughts, he could feel his tired old eyes misting over. Although it was almost sixty years to the day since, at the age of nearly thirteen, he left his home in Nottinghamshire and walked to Grimsby to become a fisherman and make his fortune, it seemed just like yesterday.

Many years may have passed but, Jacob's memories of the constant danger, hardship and cruelty that he and fellow fishermen had endured, and all the good friends who were lost at sea remain so vividly clear and still so raw. Equally clear, and no less raw in his memory, was why he had left his home and walked the fifty-five miles or so to Grimsby in the first place. Hardly a day went by when he didn't think of his beloved mother, who had encouraged him to make the journey.

On the rug at Jacob's feet sat, thirteen year old Daniel, his brother Gabriel, who was nearly eleven, and their nine year old sister, Grace. These were the only grandchildren Jacob had been blessed with. His only daughter, whom he had called Sarah-Eliza in memory of his mother and a favourite aunt, had lost her husband, Lieutenant Harold Enderby, during the Great War. In the thick of the fighting, Harold had gone over the top and along with many other brave Grimsby lads, had been killed. He was reported as missing in action - his remains were never found. Their daughter Grace had been born just a month earlier, but Harold never knew that, he was in the battlefields of Northern France serving King and country and died before Sarah-Eliza's letter reached him... She never married again!

All warm and snug by the fireside, the children sat quietly, eagerly waiting to be entranced with another story about Jacob's life. Even though they suspected that most of the stories he told them were made up, rather than what really happened, they still liked to hear them. Jacob was a master story teller. For his grandchildren's entertainment, he did sometimes make a story up. But, more often than not, his stories were based on actual facts, which he embellished or exaggerated a little. Jacob could certainly spin a yarn or two.

Over many a pint of ale, Jacob had often kept an audience entertained in the *Lord Raglan* or *Dogger Bank* pubs, which were just two of the favourite ale-houses for fisherman, being situated as they were close by the docks. In the bars, dimly lit by gas lights and the air thick with the sweet smell of burning tobacco from many pipes, he and other fishermen relived their lives and shared their experiences. You could never be sure whether the stories were fact, well developed fantasies, or just a bunch of old fishermen trying to out-do each other with their story telling. Many an argument and even fights had started because of this need to be more dramatic than the last with the story they told.

The flames and glow from the fire lit up the children's expectant faces as they looked up at this kindly old man with his white hair, mutton chop sideburns and luxurious moustache. Jacob sat quite still, not drawing from the pipe he held in his gnarled old hands. Hoping for a reaction from his grandad, Daniel, never the most patient child, glanced at the others and dramatically sighed. Finally he could wait no longer.

'...Grandad, are you all right?' he asked with some concern.

Not a flicker of emotion or even a recognition of Daniel's question crossed Jacob's weathered face as he continued to stare into the distance. For the moment, he was lost in a world of his own.

'Granddad, is something the matter?' Daniel was now becoming exasperated and more than a little miffed. Finally, in a raised petulant voice he exclaimed, 'Grandad!'

Jacob continued to stare out of the window before turning to face Daniel.

'Eh... oh yes, sorry, where was I?' said Jacob as he smiled at his grandchildren.

'...Do you want me to tell you another story of my life at sea as a fisherman?' Jacob asked mischievously.

He knew full well that's what they wanted to hear, even though they had heard most of them before. Jacob loved his grand-children and liked to play his little games and tease them.

'Yes... yes we do!' the children replied, almost in unison.

Grace, who had also become impatient, emphasised her answer by sticking out her lower lip and gesturing with her arms folded across her chest as young children often do.

Still he hesitated. With good reason, Jacob had decided that when he told them a story this time, it was going to be different. It was not going to be a fanciful, larger-than-life, tale of adventures and escapades. He intended to tell them the true story of his life, the real reason why he left his home and, without exaggeration, the peril and dangers of life on the sea. Although, there were parts of his story that were not suitable for children's ears, the truth had to be told. Everything, well nearly everything, would be the complete truth. He knew he would not get many more chances to do so, but where to start, he thought.

'...Well, let me see now, where shall I begin?' said Jacob drawing on his pipe before continuing. This was a habit he had when telling a story. It gave him time to think of what he was going to say next.

Jacob was a country boy from the Nottinghamshire village of Calthorpe, which was situated close to Newark on the main road to Lincoln. He was born in 1852, the first child of William Rawlings and his wife Sarah, who had married in the parish church of St Joseph's the previous year. William and Sarah had married young. He was not quite twenty years old and she was just eighteen.

Sarah was the youngest of five daughters born to Nathaniel Palmer, a carpenter and wheelwright, and his wife Judith. She was a likeable, stunningly attractive, slender built woman with almost black hair and deep-set brown eyes, which men found alluring and captivating. Many of the boys in the neighbourhood had their eye on her and, would gladly take her as their wife, given half a chance. When she was growing up, being the youngest, Sarah was spoiled by her parents and her older sisters.

William, the third son of an agricultural labourer, was a handsome, hard-working, strapping young man with a quiet temperate disposition and popular within the village. Sarah and William had met and danced together at the previous year's harvest festival, when nearly everyone in the village turned out for a day of celebrations. They were instantly attracted and enjoyed each other's company. Before too long they had fallen in love.

In William, Sarah knew she had found the man she wanted to spend her life with. So much so that, just a few months after they met, with her encouragement, William rather nervously asked Sarah's father for permission to marry her. Dressed in his Sunday best, he went to see Nathaniel, who played the role of a stern father to perfection. Standing there, with his arms behind him and his back to the fireplace and adopting a comically larger-than-life intimidating pose, he stared hard at William.

'…and what can I do for you, Master Rawlings?'

William hesitated.

'C'mon now boy… spit it out,' Nathaniel said with mock severity.

'Erm… I… I would like your permission to marry Sarah, Sir,' William timidly asked in a quiet voice.

'Speak up lad… can't hear ya,' Nathaniel said holding his hand to his ear as though he were deaf. '…you want to do what with Sarah!'

'I… I would like to marry her, Sir,' William said, only louder this time.

'Marry her indeed…do you love her…can you support her?' Nathaniel asked.

William was becoming even more nervous. He could feel the beads of sweat forming on his forehead.

'Yes Sir… I do love her… and I can support her,' he replied.

'Harrumph… Eh… erm… well let me see now… I'm not sure,' Nathaniel muttered

'Papa, don't be such a tease!' said Sarah, who was stood behind William and was starting to giggle.

Nathaniel looked at Sarah then back at William. His face broke into the broadest grin.

'Of course you can marry her… but, William, you must look after her, she's my baby,' he said as he stepped forward to warmly shake William's hand.

'Yes Sir, I will… thank you,' William said before turning to hug Sarah, who had started to gently weep tears of happiness.

'Thank you papa,' Sarah said, letting go of William and hugging her father.

They married a month later. It was a very happy wedding. Many of their neighbours joined in the joyous occasion, toasting William and Sarah's happiness and wishing them good fortune. The drinking and dancing continued long after the sun had gone down. Several of the village's young men were envious of William and, didn't hesitate to let their feelings be known.

'You're a lucky old bugger,' William was good naturedly told more than once, causing him to smile. He knew that he was.

As the day wore on, with the copious amounts of beer being drunk, everyone was having a good time. The revelries and feasting became louder, the dancing more wild and abandoned and the jokes and banter, more earthy and bawdy. One or two of William's friends, letting the drink do their talking, pushed their luck a little with coarse and vulgar observations of how lucky William was and, how lucky he would be that night. Some of his friends even questioned whether he was man enough for Sarah and, offered to do the honours for him, if he was not.

'Best not have too much of that ale young Will, or I'll have to come and help you out later,' one of the local lads said.

'That won't be necessary… but thanks for the offer… besides, you can hardly stand up yourself,' William replied with a laugh.

This was not a day for taking offence. William took all the remarks in good spirit. He certainly felt lucky as he gazed across and watched beautiful Sarah dancing and laughing with his friends.

…After their wedding, William and Sarah lived in a small, two bed-roomed cottage, which they rented from one of the local farmers. The single story stone building, with its slate tiled roof and blue door, was situated alongside the turnpike on the northern outskirts of the village. Though small, it was perfect for them. At the front was a neat flower garden surrounded by a low stone wall and a picket gate. The garden at the side of the cottage and round towards the back, being south facing and with good soil was ideal for creating a vegetable garden. Further round the back, was a stone enclosure, which would be perfect for keeping pigs, they thought. William and Sarah were so excited and happy the day that they moved into the cottage. Eleven months after they had married, Jacob was born there…

…Calthorpe was a 'forest village' in the Sherwood region of Nottinghamshire. Many of the village's one hundred or so houses and cottages were situated on either side of the main Newark to Lincoln turnpike. Some of the finer houses of the village sat round the edge of the village green. Also, on the edge of the green, stood the butcher's shop, two general stores and the pub, now quaintly named the *Dog and Duck*. It had formerly been a coaching inn called the *White Hart*. With the expansion of the railways, fewer and fewer horse drawn carriages stopped there when Jacob was growing up in the village.

It was a pleasant friendly area to live in. Growing up there, you would know, or at least know of, nearly everyone in the village. There were no strangers. The majority of the four hundred and eighty people who lived in the village and surrounding area, made their living from cottage industries such as crafts, textiles and weaving at home. A small number, like William, still earned their living on the land as agricultural labourers.

Unless you were tied to a farm, which William was, agricultural labouring work was becoming increasingly harder to find. Much of this work had started to be done by horse and steam driven mechanised farm machines. Machines, such as the accursed 'threshing machine', designed for rapidly removing the husks from grain, were such an advance that soon most of the farms had them. Unfortunately, farm labourers didn't always have the knowledge of the hazards of these machines and did not adopt the necessary vigilance.

In the summer months, farm labourers were served beer, the only safe cool drink available. To provide for their workmen, some farms even had their own brewery. At the height of summer, it was not uncommon for each labourer to consume as much as six pints in a day whilst they worked in the fields in the hot weather. Machinery and ale - it was a potentially deadly combination.

William and Sarah loved each other deeply. Their life together was very happy and contented until a tragic event that changed Sarah and baby Jacob's lives forever. On that dreadful and disastrous day, William, as he did every morning when he left the cottage, tenderly kissed Sarah and Jacob goodbye.

'Good bye dearest… I'll see you later… it looks like it's going to be a fine day,' William said.

He gently put his hand on Sarah's stomach and smiled at her. Soon there would be another mouth to feed. Holding his lunch of pork pie and a cheese sandwich wrapped in a piece of mutton cloth and, with a bottle of cold milky tea, William, kissed Sarah again and set off to work. With Jacob beside her, she stood by the door of their tiny cottage, watching as her man shut the gate and walked off down the dusty road.

'Wave to daddy Jacob,' said Sarah, as she bent down and lifted his little arm to encourage him to wave.

'Dada… dada,' Jacob called out as he waved at his father.

'William!' Sarah shouted excitedly, '…William, Jacob's waving.'

William stopped and turned round to look back. He smiled, waved and set off again. Sarah's face was a picture of contentment as she watched William's back disappearing down the road.

'Jacob, I'm going to make daddy something special for his dinner!' she said, not expecting that he would answer. Holding Jacob's hand and merrily humming and singing, she skipped back into the cottage.

In her worse nightmare, Sarah could not begin to imagine that her perfect world of tender love and happiness would collapse just a few hours later. Never again would she and William hold each other in their arms. They had spoken their last words to each other and spent their last night together.

It was early in the afternoon on what was turning out to be a lovely warm summer day. The weather had been unsettled for a few days, so the warm sunshine was welcomed. The sky was blue, skylarks were singing, chickens were scurrying about in the yard and Betsy their sow, who had recently given birth to seven piglets, could be heard noisily grunting and snuffling about in her sty. Jacob was quite content playing with a stick in the dirt. Close by, their scruffy mongrel dog, whom William had taken in as a stray and, inappropriately called Hector after a hero he had learned about at school, lazily lifted his head, looked around, yawned and promptly went back to sleep in the sun.

Taking advantage of the clear skies, Sarah was hanging out the washing when she spotted two men pushing a handcart and walking hurriedly up the road towards the cottage. As the cart drew closer, she recognised Tom Kite and Richard Middleton, two labourers, from the farm where William was currently working. Tom Kite had known her since she was a baby. He was an old friend of her father, Nathaniel, and also her god-father. He'd watched Sarah grow up and was one of the main guests at her wedding.

From the distance, Sarah couldn't make out what was on the cart. She couldn't see that it was William, who had been gravely injured by a threshing machine. Suffering from appalling multiple injuries, beyond all help and covered in blood, William had been carried home on the cart by his two workmates. Sarah put her washing down into a basket and started to walk towards them as they approached the cottage gate.

'Hello Tom,' Sarah said cheerily.

She nodded to Richard, whom she only knew by sight.

'What are you two up to… why aren't you at the farm?' she asked.

Tom and Richard stopped the cart several paces away from Sarah so she couldn't see what was in it. Not a word was spoken. Noticing their grim, ashen and drawn faces, Sarah suddenly felt cold even though it was sunny. She sensed something was wrong. Her cheeriness quickly vanished to be replaced by one of dread, causing her to shiver a little.

Sarah walked towards them and the cart.

'What's the matter Tom?' she asked anxiously.

Neither Tom, nor Richard replied. Raising her voice and with more emphasis Sarah again asked,

'Tom… what's happened?'

Still Tom didn't reply. He kept his head down, purposely avoiding looking directly at Sarah.

'Tom, what's going on… tell me... what has happened.'

Her voice was now becoming desperate and starting to break with emotion. Tom shuffled about uncomfortably and Richard looked down at his feet. Neither of them wanted to look at Sarah. Heaving a big sigh, Tom slowly raised his head, cleared his throat and without making eye contact, looked at her and then hesitantly spoke.

'Uh… I'm… I'm so sorry Sarah.'

'Sorry, what do you mean you are so sorry…I don't understand?' Sarah replied fearfully, walking ever closer to the cart.

'There's… there's been a serious accident… erm… William's been badly hurt,' Tom mumbled, still unable to look Sarah in the eye, as she drew ever closer.

'What do you mean accident, Tom… what are you talking about?'

Tom could feel his throat tightening up.

'Uh… William,' he said quietly, whilst again trying to clear his throat.

'…William was on his own feeding some corn into the threshing machine. He slipped and stepped on to the revolving drum…he was immediately drawn in by his leg.'

'Oh dear god no.' Sarah screamed as she dashed forward and saw William's unconscious, bloody and broken body stretched out on the cart. The full extent of William's injuries couldn't be seen as the lower part of his body was covered with an old blanket. What could be seen was distressing enough.

Sarah screamed, 'Oh God no, no, no!'

Shaking her head from side to side she began sobbing uncontrollably.

'He… he's going to be alright isn't he Tom?'

'He's not going to die is he… tell me he's going to be alright,' she implored. Sarah looked first at Tom and then Richard, seeking a reassurance that wasn't going to be given.

'Sarah… William has been badly hurt,' Tom replied.

Again, Tom hesitated before continuing,

'…Part of William's left leg was torn away and smashed to a pulp before anyone could stop the machine and get him out.' As he said it, Tom, instantly regretted being so graphic.

Sarah by now, wasn't really listening, she stared in horror at William in the cart, her arms wrapped tightly across her chest. Her breathing was becoming more rapid and shallow.

'We've stopped the bleeding with a tourniquet as best we could and sent for the doctor,' said Richard.

Sarah's knees buckled as she instantly went into a faint and would have fallen heavily to the floor had it not been for Richard's quick reactions who managed to catch her.

'We need to give her some air,' said Tom, as he loosened the clothing around her neck.

With Richard supporting her, Tom sat Sarah down on a log pile that was nearby in the yard and mopped her brow with cold water from the pump until she fully regained consciousness. Sarah roused, saw the cart with its distressing load and immediately became hysterical repeatedly calling out William's name. She would have fallen to the ground again had Tom not wrapped his arms around her trying to offer some comfort.

'My god what can we do,' asked Sarah. 'Was he drunk?'

'…Why don't you do something?' she shrieked.

The questions came tumbling out. She was beside herself and distraught with grief.

'Do something Tom, do something.' She begged.

'I'm… erm… I'm afraid there's nothing much we can do Sarah,' Tom replied.

'William's life is in the hands of the Lord now.'

Tom knew that William was dying. Still holding Sarah tightly, his shirt now wet with her tears, Tom spoke softly,

'Sarah, we've to get William inside. The doctor is on his way and should be here soon.'

Sarah didn't respond. No one moved.

'Sarah, we've to get William into the cottage,' Tom said again.

Sarah glanced up and nodded. Still sobbing, she let go of Tom and moved slightly away from the cart. Very gently, Tom and Richard removed the old blanket and lifted William to carry him through the gate and into the cottage.

'Oh dear Lord,' Sarah exclaimed with a sharp intake of breath, bringing her hand to her mouth, when she saw William's terrible injuries. '...Oh dear lord no!'

She swayed unsteadily on her feet and would have fainted again had it not been for Jacob, who had been completely forgotten about. When Jacob saw the blood soaked body of his father, being carried past him, even though he was too young to understand what had happened, he became frightened by what he saw. He burst into tears and started to wail as he toddled towards Sarah holding out his little arms.

'Mama...mama.'

Hearing Jacob's distress, Sarah's own grief was momentarily forgotten, the mothering instinct in her took over. She stopped sobbing and swept Jacob up into her arms and, pulling him closely into her chest, gently rocked him.

'Hush... Hush,' Sarah whispered in Jacob's ear.

Jacob's crying soon became a whimper before stopping altogether. So that he couldn't see how badly his father was hurt, Sarah took Jacob to one side and out of the way. Tom and Richard carried William into the cottage and laid him on the cast iron and brass bedstead.

Although the doctor arrived shortly afterwards and did the best that he could, Sarah soon realised there was no hope. William's injuries were so grave and he had lost so much blood, it could only be a matter of time. He clung on to life until the next morning, when he passed away without regaining consciousness. It was barely a month after his twenty-third birthday. Sarah, who had held his hand all night praying for him to open his eyes, at twenty-one years old and nearly eight months pregnant, became a widow. Jacob was not quite two years old...

...William's funeral took place, at St Joseph's church two days after the accident. Nearly everyone in the village, many of whom had been at the wedding just three years before, made their way to the church to pay their respects. Farmer McBride, whose farm William was working on when the accident happened, attended along with his wife. So large was the congregation, several had to stand outside the little church. William had been a popular young man and the horrendous nature of the accident had shocked everyone.

With her father, Nathaniel, and Tom Kite supporting her and, refusing to let her legs buckle and let her down, Sarah, heavily pregnant, slowly walked behind William's coffin into the church. William's three brothers and a close friend were the pall bearers. Sarah's sisters and William's elderly father and mother sat in grim faced silence in the front pews. Jacob had been left in the care of a neighbour. As she tearfully made her way up the aisle, oblivious to all around her, each step more difficult to take than the last one, all eyes were on Sarah.

Nearly everyone was feeling her grief and suffering. Several women wiped tears away with their handkerchiefs. Others just wrung their hands in anguish. Many men stood with their head respectfully bowed. Sarah's sisters had placed flowers around where the coffin would stand but, because of William's age and the tragic circumstances of his death, it was still a very sombre and desperately sad affair.

Amongst all the grief, sorrow and sadness, despite the fact this was a funeral, Sarah was already being watched and looked upon with covetous eyes by some of the young men and, not so young men, from the village. Even though nothing was being said between them, it was clear that many were thinking what would Sarah do now she was all alone? First among them was Thaddeus Stone, a powerful heavy set man who stood over six feet tall, and worked in a slaughter house in nearby Norton-by-Spital. Although, he was considered to be ruggedly handsome, there was an air of menace about Thaddeus Stone.

Despite being fourteen years Sarah's senior, in an oafish manner, typical of bullies used to getting their own way, he had made his interest in her clear to other drunken men at her wedding. He wasn't an invited guest, but had chosen to join in with the drinking and dancing anyway. Full of drink and grotesquely grabbing his crutch, his vulgar and lewd drunken comments went far beyond good natured banter. Thaddeus had been careful though not to let William or Sarah see his gestures, or hear his comments. As big a man as he was, William would not have taken this behaviour lightly. Even among so called friends, there is a line that should not be crossed.

During the three years since William and Sarah had married, Thaddeus occasionally walked past the cottage, hoping to catch sight of Sarah and draw her into conversation if she was working in her gardens. He would stop and talk to her whenever they met in the street. In her innocence and naivety, Sarah, thought he was only being friendly and the frequent meetings coincidental. She had no idea of the dark, brooding and lecherous thoughts that were hidden behind Thaddeus's outwardly affable manner, as he secretively watched and monitored her every move…

…Sobbing throughout and constantly staring at William's coffin, for Sarah the funeral service passed in a haze; she had no recollection of the sermon, what hymns were sung, or the words of comfort spoken in the eulogies offered by some of William's friends. When the coffin was lifted, to be carried outside for the burial, Sarah had to be prompted unsteadily to her feet by her father. With hers and William's family around, helping her to walk, ready to catch her if she stumbled, Sarah hesitantly followed the coffin from the church to the graveside.

'…Forasmuch as it hath pleased almighty God of his great mercy to take unto himself the soul of our dear brother William here departed…' the priest intoned in a voice totally devoid of emotion.

Wretchedly tearful and moaning softly to herself, Sarah watched as the coffin was slowly lowered into the ground.

'…We therefore commit his body to the ground; earth to earth, ashes to ashes, dust to dust…'

Throwing soil on to the coffin, the priest gestured to Sarah to do the same. As Sarah bent forward to pick up some soil to throw, with an ear piercing scream she suddenly fell to her knees, her face contorted in pain. The priest stopped his prayer.

Clutching her stomach, bewildered, frightened and clearly in discomfort she cried out,

'Aagh... the baby is coming... I think it's started, the baby is coming.'

Sarah was deeply distressed. Shocked and alarmed, her father and sisters rushed forward to help. As they gathered and fussed around her, Nathaniel knew they had to act quickly before her waters broke.

'Be careful,' Nathaniel said to nobody in particular. '...We've got to get her home.'

'Sarah... we've got to get you home.' He said softly as he knelt beside her.

'Give a hand Tom... we'll take her to my house, it's nearer than Sarah's cottage.'

As gently as they could, they raised Sarah to her feet. Nathaniel then lifted her completely. With Tom's help he quickly carried his daughter the two hundred yards or so to his house. Sarah's sisters hitched their long skirts up and followed hurriedly behind.

Surprised by this turn of events, one by one the mourners started to slowly move away from the graveside, throwing soil onto the coffin as they passed. The women chattered excitedly to each other about the impending birth. Some of the mourners made their way towards the *Dog and Duck*. Although there would be no organised wake, several of William's friends still wanted to raise a glass to his memory.

Standing in the cemetery alone and apart from the other mourners, Thaddeus Stone watched as the drama unfolded and the mourners departed. Even as the earth was being shovelled onto William's coffin, a cruel smile crossed his face. 'Once she's dropped that chit, we'll see what's to do...,' he crudely thought to himself. Already Thaddeus had made up his mind that Sarah, beautiful Sarah, was going to be his. This would be his chance...

...Just nine hours after William's coffin had been lowered into the ground, at eight o'clock in the evening, Sarah, with her sisters around her acting as the midwives, was delivered of a baby boy whom she called Joshua. It was a bitter sweet moment. As she lay there exhausted, the baby was placed on her breast and with a little coaxing, started to suckle. In this moment of tenderness, Sarah's thoughts turned to her beloved William. She started to cry.

'What's going to become of us papa?' she asked Nathaniel.

'…How am I going to manage?'

Nathaniel was a caring and loving father, but a widower himself. He had lost his beloved wife, Judith, to pneumonia when Sarah was only twelve years old. Although he was troubled about her future and welfare, he didn't show it. He knew it wasn't going to be easy for Sarah, a young widow with two children. And, as he was getting older and, had recently started to feel unwell, there was only so much he would be able to do for her.

'You'll be fine Sarah… you'll be fine,' he said reassuringly as he gently held her hand. '…We'll all help to look after you and your boys.'

Too weak to return to her cottage, Nathaniel decided that Sarah, Jacob and baby Joshua would stay with him while she regained her strength. He, and her sister, Eliza, who was two years old than Sarah, unmarried and still lived at home, could provide all the care she needed. Sarah's three other sisters, though married themselves all lived nearby and, would be on hand to help if necessary. With their love and attention, each day Sarah should grow a little stronger.

Baby Joshua, even though a month premature, at first seemed to be doing well until, without explanation, he suddenly stopped suckling on Sarah. No matter how much she tried, Joshua refused to take her breast. The Doctor was sent for but, he had no answers that Sarah wanted to hear. In desperation, thinking there may be something not quite right with her breast milk, Sarah's sisters found a local 'wet-nurse', who tried for two days to feed Joshua. She was unsuccessful. Late in the afternoon on the eighth day after he was born, Joshua died.

Totally exhausted, Sarah had dropped off to sleep with Joshua beside her in the crib, which Nathaniel had made many years before for his own children. When she woke, Joshua was dead. Life had again dealt her a particularly punishing blow... She was distraught with grief.

News of Joshua's death soon spread around the village. Although it was not uncommon in those days for babies to die in the early days of their life, Joshua's death coming so soon after William's made for a very tragic affair. Sarah found it hard to come to terms with her wretched misfortune. In the space of only ten days, her life had changed forever. Love and happiness had been replaced with extreme sadness and despair from which she thought she would never ever recover.

Though still weak and in poor health from giving birth, Sarah insisted on going to the private family funeral at St Josephs. Only the immediate family were there when Joshua, with the minimum of fuss, was buried in the same grave as his father...

'...so you see children,' Jacob said to his young audience. '...both, my father and my brother, died within a few days of each other when I was little more than a baby myself.'

'...I was only two years old.'

The two boys and Grace had been stunned into silence. They looked at each other in wide eyed amazement. This was very different. Grandad had never told this story before. Unsure what to think and trying hard to understand, Gabriel asked with the purity of innocence all young children possess.

'Were you sad Grandad... is that why you ran away from home and became a fisherman?'

'Don't be so daft Gabriel,' Daniel said smugly whilst, tut-tutting away to himself.

'...What a stupid question,' he said, before digging Gabriel in the arm causing him to yelp.

Jacob frowned at Daniel.

'Erm... well not quite,' replied Jacob smiling warmly at Gabriel.

'...You see Gabriel, I was too young to be sad... many, many other very bad things happened long before I ran away to become a fisherman.'

Jacob paused. He put his pipe in his mouth and looked out the window for a few moments. He was thinking how best to continue with the story…

Chapter 2

Thaddeus Stone Seizes His Chance

Even though the rain had stopped, the windows still occasionally rattled from the gusts of the bitterly cold wind, which was still blowing quite strongly. Jacob had been talking to his grand-children for a couple of hours. Neither he, nor the children, had noticed how quickly the time had passed. It was getting dark outside and would soon be night time. Sarah-Eliza was busy in the kitchen preparing dinner. She could see her children sat listening intently to her father, but couldn't hear what he was saying. They were all staying with her father that weekend, so Jacob had plenty of time to tell the story he wanted them to hear. 'I wonder what fanciful nonsense he's filling their heads with this time.' Sarah-Eliza thought smiling to herself.

'...I was not much older than you children are now when I left my home and family... I was little more than a boy... About as old as you are now Daniel,' said Jacob.

'It wasn't really my choice but, there were no other options.'

'Why, what happened, Grandad?' asked Daniel.

'Tell us what happened.' Gabriel said just as eagerly.

Grace stared at her grandad expectantly.

Jacob looked down at their impatient young faces. Having decided to tell them the whole true story of his life, he was not going to be rushed. He had to think carefully about what he was going to say, and how he was going to tell it.

'Patience children, patience', Jacob said.

Again he drew heavily on his pipe before tapping it on the sole of his boot to remove the tobacco ashes.

'In 1865, something very nasty happened which changed my life for ever and determined the journey I would have to take,' said Jacob.

'…but, for you to understand this and why I had to leave my home, I need to tell you more about your wonderful great-grandmother Sarah and what happened to her, after your great-grandfather William died in 1854…'

'…Sarah stayed with her father and her sister for more than two months. Initially, the shock and stress of William's accident, the funeral and Joshua's birth and death was all too much for her. In the deepest pit of despair from her shattering grief, Sarah took to her bed. Even though she needed care, for many days at a time Sarah did not want people, including her family, around her any more than was necessary. Eating very little and only picking at it when she did, Sarah wanted to be left alone with her thoughts and allowed to mourn her losses in her own way…

She spent hours with the door of her room closed and sometimes locked. Her crying and sobbing clearly heard through the thin walls of the house. Occasionally she would get out of bed, the creaking floorboards testimony to her pacing around the room in the dark hours of the night…'

Jacob, who was confused at first with all that had happened, was looked after by Eliza. He saw very little of his mother in those first few weeks. Eliza compensated for Sarah's absence and lack of concern for Jacob as best she was able. She played with Jacob, fed him, hugged him and sang lullabies to him when she laid him down at night. He was certainly much loved, so no real harm was being done.

'As much as Nathaniel respected his daughters' wishes, her frailty and not eating alarmed him. She was wasting away! And, she was still recovering from giving birth to Joshua. He could not allow this to continue. He, Eliza and her other sisters decided she had had enough time to grieve alone. Sarah needed to be reminded that she still had her whole life in front of her. After all, she was only twenty-one years old and was a mother with a child, who needed her. Nathaniel would have to speak to her…

Nathaniel walked slowly up the stairs to Sarah's room. He wasn't looking forward to this. He didn't want to upset her, but it needed to be done. Eliza followed a few paces behind. Standing on the landing, outside her room, he could hear crying. Nathaniel knocked gently on the door and softly called out her name,

'...Sarah!'

After a moment's pause, he knocked lightly again.

'Sarah, its papa... Can I come in and talk to you?'

Still Sarah didn't answer.

Raising his voice a little, 'You can't keep locking yourself away like this Sarah... Open the door and talk to me.'

'Jacob needs you... We need you,' he said earnestly.

After a few moments, Nathaniel could hear Sarah stirring and shuffling slowly across the room. She opened the door. Her forlorn appearance shocked Nathaniel. The tracks of her tears were clearly evident on her cheeks. Her face was all puffy, the dark eyes, which so many found alluring, were swollen and bloodshot. Her arms and hands hung limply by her sides. Sarah looked like hell.

'Oh... come here my precious,' Nathaniel said, holding out his arms to her, his face the epitome of fatherly concern. Sarah took a tentative step forward and then collapsed sobbing pitifully into her father's arms.

'Oh papa,' she sobbed. 'Papa, what am I going to do without him...I loved him so much,' she cried, her voice breaking with despair.

'...How... oh-oh-oh,' Sarah, struggled to speak through her sobs. '...how will I live without him, papa?'

'It will get easier Sarah... it will get easier,' said Nathaniel as he gently, but firmly held her.

'Sarah... I lost your mama when you were only twelve years old... Like you with William, I loved her so much that I thought my world had ended and, for a time it had... but, I still had you and your sisters to look after.'

'...I had to cope, there was no other way.'

As he spoke those words, Nathaniel could picture his lovely wife Judith, and thought how cruel life could be. She

32

was only thirty-nine years old when God took her, just eight years before. Not a day went by when he didn't think of her. Remembering his deep love for Judith and, seeing his daughter looking so pitiful, he felt the tears well up in his eyes.

'Oh papa, help me,' Sarah pleaded.

Nathaniel pulled Sarah closer to him so she couldn't see his distress. This was not a time for Sarah to pity him, or for him to say anymore. He just held her tightly, gently stroking her back as she sobbed and sobbed and sobbed.

Eliza, who was standing just a few feet away in the corridor watched with a screwed up handkerchief in her hands, which she dabbed lightly at her eyes. She had been moved to tears at the words and tenderness of her papa and, the sight of her sister's sadness at the loss of her much loved husband. Eliza had not yet found love and could only imagine how heart breaking it must be to lose someone you love more than life itself.

This great outpouring of grief was the turning point in Sarah coming to terms with William and Joshua's deaths. She was almost cried out. Eventually, her sobbing eased. Nathaniel tenderly suggested that she might like to come downstairs, see Jacob and perhaps have something to eat. Without speaking, Sarah looked up at her papa and nodded her agreement. Slowly and gradually Nathaniel loosened his hold and let her go. At which point, Eliza took over. Taking Sarah by the arm she led her back into the bedroom.

'Jacob wouldn't like to see you looking like this Sarah, would he,' she said. '…Let's see if we can tidy you up a bit.'

Ever so softly, 'No, he wouldn't,' Sarah replied, trying to smile.

Struggling to contain his tears, Nathaniel walked back down the stairs. He now felt sure that Sarah was going to be alright. That evening, for the first time in nearly three weeks, Sarah sat at the kitchen table with Jacob, Nathaniel and Eliza. She drank some soup and nibbled at a small piece of fruit cake, which Eliza had made that morning. As little as it was, at least she was eating something. Sarah was going to be fine.

Little by little, with Eliza and her other sisters fussing around her and making her eat, Sarah started to regain her strength. In the days that followed, several of the women in the village stopped by, and brought Sarah their secret home recipe drinks and soups, which they all guaranteed would soon have her back on her feet. Thanking them for their concern and gifts, Eliza and her sisters would often burst into fits of the giggles immediately when the door had been shut after each woman had left.

'I wonder what the secret ingredient is in this one.' One of the sisters would ask.

'Fillet of fenny snake, in the cauldron boil and bake; Eye of newt and toe of frog, Wool of bat and tongue of dog, Adders fork and blind-worms sting...' Eliza replied, cackling like a witch from Macbeth. Reducing them all, including Sarah, to fall about in fits of laughter.

Sarah took an interest in Jacob again and slowly her life returned to normal. Often, she would sit and think about William and the life they had. It was difficult at first to do so without crying. But, as the days and weeks went by, she became more able. Sarah found herself wanting to talk to her family about William and the things that he did, which made her love him so much. She even started to laugh once more at some of his antics. Like the time when old Betsy, their sow, knocked him over in the pig sty and the image of William walking back into the cottage covered in pig shite...

When Sarah ventured out and took Jacob for short walks in the village, she started to face people again. At first, it was uncomfortable, when friends and acquaintances stopped her to offer their condolences, as she knew it would be. She just smiled and thanked them for their kindness. Each day, Sarah's ability to cope grew stronger. Before too long she was able to go into the village shops without feeling apprehensive or embarrassed. She started to help with the housekeeping and the cooking and, though still mourning for William and Joshua, became a much cheerier person...

A little over eight weeks after Joshua died Sarah decided it was time for her to return to the cottage. She couldn't put it off any longer. Her life couldn't move forward until she confronted any bad memories or demons that being alone at the cottage may present her with. That evening, over dinner, she told Nathaniel and Eliza of her decision.

'Sarah... are you sure you're ready to go?' Nathaniel asked.

His manner expressed both his surprise and unease. Nathaniel had known all along that, sooner or later this moment would come, but he had hoped it would be later rather than sooner.

'You don't have to go, you can stay here for as long as you like,' he said.

'...What's the rush?'

'Yes!' said Eliza, 'Do stay here with us... Please do, Sarah.'

Eliza liked having Sarah at home, especially as she was able to look after and play with Jacob. She had begun to doubt whether she would ever have children of her own. Being Aunt Eliza may be her role in life.

'I've been thinking about this for a few days,' Sarah replied.

'Thank you Papa. Thank you Eliza but my mind is made up...I have to go home and find my own way to provide for myself and Jacob.'

Sarah reached across the table and held both her sister's and her father's hands.

'I need both of you to understand why I have to do this now.'

Although they discussed the matter for some time, Sarah would not be swayed from her decision. Eliza even offered to come and stay with her at the cottage.

'No Eliza,' Sarah said softly but firmly. 'Thank you; this is something I have to do on my own.'

Gently squeezing Eliza's hand, Sarah added,

'You can come to see Jacob and me whenever you like, but I have to learn how to manage.'

Eliza looked at Sarah and then at Nathaniel, her eyes pleading with her papa to persuade Sarah to stay a little longer.

Nathaniel shook his head. He knew that Sarah wouldn't be dissuaded once her mind was made up. She was so headstrong, just like her mother. Sarah knew that he knew…'

'While she had been staying at her father's house, Tom Kite had looked after the cottage. He called by every day and made sure that Betsy and her piglets, which were rapidly growing, and the chickens were properly fed. The piglets would soon be ready for the market, Tom thought to himself. Sarah's going to need the money she'd get for them. He must speak to her and arrange for them to be sold. Hector, the scruffy mongrel dog, he took home to stay with him until Sarah was ready to return to the cottage. Tom had quite taken to Hector, who of an evening would sit at his feet by the fireside. If Sarah wanted to let him go, he would gladly keep him…

Tom had also removed all visible signs of the accident. The cart was gone, as were all the blood stained sheets and blankets. They had been taken and washed by Tom's wife. Other than what was in her mind's eye, there would be nothing left of the dreadful accident to cause Sarah further distress and upset. Knowing she would need to earn a living, he had also made sure that Sarah's spinning wheel and the hand loom for weaving woollen flannel cloth, were working properly...

Tom was a loyal and good family friend. He and his wife, Charlotte, who Nathaniel's daughters, especially Sarah, called Mrs Tom, had not been blessed with children. Through the years, they helped looked after Nathaniel's children as though they were theirs. When Judith died, it was Tom and Charlotte that Nathaniel turned to for help to deal with his loss. Being Sarah's god-parents, they loved and cared about her as though she was their own daughter. At no little personal danger to him, Tom would continue to look out for Sarah in the weeks and years to come…

Two days after discussing it with her father, Sarah and Jacob returned home to the cottage. Nathaniel and Eliza went with them to make sure everything was alright. Rather nervously, Sarah pushed open the cottage door and holding

Jacob's hand she stepped inside. Half expecting to be upset, she was surprised when she wasn't.

Sarah looked around. Everything was neat and tidy and in its place, as she liked it to be. The stone floor had been swept and the rug, which was a wedding gift, Tom had taken outside and beaten the day before, was back on the floor. William's favourite spindle backed chair was by the fireside. Newly chopped wood was in a bucket by the hearth where a fire burned brightly. Fresh candles, not yet lit, stood in their brass holders either side of the fire mantle shelf and on the chest of pine drawers in the corner of the room. Sarah allowed herself the briefest of smiles when she saw the pair of Staffordshire pot dogs, which William had bought shortly before he died. She could remember being cross with him for wasting money they could ill-afford...

She noticed the flowers Tom's wife had put in a small vase on the table along with some cheese and cake. The smell of fresh bread that was cooling by the oven filled the room. That was Charlotte's idea.

'There's nothing more welcoming than a warm oven and the smell of fresh bread.' She had told Tom. 'I'll go to the cottage first thing and prepare it before Sarah gets there.'

'Hello Mrs Tom.' said Sarah.

'Welcome home my dear,' said Charlotte.

Charlotte was a jovial, plump lady with a large voice who, with Tom, had been waiting in the scullery. Rushing forward, she drew Sarah into her ample bosoms and hugged her.

'Welcome home Sarah... now sit yourself down my dear, I've made some tea for you,' she said.

'Come along Nathaniel... come on Eliza, sit you down.' Charlotte good naturedly ordered.

Sarah sat down, a touch bewildered by it all. She knew Mrs Tom meant well but, at that moment, tea, warm bread and cheese was the last thing she wanted. She needed to be left alone with Jacob.

After what seemed like an age to Sarah, the tea was drunk and some bread and cheese ate. Nathaniel, who could sense Sarah's unease, rose to leave.

'Come on Eliza, let's leave Sarah to it,' he said.

Gesturing with his head, Nathaniel indicated to Tom and Mrs Tom, it was time for them to leave.

'Come on Charlotte,' Tom said to his wife. '…we need to be going, too.'

'Yes… yes we do,' Charlotte replied. She had also seen the signal Nathaniel had made to Tom.

Everyone hugged Sarah, said their goodbyes and, promising to call in on her the next day, filed out of the cottage.

'Thank you Tom… thank you Mrs Tom,' said Sarah.

'God bless you child,' said Mrs Tom as she embraced Sarah so hard it nearly took her breath away. 'God bless and protect you.'

'Thank you Mrs Tom… I sure he will.' Sarah replied.

'Thank you Eliza…thank you papa,' Sarah said hugging Nathaniel who was the last to leave. '…don't worry… I'll be OK.'

With Jacob by her side, Sarah stood at the cottage door and watched as her family and friends walked down the road. Picking Jacob up, Sarah turned and walked back into the cottage and shut the door. She was now alone. Sarah leant back against the blue door and looking again at the pot dogs, promptly burst into tears. Jacob stared up at his mother. He'd seen her cry many times in the past weeks, but, these would be the last tears Sarah would shed for William…'

'There was no time for feeling sorry for herself and moping about. Within a few days, Sarah started to become organised. Her vegetable garden, which Tom had kept his eye on was flourishing and began to yield some lovely crops, the surplus of which, although not much, Sarah could sell. The cabbages were a disaster having been attacked by the Cabbage White Butterfly. Still they would feed Betsy, who would soon be mated again with the Farmer McBride's boar.

Tom slaughtered and butchered one of the piglets, now grown into pigs and showed Sarah how to cure the meat. The other six pigs were taken to market and sold giving Sarah some much needed income. Sarah even arranged to sell small quantities of woollen flannel cloth, which she wove on her hand loom. Nathaniel and Eliza called in nearly every day to make sure she was coping.

Things were improving for her. Most of the village now knew that she had returned to the cottage. Inevitably, it wasn't too long before young men, some of whom were William's friends, started calling at the cottage, offering to chop wood, do odd jobs and to help her. All of which Sarah graciously declined. Her father Nathaniel and Tom were wise to what their motives really were. After all, she was a very attractive desirable woman and now only had one child. Not too much of a burden for a young man to take on, they reasoned…

Whenever some of the younger men met in the *Dog and Duck*, Sarah's attractiveness, and the fact she now lived alone, was a frequent and bawdy topic of conversation; especially after they'd drank several pints of ale. On the few occasions when Nathaniel called in for a beer, if these men were in the bar, invariably, one or more of these would-be suitors would try to engage him in conversation and bring up the subject of Sarah. It was always the same. Nathaniel could see it coming and found it all quite wearisome.

'Erm… how's Sarah, Nathaniel?' they would ask, faking mock concern. '…is she managing on her own?' Often adding, 'If she needs any help or anything doing, I could call by, you only have to ask.'

Nathaniel just smiled and thanked them. He must have heard those questions and offers of help a hundred times or more.

'That's very kind of you,' he would reply. 'She's managing fine at the moment… Tom Kite and I are doing any odd jobs she needs attending to, so your help won't be necessary… thank you!'

The heavy emphasis on 'thank you' and the tone of his voice suggesting he knew what their little game was.

Sitting alone and saying little, Thaddeus Stone watched the antics of these luckless Lotharios and listened to their ribald comments, with mild amusement. There was only one man who would be getting into Sarah's bed he thought and, that was him. Thaddeus was well known in the area as being more than useful with his fists, with a reputation for fighting at the slightest provocation. Not many men would dare to stand in his way when his interest in Sarah finally became more widely known. For now, Thaddeus could afford to bide his time. After all he'd waited three years so far! He had made up his mind when he first set eyes on Sarah, which was not long before she married William that, one day she would be his wife. No other woman in the area interested him...

Thaddeus took to walking past the cottage again. Sometimes Sarah was outside, sometimes she was not. When she was, he stopped to talk and passed a few pleasantries with her. If he met her in the street, he would stop to ask her how she was coping and, offered to help if ever she needed it. On a few occasions, much to the surprise of others, he even attended St Joseph's on a Sunday, knowing full well that Sarah and her sisters were regular church goers. Cleverly, like a tiger stalking its prey, he never pushed it too far. Slowly, and little by little, he gained her trust and confidence and got closer to her.

As the weeks passed by, Sarah started to enjoy talking to Thaddeus on the occasions they 'accidently' met. After all, he was one of the best looking men in the village. Each time their conversation would last a little longer than the previous time. Sometimes their eyes would meet causing Sarah to blush and Thaddeus to smile. Sarah saw him as a good humoured friendly and handsome man. She knew nothing of the darker side of his character and his reputation down at the *Dog and Duck* as a drinker and fighting man. For those who really knew him, he was a man to be feared and from whom, if he was in drink, it was wise to keep your distance. Thaddeus Stone was not a man to be trifled with. Although Sarah was now twenty-two years old, she was still rather naïve.

Nathaniel and Tom knew as much as they needed to know about Thaddeus's character and reputation to dislike and be wary of him. They consider him to be an extremely bad lot with no redeeming features at all. Although they'd never seen Thaddeus fight, like most of the men in the village they had heard the story of how, only a couple of years earlier, he had nearly beaten an Irish gypsy to death in a bareknuckle fight in Newark... The gypsies pledged that one day, there would be a day of reckoning...

Before too long, with mounting unease, Nathaniel began to suspect that, even though Thaddeus was much older than Sarah, his interest in her was more than just neighbourly friendship. He also noticed that Sarah's interest in Thaddeus was subtly changing. She talked about him whenever she could. Frequently bringing his name up in conversations; especially when talking to Eliza and when she thought her father wasn't listening, or couldn't hear.

'I saw Thaddeus Stone in the village today,' Sarah would say. Or, 'Mr Stone told me…'

'Do you think he's good looking Eliza?' she asked.

'I'm sure I don't know,' Eliza replied becoming a little flustered.

She was never really comfortable when Sarah wanted to talk about Thaddeus in this manner.

'I don't know him and besides I don't look at him like that…nor should you Sarah,' said Eliza.

'Why shouldn't I?' Sarah asked with an impish twinkle in her eye.

'Well for a start… he's old isn't he?' Eliza said.

'He's not that old… not old like papa or Tom,' said Sarah, as she smiled mischievously at Eliza.

Although he was fourteen years older than her, with each passing week, Sarah had started to think differently about Thaddeus Stone. He was ruggedly handsome!

She started to look for him whenever she went into the village even though she knew, most days, he would be at work in Norton-by-Spital. At church on a Sunday, Sarah would look around the congregation hoping to see him there. When she was in her garden, she found herself looking down the road wanting him to come walking by and was disappointed if he didn't. With her growing interest in Thaddeus, Sarah was beginning to realise, the more time she spent alone, the more she felt alone. Sarah was very lonely...

During the night, lying in her bed, Sarah often found herself thinking about him. At first, it was all rather innocent. She just wondered whether she would see him the next day, or the day after. Soon, that was not all she was thinking. Lying there in the darkness, she would lightly caress herself under her night-gown. For the first time in many months, she could feel sexual emotions stirring in her that had been dormant for far too long. It was now well over a year since she had last made love with William.

Sarah found herself thinking, what would it be like to make love to Thaddeus, would he be tender or passionate she wondered? More wantonly, she thought, how would she like him to take her. Lightly caressing herself was no longer enough. Just the thought of Thaddeus entering her she found exciting. She began to pleasure herself under her nightgown. Afterwards, Sarah would lay there satisfied but confused. She didn't love Thaddeus. At best she desired him sexually. After all, in her mind, he was the best of the small number of available men in Calthorpe.

Now that the genie was out of the bottle, Sarah realised she would never look at him in the same way again. This wouldn't be the only time she would pleasure herself with the thought of making love to Thaddeus. Soon, even that wouldn't be enough. Sarah wanted to hold a naked man again. Thaddeus didn't know it, but, Sarah had begun to pursue him.

It wasn't too long before it happened.

As she went about her business in the shops and streets of the village, often with Eliza or, one of her other sisters, if they happened to meet Thaddeus, Sarah was friendly and demure. At least she appeared to be to anyone else who happened to be passing by. With Eliza, who had spent more time with Sarah in the past months than anyone, it was different. She couldn't help noticing how Sarah talked a little longer to him and, smiled at him more. Her dark eyes holding his gaze more than was appropriate. Eliza often chided her younger sister.

'Sarah… I do believe you are encouraging Mr Stone!'

'Nonsense Eliza,' replied Sarah laughing and putting her hand on Eliza arm. '…don't take on so!'

'You know our papa doesn't like Mr Stone very much,' Eliza said as they walked arm in arm down the road.

'Papa doesn't really know Thaddeus, so how can he not like him,' said Sarah.

In her conversations with Eliza, Sarah had long stopped calling him Mr Stone, it was always Thaddeus. Although when she was talking to her father, she still referred to him as Mr Stone. Eliza was not so familiar. To her, he was and always would be, Mr Stone. She didn't like him at all.

If Sarah was alone in her garden, or out of public sight when she 'accidently' met Thaddeus, her behaviour towards him was decidedly more coquettish and flirtatious. Thaddeus could sense Sarah's interest and knew that things were changing between them. He knew it was no longer a question of will she, now it was, when will she?

It was a bright, but crisp November morning the day it happened. Sarah was in her garden feeding the chickens and Betsy, who had had another litter of piglets. Thaddeus came walking up the road with a shotgun under his arm and a brace of pheasants in his hands.

'Good morning Sarah, how are you this beautiful morning?' he called out.

'Oh, as well as could be expected,' she replied pleased to see him. '...What's that you have there, Thaddeus?'

'A brace of birds I shot earlier this morning... I thought you might like them for your dinner.'

'That's very kind of you... Yes, I would,' said Sarah as she opened her gate to let him in to the garden.

'Can you just hang them in the shed for me please?' Sarah asked.

As Thaddeus walked over to the shed, he accidently and ever so lightly brushed against her as he passed, causing her to shiver. So much so that he couldn't fail to notice. They looked at each other and for the briefest of moments held eye contact until Sarah, who could feel her face going red, had to turn away and avert his gaze. Thaddeus went into the shed.

By the time he came out, he had taken longer than was necessary to find a cool place to hang the birds, Sarah had regained her composure.

'I'll be off then, Sarah,' said Thaddeus falsely. He knew he wasn't going anywhere.

'Well…you could stop for while if you like… I'll make us some tea,' Sarah suggested.

'Thank you, I'll do that… Tea would be most welcome,' he replied.

'Shall I make myself useful and chop some wood while you are making the tea?'

'Yes please… that will be helpful,' said Sarah as she went into the cottage to put the kettle on the stove. She felt a little light headed and strangely excited.

Thaddeus walked over to the wood pile, picked up the axe and started chopping. After only a few strokes of the axe he stopped, removed his coat, hung it on a nail on the shed door and rolled his shirt sleeves up. Before long he had worked up a sweat causing his shirt to stick to his back and muscular arms. Stopping to wipe the sweat from his brow, he could see Sarah watching him through the window. He knew she had been watching him for a while.

He carried on chopping the wood until Sarah called to tell him that the tea was ready.

'Come on in Thaddeus,' she shouted.

Thaddeus put down the axe, took hold of his coat and slowly walked over to the cottage. He had never been inside the cottage before. Sarah watched him walking towards her. Her heart was thumping in her chest. Other than her father, Tom Kite and William's brothers who sporadically had called to see her, no other man had set foot in the cottage since William died.

With the sun at his back, Thaddeus stood in the doorway. The door frame highlighted just how big a man he was. He looked at Sarah, she looked back. Only this time she was invitingly holding his gaze. There they stood until Sarah smiled and slightly nodded her head. Thaddeus dropped his coat, stepped forward, without a word being spoken picked

Sarah up in his powerful arms and carried her to the bedroom. For the moment, the tea was quite forgotten.

Afterwards there were no embarrassed silences or feelings of regret. Thaddeus became a regular visitor to the cottage. Sarah thought, for the time being, it was perhaps best to keep their secret to themselves. Thaddeus agreed. In a small village like Calthorpe it would only be possible to do so for a short while. It was the type of village where very quickly things got noticed and everyone knew just about everything that was going on…'

This had not been an easy part of the story for Jacob to tell. From his own memories, what his mama told him and what Aunt Eliza told him years later, he knew in explicit detail how his mama and Thaddeus had got together. As it was inappropriate, although so clearly recalled in his mind, some of the truth he kept from the children. After all, they were only children and far too young to hear such lurid details. Jacob had picked his words carefully and was circumspect in what he told them. What he could recall and see in his mind's eye, and what he told them, were two different things.

'…and so you see children,' said Jacob. 'Your great-grandmother Sarah and Thaddeus Stone got together, seemingly unaware or uncaring about the distress it would cause to the people who loved her...'

'Grandad was she a bad lady?' asked Grace trying hard to take in what she had heard.

'No… no… she wasn't. She was a wonderful woman and the most generous, caring, loving mother a boy could wish for,' Jacob replied.

'…But, after your great-grandfather William died, she was vulnerable and very, very lonely. She'd had her head turned by Thaddeus Stone…'

With uncomprehending faces, the children looked at each other. They'd never heard this expression before and were unsure what it meant. Laughing and pulling faces they all started to turn their head to see who could turn their head round the furthest. Their antics caused Jacob to laugh with them.

Chapter 3

Tom Kite Makes an Enemy

'…As you might expect in a small village like Calthorpe, it wasn't too long before people started talking about your great-grandmother Sarah. Gossip and rumours spread, around the village and, especially in the pub,' said Jacob. '…Thaddeus was to blame.'

…One evening, in early February 1856, while in his cups through a beer too many, Thaddeus let something slip. A group of young men were drunkenly and lewdly talking about Sarah when, with a sweep of his arm, Thaddeus pushed them aside to get to the bar. He had been listening to every word they were saying. Without thinking, unsteady on his feet and his face red and flushed from the ale, he turned and faced them. They all looked back at him and immediately stopped talking. Thaddeus had that effect on people. Slurring his words and in a loud voice, seeming not to care who heard, Thaddeus said,

'You're all wasting your time lads.'

'…None of you… you puny wastrels, has any chance at all with Sarah.'

Waving and gesturing drunkenly with his arm, he added.

'Sarah's… Sarah's already made up her mind who she wants and… it's not one of you miserable lot.' Thaddeus said, as he gripped the bar to steady himself and aggressively pointed his finger towards them.

'Sarah wants a real man… not you little boys,' he added mockingly laughing at them.

Thaddeus turned back to face the bar and ordered another pint of black beer.

Everyone within earshot was stunned into silence. No one spoke. Not because this was Thaddeus Stone, the fighter, or

46

because of what had been said. But, the fact that for the very first time Thaddeus had publically said something about Sarah. The manner in which he had referred to her, suggested a familiarity, which caught everyone by surprise. On all previous occasions when Sarah's good looks and availability were being discussed in the bar, Thaddeus had remained silent. Not this time. The men looked at each other knowingly. Very quickly elaborated gossip spread around the pub.

After Thaddeus's indiscreet outburst, whenever Nathaniel or Tom walked into the *Dog and Duck*, people would stop talking and look away in embarrassment. The feeling of awkwardness in the bar was palpable. When they greeted old friends and acquaintances, although their greeting would be acknowledged, Nathaniel and Tom weren't drawn into conversations. Often, the person they had greeted would move away and, in exaggerated animation, start another conversation with someone else, which excluded and surprised them. They had no idea why friends, some they'd known for many years, started to behave this way.

Rather than cause a scene in the pub, for the time being Tom and Nathaniel agreed not to ask why. Nathaniel had not been keeping the best of health of late, he'd been having coughing fits, so a disagreement in a public bar was the last thing they needed. They just ordered their beer and went and sat down and kept to themselves.

Not wishing to upset his old friend, Tom kept his thoughts to himself but was determined to get to the bottom of this. One evening after visiting the pub, he discussed the matter with his wife.

'Charlotte, there's something going on, which Nathaniel and I don't know about,' said Tom. '…People at the pub seem reluctant or embarrassed to talk to us… I don't understand why.'

'Oh!' she exclaimed.

Charlotte's lifted her hands to her mouth. Before anything else was said, she took a sharp intake of breath, looked at her husband and hesitantly spoke.

'Tom, you're not going to like this... but, there's been talk in the village.'

'Talk... what talk?' asked Tom.

'Improper talk and rumours about Sarah and Thaddeus Stone,' Charlotte replied.

Without needing for her to spell it out, Tom still asked the question.

'What about Sarah and Thaddeus Stone...what is there to talk about?'

'What rumours?' he asked again.

Charlotte wavered before replying. She was disinclined to give Tom the answer she suspected he may already know.

'Mr Stone has been seen on more than one occasion entering Sarah's cottage of an evening and not leaving until several hours later.'

'...That's not all,' she added. '...he has also been bragging at his workplace in Norton-by-Spital about how he has had carnal knowledge of a young widow woman in Calthorpe.'

Charlotte couldn't bring herself to say making love.

'How long has this talk been going on?' Tom asked,

His voice was beginning to show his anger and, Charlotte knew it.

'Well... I heard it in the village store a few days ago... and, then again in the butchers shop, today,' Charlotte said as she started to become upset.

'I'm sorry Tom... I'm sorry I didn't tell you... I suppose I was hoping that the rumours were untrue and the talk would go away.'

'It's not your fault dear,' Tom said soothingly to his wife. '...It's not your fault but, you should have told me.'

Tom was furious, but not with Charlotte. Even if it was true and Sarah had let him into her bed, not only was Thaddeus Stone a bully, he was also a braggart with no respect for women. For his own arrogant reasons it seems he was prepared to drag Sarah's reputation and the good name of her family into disrepute by bragging and gossiping about having his way with her. Tom had decided he needed to confront Thaddeus about his boasting. He told Charlotte his intentions.

Charlotte, who was well aware of Stone's reputation, immediately became worried and anxiously questioned whether confronting Thaddeus was a wise thing for Tom to do.

'Oh do be careful Tom…after all they may only be malicious rumours.' Even as she said it, Charlotte didn't believe her own words.

'…Mr Stone won't take too kindly to you accusing him of anything improper.'

Tom would not be swayed. 'We both know that I have to do this,' he replied.

It was the least he could do for his best friend Nathaniel. Although what he hoped to achieve he still wasn't sure...

…For several consecutive nights Tom went to the *Dog and Duck*. Sitting alone, smoking his pipe and making his beer last longer than normal, he watched and waited for Thaddeus coming into the pub. After three nights of waiting in vain, at about seven o'clock in the evening on the fourth day, Thaddeus stood before him at the bar. Still unsure about what he was going to do, for two hours Tom patiently watched Thaddeus drinking and talking to other drinkers on the opposite side of the bar. When Thaddeus finally got up to leave, Tom nervously followed him out into the darkness of the cold, dank street. It had begun to rain heavily.

Keeping a short distance between them, Tom walked down the road behind Thaddeus for about forty paces. Tom stopped and, with a growing sense of apprehension and fear, shouted.

'Stone... I want a word with you!'

Thaddeus carried on walking.

'Stone… stop damn you!' Tom shouted louder. 'I want to talk to you.'

Thaddeus stopped walking and turned. When he saw Tom, he knew exactly what he wanted to have a word about. Clenching and unclenching his fists in a sinister way designed to intimidate, Thaddeus walked slowly back towards Tom. Tom couldn't help but see how cold and threatening Thaddeus's eyes were. He hoped that the fear in his wasn't so obvious.

As they stood, several paces apart, facing each other, both of them were now wet through. The heavy rain added to the heightening tension between the two men.

'Well, well… if it isn't Tom Kite,' Thaddeus said menacingly.

'…And, what can I do for you Mr Kite?'

Tom walked a few steps nearer to Thaddeus and then stopped. He was still unsure of what he was going to say or do next. With good reason, he felt more apprehensive. Thaddeus stood at least half a foot taller than him and, Tom was no fighter. They were now only a few feet apart.

'It's about Sarah Rawlings and the malicious rumours you've been putting about of how she invites you into her bed,' Tom said.

It sounded weak and pathetic, but it was said and out in the open.

'What's it got to do with you Kite,' said Thaddeus. '…it ain't no concern of yours!'

'She's a family friend… and I'm her god-father, so I'm making it my concern,' replied Tom.

'What's your point then… god-father Tom?' Thaddeus asked contemptuously.

'After all she's been through in the past year… why do you have to blacken her good name and the reputation of her family by spreading nasty and spiteful lies and rumours?' Tom asked.

'…nasty lies, spiteful rumours… it is eh?' Thaddeus said questioningly. '…how do you know they're only lies Tom?'

'…Are you sure she doesn't invite me… can you be certain it's not what Sarah wants?'

He was now laughing and sneering at the same time. Thaddeus Stone had no fear of Tom Kite.

'Are you jealous Kite, is that it…eh?'

The tone of Thaddeus's voice had suddenly and ominously changed. Tom just stood there listening as Thaddeus spat out his bile.

'…Would you like beautiful Sarah to invite you into her bed…instead of you being with that fat, loud mouthed wife of yours ...Do you want to fuck her?'

'Is that why you are always at the cottage being so helpful to Sarah?' Thaddeus said derisively.

'…is that the real reason Tom… eh?'

Thaddeus was taunting and goading Tom and Tom knew it. He could feel the anger rapidly rising up inside him. There was no turning back now; this was the moment Tom knew what he had to do.

'You evil minded, foul mouthed, bastard,' said Tom as he sprang forward.

Catching Thaddeus unawares, Tom managed to land a half decent punch on his chin. Though the blow surprised Thaddeus and split his lip, causing it to bleed, he wasn't really hurt. He had received much worse in the past. Wiping the back of his hand across his mouth and seeing the blood, Thaddeus licked his lips and sardonically smiled.

'Is that all you have, Kite?' Thaddeus said, pausing to let his words sink in before jeering at Tom again.

'…Is that ALL there is?'

Suddenly, moving very quickly for a big man, Thaddeus grabbed hold of Tom by the front of his coat and viciously slammed him into the wall of a nearby building. Pulling a massive ham sized fist back, he was about to hit Tom before thinking better of it. If he hurt Tom, Sarah would find out and that was something he didn't want.

Grabbing Tom's coat tighter, he pushed him harder against the wall. Tom's hat, which had been knocked off when Thaddeus grabbed him, was lying in a puddle. The heavy rain matted their hair to their heads and ran down their faces. Thaddeus had a trail of blood running from his lip. He furiously bunched Tom's coat up under his chin forcing Tom to look upward at him. Their faces were only inches apart. Tom was nearly retching from the pressure on his throat and the smell of stale beer and tobacco on Thaddeus's breath. Wild eyed, Thaddeus glared at Tom and in a voice that was both sarcastic and scornful said.

'Thomas Kite, this is your lucky day…'

'…I'm not going to hit you this time,' he said, emphasising 'this time.' '…because I think that's really what you want me to do.'

'So, do yourself a favour Kite and piss off home to your wife.'

In a voice heavy with intimidation, Thaddeus started to mock Tom.

'You may as well get used to it god-father Kite. Sarah and I are going to be together, and there is nothing that you, Nathaniel, or that silly simpering sister of hers can do about it.'

'Not if I have anything to do with it you won't.' said Tom defiantly.

'We'll see, Kite… we'll see,' said Thaddeus.

With an open hand, Thaddeus lightly tapped Tom a couple of times on his cheek and, smiling cruelly at him, threatened.

'You'll be well advised Kite not to start meddlin', or getting involved.'

'…you may live to regret it!' Thaddeus snarled.

Thaddeus let go of Tom's coat and set off down the street.

Standing there in the rain, shaking and frightened, but still very angry, Tom yelled after him,

'You don't frighten me Stone!'

'…I'll be watching you, mark my words I'll be watching you… YOU FUCKING BASTARD!'

With the nonchalance that bullies, who know when they have the upper hand, often display, Thaddeus raised his arm and waved without even looking back…

'…Children, truly Tom Kite was a really good friend to your great-great-grandfather Nathaniel. Being concerned for his old friend's health, which was deteriorating, Tom was certain of what he now had to do. Even though the confrontation with Thaddeus had frightened him far more than he expected it to, he had to talk to Sarah…' Jacob explained.

…Watching Thaddeus walk away, Tom, wet, bedraggled and with a heavy heart picked up his hat, which Stone had deliberately trodden on, and trudged back home to his wife.

When he walked through the door of his home, his dirty and dishevelled appearance startled Charlotte.

'Oh Tom, are you alright...you're not hurt are you?' she asked anxiously. 'Get that wet coat and those muddy boots off and come and get warmed up.'

Looking very dejected, Tom removed his hat and coat, hung them on the back of the door and slowly walked to sit by the fire, before answering.

'No dear, I'm fine... only my pride is hurt.' He said despondently as he sank into his chair.

Charlotte knelt down and started to unlace and remove his boots.

'Why...what has happened Tom, have you seen Thaddeus?'

'Yes, I've seen him... for all the good it's done me,' he replied.

Tom paused, looked at his wife and said,

'They're not rumours Charlotte, it is all true... Thaddeus even bragged to me about how he and Sarah were going to be together.'

Not wanting to alarm and distress his wife further, Tom chose not to mention that he had punched Thaddeus and the threats Thaddeus made in return. Charlotte was not stupid, she knew something had happened but chose not to question Tom. Still kneeling at his feet, Charlotte started to weep.

'Poor Sarah... poor Nathaniel,' she wailed.

Taking his wife's hands in his and thinking of his old friend's failing health.

'Charlotte... Nathaniel must not know... he must not know,' said Tom earnestly.

'But Tom, he needs to be told,' Charlotte replied.

'Yes I agree, but not yet... I'll go and see Sarah in the morning and see if I can talk some sense into her.' Tom replied.

True to his word, Tom went to see Sarah the next day. It was a fruitless journey and may have even made matters worse, because it all came to a head only a few days later.

As she had always done, Sarah made Tom very welcome and offered him some tea. They drank their tea and exchanged a few general and banal pleasantries, before Tom warily raised the subject of Thaddeus Stone and the gossip that was rife in the village. Immediately Sarah's mood darkened and her whole demeanour changed. She became defiant, almost to the point of being aggressive. Her reaction shook Tom. He knew Sarah could be headstrong and wilful, but this was a different Sarah.

'What's my situation go to do with any of them... the spiteful tattle-tails,' she spat out.

'Do I gossip about them?' Sarah asked.

She was now quite incensed and agitated. Speaking softly, Tom managed to calm her. He tried to reason with her. Tom cared for Sarah and didn't want to hurt, or alienate her, so he chose his words carefully. She'd always listened to him before, but not this time. No amount of persuasion or argument would deter her. No matter what he said about Thaddeus, she would not listen or be dissuaded. Tom realised that something had changed in Sarah.

Tom felt very despondent when he got up to leave the cottage. He knew there was going to be trouble ahead, although quite how much trouble for him personally never crossed his mind. After he left, Sarah was still angry, though not with Tom. He was too good a family friend and was only looking out for her. Her anger was aimed at the others in the village who chose to take an interest in her affairs.

Sarah's fury had hardly abated, when Thaddeus called that evening. He listened intently as she told him about Tom's visit and what he'd said. Without letting his expression betray his mind and irritation, Thaddeus thought to himself.

'Tom Kite, you're becoming a meddlesome nuisance and will have to be dealt with.'

Sarah did not know, and didn't find out until a long time after, about the confrontation between Thaddeus and Tom the previous evening. Nor did she know, or even begin to suspect, that Tom would eventually suffer the consequence of what she had just told Thaddeus. She had more pressing matters on her mind.

'Thaddeus, forget about Tom Kite… I have something more important I need to tell you.'

'Why… what's on your mind, Sarah?' replied Thaddeus.

'Soon, we'll not have to worry about the gossip of interfering old busy-bodies…they'll be able to see for themselves,' Sarah said. 'They'll think much worse of me now.'

'Why… what do you mean?' Thaddeus asked rather naively.

'You simpleton Thaddeus… do I have to spell it out? I'm carrying your baby,' said Sarah laughingly. Her face was becoming flushed with the exhilaration of telling Thaddeus her news.

Thaddeus looked at Sarah for a moment before replying, 'Are you sure?'

'Yes, of course I'm sure…what did you expect after sharing my bed these past three months or more?' After a brief pause Sarah added, '…I'm now two months gone.'

'Well… there's only one thing to do then,' said Thaddeus with a wide smile on his face.

'Yes,' said Sarah. '...There is something we must do.'

The children were spellbound by the story they were hearing. As young as they were, they knew the importance of what their grandad had just told them…

'…Two days after telling Thaddeus, she was having his baby your great-grandmother Sarah asked all her family to meet at their father's house where she announced she was going to marry Thaddeus Stone. Nathaniel was very, very angry,' said Jacob…

'…There was no easy way to do it, so without mincing her words Sarah came straight to the point. Momentarily, everyone in the room was stunned into silence and stood there open mouthed in amazement. They couldn't believe what they had just heard. Nathaniel, coughing and struggling to get his breath, his face bright red and eyes bulging exclaimed in a voice so full of rage, none of his daughters had ever seen before.

'You're what!' Huffing and puffing Nathaniel added. '…What's that you say?'

Staring right back at her father, Sarah answered firmly, 'Thaddeus and I are going to get married.'

'Have you completely taken leave of your senses woman?' her father asked angrily.

Never before had Nathaniel derogatorily called any of his daughters 'woman'. Although shaken by his wrath, Sarah stood her ground

'I'm going to marry him papa… with or without your blessing,' Sarah said defiantly.

'Sarah, listen to me… Thaddeus Stone is not a suitable man for you… he's not the man you think he is.' Nathaniel said angrily as he paced around the room.

No one else dared to speak. Though not as red as it was, Nathaniel's face still displayed the full extent of his displeasure. He stopped pacing and stood in front of Eliza.

'Did you know about this?' he asked accusingly, whilst looking directly into her eyes.

'No papa, I didn't… I had no idea,' Eliza replied, not quite telling the truth and dropping her head to avert her father's questioning and accusing gaze.

Turning to face his other daughters and looking from one daughter and their husbands to the next.

'Did any of you know about this?' Nathaniel asked angrily.

Although they had heard and discussed the village gossip between them, each of them shook their head, claiming to be just as surprised as he was.

Trying to become less agitated and collect his thoughts Nathaniel paced around the room. No one spoke. His daughters watched and remained silent and averted their eyes when he looked at them. Never before had they seen him so angry. Their husbands kept quiet, not really wanting to be part of this. This was between Nathaniel and his daughters. Finally in a calmer voice he asked,

'Sarah, why do you have to do this?'

'Papa, I'm now twenty-three years old, a grown woman and know what I want…I don't want to live alone… I know Thaddeus cares for me and will look after me.'

'Yes dear, I can understand why you think that…' replied Nathaniel who was starting to settle down a little.

'…I know you are lonely, but Thaddeus is not the man for you Sarah… there are plenty of others, nearer your age, who would marry you and care for you.'

Almost pleading Nathaniel said. 'Marry if you wish, but not now and not to Thaddeus Stone.'

Sarah hesitated before replying, 'Papa, there are not plenty of others…I'm sorry, but I have to marry Thaddeus… I am carrying his child.' She paused then added,

'…I'm two months pregnant.'

Almost in unison, there was a mutual sharp intake of breath as everyone gasped. Sarah's sisters and their husbands look at each other in astonishment as the enormity of what Sarah had said sank in. Too shocked to speak, Nathaniel staggered a little before collapsing into a chair in a fit of coughing and struggling to breathe…

'Papa, papa, I'm so sorry,' cried Sarah as she rushed across the room to him. She loved her father dearly and was now concerned for what she had reduced him to. But, she was going to marry Thaddeus Stone…'

Jacob looked at his grand-children and, with a sad expression, slowly shook his head.

'…your great-great-grandfather Nathaniel recovered from his coughing fit and, although Sarah was with child, he still tried to persuade her not to marry Thaddeus. He told her, they would find a way to deal with the baby she was carrying… it was all to no avail. No amount of arguing or pleading with Sarah would change her mind. Even though it would break her father's heart, when I was four years old, my mother and Thaddeus Stone got married... A decision, both my mother and me, would very soon come to bitterly regret… There was a hard road ahead!'

'…Nineteen months after William had died, Sarah, who was nearly three months pregnant, married Thaddeus Stone at

St Joseph's church on a grey and gloomy day in April 1856. Even though the marriage was against his wishes and, in a mood as black as the overcast sky, Nathaniel attended Sarah's wedding. He loved all his daughters, especially Sarah as she was the youngest and the baby of the family. Nathaniel was also fulfilling the promises he had made to Judith as she lay dying, to look after their daughters. He would not shame Sarah by not being there…

It was a very simple wedding, mainly family. To show support for Nathaniel and Sarah, Tom Kite and Charlotte attended. Like Nathaniel, they didn't really wanted to be there and, in their hearts wished it wasn't happening. Not many of the villagers, none of whom knew Sarah was with child, were invited, or even bothered to attend the church to watch the wedding and wish them well. Thaddeus didn't have a wide circle of friends and was held in very low regard in the village. He didn't care. He now had what he'd always wanted; the most beautiful girl in the village was his wife…She was his trophy, his prize possession for him to brag about.

It was all so very different from William and Sarah's wedding five years before, which had been such a joyful occasion. There was no all-day feasting and dancing at this wedding, just a small muted wedding breakfast, attended only by family and, a very small number of close family friends. Nathaniel, who only wanted the best for his daughters, tried to smile and look pleased for Sarah. Her sisters fussed around and endeavoured to make it a happy affair. Despite their best efforts, it was a very strained celebration.

Thaddeus watched and waited for the right moment to speak to Tom Kite alone. When the chance, which wasn't long in coming, came, Thaddeus walked over and holding Tom's arm in a vice like grip, led him out of the earshot of others. Unaware that Charlotte was watching him, and in a voice heavy with malice he advised Tom of the consequences of him taking too keen an interest in Sarah's welfare in the future.

'Kite, I'm sure that Charlotte wouldn't want anything to happen to you, would she now!' Thaddeus said. 'Take this advice as my wedding gift to you god-father Tom. You'll do well to heed it... it won't be given again... keep your nose out of my affairs.'

Too stunned to reply, from the menacing tone of Thaddeus's voice, Tom he had been warned.

Seeing that Thaddeus had finished talking and had gone to sit back down with Sarah, Charlotte wandered over to her husband.

'Tom, what did Thaddeus want?' she asked.

'Oh, nothing much,' Tom lied. '...He just wanted to thank us for coming to the wedding.'

Charlotte could tell by the worried expression on Tom's face that he was lying. They both turned and looked over towards Thaddeus and Sarah. With steely eyes, Thaddeus returned their gaze and slowly rose to his feet. Looking directly at Tom, he stared and then winked before raising his glass in a provocative toast to Tom. Thaddeus smiled. Tom felt a cold shiver run down his spine.

Chapter 4

A marriage made in hell!

'...After the wedding, Thaddeus moved into the cottage. For the first few months they lived together everything seemed to be fine. Their daily life was distinguished only by its normality. Thaddeus would go off to work leaving Sarah at home to look after Jacob, the vegetable garden, their chickens and old Betsy. Occasionally, on his way home, he would call at the *Dog and Duck*, but never stayed for more than a couple of pints. His dinner would be on the table waiting for him.

Sarah accepted that living with Thaddeus, was not quite the same as being married to William. The love she had had for him could not be replaced. Nevertheless, at first she was contented. People in the village stopped gossiping about her and her pregnancy. Thaddeus had done the right thing by her. Nathaniel, Eliza and her other sisters regularly called by to make sure she was keeping well. As Sarah grew larger with the child she was carrying, her sister's visits became more frequent. Life for Sarah appeared to be happy again. Before long, even Nathaniel began to think he may have misjudged Thaddeus...

Tom Kite wasn't convinced. Other than Charlotte, and she didn't know about the threats that had been made, no one else knew of Tom's disagreements with Thaddeus. In those first months after the wedding, even though Thaddeus would be at work, four miles away at Norton-by-Spital, Tom never set foot inside Sarah's cottage. He didn't want to give Thaddeus any reasons at all for him to be angry with Sarah. If he happened to be passing by and saw her in the garden, or in the street, he would stop and speak. Outwardly Tom's behaviour towards

Sarah did not change. She suspected nothing. Tom watched out for her from a distance…

Unfortunately for Sarah everything changed for the worse when, heavily pregnant with his child, she started to say no when Thaddeus wanted to make love to her. The first time she refused him, although annoyed, Thaddeus appeared to understand the physical discomfort making love had begun to cause her. Regrettably, his understanding attitude was very short lived. Sarah soon discovered, to her cost, the true brutal nature of the man. After several nights of being rejected, Thaddeus forced himself upon her. This was not making love, this was rape!

Thaddeus couldn't bear being rejected by Sarah. He brutally took what he wanted, whenever he wanted and, continued to do so. Each time, when it was over and Thaddeus had gone to sleep, Sarah would lie there in the darkness, wide awake, sometimes quietly weeping. She tried to convince herself that things would be alright again after the baby was born. But, she couldn't help wondering whether her father, and Tom, had been right all along…'

Again Jacob was being very careful in what he told the children. Although, he wanted them to understand how his and his mother's life changed after she married Thaddeus, there were certain things that happened, like Thaddeus forcing himself on Sarah, which they didn't really need to know. He wasn't about to tell his beloved grandchildren that their great-grandmother was repeatedly raped by her second husband.

'…In September 1856, after a particularly difficult fourteen hours in labour, your great-grandmother Sarah had a baby daughter, whom she called Hannah. Hannah was a very pretty baby… and my first half-sister… As much as she was beginning to regret marrying Thaddeus, Sarah loved all her children dearly, '*They're my reason for living and always bring me great joy',* my mama used to say.' said Jacob.

Deep in thought and looking down at his grandchildren, Jacob paused. He slowly refilled his pipe with tobacco and lit it from the fire with the taper Daniel had handed to him.

'Thank you Daniel,' he said.

Jacob drew deeply on the pipe, savouring the fresh tobacco, before he continued.

'In the days following Hannah's birth, Eliza would call every day. She would arrive early in the morning and stay with Sarah all day long until it became dark. Sarah found her a great help in looking after Jacob, preparing meals and doing whatever needed doing. Sarah's other sisters called in whenever they could. They had their own families to look after.

Thaddeus would go off to work, before Eliza or any of the other sisters arrived. There were no goodbye hugs or kisses when he left the cottage. Most mornings, he would just pick up his hat and coat and storm out of the cottage without even saying a word. Sarah no longer watched from the door, or waved goodbye as he went down the road.

In the evenings when Thaddeus stopped off at the *Dog and Duck*, which now happened nearly every day, he started staying there longer and drinking more than before. Sometimes, Eliza would still be at the cottage when Thaddeus stumbled through the door. Living with a regular drunkard was something Sarah and Eliza were not used to. Only once in their life, had they seen their father drunk. And, that was after a wedding! He was a happy drunk. Nathaniel had come home swaying and singing, he flopped into a chair and promptly fell asleep. With Thaddeus it was different. Eliza started to become concerned for Sarah's safety... When he was drunk, Thaddeus frightened Eliza…

One morning, when Thaddeus was at work, Eliza told Sarah of her fears. Even though Sarah knew things had changed between her and Thaddeus, she tried to laugh it off and reassure her sister that she was alright. No matter what she said, Eliza wasn't persuaded. But, decided to let the matter rest for the time being.

Sarah didn't stay confined to bed for long after giving birth to Hannah. Eliza still called every day and fussed around, helping and making sure Sarah didn't try to do too much. Unfortunately, Thaddeus didn't show Sarah the same care and consideration. Staying later at the pub each evening and coming home drunk became a regular occurrence. If Eliza was still at the cottage, Thaddeus would angrily turn on Sarah…

'What's she still doing 'ere?' he'd slur. '…why does she need to come 'ere every day…? You're not helpless, are you?'

'Oh… don't fret so! Thaddeus… she's my sister and wants to help me.' Sarah replied trying to lighten the atmosphere.

'You don't need any help… do you?' Thaddeus asked facetiously.

Trying to reassure Eliza, Sarah smiled, put her hand on Eliza's arm and said with fake jauntiness,

'Off you go now Eliza, I'll be alright.'

'Yes… bugger off, spinster sister,' Thaddeus snarled contemptuously at Eliza, before slumping into a chair and bawling at Sarah,

'Take my boots off, wife… where's me dinner?' He expected to be waited on hand and foot.

Walking Eliza to the door, Sarah whispered,

'Perhaps it might be better, Eliza, if you don't come round for a few days… Don't worry, I'll be fine… I can manage.'

'OK… OK, but only if you're sure that's what you want,' said Eliza.

Sarah nodded and silently mouthed, 'Yes… it's what I want'.

As troubled as she was, Eliza reluctantly bowed her head in agreement. She hugged Sarah and set off home. Nathaniel had recently started coughing up blood, which the doctor had diagnosed as consumption. Distressing him about Sarah's circumstances would not help his health at all, Eliza thought. She made up her mind to say nothing to her father but, would discuss the matter with Tom Kite and Mrs Tom instead. They would know what to do.

When Eliza went to see them a day or so later and shared her worries, their response surprised her. They were both reluctant to interfere. Eliza couldn't understand why.

'Eliza, Sarah is Thaddeus's wife now…it's no concern of ours if he comes home drunk,' Tom said before asking. 'He's not mistreating her… is he?'

'No, I... I don't think so,' said Eliza even though she wasn't sure.

'Well then, we've nothing to worry about... have we!' said Tom.

'I suppose not,' said Eliza, who was still unconvinced.

Eliza would have been more reassured if she had known what thoughts were going through Tom's mind. He, quite wisely, had decided it would be best, especially for Sarah, if he appeared not to be getting involved...

With each passing day, Sarah began to see less and less of the gentler and kinder side of Thaddeus's nature, which had charmed her not that many months before. Sober, he could be very different, or so she thought. Before long though, Sarah began to see the true character of the man she was now living with. Drunk or sober, Thaddeus became a critical and controlling bully and made demands on her...'

Only three weeks after she had giving birth to Hannah, Thaddeus forced himself on Sarah again and, would do so most nights thereafter. Often he was too drunk to notice, or even care about the physical and emotional hurt, he was causing her. Thaddeus was taking what he wanted, when he wanted. Sarah would lie there and endure his embrace in silence. The sound of Thaddeus's grunting and heavy breathing could be clearly heard through the thin wall, which separated the two bedrooms in the cottage.

As Jacob grew older, and had some idea of what was happening to his mama in the next room, he would pull his blankets and pillows up tight around his head to block out the sound. On many nights, he cried himself to sleep. Sometimes, when Thaddeus arrived home from the pub he was so drunk, he could hardly stand, which in a strange way pleased Sarah and Jacob. At least when he was in that state, he left her alone and just fell asleep.

In drink, Thaddeus's temper was quick and vile. If Hector, the dog, got in his way, he would kick out at him and send him yelping into the scullery, or the yard if the door was open. Every now and then, Hector was kicked just because it amused Thaddeus to do so. His patience with baby Hannah was also short. He never picked her up or, cuddled her; he would just yell at Sarah to, *'shut that chit up'*, if the baby was crying.

Sarah never knew when she could expect Thaddeus to arrive home of an evening. No matter what time it was when he walked through the door, he expected his dinner to be on the table. Sarah had to keep looking through the cottage window and watch out for him walking down the road. She was always on edge and often thought to herself, please god, let him be in good humour this night. Sometimes Sarah got it right, sometimes not. If his meal was not on the table, Thaddeus would fly into a rage. He would shout threateningly at Sarah, lash out at Hector and frighten Jacob, who would hide behind his mother's skirts.

Frequently, Thaddeus would find faults, even where none existed. He seemed to delight in reducing Sarah to a tearful, cowering shadow of the headstrong woman she had been when they first married. Sarah's self-esteem was getting lower and lower. If he thought the dinner was too cold, and sometimes even if it wasn't, he would pick it up and throw it at the wall, or even Sarah. Or, he would give it to Hector, yelling it was only good for dog food and demanding that Sarah cook him something else. When he was in those moods, he had a black heart and it was a difficult time for her.

Sadly, it became the regular pattern of her life, Sarah was often afraid of Thaddeus. She found herself regretting ever letting him into her bed and into her life in the first place. How she wished she had listened to her papa and Tom. But, she had made her bed, now she had to lie on it. Becoming increasingly unhappy she kept her thoughts to herself. Often it crossed her mind, why couldn't Thaddeus have an accident at work - why did it have to happen to a wonderful man like William, but not to a brutal thug like Thaddeus?

With each passing week, Thaddeus became more and more controlling. He delighted in speaking cruelly to her. He demanded to know who Sarah had seen, where she had been and why. He wanted to know who she had talked to, what was said and, what she had been doing all day. Thaddeus wanted to know everything. She was left in no doubt when Thaddeus was unhappy with what she told him. She started to feel like her life wasn't her own anymore. He wanted to own her body and soul.

When Thaddeus was at home he made it clear that he didn't welcome visitors. With his abrasive manner and brooding presence, anyone who did call was made to feel awkward and uncomfortable and, never stayed for too long. Sarah's sisters, even Eliza, stopped visiting altogether if Thaddeus was there. This was exactly what he wanted. Sarah's family would not be able to see how nervous and fearful she had become whenever she was around him.

Before too long, Sarah even announced to her sisters that, it wasn't necessary for them to call on her so often when she was home alone during the day. Although, Sarah said Nathaniel's consumption and failing health should be their main concern and not her, they all knew that Sarah was being coerced by Thaddeus. In truth, she was being more than coerced. She was gradually being isolated from her family and friends and, appeared to be going along with all Thaddeus's wishes. He was treating her like a chattel to do whatever he wanted with her. Much to her family's concern, in April 1857, Sarah fell pregnant again.

Thaddeus continued to abuse her throughout the nine months she carried the baby. Sarah had long ago given up all ideas of willingly making love to Thaddeus. Disgusted with herself, she allowed him to use her. Not that she had much choice in the matter. If she had wanted to fight him off, she wouldn't have been able. As her term advanced, Thaddeus knew that, Sarah would soon need the help of her sisters. Better them than some nosey midwife, who would spread gossip around the village. Eliza and the sisters started to call again.

Six months into her second pregnancy, Thaddeus struck Sarah for the first time. Although he had made threats many times before, he had never actually hit her. He had always managed to restrain himself. Not this time!

'Don't you dare back mouth me, wife… you'll feel the back of my hand if you talk to me like that', he would threaten. *'I'll*

take my belt off to you', was another of his malevolent promises.

As much as he frightened Sarah, these were normally idle threats. Although Thaddeus had been drinking, he was not drunk, when he struck Sarah for the first time. He knew exactly what he was doing.

The evening had all started off pleasantly enough. The cottage was welcoming, there was a fire burning brightly in the hearth. An oil lamp and fresh candles, which Sarah had lit, flickered and spluttered creating a hospitable warm amber glow throughout the room. For Thaddeus's dinner, Sarah had prepared a rabbit stew and fresh bread, which she had baked that morning. It was already on the table when he walked through the door. Jacob and Hannah were asleep in bed. Sarah hoped for a peaceful evening. She was trying to make the best of a desperately bad situation.

'Hello Thaddeus… give me your coat,' she said trying to be cheerful. '…your dinner's ready on the table.'

'Hello Sarah… it certainly smells good,' Thaddeus replied affably.

There was no longer any embracing when they greeted each other. That had ended before Hannah was born. If he was in good humour, they just smiled, or said very little when he was not. Thaddeus took off his coat and handed it to Sarah. He leant the heavy cudgel style walking stick, which he had recently taken to carrying, against the door and sat down at the table. Sarah hung up his coat.

'Do you want me to unlace your boots before you eat Thaddeus? Sarah asked.

Thaddeus replied, 'No… don't bother. I'll eat first.'

Thaddeus seemed to be in a good mood. Sarah relaxed. She walked to the table and standing next to Thaddeus, started ladling a generous portion of the rabbit stew into a bowl for him. Looking around the room, Thaddeus nonchalantly asked,

'Where's that flea-bitten dog… where's Hector?

'Oh… he's gone Thaddeus,' said Sarah lightly.

'What?' Thaddeus asked.

Thaddeus looked up at Sarah and took hold of her wrist, stopping her from ladling the stew into the bowl, which surprised her. He started to twist her arm.

'Thaddeus, let go of my arm… you're hurting me!' Sarah cried.

The atmosphere in the room had suddenly changed. There was now an air of menace. Ignoring her cry of pain, and still holding her arm, but now gripping it even tighter.

'Gone… what do you mean he's gone?' Thaddeus demanded to know. 'Where's he gone?'

'I've given him away… Thaddeus,' Sarah replied. She was grimacing as he continued to twist her arm.

'Why have you done that?' Thaddeus asked.

'Thaddeus, I'm six months with child and won't be able to cope with Hector in the next few weeks.' Sarah explained, adding, '…You didn't like the dog anyway!'

'I'll decide what I like… not you Mrs Stone,' Thaddeus scowled. He stared hard at Sarah.

'…Did you ask me if you could give him away… eh, eh…? Did you?' Thaddeus said intimidatingly and continued to rage.

'…Was it not worth asking me… had you already made up your mind… eh? Don't you need my advice any more… is that it?'

'IS THAT IT?' he shouted aggressively.

Thaddeus was beginning to lose his temper.

Sarah didn't reply; she just shook her head. Still holding on to her, Thaddeus asked,

'Who have you given him to, Sarah… who's got him?'

'Tom Kite… I've given him to Tom,' Sarah replied.

'You've done WHAT? Thaddeus said, becoming more infuriated at just hearing Tom Kite's name.

He was now standing, towering above Sarah and still holding her arm.

'I've given him to Tom… he called and collected him this morning,' said Sarah. '…I asked Eliza, to ask Tom to call.'

'Kite's been here… today… while I was at work!' Thaddeus said.

By now, Thaddeus was very angry, but Sarah didn't understand why. She couldn't see a problem with giving a dog away to Tom. Even though she thought it strange that Tom had kept his distance of late, Sarah didn't know that there was very bad blood between them and that Thaddeus had an irrational hatred of Tom.

'I don't understand Thaddeus… what's the problem, it's only a dog.' Sarah said nervously.

'I'll tell you what the problem is… you're the fucking problem Sarah,' Thaddeus angrily spat out. '…you're the fucking problem... reject me... push me away will you… YOU WHORE!'

Thaddeus's real innermost raging fury was now violently evident.

'…I'll teach you to push me away,' he ranted.

At that moment, Thaddeus gave reign to his rising temper. Sarah didn't see the blow coming. He hit her across the face with the back of his free hand, whilst he held on to her with the other.

'…Tom Kite's been here today… has he!' Thaddeus asked. His voice was full of venom.

This time Sarah was knocked to the floor.

'If Hector can go… these fucking dogs can go to Kite as well.' Thaddeus said angrily.

In an act of extreme spitefulness, he took William's Staffordshire pot dogs off the mantelshelf and smashed them to smithereens on the stone floor.

Thaddeus stormed towards the cottage door and put on his coat. He picked up his cudgel and, looking contemptuously at Sarah, used it to sweep the rabbit stew, bread and all the crockery off the table.

'I'm going to the pub… that lot had better be cleared up by the time I get back,'

Sarah lay there hurt, shocked and uncomprehending of how quickly and viciously Thaddeus's mood had changed. Her nose was bleeding and the side of face was red and starting to bruise. She was splattered with rabbit stew. Sarah started to cry. What had she done to deserve this? All she ever wanted was to be happily married with her children, and eventually her grandchildren, around her, she thought. As Sarah slowly started to rise to her feet, she saw Jacob standing in the bedroom doorway in his nightshirt. Thaddeus's shouting had woken him. Jacob was crying!

'...Children,' Jacob said sadly shaking his head. '...It really pains me to tell you this, but sadly that was not the only time, I saw my mama being beaten.'

'As distressing as it is... I want you to understand how Thaddeus Stone's brutality dominated your great-grandmother and, how it ultimately led to me having to leave home.'

'...After that first time, Thaddeus beat her more frequently. It became such a regular part of my childhood that I began to expect it and almost thought it was normal. Strangely, when I look back, I started to associate the smell of stale beer and tobacco, which Thaddeus always reeked of, with being beaten, especially after he had started to hit me as well... Often, it was so difficult to tell what sort of mood he would be in. Time and again, the slightest incident would send him into a rage. He would lash out, sometimes with his fists, sometimes with his belt. Whereas, on other occasions, he would let the incident pass and even laugh it off...

He was playing mind games with Sarah and me... Your great-grandmother never knew when or where the next blow was coming from. Most of the times when Thaddeus hit Sarah, he avoided her face. He would punch her in the stomach or lash her across the back with his belt or a stick. He was always careful not to mark her where others could see what he had done. Thaddeus Stone was a sadistic, brutal and cruel man, who took pleasure out of the misery he caused...'

Jacob could see that his grandchildren, who had been sat so quietly and listening intently, were starting to become upset, but decided to carry on with his story. At seventy-three years old, he knew that, he would not have many more opportunities left to tell the whole hidden truth of the story of his life. He was an old man seeking some sort of moral redemption and wanted to put the record straight.

Before he continued, he gently touched Daniel and Gabriel on the face to reassure them. He gestured to Grace, who looked as though she may burst into tears at any moment, to come and sit beside him. Putting his arm protectively around her, he carried on.

'...now don't upset yourself, children, you'll see that eventually some good came out it.'

'If these bad things hadn't happened, I wouldn't have left home to become a fisherman and I wouldn't have met your grandma. And...' he said smiling at them,

'...without meeting your grandma... your mother, Sarah-Eliza, would not have been born and neither would you... My very precious grandchildren...'

Just before Christmas in 1857, less than three months after Thaddeus first hit her, with Eliza and her sisters around her Sarah gave birth to her fourth child. This was the second daughter she had produced with Thaddeus. Just like her older sister, Hannah, she was a beautiful baby, whom Sarah named Harriett. Sarah liked to use names from the bible, which she had taken to reading more and more as the years passed.

In the presence of his sisters-in-laws, Thaddeus made the effort to look pleased and proud. In private, he was scornful that Sarah had produced yet another girl. According to him, she couldn't do anything right. Babies and especially girls, he thought, were an inconvenience.

After Harriett was born, Sarah and Thaddeus's life together settled into a cold and loveless union. For him, it was a daily routine of work, pub, home, bed and taking Sarah whenever he wanted to. For Sarah, it became a life of drudgery and trepidation. When she was not pregnant, she looked haggard and drawn. Her eyes, which used to captivate so many, had lost all their allure and sparkle. She looked like a lost soul in permanent torment and lived in constant fear of Thaddeus.

Never again did she wish for a better life with him, she wanted rid of him. She wished him dead. Even though it went against all her Christian instincts and values, each night she prayed, beseeching the devil to rise from Hell to take him. But, that wasn't going to happen, no matter how hard she prayed.

Sarah became reclusive. She kept her visits to the shops in the village to a minimum. Other than the times when she went to see her father, who because of his illness was becoming weaker, she saw very little of her sisters, or her brothers-in-laws. Not wanting to provoke Thaddeus, which became increasingly easy to do, Sarah never told him of her visits to see Nathaniel, nor, whenever she happened to bump into Tom Kite or Mrs Tom.

Tom had suggested, shortly before she gave birth to Harriett, it would perhaps be best if she never mentioned to Thaddeus that she'd seen him, or even Charlotte. After his extraordinary outburst over her giving Tom the dog, Sarah understood fully why Tom would advise her in that way. A disturbing chain of events would soon show that Tom's advice had been soundly given…

One night when Thaddeus was drinking alone in the *Dog and Duck,* Tom walked in. The pub was quite crowded. Tom went up to the bar and ordered his pint of ale. He then had to walk past Thaddeus to get to some friends he wanted to talk to. As he did, their eyes met. Anyone who may have been watching couldn't help but see the mutual hatred between them. Staring coldly at Tom, Thaddeus remembered he had some unfinished business he needed to deal with.

'…you keeping well, Kite?' Thaddeus sneered.

Despite being a little apprehensive, Tom was not going to show it and back away.

'I'm fine… if it's all the same to you Stone,' Tom replied trying to keep any fear out of his voice.

'Make sure you stay that way Kite,' said Thaddeus warningly, before adding, '…and how's that dog of yours… or should I say mine?'

'The dog's fine… he was never yours in the first place Stone, he was William's,' Tom said as he pushed past Thaddeus.

At that moment, Thaddeus nearly lost control. In his warped and twisted mind, instead of hearing Tom say, Hector,

72

the dog wasn't his in the first place, he heard, 'She was never yours in the first place, she was William's.' Although Tom had not said that… that was what Thaddeus had heard. Tom Kite was laughing at him, or so he thought.

Thaddeus finished his beer, glared across at Tom, who was now in conversation with his friends, and stormed out of the pub. Thaddeus was ominously thinking to himself, all will soon be settled. Tom would have been most uncomfortable if he had known the dark thoughts that were racing through Thaddeus's mind. He didn't have to wait too long to find out!

The very next morning, when Tom left for work, there was a pair of freshly killed crows hanging on his gate. Tom looked around, there was nobody in sight. Deciding not to alarm Charlotte, he said nothing. He cut the crows down and took them with him. When he was far enough away from his house, he tossed them over a hedge. The foxes will find them he thought. The incident had troubled Tom. Worse was to come!

Two mornings later, a dead badger hung on his gate. Its belly had been slit open and the entrails left to dangle. Dead crows were one thing, but this was something far more serious. In the vilest manner, Tom was being warned and, he knew who by. Other than Thaddeus, Tom had no other enemies in the village. Verbal threats he could tolerate, dead and mutilated animal carcasses on his gate; this was very sadistic and unnerved him.

Tom was unsure how to deal with it. He didn't want to upset Charlotte and he couldn't really talk to Nathaniel, or Sarah, or any of her sisters. He would have to deal with this on his own. Even though he knew Thaddeus was responsible, it would be unwise to confront and accuse him without any evidence that he was responsible. Again Tom chose not to tell Charlotte. He took the badger's remains and buried them in a nearby field.

A few days after the badger incident, when Tom came home from work, Charlotte was waiting for him at their garden gate. With an unhappy face, she embraced and greeted him.

'Hello Tom.'

73

'Hey... why the sad face Charlotte... Nobody's died have they?' Tom said jokingly.

'Oh Tom... I've got some bad news.' said Charlotte.

'What bad news... Charlotte... it's not Nathaniel is it?' Tom asked earnestly.

'...No, it's not Nathaniel... it's Hector. He's dead... he's been poisoned,' she replied. 'He's lying over near the shed... I've covered him up.'

Grim faced, Tom walked over to where Hector lay. He removed the old blanket that was covering the dog. From the froth that had dried around his muzzle, his tongue hanging out and the look on the old dog's face, Tom could see Hector had died in agony. Probably from rat-poison, he thought. Just like the two previous warnings, this had all the indications of being Thaddeus Stone's handiwork. Tom knew this intimidation couldn't go on much longer like this. Thaddeus Stone had thrown down the gauntlet; he was challenging Tom to face up to him.

Telling Charlotte to go back into the house, Tom gently picked Hector up and walked to the bottom of their garden, where he buried him. Afterwards Tom stood there for a moment deep in thought trying to make up his mind what to do. This incident had shaken him. If Thaddeus could do these evil things, especially to the badger and poor old Hector without being seen, what else might he be capable of?

Was Charlotte now in danger? Where would it all end? If Tom told the village constable, what would he be able to do? Without evidence, Tom's suspicions were worthless. Tom knew that he had no option but to accept Thaddeus's challenge and confront him. But first, he had to tell Charlotte about the threats, the crows and the badger.

'...Less than a week later, in 1858, when I was six years old, Tom Kite was found dead...' said Jacob.

Chapter 5

I had to kill him!

'...For many years, no one knew what had really happened to Tom. Some farm labourers, walking to work early in the morning, found him floating face down in one of the drains that ran alongside the fields. Although he had bruises on his face, Tom had been drowned...

...In her heart, Charlotte, knew it was Thaddeus who had killed Tom. She told the local constable about her suspicions, the threats, Hector being poisoned and the dead things being left on the gate, but there was little that the constable could do. Although he questioned Thaddeus, who of course denied everything, without any real evidence, other than Charlotte's suspicions, no prosecution could be brought. She even went to the main police station in Newark, but to no avail. Without any evidence there was nothing they could do.

When Sarah heard that Tom had died, she also thought Thaddeus was responsible, but said nothing. She despaired at losing her god-father who was a valuable friend, and started to fear for the safety of her own family.'

'Did Thaddeus kill Mr Kite?' Daniel asked his grandad.

'Yes... yes Daniel, he did,' replied Jacob. 'Several months later, when he was drunk, he bragged to Sarah about killing Tom ...

'...Where's your precious Tom Kite to protect you now', he had taunted her. Knowing she wouldn't be able to testify against him. He took sadistic delight in telling her what he'd done...'

'...Tom had gone to the *Dog and Duck* to confront Thaddeus. For his own safety, he had decided to challenge him in public where there would be witnesses. Tom sat waiting,

75

sipping his pint and smoking his pipe. He was nervous. Just as he was about to enter the pub, Thaddeus saw Tom through the pub window and chose not to go in. Instead, he waited outside in the dark for him to leave. Tom didn't know that he was out there. After a while, thinking that Thaddeus wouldn't be coming in to the pub that night, Tom elected to leave and come back the next night. He was determined one way or another to end the feud between him and Thaddeus...

When Tom left the pub, he didn't see Thaddeus lurking in the shadows. This time, quietly and furtively, making sure no-one else could see them, as Tom made his way home, Thaddeus followed behind. Thaddeus knew that Tom and Charlotte lived on the outskirts of the village on a stretch of road where there were few houses. He kept his distance. Thaddeus didn't want Tom to know that he was behind him until they reached a secluded spot. When he thought they were out-of-the-way and making sure no one else was around, Thaddeus called out to Tom to stop.

Thaddeus boasted to Sarah about how startled and alarmed Tom was when he turned round and saw who was coming towards him out of the darkness...

'...Old Tom nearly pissed himself,' Thaddeus laughed cruelly.

'Trembled like a little girl... did your precious Tom Kite... I thought he was going to start crying for his mummy.' Thaddeus told her.

He was trying to hurt Sarah by belittling the reputation of the man, who had looked out for her since she was a baby and, whom she had looked up to. It would take more than Thaddeus's vile taunts to do that.

He took great delight in telling Sarah in unpleasant detail of how they had fought an uneven match, which didn't last long. Tom had no option but to defend himself and fight. Although he fought as hard as he could, he was soon knocked unconscious. Tom wouldn't have known that he was fighting for his life against this much larger and younger fighting man.

With relative ease, Thaddeus picked up Tom's unconscious body and carried him to the drain, and threw him into the shallow water. He then stood with his foot on Tom's back until he was sure he had drowned. The fight and the drowning were both over in a matter of minutes. Tom was left for dead in the drain. Making sure he hadn't been seen, Thaddeus took a short cut through the fields rather than going back down the road, and hurried back to Sarah and the cottage.

Listening to this sorry tale, Sarah, could remember him coming home one evening all agitated and animated. At the time she thought it was just Thaddeus being in one of his strange moods. Now she knew that must have been the night he killed Tom Kite. In fear of her own life, Sarah never told anyone what Thaddeus had told her until several years later. Shortly before she died, Sarah told Charlotte what she knew about how her beloved Tom had died…

Children, your great-great-grandfather, Nathaniel, had been friends with Tom Kite for over thirty-five years. He was distraught when he heard that his old friend was dead, especially when he was told the circumstances of how he had died. After Tom's death, Nathaniel, seemed to just give up. He weakened more rapidly; his consumption worsened and he took to his bed. Nathaniel was never seen outside his house again. Eliza and her sisters looked after him. Sarah would call whenever she could. But, she had serious problems of her own, which she wasn't of a mind to share with her sisters, or tell her father...'

Jacob stopped talking and paused for a moment to gather his thoughts. He sucked on his pipe, before continuing. He had told them this much and wasn't going to stop now. The rest of the story, however disturbing, needs to be told and told truthfully, he thought.

'…When I was a child, it seemed to me, that my mother was always expecting another baby,' said Jacob.

…About a year after Tom had been found dead, Sarah became pregnant again. She only carried this child for five months before miscarrying following yet another beating from Thaddeus. On the day she miscarried, something, Sarah didn't know what, had upset him. He slapped her and punched her in the stomach and stormed out of the cottage, leaving Sarah in pain on the floor. Thaddeus didn't know that his punch would cause Sarah to lose the baby. All alone, amongst the pots and pans and lying next to the coal scuttle, in absolute agony Sarah miscarried on the dirty scullery floor...'

Jacob, who was then seven years old, wasn't in the cottage when Sarah miscarried. He was at the 'Dame' school, which he had been attending for about a year. When he returned home, later in the day, he found his mother, white faced and haggard, sobbing and holding a bundle in her arms. Sarah had managed to get up, tidy herself up a little and had wrapped the miscarried child, which was a boy, in an old bed sheet. She told Jacob to run down the road and fetch Aunt Eliza.

Eliza came to the cottage and did whatever she could to make sure that Sarah was alright. Not that there was much she could do. She even tried to persuade Sarah to come home with her, but Sarah would not listen. I have to stay at the cottage with the children, she told Eliza. The miscarriage meant that the dead baby needed to be quickly buried. So they agreed that, Eliza would take him away, before Thaddeus returned home, and go to St Joseph's and arrange for his burial.

Although fearing for her sister because she was unsure how Thaddeus was going to react, Eliza did as she was asked. She left the cottage and took the dead baby with her. With the minimum of fuss and, after telling him the circumstances of the miscarriage, she arranged with the priest for the baby to be quietly buried in St Joseph's church yard.

When Thaddeus returned home drunk later that evening and was told, he was uncaring and unbelievably dismissive about what had happened. Fortunately for Sarah, he left her alone that night and for several more nights after.

Regrettably, Sarah's and Jacob's life would get much worse in the years to come...

'...The next six years of my life were hard and very difficult to bear... I frequently cried myself to sleep at night,' said Jacob.

'Much of the time, because I was a child, I couldn't understand why things happened in the manner that they did. Thaddeus would slap, or hit me with the back of his hand for the slightest provocation. I was regularly beaten, but had no idea why. It was only when I got older that I realised, Thaddeus disliked and resented me. He resented me because I was William's son, born out of a deep loving relationship and, had brought great joy to both my mama and papa…

…Although weak, my grandfather Nathaniel lived bedridden for another year and passed away in 1860, when I was eight years old. He died in the same year my mama gave birth to Thaddeus's only son, whom she called John. Thaddeus seem genuinely pleased that he now had a son. Unfortunately for me... his pleasure in his son John only increased his displeasure in me. The slaps and blows became more frequent and harder. I took to keeping out his way as much as I could. Even hiding and sleeping in the shed when Thaddeus was drunk.

Resigned to her sorry fate in life and what Thaddeus had reduced her too, your great-grandmother had more children with Thaddeus. My half-sister Miriam was born in 1861 and eighteen months later she had another daughter, Rebecca. Two years after giving birth to Rebecca, my mama was heavily pregnant again, when the events happened that made it necessary for me to run away from home.

It was a lovely evening in August 1865, just two weeks before my thirteenth birthday. My mama, John, Miriam, Rebecca and me, were at home in the cottage. Hannah and Harriett had gone to stay with Aunt Eliza after our grandfather Nathaniel died. Eliza now had a much larger home and welcomed her nieces' company. I can remember thinking as we all sat merrily talking that evening, how my mother looked much better than she had done for a long time. She was laughing and joking with us when with a loud crash the door burst open. Thaddeus stood there, battered and bleeding…

…For various wagers, at the age of forty-six, he had started bareknuckle fighting again. The Irish navvies and gypsies who lived around Newark hadn't forgotten, how, in a bareknuckle fight several years before, Thaddeus had nearly beaten one of their people to death. They were out for revenge! A few easier fights were arranged, which the unsuspecting

Thaddeus won. They were testing him out, trying to establish how much the passing years had diminished his fighting skills. The navvies and gypsies had a plan, which Thaddeus couldn't see, but was slowly being drawn into...

The more times Thaddeus fought, the more brutal he became at home. It was as though the thrill of hurting someone was coursing through his very being. Their plan was working. When they were ready, the navvies offered Thaddeus a wager to fight a Limerick man whose name I never knew, that had recently come over from Ireland...

Convinced of his own invincibility Thaddeus took the wager and bet all the money he possessed on the outcome. So sure that he would win, he even borrowed money from some of the men he worked with at the slaughter house. Thaddeus wasn't to know that this Limerick man was half his age, just as big and, had never been beaten. And, like Thaddeus, he too, had a reputation for the ferocity and brutality of his fighting.

The outcome was inevitable. Thaddeus was soundly beaten and he lost all his and, his workmates, money. His arrogance and self-confidence had been his downfall. Though they wanted to hurt him badly, the navvies had the good sense to know when enough was enough. As much as they may have wanted to, the navvies and gypsies were not going to kill him. The last thing they needed was an excuse for the constabulary to come around asking them questions…

There Thaddeus stood in the cottage doorway, battered, bleeding and angry. Alarmed, my mother told the younger children to quickly go to their bedroom and to shut the door and not to come out until she came to fetch them. I was concerned for my mother's safety, so I chose to stay in the room. We'd never seen Thaddeus like this before and, we had no idea how he was going to react...

Thaddeus slammed the door shut and staggered over to a chair and sat down. Though my mother hated him and was inwardly pleased he had taken a beating, he needed his facial injuries tending to. Drawing some fresh water from the pump and with a piece of cloth, she went over and started to clean up his face. Thaddeus's left eye was closing, it looked like his nose was broken and he'd lost some teeth. He looked a sorry sight.

Occasionally flinching with the pain, he allowed my mother to tend his injuries. What she couldn't tend to, was the hurt that was welling up inside him. Thaddeus had been shamed, he was embarrassed. Nobody had bettered him before. Not only had he been bettered, the navvies had humiliated him. His young opponent had taunted him and, towards the end of the fight, hit him at will. Someone had to pay. Someone was going to pay for his shame. That someone would be my mother.

After she had finished cleaning and dressing his injuries Thaddeus sat there in ominous silence, thinking and brooding. His mind was in turmoil. He refused all offers of food, but accepted a flagon of ale. As he drank, his expression darkened and his mood became blacker and blacker. He suddenly rose to his feet and exploded with rage. Turning towards my mother and with a voice full of menace, he bawled at her,

'This is entirely your fault!'

'Why... why Thaddeus what have I done now?' mother replied fearfully.

She had become frightened at how suddenly she was being blamed for something she'd had nothing at all to do with.

'...It's always your fault, Sarah... you make me do these things.' Thaddeus ranted.

My mother couldn't understand why he was talking nonsense like this, but she knew exactly what was coming.

'...Why do you make me do these things... you fucking bitch?' he snarled viciously at her.

Now very fearful, 'I don't make you do anything Thaddeus... you're your own man,' my mother pleaded.

'...Yes you do... yes you FUCKING DO!' he yelled. Thaddeus had totally lost his mind.

With that, he moved forward towards my mother, and although he winced from the pain of bruised and possibly broken ribs, he managed to get hold of her. I rushed over and tried to get between them, but he just brushed me away as easy as swatting a fly off his coat...'

The children looked at each other a little concerned. They could see that Jacob was starting to become quite agitated. As he remembered in explicit detail what happened that night, he became slightly breathless and much redder in the face. Although, when he told the story to the children, he hadn't used the swear words he so graphically recalled. They were imprinted on his brain and still made him angry all these years later. He could still hear them.

'…Thaddeus attacked my mother and began hitting her harder and more viciously than ever before. He even punched her in the face. She held her arms up around her head as she tried to defend herself. I could hear her screaming with each blow. Thaddeus had really had lost his mind. He was like a man possessed and totally out of control.

'No Thaddeus… NO,' she cried out. '…You're killing me.'

'You fucking bitch,' he shouted at her.

The thudding of the blows and my mother's screams cut through me like a knife. I couldn't stand it any longer. Grabbing the nearest thing to hand, which happened to be Thaddeus's own cudgel, I hit him as hard as I could over the back of the head. Not just once, but three times. All the years of hurt, which was bottled up inside me, went into those three blows. I was so angry.

The first blow stunned Thaddeus. I actually heard his skull crack. He let go of my mother and sank to his knees. After the second and third blows, he fell to the floor dead… his skull was broken. Thaddeus died as he lived his life; violently. Blood oozed from his head, staining the rug and floor. I dropped the blood stained cudgel to the floor. I had killed Thaddeus Stone.

My mother and I stared at each other. She was bleeding from the mouth and nose and was breathing heavily. I stood there trembling in shock, not quite believing what had just happened. And, what I'd just done.

'Oh Jacob… oh my precious son, what have you done… what have you done?' my mother asked.

'I… I've killed him… for you mama… he can't hurt you no more,' I said before bursting into tears.

'I know son… I know,' my mother replied. 'Come here, Jacob.'

Although it was all those years ago, I can still remember clearly how my mama came over and wrapped her arms around me. We just stood in silence for a short while. She was already starting to think of the consequences of what had happened. Becoming panic stricken mama started crying.

'Oh no… Oh no,' she cried. 'The constable will come and take you away…'

'…you'll be tried for murder, Jacob… they will hang you…' she said.

Taking hold of me by the shoulders and looking straight into my eyes said,

'…You can't stay here… I can't let them take you.' Mama wept.

We looked at each other, we were both crying. Again she hugged me tightly.

'Oh Jacob… Jacob!' she sobbed.

In our hearts, we both knew that I would have to flee and get far away from Calthorpe as fast as I could…'

Jacob stopped talking, he was breathing heavily. His face flushed with the emotion and turmoil of telling this part of the story. His grandchildren looked at him horrified. Grace was a little frightened. Not knowing what to say or do. For a while no one spoke.

'…You really killed him… I mean, really killed him, grandad,' said Daniel in wide eyed astonishment.

Gabriel and Grace were too shocked to say anything. They just stared, incredulous and unbelieving at what their grandad had just told them. He was a murderer!

'Yes… yes I did… I'm sorry to say… I'm not sorry that I did it, but, I am sorry I have to tell you, my lovely grandchildren, that I killed someone.' Jacob replied.

'…On the twenty-second of August 1865, I murdered Thaddeus Stone.'

They all sat for a moment in silence. The redness of Jacob's face started to fade. Looking out of the window, he sucked on his pipe and in a calmer voice, said.

'That's the first time in many years; I've told anyone the real reason why I left home… Even my wife, God bless her, and my wonderful daughter, your mama, doesn't know. For reasons which I will explain to you, the truth has been hidden for so many years.'

'Now I know father,' they heard a voice say. '…Now I know!'

Startled and disturbed, Jacob spun round and looked aghast when he saw his daughter.

Sarah-Eliza was sat in the corner of the room. She'd stopped working in the kitchen and had come to tell them that dinner wouldn't be too long. But, seeing her children so attentive, obviously enraptured with what her father was telling them, decided not to disturb them. Stepping quietly into the room she had sat down to listen to him for a while. Neither Jacob, nor the children knew she was there. Sarah-Eliza couldn't believe what she had just heard. Her father had killed someone.

Regaining his composure, Jacob looked at his daughter and asked her to come over and sit with them. She walked across the room and pulled a chair closer to the fireside and sat down. Grace got off Jacob's knee and went and sat with her mother.

Apologising to Sarah-Eliza, Jacob asked her not to be angry with him. After keeping the secret for nigh on sixty years, he explained that he'd only decided that very day to tell the children the true story of why he left Calthorpe. And, he had planned to tell Sarah-Eliza the complete true story, [including Thaddeus raping his mama, which he had left out of the story he told to the children], after they had been put to bed.

'What did you hear Sarah-Eliza?' Jacob asked.

'Not all… but, enough, father,' she replied.

'Well… don't judge me too harshly Sarah-Eliza… before I tell you the whole story,' said Jacob.

Sarah-Eliza loved her father and wasn't going to get angry with him in front of the children. Though there was so much she now needed to ask him, including why had he chosen to tell the whole story now. This troubled her. She said nothing more and decided to hold her tongue but resolved to discuss the matter at a more convenient time later in the evening.

Daniel and Gabriel weren't really bothered about such trivial details, as to why their mother hadn't been told. They wanted their grandad to carry on with the story and had questions of their own to ask.

'Carry on telling your story father,' said Sarah-Eliza. '…we'll talk some more later on tonight.'

'Yes carry on grandad… please.' Gabriel implored.

This time, Jacob really needed to suck on his pipe, taste the tobacco, and gather his thoughts rather than use it for dramatic affect. Before he could speak again, ever impatient Daniel, trying so hard to be grown up and understand what he had just heard asked,

'…Grandad, would they really have put you on trial for murder… you were only protecting your mother… I mean would they really have taken you away?'

'Yes, Daniel they would… even though I was trying to stop my mama from being hurt… I had killed a man… I have no regrets… He was an evil, vile, sadistic man, who in my opinion needed killing.'

'Father… that's enough of talk like that,' Sarah-Eliza said disapprovingly.

'Yes dear… sorry, you are right… perhaps I've got a bit too carried away with the emotion of recalling all that really happened that night.'

'Yes, father… maybe you have!' Sarah-Eliza replied, frowning reproachfully at her father.

'After you killed him, what did you do Grandad… why didn't the police come and catch you?' asked Gabriel.

'Quite simple Gabriel… because, the police weren't looking for me… although I didn't know that at the time,' Jacob replied.

'What!' Gabriel and Daniel exclaimed together.

Sarah-Eliza and the children looked at each other and then back at Jacob. Now they were even more confused…'

… After Thaddeus died and when they were both calmer and thinking more rationally, Sarah sat Jacob down and together they planned how to deal with this catastrophe. Sarah's love for her son took over. She was determined that the police were not going to take Jacob. He would soon be thirteen years old and had his whole life in front of him. She had to get him away from the village, before anyone else found out what had happened to Thaddeus…

'Jacob… you do realise that you can't stay here anymore, don't you?' Sarah asked, adding

'…In the morning the constable will have to be told about Thaddeus and you cannot be here when he is… You do understand that don't you?'

'Yes mama, I think I do… but, where will I go… what shall I do.' Jacob replied fretfully. 'How will I manage on my own?'

Jacob started crying and shaking again, his face a picture of anxiety and misery. He was fearful of what his mama said needed to happen.

'I…I… don't want to go… Why can't I stay here mama?' he pleaded.

'Now you listen to me Jacob and listen well… if you stay here the constable will certainly take you away to prison and I may never see you again.' Sarah said firmly. '…I need you to be strong!'

'…You must leave here and go to one of the towns or cities where no one will know you… and never ever come back or contact me until I tell you to do so.'

'Yes mama… but, what will I do on my own?' asked Jacob, still sobbing.

'Son, listen to me…these days, people are moving around the country all the time now to find work in the new industries… You must do what others are doing, go and find work… become a man and make your father and I proud of you,' Sarah said insistently.

'Go and make something of yourself, Jacob… live a rich and rewarding life, which you won't be able to do if you stay here.'

Very reluctantly Jacob had to agree. Though apprehensive, he knew his mother was right. There was no other way out of this terrible mess.

'But… what will you do mama?' he asked.

'Don't you worry about me… I'll send for Aunt Eliza and together we'll think of something to tell the constable… but, not until after you've gone.' Sarah replied.

'…First I have to make sure that you're safe.'

Sarah already had a plan in mind. She knew what she was going to do once Jacob had got away, but she kept these thoughts to herself. He didn't need to know...

…Having decided that Jacob had to flee, they prepared for him to leave. Sarah bundled together a few clothes and made sure Jacob had his warmest clothes on. She walked over to the pine chest of drawers and from the back of one of the drawers, took out a poke of money. Some of the money she'd earned from weaving at her loom, she'd saved and hidden away from Thaddeus. Just a little bit at a time so that he didn't notice or become suspicious. There was no need to hide it now.

Sarah gave Jacob fifteen shillings, which was about a week's wages for a labourer and, told him to keep it safe in his pockets and not tell anyone that he had it.

'Trust no one son until you think you know them well…and even then still be wary,' she cautioned Jacob.

From the pocket on her skirt, Sarah took out the wedding ring William had given her fourteen years before and, with a leather thong, tied it around Jacob's neck. She had managed to also keep the ring hidden all the years she was with Thaddeus.

'Jacob… your papa and I were so in love when he gave me this ring… you were the result of our love… It's your ring now; give it to your wife when the day comes.' Sarah said, her voice faltering with the emotion of what she was remembering and saying to Jacob.

Tearfully, she hugged Jacob and kissed him on the cheek, not wanting to let him go, but knowing she must.

'Go now my son… go and prosper… become someone and then all these years of hurt will have been worthwhile,' Sarah said as she wiped tears from hers and Jacob's face.

'...Go to Lincoln and from there maybe go on to Grimsby. I've heard tell that there's work to be had there in the fishing industry.'

'What do I know about fishing,' Jacob replied.

'What does anyone know... go and find out... learn, prosper and make your fortune,' Sarah told him before adding,

'You mustn't write to me...we can't let the police know where you are... Let some years pass and then write to your Aunt Eliza, when you're safely settled... she can then tell me how you're doing... I'll be able to come and see you.'

Jacob nodded and trying to stifle his sobs, he opened the cottage door and, even though it was late at night, stepped out into the darkness to walk the fourteen miles to Lincoln. Embracing and kissing his mother for one last time, with fifteen shillings in his pocket and his bundle over his shoulder, Jacob set off down the road into the unknown.

'Don't look back, Jacob...and don't ever come back until I tell you too.' Sarah tearfully shouted.

Jacob didn't look back. He wasn't to know he would never see or speak to his mother again...

...Once Jacob had gone, Sarah shut the blue door and sat down sobbing. Looking at Thaddeus's dead body, she could feel all the hatred she had for him, eating her up inside. She was determined that some good will come out of this. Sarah never slept that night, she sat there, in the candle light, reading her bible and thinking about what was going to happen in the days to follow.

At first light in the morning, after she had covered Thaddeus's body up, Sarah woke up John, Miriam and Rebecca, and took them to Eliza's house. Eliza couldn't believe her eyes when she saw Sarah bruised face, or her ears, when Sarah told her what had happened and what she intended to do about it.

'Sarah, is that wise... what if they don't believe you?' Eliza asked earnestly.

'They will Eliza... they have to,' Sarah replied.

'…I have to protect Jacob… and I need you to help me to do it,' Sarah said. '…Jacob wouldn't stand up to police questioning… I really have to do this.'

'…Jacob is his father's son and needs a better chance in life than William had… I'm going to make sure he gets it.' Sarah said passionately.

Although she feared for her sister's welfare, Eliza reluctantly agreed to go along with Sarah's plan and agreed that the children could stay with her. Hannah and Harriett were already living there anyway.

Sarah left the children with Eliza and went to find the constable, who was new to the village. He'd only been there a few months and was relatively inexperienced. After he was found, she took him to the cottage. When Sarah pulled the cover off Thaddeus's dead body, he was startled and staggered back in horror at the sight of the injuries and the coagulated blood on the body and the floor. From the look on his face, Sarah thought he was going to retch. The constable managed to control himself, but was very white faced and unsteady on his feet when he asked her what had happened. Sarah explained how Thaddeus had attacked her, the evidence was still plain to see on her face, and in self-defence she had hit Thaddeus several times with the cudgel.

Unsure what to do or say, the young constable was out of his depth. Chicken stealing and drunken men, he could deal with, but battered dead bodies were another matter. Apologetically, he said he'd have to take Sarah into custody, while he sent for the local sergeant or a more senior officer from Newark to come and investigate the matter. Thaddeus's body was removed to the police station, prior to its burial. Sarah was taken into custody and the cottage locked up.

When the senior officers from Newark investigated the killing, Sarah lied about Jacob's absence by saying he'd run away terrified by Thaddeus and would probably be hiding in the woods, or somewhere nearby and, would return before long. The police officers were not at all interested in a boy, not yet thirteen years old, running away. *'Happens all the time',* they said dismissively and, gave Jacob no more thought. So far so good, Sarah thought to herself.

At first the police appeared to accept Sarah's confession that she had struck out in self-defence. Thaddeus's other extensive injuries, which he had sustained in the bareknuckle fight, told a different story and needed explaining. The police had no doubt that Thaddeus had hit Sarah. But, as they couldn't find anyone to confirm that the bareknuckle fight had actually happened, they concluded, quite wrongly, that she had caused all of Thaddeus's head and facial injuries.

Sarah was charged with the wilful murder of Thaddeus Stone by attacking him with his own cudgel, while he was probably sleeping off a heavy drinking session. She was nearly six months pregnant, with the last child she would carry, when they imprisoned her in Newark jail. Sarah was held in jail for eight weeks until her trial at the next Assizes in Nottingham. This was not at all what she had expected to happen.

The jail was overcrowded and filthy. All types of prisoners were herded together with no separation of men and women, the young and the old, the convicted and the un-convicted, or the sane and the insane. Conditions in the prison were very basic and she suffered intolerable discomfort. No allowance was made for the fact she was pregnant. Sarah wasn't unique. Many women in the prison were pregnant. Some even became pregnant whilst in prison. Her cell was cold and bare, with a hard wooden bed, the food was monotonous and there were few activities to relieve the boredom. Prison was a deterrent. Visits from family were limited and controlled.

When Sarah's case came to trial, she had no legal representation. Unfortunately for her, the police made a compelling and damning case. Even with legal representation it would have been hard to argue against the police's contentions. Her family and friends stood by her and did what they could. Several witnesses, including the parish priest from St Joseph's church, testified as to her character and good name but, there were none that could give reliable evidence about how frequently Thaddeus had beaten her. Sadly, how he had managed to isolate Sarah from her family and friends, and her own determination that no one would know she was being abused would count against her. Sarah was found guilty of murdering Thaddeus Stone in a frenzied attack while he was sleeping.

The case against Sarah was won by the seriousness of Thaddeus's facial and head injuries and, because nobody came forward to give evidence to corroborate her contention that they had been sustained in a bareknuckle fight. The Irish navvies didn't want to become involved and denied that there'd been any fight. Ironically the consequence of Thaddeus Stone's violent last day on earth in this life was Sarah's undoing!

When the judge put the black cap over his wig, there was a loud gasp from the crowded public gallery. Some cheered, some shouted 'shame'. The spectators loved a good murder case and knew what the sentence would be. Gripping the rails of the dock, Sarah stood there trembling, but steadfast as the judge sentenced her to hang by the neck until dead.

Hearing the verdict and the sentence, Eliza, her other sisters and Mrs Tom, who were sat in the public gallery, began to wail and sob in anguish. Sarah looked up at them and tried to smile as she was taken down to the cells. She could not let them see how terrified she was. As she was now seven months pregnant, the death sentence would not be carried out until after she had been delivered of the baby. There was still a chance that the sentence may be commuted into a jail term. Through the prison reforms, in Victorian England, there was an increasing reluctance to hang women. But, on the day of the trial, Sarah went back to her cell knowing she had less than two months of her life left to live in Nottingham jail. This was not the outcome she had planned.

Eliza and her sisters visited Sarah whenever they were allowed. During one of these visits, shortly before she went in to labour, Sarah gave Eliza a letter.

'Will you give this to Mrs Tom? ...She needs to know what really happened to Tom,' said Sarah. '...tell her I'm dreadfully sorry... I should have told her much sooner.'

Eliza promised to deliver the letter to Charlotte,

'Thank you for looking after my children,' Sarah said to Eliza, who was sobbing. '…It's a comfort to me to know that they are safe and well cared for.'

'Every day… tell them how much I love them.'

'I'll do my best Sarah,' Eliza tearfully replied as she rose to leave.

The sisters looked each other in the eyes. Both knew that although not a word was spoken, all that could be said was being said at that moment. They hugged in a long embrace.

'My dear sister… I'll love them like you do.' Eliza said.

'I… I know you will,' Sarah replied. 'I… know you will… Off you go now; I'll see you again soon.'

Tearfully Eliza left. She never saw Sarah again.

Two days after her visit, Sarah went into labour. After ten painful hours and only basic care, she was delivered of a baby girl, but died shortly after giving birth. All the beatings and the events that led to Sarah being imprisoned and, the imprisonment itself, had left her very weak. She didn't have the strength, or the will to fight anymore. At the age of thirty-two on the 28th November 1865, as Sarah gave life, she gave up her own life - knowing that her beloved Jacob was now safe.

Being a convicted murderer, Sarah was buried with the minimum of ceremony in an unmarked grave in the prison grounds. Eliza collected the baby from the prison and took her home to be raised with her sisters and brother. As Sarah had asked her to, she named the baby Charlotte, after Mrs Tom. Eliza became the mother and provider for all of Sarah and Thaddeus's six children.

Eliza had no way of contacting Jacob, to tell him that his mother was dead. He had heeded her advice, about letting people know where he was. It would be four more years, before Jacob, when he was seventeen, wrote to his Aunt Eliza giving an address where she could contact him…

It was now totally dark outside and way past Grace's bedtime. Sarah-Eliza rose to her feet and went over to draw the curtains across the window. As she did, the clock on the mahogany chiffonier chimed eight o'clock. Sarah-Eliza realised just how long they had been sat listening to Jacob. He really was a master story teller, she thought. Although she had missed the earlier part of his story, Sarah-Eliza had been just as captivated as the children were with the part of the story she had heard.

Sarah-Eliza spoke, '...that's enough for today, father... it's already past Grace's bedtime and we haven't eaten yet.'

'...come along all of you let's go and have our dinner before it is totally ruined.'

'Oh mother... do we have to?' asked Daniel.

He wanted his grandfather to carry on and would sit there listening all evening, if his mother would let him. There was so much he wanted to know.

'Yes Daniel, we do,' she replied firmly. 'Grandad can carry on with his story in the morning... won't you father?'

'Yes... yes of course I will... Come along children, let's all go and eat,' Jacob answered.

'Oh bother... bother!' Daniel muttered under his breath.

Reluctantly, the children got up and followed their mother out of the room. Jacob walked along behind them.

...After they'd eaten and the children had been put to bed, sat by the warmth of the fireside Jacob told Sarah-Eliza the whole truthful story. She sobbed and looked aghast when he told her of the repeated rapes and the beatings his mother had endured. The beatings that he had taken, which he played down a little, and the murder of Tom Kite distressed Sarah-Eliza even further. Most of all, she sobbed because, only now, she was hearing what her father had had to endure as a child. She wished he'd told her about his childhood much sooner. Why was he telling her all this now? She wondered.

As Sarah-Eliza sat looking at her father, who was also becoming upset and moist eyed, she fiddled with and twisted a gold ring she had on her finger. Jacob had given it to her after his wife died, saying, she would have wanted her to have it. Sarah-Eliza assumed he had meant her mother, because that was the ring Jacob had put on her finger when they married. Now she knew the ring that her father had given her, was the

one his mother had tied around his neck the night he had left
Calthorpe…

Part 2

Chapter 6

The Road To Our Fortune Won't Get Any Shorter!

When the curtains were drawn open the next morning, even though it was November, it was bright and sunny. The wind had eased, the smog had lifted and there were only light clouds in the sky. It looked like it was going to be a nice day. Totally different from the previous day, when the weather had been as cheerless as parts of the story their grandad had told them.

Normally, it was difficult to get the children out of their bed. Not this day. Daniel and Gabriel got up at the first time of asking. They washed the sleep from their eyes, dressed quickly and hurried down stairs for breakfast. Grace took a little longer. The boys were sharing a bedroom and had talked excitedly, long into the night, about their grandad killing someone, 'who needed killing.' In the manner of adolescent young boys, both spoke with exaggerated bravado and imagination about what they would have done, had they been Jacob.

'I would have killed him… biff, bash… Take that Thaddeus Stone,' said Daniel, as he punched and pummelled his pillows, which he had stood upright against the bed-head to represent Thaddeus.

'So would I,' said Gabriel, not to be outdone by his brother.

The boys wanted to know how their grandad had got away with murder and couldn't wait for him to continue telling his story. During breakfast, Sarah-Eliza had had to chide both her boys for eating far too quickly.

'Grandad will only tell the story, when he's ready… so stop gulping your food down and be patient,' she said. '…Isn't that right father?'

'Yes… yes dear… that's right,' said Jacob, as he gave a crafty wink to the two boys.

'Father, I saw that… you're incorrigible,' said Sarah-Eliza.

When breakfast was finished and the pots cleared away, the children and Sarah-Eliza went into the sitting room and sat around Jacob. After listening to her father the previous evening, Sarah-Eliza now needed to hear the whole story. This was important to her, because she knew that her father was talking from the heart and not making up a far-fetched yarn. They sat waiting patiently.

Jacob, put his pipe in his mouth and looking at the children, took the time to light it with a taper from the fire. He was smiling but, not being hurried. After blowing out the taper he drew hard on the pipe and savoured the taste of the tobacco before exhaling. He was deep in thought. Then he began.

'Be brave, be strong Jacob. Don't let mama see you're upset, I told myself as I walked away from the cottage…

…I heard my mama shout, *'don't look back, Jacob… and don't ever come back'*. I wanted to turn round and say something to her, like 'I love you mama', but I knew that if I did, I wouldn't have left her. So I didn't, I said nothing. I had to keep walking. With my mama's words ringing in my ears, I quickened my footsteps to carry me away from the cottage as fast as they could. I set off towards the main road, where I had to choose to go right or left. I chose to go to the right as this was the road into Lincoln.

That night, the sky was clear and there was a three-quarter moon. So it wasn't as dark as it could have been. As I walked along the road, I could see quite well. Well enough to spot some animals scurrying and darting about. I wasn't alone. Sometimes, in the moonlight, I could just see their eyes staring out from the hedgerows and bushes. As I walked, several foxes and badgers crossed my path. Many times I heard the screeching and hooting of owls as they hunted their prey. Two or three times, barn owls flew close by me like white ghosts in the sky, making me jump.

'Were you frightened of the dark grandad…I would be?' asked Gabriel.

'Me too!' said Grace.

Daniel, trying to be clever, just tut -tutted, causing his mother to look across at him sternly.

'No... I wasn't scared of the dark... In those days there were no street lights on the country roads and in the villages, not like we have now, so I was used to walking around in the darkness of the night.'

'Mind you... when I came to stretches of the road, where it passed through the woodlands and forests I walked a lot quicker...' For dramatic effect, Jacob leant towards the children, lowered his voice and spoke slowly.

'...There's something quite scary, eerie and ethereal about forests and woodlands in the dead of night that fuels our imagination and frightens the inherent primeval legacy that's in all of us...'

Jacob leant back in his chair. His weathered, old face beamed with a broad grin. Looking at the children's puzzled faces, he felt sure that none of them had understood a word of what he had just said. He smiled.

'... I must have walked for about three hours before I felt tired and a little cold, so I looked for somewhere warm to sleep for a couple of hours. From the number of times I had hidden from Thaddeus, I was quite used to sleeping outside in sheds and similar shelters. For a while, I thought I may have to sleep in the hedgerow when, lucky for me, I saw a small barn type shelter close by the road. And, I could get in.

Curled up snug in pile of hay, I felt safe for the first time in several hours. As I lay there wondering what my mama was doing, I fell into a deep sleep and slept for about four hours. I couldn't really be sure how long, as I had no watch, or any other means of telling the time. When I woke up, it was just starting to get light. So I'd better scarper I thought, before anyone comes along and finds me there.

Cautiously I looked out... nobody was about. I left the barn and went back to the road to continue my journey. After I'd walked just a few hundred yards more, rounded a bend in the road, I was surprised to see Lincoln Cathedral on the skyline, less than two miles away. Although I'd never been to Lincoln before, my mama had. And, I knew from things she told me, that Lincoln had a massive cathedral, which sat on top of a hill, next to a castle and could be seen from miles away. That's Lincoln over there I thought.

So, I must have walked about twelve miles before I stopped to sleep. I felt really pleased with myself. That was, until I remembered why I was on the road to Lincoln in the first place. *'Go and make something of your life Jacob... go and prosper'*, my mama had said. Ahead of me was the future. My future...

Less than an hour later, I arrived in the south side of Lincoln and walked up the High Street. Before that day, I'd never been more than four miles out of Calthorpe and, was amazed by the sights, which greeted me that morning. In the early morning sunlight Lincoln Castle and the imposing Cathedral were straight ahead of me on top of the hill. I walked slowly up the High Street, trying to take everything in. Looking in the shop windows, I couldn't believe how many different types of shops there were and, the numerous things, many of which I'd never seen before, that were being sold. Calthorpe had only two general stores, a butchers shop and a pub. There was five times that number of shops on one side of the High Street alone and, about six or seven pubs...

The city was beginning to stir. With each passing minute, more and more people emerged onto the street. Men were going off to work, the shops were opening, horses and carts started to trundle down the road. I could hear the horses snorting and their hooves beat out a steady clip-clop rhythm as the drivers coaxed them forward with their whips. Every now and then, I heard the ripe language of the drivers as they cursed and swore at their horses for not doing what they wanted them to do.

People were going about their business; shouting out good humoured greetings to each other, or to attract interest in whatever they were trying to sell. Amongst all these people and horses, several dusty and mangy stray dogs were scavenging and wandering around, occasionally barking or yelping as they were moved out the way by the toe end of someone's boot. Gradually, the High Street became a noisy cacophony of sound. Unlike anything I had ever seen or heard before. It was the start of another working day in Lincoln...

Further up the High Street, I saw smoke billowing from the chimney of a steam train, that was about to depart from the station. I had never been as close as this to a steam train before and was astonished at how big they were. The crossing gate, where the rail track crosses the High Street, had been closed. I was so excited to stand there and watch as the train, with steam hissing from its engine and pulling four coaches crowded with people, leave the station and pass by, right in front of me. The driver of the train waved to us and with two shrill blasts on the engine's whistle, which startled several people, the train picked up speed and was gone. I had never heard anything so loud in my life... Even today, in my imagination, I can still smell the mixture of smoke, oil and steam from the train, my first train, as it went past. For the briefest of instants, I had forgotten all the awfulness and nastiness of less than twelve hours before. Like most children would be, I was captivated by the sight and sounds of that train as it passed by...' said Jacob.

'...With the train gone, I could move forward up the street again. I hadn't walked too far when I saw a policeman. I panicked, which was only natural, I suppose. As it happens, that policeman couldn't have been looking for me anyway. It was still early in the morning and my mama, wouldn't have yet told the constable in Calthorpe, which was fourteen miles away. But, panic I did. I darted into an alleyway at the side of one of the pubs to hide out of the policeman's sight.

'...You on the run from the rozzers?' I heard a voice from behind me say.

I turned round and there in the shadows, hiding behind a pair of up-turned barrels, was a dirty, ginger haired, freckled face, raggedly dressed boy, not that much bigger or older than me.

'What did you say?' I said to him, not being sure what he had actually said to me.

'For sure, you're on the run... aren't you?' he said, in a really broad accent that I'd never heard before.

'No... no, I'm not!' I bristled. '...what makes you think that?'

'Well now,' he said, as he came out from behind the barrels. '...by the way you dashed into this alley, when you saw that crusher on the corner... I'd say you were.'

Rozzers, crushers, this boy was talking in an accent that was strange to me and using words, which I'd never heard before.

'Don't worry... I'm not going to dob you in it,' he said. '...I'm on the run too.'

He went to the top of the alley to see where the policeman was and came back and sat down on one of the barrels.

'He's gone, the crusher's gone... so panic over,' he said, gesturing for me to sit beside him.

I walked over and sat on the barrel next to him.

'Well then... what's your name?' he asked. '...mine's Finbar McHugh.'

'Finbar... Finbar! What sort of name is that...?' I asked laughingly, because I'd never heard it before.

'It's a fine Irish name, cos I'm from Ireland... and for sure, it's nothing to laugh about,' Finbar said. '...What's your name anyway?'

Although my mama had told me not to trust anyone, there was something about this lad. I decided I liked Finbar. So I told him my name.

'My name is Jacob Rawlings,' I said.

'That's a fine name too Jacob, for sure... but, I think I'm going to call you Jake,' said Finbar.

'Why?' I asked.

'Because I like the name Jake... Jacob's fine... Jake is better,' he replied.

'Well in that case,' I said. 'I'm going to call you Barf... no, no that won't do at all... I'm going to call you Barney...Yes, that's it, Barney.'

'Well then Jake, meet Barney and... I'm very pleased to know you,' Barney said holding out his hand, which I shook, before we both started laughing...'

'…That children, is how I met Barney McHugh, who became my life-long best friend…' said Jacob.

Sarah-Eliza was smiling and the children were laughing at how their grandad had told this part of the story.

'…Barney was from County Down and had come over from Ireland with his mammy and daddy about three years before. He wasn't sure exactly how long he'd been in England, but knew that he had experienced three English winters. His father was one of the many thousands of navvies who had come over from Ireland to find work building the railways and the canals. When they came over, his mammy had left Barney's younger sisters and brothers with relatives and, promised to send for them once they were able to. I don't think she ever did…'

'…Why are you on the run Barney… what are you running away from?' I asked him.

'From the workhouse… from Suth'ell Union Workhouse,' he replied.

I wasn't sure at first where he was referring to, until I remembered that the town of Southwell, which is not that many miles from Calthorpe and Newark, is pronounced Suth'ell and it had a workhouse. His strange accent had thrown me...

'Why were you in the workhouse… where's your mother and father?' I asked.

'Gone… both are gone,' he replied.

'Gone… gone where…where have they gone to?' I asked him.

I was suddenly starting to feel sorry for Barney...

…He waited for a while before he replied to me. Taking a sharp intake of breath, and becoming visibly upset, but managing to hold back the tears, he told me that his father, whom he loved, had being killed working on the railway. They were working in Derbyshire, blasting the way through some rocks. Before all the navvies had cleared the area, the dynamite detonated too soon. His father was caught in the explosion... they never found much of him.

Shortly after his father died, his mammy took up with another man. Barney endured living with them for about a year. One morning when he woke up, they were gone. His mammy and her new man had run off, leaving him behind to fend for himself. Nobody knew where they had gone. The general manager of the railway company said Barney couldn't stay at the works and arranged, with the police, for him to go to the Southwell Union workhouse. Before the children could ask, Jacob explained what the workhouse was.

'...The workhouse was where they put you, if you had no job, nowhere to live, was a tramp, or was an orphan with no one to look after you,' said old Jacob. '...You received food and somewhere to sleep but, in most workhouses you lived in horrible conditions...

At Southwell, Barney had to work all day, either breaking stones into smaller pieces, which could be sold for road-making. Or, oakham picking, which involved teasing out the fibres from old hemp ropes and nearly broke your fingers. The fibres were sold to ship builders to be mixed with tar and used to seal the lining of wooden ships. For a young boy, it would have been hard work. Discipline was harsh. Often the punishment for transgressions, even minor ones, was being whipped. Barney lived there for nearly a year and was whipped on three occasions before he absconded...'

I asked Barney, 'How long have you been on the run?'

'Four days since.' Barney replied. '...I haven't eaten for two days...I'm right starvin'.'

'You've not got any scran in that there bundle have you?' he asked.

I was confused, 'Scran...what's scran?'

'Scran is snap... scoff... food!' he said looking at me as though I was an imbecile.

'No I haven't, but I do have sixpence... we could buy something with that... I'm hungry too.'

Even though I'd decided I liked Barney, I wasn't going to let him know that I had fifteen shillings in my pocket.

'Well, that's just fine and dandy,' Barney said with a smile. '...Let's go find something to eat.'

'…We left the alleyway and walked up towards Steep Hill and the Cathedral until we found a pie shop. With the sixpence, I bought two meat pies for penny and halfpenny each and, a loaf of bread for one penny and three farthings, which left me with one penny and farthing change from the sixpence. We took our food and sat by the River Witham, which was only a few yards from the pie shop and ate our breakfast…'

'What about you Jake, what are you running away from?' Barney asked me.

'What's your story?'

'…I told him about the accident and my father William dying, and about my wonderful mama. I also told him how brutal and vicious Thaddeus was and, how he had fooled my mama into thinking he was the man for her. And, I told him about Hector being poisoned and Tom Kite's murder. I didn't tell him that Thaddeus was dead and had been killed by me…Barney thought that I was just running away from a brutal, sadistic stepfather who was still alive. Which, in one sense I was. But, I never told him Thaddeus was still alive I just didn't correct him…He had listened intently…'

'Jake, for sure, we are so alike,' he said.

'…Our fathers were both killed in accidents, your daddy was mangled and mine was blown apart…our mammies took up with other men, who we didn't like and who beat us… And, now we are both runaways,' he said earnestly.

'Barney could certainly talk. I had noticed that he said, *'for sure'* quite a bit and, often started his sentences with *'well now'*.'

'Jake, we're almost like brothers…'

'I nodded, but said nothing. In the sense of what had happened to us both, Barney and I were very similar...'

'…What are you going to do now…where are you going?' he asked me.

I hesitated before replying. Then decided I could trust Barney.

'I think I'm going to go to Grimsby…my mama told me that there's work to be had there in the fishing trade…and fortunes can be made.' I replied.

'Well then, Jake Rawlings… Barney McHugh is coming with you,' he said. 'That is… if you could do with some company on the road.'

'That's fine with me,' said I. Thankful for finding a friend so soon.

'Well come on then Jake… for sure, there's no time to waste, let's get moving… The road to our fortunes won't get any shorter.'

We both laughed and set off to walk to Grimsby, which was a journey of about forty miles…'

'…Mingling with the people as they went about their business and, being careful not to draw attention to ourselves, especially from the 'rozzers', we carried on walking up Steep Hill, towards the castle and cathedral. There we stopped to gaze in wonderment at them both...

'Well now Jake… did you ever see anything like that before?' said Barney.

…We stared, open mouthed in bewilderment at the sheer size and architecture of Lincoln Cathedral. I'd only been in Lincoln for a few hours and already there had been one surprise after another. First of all, there were all the shops and pubs in the High Street, and then seeing and being so close to the steam train as it passed by. Finding a friend so soon after leaving home feeling all alone and, standing with him in front of this massive cathedral, with a medieval castle behind me, made me realise, just how small Calthorpe village had been. I also realised how little I knew of the world outside Calthorpe. Having a street-wise friend like Barney was a god-send, especially as there would be many more surprises in the days, months and years to come…

'No I never have, Barney… I didn't think that men could build something as large as this.' I replied.

'For sure, neither did I… the Irish must have helped,' Barney joked with a smile on his face. He really had a pleasing way with him.

'We stood and stared only for a short while before deciding we had better get a move on. After all, we were both runaways. There were too many policemen in Lincoln. It was best that we got out of there as soon as we could. We had no maps to guide us and only had a vague idea of the direction we needed to take, so we headed north out of Lincoln through the Bail-gate...

Nobody appeared to take any notice of us as we walked up the road. Very soon we were out of Lincoln, and set off at a steady pace in the general direction we thought would take us to Grimsby. As we walked, we talked and got to know each other. I discovered that Barney could neither read nor write. He wasn't even sure how old he was. His mammy used to tell him his age. He thought he was about fifteen. So we decided from now on, his birthday would be celebrated on the twenty-third of August, because that was the day he had met me. And that, the 23rd August 1865, the first day of my new life, had been his fifteenth birthday and we'd celebrated it with a meat pie each...

After originally lying to him about how much money I had, I lied to him again, when he asked my age. I told him I was fourteen. They were the last and only lies I ever told Barney McHugh. He became my best and most valuable, loyal life-long friend...'

'...Other than getting lost, it was an uneventful first day of a walk that took us nearly three days to complete. We would have reached Grimsby sooner had we taken the right road out of Lincoln in the first place. Although the Bail-gate route took us north and out of the city, we should have gone up Lindum Hill, and left Lincoln by a road that took us in a north-easterly direction. But, we weren't to know that. I suppose I should have realised something was wrong, when I didn't see any milestone markers on the edge of road, showing the distance to Grimsby. But, perhaps I wasn't too bright in those days...'

'How far did you walk father, before you knew you were wrong?' Sarah-Eliza asked.

'Yes grandad, how many miles had you gone?' Gabriel wanted to know.

'Let me see,' said Jacob as he put his pipe into his mouth. 'I think we'd walked for about five hours, don't forget I didn't have a watch... so I'd say about fifteen miles.'

'How did you know, you were on the wrong road, grandad?' Daniel asked.

Grace wasn't interested in such detail and for the moment looked bored.

'We had a stroke of luck... A young farm labourer about twenty five years old, his name I can't remember, who was driving a horse and cart loaded with hay came down the road towards us..' said Jacob.

'Good afternoon lads... where are you going to?' he asked pleasantly as he stopped his cart.

Unsure how to reply, Barney and I looked at each other and hesitated before answering. The cart driver smiled at us and knowingly said,

'You're runaways from a workhouse or orphanage, aren't you?'

'How do you know we're runaways?' I naively asked, realising I'd just confirmed that we were.

He laughed.

'To me, that's easy... you look like runaways... You've got a bundle, and scruffy ginger here hasn't had a wash for few days... Don't worry lads, it's not my business and besides, I was a runaway once.' He said genially.

'Well then... in that case, the name's Barney and not ginger. And for sure I am a bit scruffy... but I mean well.'

'We're going to Grimsby to become fishermen to make our fortunes.' Barney said, deciding he could be honest with this man.

'Not on this road you ain't,' the cart-driver replied light-heartedly.

'Why's that then?' I asked.

'This ain't the road to Grimsby... that's why!' he said.

'You should have turned off about three miles back... You've come too far up this road.'

Seeing the confused look on our faces, he asked,

'Do you know the way... do you know how to get to Grimsby?'

'Not really... or for sure, we wouldn't be on this road now, would we?' Barney said, becoming a little irritated.

'Look lads… I'm going the way you need to go back… Climb onto the cart and I'll take you to a crossroads and put you on the right road for Grimsby.' He offered.

…We didn't need to be asked twice. Sitting comfortably in the hay, we enjoyed the ride back to the crossroads where we should have turned off…

'Ok lads, off you get… Don't forget, keep on this road until you get to Market Rasen and from there follow the signposts for Caistor. Once you get to Caistor you've only got about twelve miles to go.'

'Good luck lads!' he shouted as he drove his cart down the road.

'We walked for a few more hours that day, before deciding to rest and sleep in the shelter of a hedgerow. It was August and a warm night, the grass under the hedgerow was lush and made a restful bed. We were not too uncomfortable…

As we sat talking before going to sleep, I made a decision, which I have never for one second in my life, regretted. I decided, against my mama's advice, to tell Barney how much money I had in my pocket. I did so, because the next day, I would have to buy some food for us and, he would then know I had more money anyway…

'There was just something about him, I felt I could trust. Children… in all the years I knew him, Barney McHugh, never ever abused my trust!' said Jacob.

'Barney was astonished when I told him how much money I had, and wondered where I'd got it from. So, I told him about my mama saving and hiding the money from Thaddeus and showed him the ring she had tied around my neck. He thought fifteen shillings was a fortune. He had never seen, or held that much money in his hands before and asked if he could hold it. Without any hesitation, I took the money out of my pocket and placed it in his hands. Barney closed his fingers around the coins and with a look of childish delight on his face, he shook his hands a few times to make them rattle. He then thanked me and hurriedly put the money back into my hand…

That's when I made a bond with Barney that was to last a lifetime. I gave back to him, half the money; seven shillings and three pence. You keep that in your pocket, in case we get separated, I told him. This way, we'll both have money to keep us going until we find work. I'm sure you'll find a means to pay me back one day. Barney, stared at the money I'd put into his hands and then stared at me. For once, he was lost for words. When he spoke, he looked me in the eye and said,

'Well now Jake, you've just given me half of all you possess… I'll swear an oath to you. This will be returned a hundredfold or more,' he said.

'Together, we will make our fortune and we will watch out for each other… For sure, we are now brothers…for life.'

I could tell that he meant it. Not taking his eyes off mine, Barney held out his hand and grasping my hand in his, he shook it. We nodded to each other and not another word was said on the matter. It didn't need to be. We said goodnight and lay there in the grass thinking about the bond we had just agreed. I drifted off to sleep and slept well.

When we woke the next day the weather was again kind. I looked at Barney and thought, the cart-driver was right. With his dirty and torn shirt, he looked a scruffy mess. I told him to take his shirt off and I would give him one of mine from my bundle. Barney was reluctant at first before being persuaded. When he removed his shirt, I saw why he had been reluctant. Across his back, he carried the scars from the whippings he had received at Southwell. Barney looked at me and put on the clean shirt. I never said anything and neither did he…

After going to the toilet behind the hedge, we set off…'

'Father, that will do… did the children really need to know that?' Sarah-Eliza exclaimed.

'No dear, I'm sorry… I suppose they didn't.' I replied.

The boys just giggled.

'…In just a couple of hours we had made it to Market Rasen, where we bought some food from the store in the market square. Without dawdling unnecessarily, just as the cart-driver told us to, we followed the signposts to Caistor, which we reached and, passed through by late afternoon. We were both getting excited at the thought of only being a few miles away from our destination. All the problems I had left behind in Calthorpe, though only two days before seemed such a long time ago. About an hour or so after leaving Caistor, we rested and spent a second night asleep under a hedge by the side of the road.

With the rising of the sun the next day, we couldn't wait to get walking. There was less than ten miles to go. With happy hearts and a smile on our faces we strode out those last miles. Within three hours, we stood at the top of Irby Hill. There in front of us, with the sun shimmering off the water was the River Humber and the port of Grimsby. Fishing smacks and larger sailing vessels could be seen tacking up the river to the port, or heading towards the mouth of the river and the open sea beyond.

A magnificent huge red brick tower was bathed in sunlight and stood out like a welcoming beacon. We later learned that this was the iconic Grimsby Dock tower, which had only been built just a few years before we arrived in the town. Over the years that tower would be a most welcome sight for us, other fishermen and sailors, as our vessels made their way back up the River Humber and the safety of the port. From the top of Irby Hill, we could make out a forest of masts and sails of fishing smacks and other vessels that were tied up in the docks.

'Do you see that Barney… do you see that?' I said excitedly.

'There's were we're going to make our fortune.'

'For sure I see it… and a beautiful sight it is Jake,' he replied. '…One day we'll own one of those boats.'

'Only one,' said I, '...that won't do at all!'

Laughing and joking with each other, we set off down the hill…'

'Little more than an hour later we walked into Grimsby. Our route had brought us into the town along a turnpike that finished near to the parish church of St James and the newly built train station. In fact not far from where we are now,' Jacob told the children. 'But, what you now see as roads with fine houses and the ornamental public park, in those days, it was all open farm land and fields. The historic old town of Grimsby, when Barney and I arrived was centred on the church and the River Head... We knew that if we were to make our fortune, we needed to be in the dockland area, which was about a mile away from the church. So that's where we headed.

Though only a short distance from the old town centre, the area we now know as the East Marsh, was almost a different town from the old town of Grimsby. It was a sprawling estate of closely packed, working class, back-to-back, cheaply built terraced housing for letting. Many owners had built and, crammed as many tenements as they could into small parcels of land. There was intolerable overcrowding and appalling living conditions. The area had a reputation for containing some of the worst slums in Grimsby. These houses were really not fit for dogs to live in, but, Barney and I had to find lodgings there. It was too late in the day to start looking for work.

On our first night in Grimsby, we found lodgings in Ellis's buildings, which was entered by a covered rat-run passageway. The courtyard contained twelve two-storied houses with only a ten-foot width between opposing houses. The houses had no back doors; over sixty people lived here and, shared the court's six communal box privies, which faced the front of the houses close to the doors of the living rooms. All manner of humanity and, the dregs of society lived in these courts and tenements. In an area like this, it was inevitable that muggings, drunkenness, disorderly conduct and violence thrived and were commonplace. To survive, you needed to be street-wise, which I wasn't. But, Barney was!

The room that Barney and I took that first night cost us two-pence a day each, which we paid, taking care not to let anyone see how much money we had. Worst of all, we had to share the room with seven other adult lodgers, who had come to Grimsby from Manchester, Leeds, Nottingham and elsewhere to find work...'

'In our room, there were only three beds, between the nine of us!' said Jacob. '...and the bedding was none too clean.'

'What! Only three beds and dirty bed sheets,' Daniel asked, screwing his face up in disgust.

'That sounds awful... how did you sleep father?' Sarah-Eliza wanted to know.

'We all slept top to tail and three to a bed... unfortunately for us. Barney and I shared our bed with a fat, smelly man from Hull... not that we had a thimbleful of choice in the matter,' Jacob said, before adding.

'We'd just got into bed, fully clothed and keeping our money tight by us when, he, the foul smelling man, came into the room. He reeked of beer, tobacco, stale sweat and a stench I couldn't identify. In the candle light he saw space in our bed.

'Right, shift over, you skinny pair of sprats... make way... I'm sharing this bed with you tonight,' he said. With that, he took his boots off, loudly broke wind, relieved himself in a chamber pot, pushed us over and got into bed and promptly fell fast asleep. It was my misfortune to be in the middle, I was the one sleeping next to him. Barney was on the edge of the bed.

'It was a long time before either of us fell asleep... but sleep we eventually did.'

'Oh! How dreadful,' Sarah-Eliza uttered with a look of revulsion on her face.

The children said nothing intelligible. They just sat there, pulling faces, holding their noses and going, phew! And eurgh!

'The next morning, Barney and I couldn't get out of bed fast enough. Putting our boots on, which we had kept in bed with us, we left the lodgings and headed towards the docks and our future. We had been advised to keep our boots close by, so that they weren't stolen during the night,' said Jacob.

'It was only a short walk from the lodgings and I wasn't really sure what I was expecting to find... The strange sights, sounds and the smell of the docks literally took my breath away. For me, being a country boy, this was a whole new world. Barney had seen the docks at Liverpool when he came over from Ireland with his mammy and daddy so he was not as impressed as me...

As a town and fishing port, Grimsby had grown rapidly after the railway arrived in 1848. By 1865, the year when we arrived, the population of the town was about eleven thousand.

Over the next forty years, the population would grow by another fifty thousand and more, into the much larger town that you children know. Almost all of these people and, in some cases their families, had come to Grimsby, to be part of the growing fishing trade and support businesses and, hopefully to make their fortunes... Barney and I were no different. We were just two more souls among those thousands who had been drawn here seeking a better life…

We walked around the docks and stared in wonder at what we saw. The dock, which is now called the Royal Dock, was full of barques, barges, brigs and handsome iron hulled three mast sailing ships, with interesting names such as *'Lady Harewood'* and *'Spirit of the Sea'*. Where they were from, or where they were bound for, we didn't know and could only imagine! For a while, absolutely transfixed, we stood and watched and listened to cargo being loaded and unloaded. There was coal, timber, dozens of barrels of who knows what, countless sacks of grain, bales of wool and all manner of things. Steam cranes were hissing and clanging away, ropes were being hauled on derricks and large carts, which were pulled by heavy shire-horses, were being loaded...

Some of the cargoes were being loaded directly onto railway wagons that were waiting on the tracks that ran alongside the dockside. Only four days before in Lincoln, I had gazed in awe at my first steam train. On that morning and every day on the Grimsby docks thereafter, there wasn't just one train there were many, all steaming away and belching smoke from their chimneys. The engine drivers, the men unloading the ships and the sailors on the ships were shouting out instructions and banter to each other in a good natured sense of urgency. There was a real vibrancy about this part of the dock. Everywhere we walked and looked, men were working.

'Well now Jake… would you like to be the captain of one of these beauties?' Barney asked as we stood alongside a magnificent three-masted ship called *'Mighty Pegasus'*.

'That I would Barney… then we could go anywhere we wanted.' I replied and asked '…What's a *Pegasus*?'

'For sure... I haven't a clue... but it's a fine name,' Barney replied.

'It was difficult for us to take it all in. We could have stood and watched all day because there was so much to see. Although we were enjoying and excited at what we were seeing, that wasn't why we were there. We needed to find work. Watching others work, would not put money into our pockets...

We wandered over to the recently built Fish Pontoon, where many species of fish had been landed and sold during the day's early morning trade. Again, I saw and heard things that I'd never seen before. The pontoon was a smelly hive of industry and cacophony of noise. It was like an orchestra of discordant sounds being played at full volume. Alongside the pontoon, there were more railway wagons and trains, hissing steam and blowing smoke. Clattering and banging, we could see and hear men shouting and loading the railway wagons with wooden tubs full of fish that were packed in ice. These trains would take the fish to Billingsgate fish market in London and to other cities such as Manchester and Sheffield... Some fish, probably for local trade, was packed in open tubs and boxes waiting to be moved to the merchants who had bought the fish...

Although there was camaraderie between the men, Barney and I soon realised that working on the fish pontoon was not the easiest of jobs. Conditions were very basic...there was no regard for human comfort or safety. Landing, selling and moving the fish was the priority. The pontoon only had a roof that was supported on steel columns and, being open on all sides, it would be numbingly cold when the wind and rain blew through during the winter months. They were very hardy men who made their living working on the pontoon... We quickly agreed it was not a job for us...

Hand barrows loaded with several boxes of fish, were being pushed about by the barrow boys. We wondered how the boys managed as the barrow loads looked impossibly heavy. In later years when the barrows got even larger and heavier, quite often, especially in the winter when the pontoon floor was icy, accidents would happen. Occasionally a barrow boy would lose control of his barrow and it, the loaded fish boxes and, sometimes the barrow boy as well, would go over the side of the pontoon into the water of the dock. The fish and the barrow would be lost... Over the years, several barrow boys fell into the dock and drowned...

For local sale, some men were filleting fish. I couldn't believe the speed at which they worked; their sharp knives moving so quickly. I was surprised they never cut their hands. But they never seemed to. Strewn all around them on the pontoon floor, there were fish guts and fish skins, which were being trod on as the workers went about their work. Frequently, an opportunist seagull, from the many herring gulls and black-headed gulls that were flying and noisily crying above the pontoon and docks, would land and take whatever they could scavenge. The oilskin clothing that the workmen wore, were covered in fish slime and scales and there was running water everywhere. The general stench of the fish and the pontoon seems to stay in your nostrils for ever. This is what our foul-smelling bed-mate from Hull had reeked off...'

'Eurgh!' said the children again.

'I'd never seen or had heard of anything like it... and neither had Barney.' Jacob told the children.

'...our senses were being bombarded, with one new experience after another.'

'Well now... tis a noisy and smelly old place, we've arrived at Jake.' Barney said with a laugh. 'Not sure it's good enough for two fine gentlemen of the road such as us.'

'It is that, Barney... It's terribly grim in Grimsby,' said I putting on a posh accent.

We both burst out laughing. I thought I was being funny. I didn't know that what I had said was one of the most often used jokes to describe the town.

'Smelly or not... for sure we're here now and we need to find some work.' Barney said.

Chapter 7

Mr Kingston Gives Us A Chance!

'...In the Fish Dock, there were about fifty, or so, of the two hundred and twenty fishing smacks that were sailing from Grimsby at that time. The other smacks were at sea, fishing the North Sea, Faroe's or Icelandic waters. Smacks that were in dock, had either just returned with their catch and unloaded it on to the pontoon, or were preparing to go back out to sea. As we looked beyond the smacks that were in the dock, we could see the mouth of River Humber and the North Sea. On this beautiful, sunny August morning, it looked so calm and inviting. We were soon to find out that was not always the case.

Barney and I wandered round to what is now called the North Wall quayside, where the smacks waiting to go to sea were moored. Talking eagerly and excited we walked up and down, looking at the boats and, even though we had no real understanding of what the life of a fisherman was like, we agreed this was where we would find work and make our fortune. But we didn't have a clue what you had to do to become a fisherman. Undecided and unknowing, we had no idea who to ask. Not that we needed to, as we walked and talked we were being watched. But, we didn't know that.

On the deck of one of the smacks, a man wearing a billycock hat and oilskin smock was washing down the deck. He'd stopped what he was doing, looked up and watched us walk past. Now that we were walking back towards him, again he ceased working and look up. And in an accent stranger and stronger than Barney's, shouted,

'Hello lads...what you'se up to?'

'Nothing much Mister... we're just looking... We're not doing any blagging,' Barney shouted back.

'Blagging', there he goes again, using words I couldn't understand, I thought. But, that was Barney. Before long I had learnt a whole new vocabulary...'

Jacob chuckled to himself at the memory of some of the words he had learned from Barney.

'...The man continued to look us up and down as we drew closer to where he was working...

'I know you're not lads... Never thought for a moment that you were,' he shouted back in an accent as thick as a Toc-H candle and added,

'Are you'se looking for work?'

We stopped walking and looked at each other and then back at him.

'Well now mister, we might be... what's it got to do with you?' Barney shouted back.

The man stopped working and quickly walked down the deck of the smack. Putting one foot on the side of the boat, he easily jumped up onto the quayside and stood in front of us. He was a ruddy faced, heavily whiskered, man in his forties, thick set and stocky, but not overly tall. His high crowned billycock hat, made him seem taller. He seemed to have an agreeable disposition.

'I'll tell you what it's got to do with me, you cheeky young bugger... I'm Henry Kingston, from Brixham,' he replied.

He pointed at the fishing smack he had been working on and the smack tied up next to it.

'...This one, the *Mary-Ann* and that one, the *Mary-Jane*, are my smacks... and I could use a couple of honest, god fearing, hard-working apprentices... Are you interested?'

'...I take it that you'se is from a workhouse or an orphanage,' he said.

We never bothered to argue whether we were from a workhouse or not. That was not important. It was only our first full day in Grimsby and already we were being offered work.

I was too dumbfounded to speak, so Barney, not that I could stop him, did the talking.

'What's the pay… what are you offering?' he asked.

Henry Kingston looked at Barney, amused by his audacity, which had brought a broad smile to his face.

'That'll depend on how old you are and what you can do,' he replied.

'Well now, I'm Barney McHugh and I'm fifteen years old… it was my birthday just the other day… and, my skinny friend here is fourteen and called Jake Rawlings,'

'I can cook… and he can read and write,' Barney added.

'I certainly need a cook… not sure I need someone just cos they can read and write,' Mr Kingston said.

'It'll be hard and dangerous work… thar's danger and death in this business… does that frighten you?'

'Not at all… Not at all!' replied Barney, whose bravado was much stronger than mine.

'Thar's much you'll have to learn.' Mr Kingston told us.

'He's a quick learner for sure… and, you take both of us or neither.' said Barney as he looked at me and nodded his head, seeking my approval.

Mr Kingston paused, looked both of us up and down and rubbed his chin before saying,

'A quick learner, you say!'

'I do!' said Barney. '…and for sure he is.'

'I…I am!' said I, not too convincingly in a squeaky voice.

'Oh now… the cat's not got your tongue then, young Jake Rawlings,' Henry Kingston said.

Again he paused. He walked around us, rubbed his chin again and continued to look us up and down. Eventually, with his hands on his hips, he spoke.

'I'll pay you both four shillings and sixpence a week and a share of the liver money… You'll have good food while we are at sea, but when we are in dock… you'sell have to fend for yourselves…'

'Are you'se interested, lads?' Mr Kingston said. '…are we agreed?'

Barney and I looked at each other…four shillings and sixpence a week each. That was a little bit more than half the money we each had left in our pockets from my mama's fifteen shillings. We both smiled and nodded our head and without knowing what it meant to be a fisherman, we agreed to become one.

'We're both agreed, Mr Kingston,' I said.

'That's good... now give me your 'and... let's shake on it,' he replied. '...we'll sort the indenture papers out later.'

With the broadest grins on our faces we shook hands with Mr Kingston.

'Look lively then... go and get your gear and come aboard... we'll be sailing on the tide at eight o'clock tonight.'

'This is our gear Mr Kingston,' I said. 'This small bundle is all we have.'

'Well, well' he said with a raucous laugh, 'you'd better come with me then... and let's get you'se suitably clarted out.'

'Mr Kingston took us to nearby marine stores and ships chandlers, where he bought a load of sea-going gear for Barney and me. Spare trousers, thick jumpers, oil frocks, sou'westers and sea-boots, anything else, he said he could provide from what he had on board the *Mary-Ann*...'

'That'll do for now,' he told Charlie Banks, the owner of the store.

'...Don't suppose you can pay for this gear... can you?'

We shook our heads.

'No Sir... we can't,' said I.

'Ok then lads... I'll sort it with Charlie,' Mr Kingston said. '...these ain't gifts... you'll be paying for them out of your wages at the end of the trip.'

'That is... if we earn anything,' he added and winked at Charlie. 'Right lads, pick 'em all up and let's be going.'

'Cheerio Charlie,' Mr Kingston said to the store owner.

'God speed Henry... I hope your trip's a good un,' Charlie replied.

'Thanks Charlie... so do I'' Mr Kingston shouted back, as we walked out of the door.

'...On the twenty-seventh of August 1865, just five days after I killed Thaddeus Stone, I signed on as an apprentice to Master Henry Obadiah Kingston on the fishing vessel, *Mary-Ann*, originally from Brixham, now registered in Grimsby.

Mama would be so proud and pleased for me, I thought. I didn't know that on the day I became an apprentice fisherman, my mama was languishing in foul conditions in Newark jail awaiting trial for murder…'

Seeing her father's sad expression, Sarah-Eliza quickly changed the subject.

'You were lucky to find work so quickly father… wasn't you?' she asked.

'No… not really dear,' Jacob replied. 'But, at the time… we thought we were.'

Jacob thought he had better explain.

'…In the 1860s, because of the railway link to London and other major cities, Grimsby's fishing trade was growing rapidly. As it was quicker and easier to get to the fishing grounds in the North Sea and northern waters from Grimsby many smack owners moved to the port. They came from places such as, Barking, Greenwich, Ramsgate, and Brixham, which is where Mr Kingston had moved from. The only problem was Grimsby didn't have a home-grown pool of experienced fishermen, which the smack owners could draw upon. It meant that the crews for the fishing vessels had to come from outside the town… Smack owners were crying out for fisherman, experienced or not, and took them from wherever and however they could…

…Although, some boys came from Grimsby, the workhouses, reformatories, foundling hospitals and orphanages became the most fertile recruiting grounds for apprentice fishermen. Just like Barney and I, many boys from all over the country became apprentices in the hope of a finding a better life. Once they went to sea, the danger and hardship that was the daily life of a fisherman quickly brought home to them the reality of what they had signed up for. In the 1860s, of all the fishing ports in the country, Grimsby had the largest number of apprentices. I later found out that approximately eighty-five percent of all the fishermen working from the port came from places other than Grimsby. So, finding work was not at all difficult…'

'I can understand that… but why did they use inexperienced apprentices, father?' Sarah-Eliza asked.

'Quite simple really… apprentices were cheap. They could be paid low or, no wages and, other than the smack's master, they had no one to protect them…' Jacob replied.

He briefly paused and then added,

'…By the 1870s, there were far more apprentices than experienced fishermen sailing on the smacks. During this period, some of the methods the smack owners used to recruit young boys from inland towns caused the recruitment of apprentices in Grimsby to be viewed with a considerable degree of disapprobation…'

'Disapprobation… what's that mean grandad?' asked Daniel, looking totally bemused.

'Oh sorry… it means dissatisfaction or unease.' Jacob replied.

'He could have said that,' Gabriel complained to Daniel.

'Gabriel, don't be so rude!' Sarah-Eliza chided him.

'Well, he could have… he could have,' a chastened Gabriel continued to mumble.

'Yes… yes I suppose I could have,' Jacob replied and smiled at Gabriel as he gently touched his face. He did like to tease them.

As it was an important part of the story Jacob was telling, he continued to explain.

'…How some apprentices were recruited was little better than legalised kidnapping. Fishermen were so hard to come by that often smack owners employed a strategy of sending out, what became known as, 'decoy ducks' into the highways and bye-ways of towns and cities to win the confidence of impressionable and sometimes desperate young men. They would beguile them with glowing pictures of the life of a fisherman, whose sky is never clouded, whose winds are forever fair, whose course is never amid the hidden shoals, rocks and reefs of the dangerous tack, but whose gold laden argosy is ever bound in bountiful shoals of fish that practically jumped onto the hooks and into the nets…'

121

For the briefest of moments, Jacob paused and smiled. He enjoyed telling stories and was pleased with himself and the manner in which he had explained that. But, before he continued his face darkened and the tone of his voice changed.

'...Much to the despair and anguish of parents, many, many young boys were lured away from their home with these false promises...

...During the first few years that I was a fisherman, I witnessed many distressed mothers and fathers pleading with smack owners to release their sons from the indentures they had signed. As the apprentice was legally bound by the indenture, very rarely were they successful in persuading the smack owner to release the boy... The smack owners needed crew...'

Jacob stopped talking. He leant forward and from his pocket, took out a letter that he had kept for nearly fifty years. Barney, found the letter in the locker of a smack he sailed on and, being unable to read very well himself, had given it to Jacob to read. Jacob showed the dog-eared letter, with its fading ink, to the children and then read it to them.

> '...Hon Sir,
>
> I beg leave most respectfully to address these few lines to you, hoping you will excuse me in troubling you at this time, and will relate the case as briefly as possible.
>
> On September 28th, 1873, my son Robert Bowman, aged 14, suddenly disappeared. I applied to every police office in London for two months. I could glean no tidings of him. At last my sister received a letter from him. She forwarded the same to me. It appears he had been decoyed from home by a lad years older. They got so badly off that they took refuge in the Romford Union. During the two days they were there a Mr Marks, smack owner, Great Grimsby, saw them, took them down, and he writes me they were legally bound to him for seven years. I have written; I have pleaded his ignorance, his youth and his inexperience

of legal documents. The boy states that it was not read over to him, but Mr Marks writes, unless I can pay the sum of £20 he will not release him or let me see him until the expiration of seven years. He, the boy, writes me he is a thorough slave, receiving no wages, and working day and night.

I am informed that it is quite illegal to bind a boy that is under 15 years of age without the consent of his parents. I am a widow with a family of seven children, Robert being the eldest. I am in exceeding low circumstances and work hard to maintain my children. I shall not, nor can I pay this man £20 to release him. The boy has just, as it were begun to help me a little to maintain himself and, the six younger children.

Your help in securing his release will be most appreciated.

I am yours sincerely
Elizabeth Bowman'

'I never knew for sure who the letter was addressed to as there was no envelope. Nor did I know whether a reply was ever sent to Mrs Bowman,' said Jacob.

'That's really awful father… was Robert released?'

'…Why did you keep the letter?' Sarah- Eliza wanted to know.

Sarah-Eliza's face was picture of concern as she looked at her children sat at her feet. As a mother, she was thinking how she would feel if anyone enticed them away.

'I kept the letter because Barney and I knew Robert Bowman… and no, he wasn't released,' said Jacob shaking his head, before solemnly adding,

'…Robert Bowman, at the age of sixteen, in 1875, was at sea on the smack *Butterfly*. In a violent storm which sank six other smacks…the skipper and mate of his vessel were soon washed overboard and lost. Terrified and fighting for his life, Robert clung onto anything he could as heavy waves continued to crash and pound into the *Butterfly*. He pleaded with God to help him – all to no avail. After the rudder head had been broken off the stricken smack lay broadside to the gale, Robert could hold on no longer and was swept overboard and drowned. Another apprentice, whose name I cannot remember, was the only survivor. He was rescued by the smack *Lily* and returned to Grimsby, where he told the port superintendent the fate of his shipmates…Sadly, from the moment he had been decoyed away from home, Robert never saw his mother again.'

Telling this story was turning out to be a poignant experience for Jacob. It was calling to mind old painful memories. Seeing her father was becoming upset, Sarah-Eliza said,

'That's enough for now father… let's have a break and a nice cup of tea and a biscuit before you carry on.'

'Yes dear… that's a good idea,' Jacob replied.

He looked at Sarah-Eliza and quickly realised why she had suggested the brief break. They smiled warmly at each other as they rose out of their chairs.

'Come along children,' said Sarah-Eliza, 'into the kitchen with you!'

After a cup of tea and a glass of cold milk for the children, they returned to the warmth of the sitting room and Jacob continued with his story.

'…Although parents of apprentices caused problems, by far the greatest number of difficulties, were caused by the smack owners themselves,' said Jacob.

'Some were unscrupulous and were prepared to accept as an apprentice any young boy who was willing, or who could be persuaded, to sign indentures... no attempt was made to ascertain whether or not the boys were acceptable. They were only interested in obtaining labour and gave no thought or consideration to the quality of that labour. Consequently, they accepted boys with unsuitable characters, boys who were rogues, thieves and incorrigible liars. Even boys who were physically unsuited to a life at sea were apprenticed… It was very wrong!'

'That's really dreadful father… I didn't know that.' Sarah-Eliza commented. She was really being drawn into Jacob's story.

'No dear… unfortunately, not many do… It's part of the history of fishing that's hidden from view and seldom talked about… I swore that if Barney and I ever owned a smack, we would never apprentice boys based on lies and them being lured away from their homes with deceitful assurances,' replied Jacob.

Jacob leant back in his chair, and deep in thought, he slowly recharged his pipe with fresh tobacco before continuing.

'…So, my dear daughter, coming back to the question you asked me before we had our tea… I suppose, Barney and I were lucky in one respect and not so lucky in another,' Jacob said, chuckling to himself as he lit the pipe.

'…We were lucky because we signed on as apprentices with Master Henry Kingston… unlike many of the masters and owners he was a kind, educated man and treat his crew fairly and honestly. Don't get me wrong… he worked all of us as hard as he worked himself…

…Unfortunately not all masters were like him, many were basically uneducated men, who could neither read nor write. Some of them simply regarded the young boys merely as part of the process for taking fish. Worst of all, scores of masters often subjected their crew, especially their apprentices to appalling cruelly whilst at sea. The masters of smacks literally had control over life and death. Some apprentices were treated no better than child slaves of the waves and had a very hard time at sea…

…You will be horrified by some of the stories I'm going to tell you about what happened time and again on board fishing smacks when they are miles away from land on stormy seas…'

'Oh wow… good oh,' said Daniel, his face flushed with excitement at the prospect of the gruesome stories his grandad was going to tell them.

'NO, no, no… it's not good oh, Daniel,' Jacob said abruptly. He frowned at Daniel before adding, '…Apprentices were supposed to be taught seamanship, but were often no more than forced labour and very frequently ill-treated. More often than not they were given the worst jobs to do...'

Jacob stopped talking. He stared directly at Daniel and said,

'...Daniel, you are thirteen years old... Can you imagine being hung up by the thumbs from a spar? Your feet are off the ground and you are being flogged, just because it amused someone to do it to you... You are hanging there in pain, crying for your mama and having no one to protect, or help you... Your pain only finishing when your tormentor got bored and cut you down...'

'...Can you imagine that?' Jacob said sternly.

Daniel's boyish comment and enthusiasm for hearing about the cruelty had stirred in Jacob upsetting memories from long ago. His very terse and angry reaction surprised Sarah-Eliza and the children. She wondered why she was seeing and hearing a side to her father that had never been seen or heard before.

Daniel, realising that his grandad was cross, replied.

'Erm... no grandad I can't,' He was quite contrite. 'Erm... I... I'm sorry.'

'It's ok Daniel... it's ok... you weren't to know... Maybe you'll all think differently by the time I finish my story,' Jacob replied soothingly whilst smiling at Daniel, who sheepishly smiled back.

Quickly changing the subject, Sarah-Eliza asked.

'If Mr Kingston was a kind master... why were you unlucky father?'

Jacob laughed out loud, which eased the tension, before replying.

'That's because daft old Barney and I didn't know how long we had signed up to be an apprentice for and, we had no idea of the difference between fishing on a cod-smack or a trawler...

As Mr Kingston thought I was fourteen, in reality, I was still a week short of my thirteenth birthday he signed me up to a seven year apprenticeship. Barney, being fifteen, made his mark for a six year apprenticeship...Officially, you shouldn't be an apprentice as young as I was without your parent's permission, or after you was twenty-one years old.

126

Occasionally, because apprentices were cheap, the rules were bent!

Henry Kingston's vessels, the *Mary-Ann* and *Mary-Jane* were cod-smacks, sometimes called cod-men or liners, because they were primarily in the business of catching cod by using fishing lines rather than nets. Quite simply, fish were caught by means of hooks and lines. Normally during the winter months, lines up to two miles long, baited with hundreds of hooks were employed and during the remainder of the year, hand lines were used...Trawlers on the other hand, towed a bag shaped net along the sea-bed and in addition to cod, haddock and ling, caught many other species of fish such as plaice, sole and halibut...'

'But, father, I still don't understand... what was the difference and, how were you unlucky,' Sarah-Eliza asked. '...You were still out there catching fish.'

'Well now... a cod-smack usually carried ten or eleven hands, four or five of whom would be men, the others were apprentices... Trawlers usually only carried five hands, the master, second hand, third hand, deck boy and cook... A cod smack went to sea for up to ten weeks or more and fished the dangerous waters around the Faroe Islands or Iceland, whereas a normal voyage for a trawl smack was eight to ten days, chiefly fishing on the Dogger Bank in the North Sea...'

'We had never ever been on board a boat yet, Barney and I signed up to a cod-man and long trips to some of the roughest and most dangerous waters in the world... It would turn out to be a hard lesson learned.'

'Oh... now I understand... how did you manage all that time at sea?' asked Sarah-Eliza.

'With difficulty at first my dear... with great difficulty!' answered Jacob, again chuckling to himself.

'...Just as Mr Kingston had said, shortly after eight o'clock on that mild August evening, the *Mary-Ann* with Barney and me on board, as two of the smack's five apprentices, set sail. With Mr Kingston on the tiller, the smack slipped through the lock gates and sailed out into the River Humber and the open sea beyond. Although Barney and I were both enthusiastic, we were more than a little apprehensive of the unknown we were sailing into. Even though this was the first of many hundreds of times, I've sailed down the River Humber, I can still remember looking back towards shore and seeing the Dock Tower silhouetted by the setting sun. It was a wonderful sight. The rays, from the sun, shone right and left and, above the tower. As we sailed away, from our ever increasing distance, it looked like a giant roman candle. Barney and I stood admiring the view, neither of us realising, it would be quite a while before we saw the Dock Tower again…

…The journey down the River Humber, which was calm, was smooth and enjoyable. *Mary-Ann* was a fine smack, ketch rigged and sailed well. As we headed towards the open sea it gently rolled on the waves. I thought to myself, 'I'm enjoying this'. Thaddeus Stone was long forgotten. At the mouth of the river, Mr Kingston turned the tiller, and we headed North by North-East in the direction of the far off fishing grounds. We had only sailed a few hundred yards on this new tack, when I realised who had control over life and death out there. It was the sea. And, as King Canute discovered, the sea will always have the last word…

Although, the sea was running only a slight swell, I would experience much worse in the days, months and years to come, the *Mary-Ann* had started rocking and rolling and pitching. The smack moved about like a cork bobbin. Even in a gentle swell, it needed strong hands on the tiller to keep the smack heading were it should be going. With all this new movement, it wasn't too long before, much to Mr Kingston's and Barney's amusement, I became reacquainted with my rather meagre dinner, which we had had at a pie shop on the docks. I only just made it to the side of the smack before I retched and brought my whole dinner up. The waves, which splashed up the side of the smack into my face, in a perverse way, washed away the food debris of my chin, they had caused. I tasted salt water for the first time. It was vile!

Barney's amusement was short lived. The swell increased as we sailed further from the shore. About an hour after I had been sick, Barney rushed to the side of the smack and violently retched, bringing up all he'd eaten in the past few hours.

'Tis a weak stomach you'se have there, Barney McHugh,' shouted Mr Kingston from the tiller. He was finding our discomfort funny.

Barney turned round to face Mr Kingston.

'Well now... weak stomach is it,' replied Barney. '...for sure, I'm chucking it as far as I can.'

Mr Kingston and some of the crew, who were working on deck, all burst out laughing... Barney McHugh had a great sense of humour and a way with words... I do miss him.' Jacob sighed.

'...Even though the *Mary-Ann* was a relatively new smack, only ten years old, the conditions on board were dreadful, very basic and primitive. All the crew, men and boys, lived, ate and slept in the same confined cabin area, which you accessed down a companionway stairs. Once we sailed I realised that we rarely saw a slice of bread at sea, only biscuits, and not soft ones at that. As there was no table we sat on the lockers, except in bad weather, when we sat on the floor. The *Mary-Ann* had no real facilities for washing – personal hygiene was not a priority. And, there were no toilets. We had to defecate and urinate over the side of the smack, or into buckets for throwing overboard. Not a particular pleasant task especially when the smack would be pitching and rolling in heavy seas with waves crashing onto the decks. We were warned about checking which way the wind was blowing before throwing anything overboard...'

'...We had so much to learn... but some things needed to be learned more quickly than others,' Jacob explained with a raucous laugh.

'Oh no... how awful!' said Sarah-Eliza, bringing her hand to her mouth and looking disgusted.

Daniel and Gabriel just said, 'eurgh!'

Grace, who hadn't worked out the consequence of throwing something into the wind, said nothing.

'Mr Kingston was a compassionate and considerate man. Over the years, I would learn much from him. Seeing that we had both been sea-sick and as it was our first trip at sea he told us to go below and get some sleep in the hammocks…

'You'se can start your learning at first light in the morning… you'll not be sea-sick by then, lads,' he said.

'Thank you Mr Kingston,' said I as we left the deck and went below.

'Thank you kindly, Sir,' Barney shouted to him, before adding with a huge grin, '…I knew we found a fine smack to sail on.'

We were grateful that Mr Kingston recognised our discomfort. But, trying to get into a hammock for the first time, in candlelight, was not the easiest thing to do. Especially in a vessel that's rolling about on the waves. It took me several attempts to get into one. Twice I fell to the deck. On the third attempt I was in mine. Barney took many more attempts.

'For the love of sweet Jesus… how do you get into one of these damn things?' he said, falling to the deck at least five or six times.

'Stop that bloody racket… will ya,' one of the other crew members shouted. '…we're trying to get some sleep 'ere.'

'Stop yer mithering!' Barney shouted back.

'For sure… who wants to sleep strung up like a skinned rabbit anyway?'

Barney cussed and swore and threatened to tip me out of mine, because I was laughing so much. Much to the relief of everyone else, eventually he finally managed to get into the hammock and we both got some sleep.

Moving with the sea, the *Mary-Ann*, creaked and groaned. All wooden smacks had their own voice. It was a sound that I came to love. Our hammocks gently swung like pendulums. Twice, during the night, I had to get out of my hammock to be sick into a bucket. It stank, so after the second retching, on wobbly legs I traipsed back up to the deck and, after checking which way the wind was blowing, I threw the bucket's contents over the side of the smack into the water. During the rest of my life as a fisherman, I was never again sea-sick, no matter how bad the weather.

Even though I was on deck because I had been sea-sick, there was something magical about being on the deck of a smack in the middle of the sea in the dead of night. Because there isn't land, buildings, trees or anything to block your view on the horizon, you begin to realise just how big the sky and the heavens above really are. For as far as the eyes could see and stretching beyond into infinity the sky and sea appear to go on and on and on...

Without knowing what lies beyond, it's no wonder then that ancient mariners never sailed far away from the coast in the dark of night, for fear of sailing off the edge of the world, which they believed they would. Out there, you are just the tiniest speck on the great expanse of water. But, on a clear night, as it was that night, you get to marvel at the many thousands of twinkling stars that you can see. They seemed so close that you could almost touch them. It's a sight I never tired of seeing and one you rarely see when you are on land...'

Chapter 8

Hardship and Life on a Fishing Smack

'At first light the next morning, the third hand, Albert Barker, unceremoniously tipped Barney and me out of our hammocks. This was the beginning of our new life working as fishermen, deck-boys and occasional cook to be precise... Just as Mr Kingston had told us the previous evening this is when our learning proper would start. There was so much for us to learn and learn as quickly as possible. Not only did we have to get to know and understand about life on board a fishing smack and how to catch, identify, gut and store fish, we also had to become skilled at sailing a smack. We had to become sailors as well as fishermen. At sea, sailors use a language that most people on shore wouldn't understand. We needed to understand the meaning and the importance of words and expressions such as: avast, beating to windward, bulwarks, furling, futtock-shrouds, ready about, larboard, starboard, for'ard, aft and, many, many more.'

'I can talk sailor talk, grandad!' said Daniel.

'...Avast ye you swabs,' he said gleefully, doing an impression of Long John Silver. '...belay or I'll keel-haul ya.'

Gabriel and Grace laughed. Jacob and Sarah-Eliza grinned. Daniel had recently started reading Robert Louis Stephenson's book, *Treasure Island*; a tale of 'buccaneers and buried gold'. Hearing his grandad talk about the sailing terms he'd had to learn, reminded Daniel of what he had read in the book.

'Erm... yes Daniel... something like that,' Jacob commented before continuing. '...now where was I?'

'...Ah yes... many years later when the steam trawlers started to replace the smacks, getting to the fishing ground was much easier. The master, pointed the boat in the direction where he wanted to go and, the engine and screw propeller took you there. Steam powered vessels could punch their way through the waves and sail into the wind... In the olden days, sailing a smack was much more difficult and far slower. You relied totally on the strength and direction of the wind and the movement of the seas. Ship's masters, like Mr Kingston, had to understand the nature of the sea, and be able to read the weather and the winds. As I told you children before, especially in the days of the sailing smacks, the sea was the real master and it never lets you forget it...

On board a smack, or any sea-going vessel, there has to be a pecking order of who was in charge. On the *Mary-Ann*, the Master was Henry Kingston, who as you now know, also owned the smack. But, not all smack owners went to sea... Some employed a skipper to take charge of the vessel on their behalf. Undoubtedly, some skippers were like Mr Kingston with sterling qualities and impeccable characters that treated their crew and the apprentices with kindness and consideration. They dealt fairly with the boys, even if at times, justice was dispensed with a firm hand. Regrettably though, some were not... They were brutal, callous and sadistic unfeeling men. Quite often, it was these employed skippers who committed, or allowed the worst acts of cruelty and viciousness towards the apprentice boys to happen...

Second in command on the *Mary-Ann* was the Mate, George Simmons. Before he became a fisherman, for a couple of years in his early teens, he had been an agricultural labourer in rural Lincolnshire. George Simmons was a likeable, genial man in his late twenties and had been fishing for fourteen years when we first met him. He had served a five year apprenticeship on the trawling smack *Scorpio*, which was owned by a Mr Mount, who came from Ramsgate. He was a smack owner who didn't go to sea... He employed a skipper, whom, as we later found out, George Simmons didn't care for very much. As we did with Mr Kingston, all the while we were apprentices we never called him by his first name. He was always Mr Simmons...

Once he got to know both Barney and me, he told us the very tragic story of how he eventually became the mate on the *Mary-Ann*... When his apprenticeship on the *Scorpio* was completed he effectively became a free agent. Within reason, he could choose who he wanted to sail with. Smack owners were always looking for experienced crew. For his first trip to sea, after completing his apprenticeship, he signed back on to the *Scorpio* as the third hand. During that voyage, a terrible incident with a young apprentice made up his mind that, once they had returned to port, he would no longer sail on any of Mr Mount's vessels...

The smack *Scorpio* was thirty-five miles out at sea. A sixteen year old apprentice, Frederick Brewer was serving on the smack as cook, and had been for six months. He was on trial from the Charlton Union workhouse near Dover. Frederick was a slight built, nervous boy and quite unsuited for sea. Most of the time, he was frightened and frequently burst into tears. He should never have been apprenticed. But, the workhouses cared little whether the boys they sent were suitable for sea, or not. Recognising his disposition and fears, Mr Simmons had tried to befriend and help Frederick Brewer whenever he could on the previous trip...

Brewer's ultimate fate was sealed following a simple act of carelessness. After trimming the mast-head light, he put away the paraffin can in such a careless manner, that it fell over and oil was lost. For this, much to Brewer's distress and pain, the skipper, John Grice, gave him several hard cuts across the shoulders with a piece of thick rope.

'How do you like this boy?' he shouted as he beat him. He seemed to get perverse pleasure from doing so... The more the boy yelped and cried, the more Grice enjoyed lashing him.

This was not the first time that the skipper had beaten Frederick. During this trip and on the previous trips beating the boy was a regular occurrence. Shortly after this latest brutal lashing, Frederick Brewer, who clearly could stand no more beatings, jumped over the side of the vessel into the sea and was drowned. No body complained to the skipper. No body dared! You complained at your peril. At sea, the skipper was master and, very strange things could happen when you were alone on deck at night...'

Jacob paused. He looked at Sarah-Eliza and then at the children and suggested they might like to go into the kitchen and help themselves to another piece of cake or biscuit, before he continued with the story. They didn't need asking twice. Jumping quickly to their feet, the three of them left the room. Jacob indicated to Sarah-Eliza to stay with him. From down the corridor of the house, Jacob and Sarah-Eliza could hear Daniel doing his Long John Silver impression, only this time Gabriel and Grace where joining in. They were all laughing. Jacob spoke.

'I've sent the children out of the room my dear, because there's something I want to tell you that's not really suitable for their ears.'

'What's that father?' Sarah-Eliza was curious.

'It's about Frederick Brewer,' said Jacob.

Jacob hesitated. It wasn't going to be easy to tell his daughter, what he wanted her to know. The types of incidences he was going to mention didn't get talked about in polite society.

'Erm... erm... John Grice, the skipper of the *Scorpio*... erm... had been committing unnatural acts on Frederick Brewer.'

'What do you mean?' Sarah-Eliza asked, not sure what her father was struggling to tell her.

Jacob hesitated.

'...He... he... frequently sodomised him when they were alone on deck during the night.'

'Oh... oh my word... how ghastly,' she gasped in disgust, hardly believing her ears.

'...he did what!' She asked again. Had she heard correctly she wondered.

Despite the look of revulsion on Sarah-Eliza's face, Jacob continued.

'It wasn't the beating that tipped Frederick over the edge that day... he was always sexually assaulted by Grice after he

135

had received a beating...The two acts of sadistic brutality seemed to be linked...'

'...Frederick knew what would be coming that night,' said Jacob. 'That's what he could no longer stand.'

'Oh no... the poor boy... Could nobody help him?' Sarah-Eliza asked.

'No dear... although some of the men knew what was happening to Frederick, no one tried to help him... No one dared. The sea can be a lonely forbidding place in the dead of night.' Jacob replied.

'...strange things can happen!'

Jacob thought he'd better explain further before the children returned.

'...Sadly, during the days of the smacks, because of the working conditions, incidences of sexual assault and sodomy, were prevalent. More often than not, young boys, who had been assaulted in this manner suffered in silence without reporting, or seeking redress for the assault... Just like Brewer, most of the boys took no action because they were afraid or ashamed to do so... or, because they did not have the vocabulary or the wit to know how to frame a complaint.'

'...Unfortunately, because Frederick Brewer was slight built, quiet spoken and a little effeminate and, looked much younger than his sixteen years, he suffered more than most,' said Jacob. '...The crew of the *Scorpio* knew John Grice for what he was, a sadistic deviant...'

George Simmons was a kind and decent man and thought something needed to be done and decided to report John Grice to the smack owner, Mr Mount. He hoped to get some sort of justice for young Brewer. Unfortunately, Mr Mount saw something else in John Grice and wasn't at all interested in George Simmons's complaint. Jacob explained.

'Oh my... those poor, poor boys... how dreadful... How sad!' Sarah-Eliza muttered.

'Yes... It was really terrible what happened to some of them, as you will hear,' said Jacob quietly.

'...Hush now dear... the children are coming back.'

Still laughing at being pirates, the children came rushing back into the room and sat down at their grandad's feet. Sarah-Eliza looked at her children. Seeing their happy and innocent faces and thinking about Frederick Brewer and the other unfortunate boys who were assaulted, she nearly burst into tears. Listening to her father, Sarah-Eliza was beginning to understand the price that was paid as Grimsby grew and prospered. The children didn't notice their mother's distress; they were too busy looking at their grandad and waiting for him to continue the story.

'Now where was I.' said Jacob. 'Ah yes... I remember, I was telling you about Mr Simmons and Frederick Brewer.'

'...When the *Scorpio* arrived back into Grimsby a few days later, Mr Simmons went to see the owner, Mr Mount, to complain about Brewer's treatment at the hands of John Grice. Mr Mount, a stern imposing man in his fifties, was sat behind a huge leather topped desk in an oak panelled office. Already feeling uneasy and anxious from being in this office, his appearance unnerved Mr Simmons further. Mr Mount was dressed in the manner that successful men of that time adopted. He was wearing a dark frock coat over a white shirt that had high winged collars, a bright waistcoat and grey cravat. Across his ample belly stretched a heavy gold double Albert chain. The outline of the pocket watch could be seen in the waistcoat pocket. He looked every inch the wealthy smack owner that he was.

Mr Simmons was made to stand and wait until Mr Mount was ready to talk to him. Eventually he looked up.

'What can I do for you, Simmons?' He asked in a cold, matter of fact tone of voice.

Intimidated and starting to sweat, Mr Simmons started to tell him of the brutality meted out to Frederick Brewer and the lashings he frequently received from Grice. Mr Mount only listened for a short while before he held his hand up signalling Mr Simmons to stop talking. He was dismissive of the whole incident and couldn't care less. John Grice, as he was paid to do, was a skipper who brought many tons of fish to port. Fish meant wealth!

'…You should remember, Simmons that these boys are the scum of the earth, for the most part… Many are the children of degraded and drunken parents – reared in the mire... Most are liars, full of the most vicious instincts… I suppose that if there is any rope-ending, it is always fully deserved,' said Mr Mount scornfully.

'Now… is that all or, is there anything else you want… I'm far too busy to concern myself about the fortunes of one sixteen year old lad from the workhouse.' He dismissively added.

George Simmons thought for a moment before replying.

'Yes Mr Mount, there is something else… you can look for another third hand… I won't ever be sailing on your smacks again.'

'…That's your choice Simmons, your choice… There's plenty more where you came from… Good-day!' said Mr Mount derisively, gesturing with his hand that Mr Simmons should leave the office.

'...Go and draw any money that's owing to you and get out of my offices,' Mr Mount barked.

'…Shut the door on your way out!'

Sarah- Eliza and the children were stunned by what Jacob had told them. Frederick Brewer's fate and the callous, dismissive attitude of the smack owner had shocked and surprised them.

'That's absolutely unbelievable Father… poor Frederick Brewer,' said Sarah- Eliza. '…how could Mr Mount be so uncaring?'

She was also thinking about what else Jacob had told her when the children were out of the room.

'…My dear,' Jacob sighed before continuing. '…not everyone has the same Christian values that we have.'

'…unfortunately Mr Mount's attitude was not unique among the smack owners at that time… and, other than accidental deaths and losses through storms, many, many boys died or suffered cruelly in similar situations to Frederick Brewer,' Jacob sadly replied.

For a moment, until Gabriel spoke, the children were stunned into open-mouthed silence.

'What happened to Mr Simmons grandad?' he asked. '…he seemed like a nice man!'

'…Yes Gabriel, he was a really decent man,' said Jacob.

'…George Simmons didn't have trouble finding work. He sailed on a few different smacks for a couple of years before he met Henry Kingston in the ale-house *The Crooked Billet* in King Street, near the docks. They got on so well with each other that, after he told the story of why he left Mr Mount's vessels, Mr Kingston offered him the berth of third hand on the *Mary-Ann*, which Mr Simmons gladly accepted.

'You'se sound just like the sort of man I need', Mr Kingston had said to him…

When we joined the *Mary-Ann*, Mr Simmons had been with the vessel for over six years and had been promoted from third hand to the mate. He claimed that he knew the smack nearly as well as Mr Kingston. He was firm but fair with all the men and helped Barney and I as much as he could during the years we sailed with him…

The third hand, Albert Barker... now he was quite a different kettle of fish. He was a grumpy, mean spirited, Grimsby man with a quick temper on him. In dock and on board the smack, whenever he could get it, he liked his drink. He would find any excuse to hit me, Barney or any of the other young apprentices, with the ropes end, especially when Mr Kingston or Mr Simmons were asleep or below deck. We disliked him intensely. For some reason, unbeknownst to us, from the first time we met him, he seemed to take against both Barney and me and gave us a hard time. Several times, Mr Kingston, or Mr Simmons, intervened on our behalf to save us from further punishment.

On one occasion, I was on the receiving end of Albert Barker's temper and was being given the rope, when Mr Kingston stepped in. He said something to him that has stayed with me since.

'BARKER... you'se stop that!' Mr Kingston bellowed from the tiller. 'What's the lad done to deserve the rope?' He frowned angrily at Barker.

'It's Rawlings... he's been lubberly and insubordinate,' Barker lied his shouted reply.

'On my vessels Mr Barker, we spare the rope... cos you can catch more flies with honey than with vinegar,' Mr Kingston shouted back. '...Do you get my drift... does you'se understand me?' He asked firmly and still staring hard at Barker.

'Yes sir... I do,' Barker replied glowering at me. He really didn't like Barney and me.

'Make sure you do, Barker... you'se leave the boy be and belay that rope!' Mr Kingston ordered. '...now get on with your work Rawlings.'

'Are you'se ok, Jake?' Barney, who was working nearby, asked with concern.

'Yeah... I'm fine, Barney... he didn't hit me too hard... Let's get on with our work before old misery guts has another go at us.'

Sarah- Eliza wanted to ask her father how often he had been lashed with a rope-end, but for the moment chose not to. Questions like that could wait. Daniel had questions of his own. He couldn't understand what his grandad had meant.

'Flies, honey, vinegar, what's that got to do with catching fish... What do you mean grandad?'

Jacob, looked at Daniel, put his pipe into his mouth and drew deeply on the freshly lit tobacco. His old eyes had a real sparkle in them. He grinned broadly at Daniel before replying.

'I'm glad you've asked me that Daniel.'

'...I've already told you that I learned much from Mr Kingston. This was one of the best things he taught me... you'll all do well to heed his advice.'

Jacob explained.

'...it's to do with getting people who work for you to do their best... just as the flies will avoid the vinegar jar and gladly settle and eat from a honey pot... people will work harder for you if they are treated kindly and spoken to respectfully… more so than by angry words and lashings from the tongue, or ropes end.'

Jacob leant back in his chair and looked at the children and then at his daughter.

'Do you all understand what Mr Kingston meant?'

'Yes,' the children said as they nodded their head.

'Grandad, it's like saying please and thank you… isn't it?' Grace said.

'Yes Grace… it's exactly like that.' Jacob replied with a broad smile on his face.

Grace smiled and Sarah- Eliza beamed at her daughter. Jacob carried on with his story.

'…I'll be telling you more about old misery guts Albert Barker in a moment… On that first trip, there was also another man, a deck-hand, whose real full name I cannot remember. For reasons which I'll explain shortly, I can picture him very clearly, but sadly, I'm sorry to say, I can't recall what his proper name was. I only remember him as Biffo Barnes from Barking. He was an agreeable experienced fisherman in his early thirties and was just over six feet tall, but walked with quite a pronounced limp, the legacy of a violent storm at sea, from about three years before…

He told me that he was sailing as third hand on the smack *Vincent*. During the height of the storm, a mizzen sail restraining sheet snapped and the mizzen boom swung across the aft deck and slammed into him and knocked him over. He fell awkwardly and shattered his leg in two places…

Unable to hardly move or help his crew mates, he was in agony for the remainder of the storm and, the nine hours it took the *Vincent* to reach the port of Berwick on Tweed, where he was put ashore for treatment…

Biffo considered himself to be fortunate. Some fishermen lost limbs in similar accidents. His leg took several months to heal well enough for him to return to sea. Because of the limp, he struggled to find work as a third hand, which is why he was sailing with Mr Kingston as a deck hand. He only sailed with us for a few trips. Experienced deck-hands regularly moved from smack to smack. Over the years, I've sailed with so many, which is why I don't always remember their names. However, in Biffo's case, about a year after I met him, Mr Kingston offered him the chance to sail again as the third hand on the *Mary-Jane*, which was skippered by Mr Kingston's brother, Charles. With our good wishes he left the *Mary-Ann* and joined the *Mary-Jane*...

Also on the *Mary-Ann*, besides the hopelessly inexperienced Barney and me, there were three other apprentices. John Phillips was seventeen and came from the Wolverhampton Union workhouse. John was only fourteen, when he had been arrested for doing nothing other than *'loafing about'* the centre of Wolverhampton. Because he was an orphan, living on the streets and looked a ragamuffin, the magistrate sent him to the workhouse. The guardians there only kept him for about a week before sending him to Grimsby to be apprenticed. Like us, John was lucky. He'd been apprenticed with Mr Kingston for three years and, was doing well.

Making his second trip on the *Mary-Ann* was sixteen year old Herbert Horton. He was a former agricultural labourer who came from Boston in Lincolnshire. Herbet was a quiet spoken, average built, fair haired lad, just over five feet six inches tall. Although he had become an apprentice with his parents' blessing, I'm not sure that the sea was really the life he wanted. He never seemed happy with his lot...

Then there was Harry Robinson, a likeable but loud-mouthed, strapping built runaway from Manchester. Harry who was eighteen had been with Mr Kingston for two years. Before he absconded and ran away to Grimsby, Harry had been apprenticed for a few months as a shoemaker. We all knew that Harry Robinson was not his real name...

At sea, names didn't matter. You learned to rely on the person not their name. They could be called the Queen of Sheba, for all we cared, as long as they did their job and watched your back as well as you watched theirs. Most fisherman, were given a nickname any way. Herbert became 'Nobby', Harry Robinson was 'Robbo' and Barney, not surprisingly became 'Paddy'. When out of his earshot, we apprentices always referred to Albert Barker as 'Misery Guts'… With the exception of Barney, to whom I was always Jake, among the apprentices, the deckhands and the third hand, I was nicknamed the 'Shrimp' because at only four feet ten inches tall, I was by far the smallest. Neither Mr Kingston nor Mr Simmons ever used the nicknames.

Mr Kingston had hoped to sign on another experienced deck-hand before we sailed, but was let down at the last minute. As the *Mary-Ann* had the bait on board, he didn't let that 'stop the ship'. We sailed on the evening tide as planned. Only now, the nine of us, including the 'wet behind the ears' Barney and me, would be doing the work of ten men…

On that first day, after a breakfast of tea and hard tack, which was a type of biscuit, we went up onto the deck. To our inexperienced eyes, it seemed like a fine day. Although, in the direction we were heading, there were some darker skudding clouds on the horizon, we didn't really pay them any mind. The sky was mainly bright and the wind that morning was not much more than a stiff breeze. The other crew members were already working on deck, preparing the lines for the day's fishing. Mr Kingston was at the tiller and with the wind blowing into his face was staring ahead…

'Morning lads… did you'se sleep well?' he asked us cheerily.

'Yes sir, we did,' said I.

'I did as well,' Barney said. '…for sure, I like those hammocky things… real easy to get in.'

'Struggled then did you Barney?' Mr Kingston said with a big grin on his face.

'…I wondered what all the banging and crashing was… even thought we might have run aground.' He joked.

'Not at all …not at all,' Barney replied as he went red in the face with embarrassment.

'Joking aside lads… do ya notice anything about the sea?' Mr Kingston asked.

'No, Sir' I replied. I thought it looked much the same as the day before. Barney said nothing.

'Look how deep the swell is getting… do ya see the white horses forming on the crest of each wave lads… can you'se see the spume being blown off?' Mr Kingston asked.

'Although, we'd never heard those expressions before, we instantly knew what he meant,' Jacob told the children.

'…As I looked out across the water I noticed that nearly every wave had a white crest, which Mr Kingston called a white horse.'

'…The early morning sunlight made each droplet of the spume sparkle like jewels being scattered into the sea. Little rainbows could be seen at the bow of the smack as the sunlight shone through the spray being created as we moved through the waves. I thought it looked so beautiful, but Mr Kingston could see something else. He could see chaos and danger…

'The wind's getting up,' he said as he looked towards the distant horizon.

'…You'se two lads are unbelievably unlucky… I hope that's not an omen of things to come.'

Neither Barney nor I had a clue what he meant by, *'an omen of things to come'*. But we could see from the expression on his face that he wasn't joking. Mr Kingston paused before adding,

'…Your first full day at sea and you'se lads is gonna have the roughest of baptisms… Thars a mighty big blow coming our way.'

'Without even looking at the weather gauge… I swear, Master Henry, can smell a storm… hours before it actually happens,' shouted George Simmons who was working nearby.

'What do you mean by a big blow, Mr Kingston,' I asked, already knowing the answer.

Although Mr Kingston chose to be honest, he tried not to frighten us and hesitated before answering.

'Well lads… I won't lie to you, lads… It's a gale force storm that'll shake us about a bit.'

'…We sailed a good distance last night… now we're too far from shore to make a run for shelter and safe harbour.'

Seeing the worried expression on our faces he added, 'Don't fret lads…the *Mary-Ann* is a sound vessel, she's a tough un… she'll tackle it head on… and we've a few hours to catch fish before we get her ready for what is surely to come.'

Mr Kingston sounded confident. I wasn't so sure.

'We'll be fine lads… nothing to worry about,' he assured us. 'My course is set to return the *Mary-Ann* home safe with a full hold… that's the objective of our endeavour.'

'And we will… God willing,' Mr Kingston said smiling at us. '…off you'se go now with Mr Simmons… he'll show you what's what and get you'se started fishing.'

As we walked across the deck towards Mr Simmons, Barney started to merrily whistle.

'STOP THAT WHISTLING LAD… you'se stops that right now,' Mr Kingston bawled at Barney. His face was a picture of anger, which surprised us.

Mr Simmons looked horrified. Others stopped working and glared daggers at Barney who stopped whistling and looked confused at the reaction his whistling had caused.

'C'mon 'ere Barney… you too Jake,' said Mr Simmons. 'Let me explain.'

'…among fishermen, whistling is generally considered to be a bad habit and very, very unlucky… Barney, in the old days, you would have been tied to the mast and flogged hard for *'Whistling up the Wind'*… The inference is that, you aren't just whistling up wind, but a raging gale and, certain disaster and catastrophe into the bargain.'

Mr Simmons then pointed to the darkening clouds on the northern horizon and said.

'Look over yonder lads… That is what the Master was just telling you… I don't think that Mother Nature's north wind is gonna need your help to give us a bad time later today, Barney… do you?'

'No Mr Simmons… I don't think it will… For sure, I'm not a good whistler anyway… only know one tune,' Barney replied, trying to make a joke.

'NO, Barney, no… this is not a joking matter,' Mr Simmons rebuked him and then explained.

'...For centuries, fishermen have had a wide range of superstitions and take them all very seriously... you'd both better learn them quickly.'

'...You don't want to become known as a Jonah or a jinx that nobody will sail with.' Mr Simmons advised us...'

Jacob thought he'd better explain more to the children about fishermen's superstitions.

'As I listened to Mr Simmons, I realised that was probably what Mr Kingston meant when he said, *'an omen of things to come'*... He was wondering whether Barney and me were only unlucky or were we jinxed. And, before you ask children, no we weren't jinxed just terribly unlucky that the big blow happened on our first day at sea...'

'Let me finish explaining,' said Jacob. '...Rough and ready conditions at sea were tolerated quite happily by most fishermen. The dangers of the job were accepted as an occupational hazard, or challenge. Unless disaster was inevitable, fishermen rarely showed any sign of fear... Courage however, was one thing and chance or bad luck another. At all costs it was important to avoid bad luck at sea...

There were so many unwritten rules at sea, which if broken were supposed to herald disaster... One of the unluckiest things a fisherman could do, was to cut a slice from a loaf of bread, if there was any on board, and then turn it bottom up on a plate. This was reliably believed to indicate that the smack would capsize and drown everyone... Tradition and superstitions die hard. Many strange customs are still observed today, quite simply because people would rather do so than run the risk of tempting providence and fate...'

'Sorry lads,' a red-faced chastened Barney shouted to the others working on deck.

'...For sure, it won't happen again.'

'Nodding their head, or waving their hand, they acknowledged Barney's apology...

Mr Simmons showed us around the smack and put into plain words all the different jobs that had to be done to catch fish. The *Mary-Ann* was a liner, which meant that fish were caught on hooks and lines...

In the winter months, long lines, which consisted of approximately sixteen dozen lines, each about thirty fathoms long were used... Attached to each long line, at about nine feet intervals were short snood lines which carried the razor sharp barbed hooks. These were usually baited with whelks, mussels or some other shell fish. When all the long lines were joined together, they formed a string stretching out several miles from the smack and, could have as many as six thousand hooks, all of which will have been baited by hand... Where several smacks were fishing the same area, it wasn't uncommon for one smack to accidently sail across the long lines of another smack... The consequences of such an accident would be settled once the smacks were safely back in port.'

Thinking about what he was going to say next, Jacob chuckled so loud that he made himself cough and splutter.

'Father, are you alright?' Sarah- Eliza asked.

'Yes dear... I'm fine.' He replied still chuckling. 'Let me see now, where was I?'

'... Ah yes... once they were back in Grimsby, in the dockland pubs, which the fishermen frequented, many fights had started when crews from the smacks came upon each other... Cut lines meant lost fish and lost wages...Two crews scrapping, knocking seven bells out of each other and others, drunk and sober joining in the fight just for the fun of it made for a right rowdy do... Tables, chairs and ale getting knocked over everywhere.'

Jacob was really laughing loudly now at the memory of these incidences. In his mind, he was back in the *Fisherman's Arms* or *Dogger Bank*, which were two notoriously rough spit and sawdust ale-houses. As they grew into men, and before they became sensible enough to not get involved, Barney and Jacob had often stood side by side, slugging it out with other fishermen. Sometimes they won, sometimes they didn't. Over the years, they'd had a few black-eyes and bloody noses between them.

'Father, did you and Uncle Barney get involved in the fighting?' Sarah- Eliza asked, not sure what to make of her father's enjoyment. She was seeing something in him that she'd never seen before.

'Once or twice my dear… once or twice,' Jacob replied, still laughing raucously.

Happy days he thought, but chose not to elaborate any further. After all, his grandchildren thought he was a respectable and successful fisherman. To regain his composure and stop laughing, he fiddled with his pipe before continuing.

'…In the summer months, Mr Simmons explained, much shorter hand-lines were used. A hand-line was normally only about thirty-five to forty fathoms in length. The hand-line, snood and hooks would be attached to a lead weight of about seven pounds, which carried the bait down to where the fish were. When the hand lines were in use, normally the smack would be hove-to and each man, apprentices and all, worked his individual line...

George Simmons was a patient man. He took the time to make sure we understood what he was saying and encouraged us to ask questions. It was all so strange and a lot to take in. I did notice though that he kept looking at the distant clouds building up and the gradual darkening of the sky. The expression on his face betrayed his concern of what was to come.

'We're gonna hove-to shortly and shoot the hand lines out for a few hours afore that big blow gets to us lads,' he said jovially. 'Then we'll see if you can catch fish.' He laughed.

'Well now, Mr Simmons… I was the best fisherman west of the Shannon,' said Barney.

Barney really had a joke for everything and never stayed subdued or downcast for too long.

'We'll see… we'll see,' Mr Simmons replied with a smile on his face.

'My, my… aren't we the cocky one!' Albert Barker, who was stood nearby, sneered.

'Easy Albert… easy, the lad's only joking,' Mr Simmons said.

148

'Harrumph… bloody Irish ginger idiot,' Albert snorted as he carried on with his work.

'…We were shown how to get the bait out of their shells and put it on the hooks, preferably without skewering the hook into our hands. Not that that prevented me from hooking my hand at the first attempt… Fortunately, the barb didn't go into my hand and the cut wasn't so severe. If the barb had penetrated the skin, the hook would have had to be cut out of my hand. This was one of the daily hazards of fishing with hooks and lines…

Until you get your sea legs and find your balance, it is not easy to do things standing on a smack that is forever moving in all directions…

We fished with hand lines, each having two hooks and on my first shoot, I caught two cod, but when I tried to haul them on board, they fell off. Albert Barker wasn't amused and told me so. I was lucky not to get the ropes end. He really was a miserable man, but a good fisherman. I did better on my second attempt though, I managed to haul aboard two cod, which I then had to gut ice and then pack away…

All the while as we fished, the sky was growing darker and the wind was becoming stronger.'

Chapter 9

Fighting For Our Lives!

'With each passing hour, the storm was ever closer. The swell was increasing and the white horses were now charging into the side of the smack and splashing over the bulwark into our faces and drenching us as we worked our hand lines. Although it was getting darker and the rumble of thunder and occasional flash of sheet lightening could be seen and heard in the distance, we fished for several hours. I can remember clearly how it became a bit of a friendly competition among the five of us apprentices to see who could catch the most. John Phillips, who had been an apprentice the longest, was nearly as fast as Albert and Biffo. He easily beat us. Barney did well though and managed to keep up with Robbo. Nobby and I were the losers but not by many. Nevertheless, we all caught plenty…

As we fished, Mr Kingston and Mr Simmons kept a close eye on the rapidly darkening clouds and the increasing swell of the sea. ..

Barney and I were learning that life at sea as a fisherman was hazardous. Every day was fraught with danger. When hauling in the hand lines we had to lean over the side of the smack… which was a very risky thing to do as the smack would be rolling, pitching and yawing in heavy seas. When the smack rolled, sometimes our faces were only inches from the water. The bulwark of a smack was quite low, falling overboard while working the lines was a daily risk. Over the years, many Grimsby fishermen and young apprentice lads were lost while bringing in the catch…

Only a couple of years before, while hauling in his hand line, John Phillips was nearly drowned. When the *Mary-Ann* was hove to and fishing the icy waters near the Faroe Islands, it was hit on the larboard side with a big wave, which caused it to roll quite suddenly and deeply. John lost his footing and fell overboard on the starboard side. Fortunately for him, Mr Kingston was stood nearby working a hand line. Before John sank beneath the waves, Mr Kingston, thinking quickly, managed to get a grip of him with a boat hook and haul him back on board. He had saved his life. John couldn't swim, not that he would have lasted long in the water. It was too cold to survive more than a few minutes…

Over the coming weeks, we were to soon learn, that fishing was carried out day and night in all but the most extreme weathers. If fish weren't caught, we didn't earn any wages. So risks would be taken! The very nature of fishing meant that we lived with the daily threat of being injured. Just as had happened with Biffo, injured fishermen often died or suffered in agony until land was reached. Besides the perils and dangers of the job itself, fishermen had to contend with being permanently cold and wet…

'Can you imagine living and sleeping in clothes that were always wet?' Jacob asked.

Not waiting for an answer, Jacob continued to talk.

'…On that first day, as the swell was becoming ever deeper, the clouds ominously darker and the wind was starting to blow much more strongly, we carried on fishing and working our hand lines for as long as we could. Though we were hove to, the *Mary-Ann* was being tossed about as it rode the crests and troughs of the increasingly angry sea.

'See what you've brought upon us with your damn whistling… you bloody Irish bog idiot,' Albert Barker snarled at Barney.

Barney was unsure what to say, so he said nothing to Albert and carried on with his work. He looked across at me and, to my surprise I could see fear in his eyes. Not fear of Albert, but fear of the storm that was coming our way.

'Do ya think we'll be alright, Jake?' he asked me. '…It doesn't look good.'

'I… I… don't know, Barney,' I replied, unsure what to think. I was also becoming nervous.

'Looks like it's gonna be a tough one, lads,' John Phillips shouted across to us. Adding '…Mr Kingston's one of the best… If anyone can bring us safely through, it's him.'

We didn't fish for much longer. The storm was too close.

'That'll do for now George… haul them hand lines in and prepare for the storm,' Mr Kingston shouted from the tiller. '…I'll put her into the wind.'

'Ok Henry,' Mr Simmons shouted back and immediately started to secure the *Mary-Ann*.

'…C'mon lads… look lively, get those lines in… let's get all the loose gear on deck and in the galley stowed away.'

'Barker and Biffo, being experienced hands didn't need telling what to do… Everyone got on with making the smack safe from the tempest that was to come… As I worked, I stopped feeling nervous, my mind was occupied with doing whatever I was told to do and, as quickly as I could. The look of fear had also left Barney's face as he set about his work… Although it's so many years ago, I can still remember that storm as though it were yesterday,' Jacob told the children.

'…Even though I was the youngest, I wasn't as scared as some of the others on the smack.'

'…About thirty minutes or so after Mr Kingston had asked for the smack to be made secure, the storm hit us. Within minutes, what had been a very strong wind turned into a shrieking maelstrom of a gale. We were being pummelled by an ear-splitting unearthly force that had to be fought and mastered before it took the *Mary-Ann* and all of us down into Davy Jones' Locker…

The wind screamed and howled and blew in ferocious gusts through the smacks rigging and sails. The mainsail, mizzen and jib sail were full and looked as though they may be ripped asunder at any moment. But they weren't! The yards, ropes, sheets and cleats were straining to contain the increasing violence of the wind. But lucky for us, they did! Although some of the wooden yards creaked and cracked, they held. As the wind strength increased, Mr Kingston ordered the rapid reefing of the mainsail, leaving only the mizzen and jib set. Set up this way, he pointed the Mary-Ann directly into the wind.

The swell of the sea was now so deep that when the *Mary-Ann* was in the trough, we couldn't see the horizon. Wave upon wave leapt into the smack – fore and aft. The deck was awash, with water gushing everywhere. Although it was only late afternoon, the sky had become as black as ink, and the heavy driving rain made for poor visibility. The wind howled, thunder boomed and sheet lightening flashed. Mountainous heavy waves pounded the *Mary-Ann*, making it roll so far over, that we wondered whether it would ever right itself. I'm certain I wasn't the only one who thought we were close to meeting our Maker that day...'

Jacob was enjoying telling this part of the story. To add to the drama and create a sense of doom, he was changing the tone of his voice and the speed at which he spoke to emphasise the danger. The children loved it and listened intently. It was as though Jacob was back in the *Lord Raglan*, trading stories with other fishermen.

'...Anything loose on deck, including the crew would have been just swept away. Mr Kingston in his oilskin and sou'wester stood solidly at the tiller on the aft deck. His powerful arms keeping the tiller and the *Mary-Ann* headed in the direction he knew they had to take. All the nous and experience he had gained from nearly thirty years as a sailor was being used to keep the smack afloat. Henry Kingston knew that if the vessel was on the wrong tack and came broadside into the wind and waves it would be swamped and would capsize. Head to wind, towards that point on the horizon from where the wind blew, it had to be. Mr Kingston was aiming for the wind's eye...

Mr Simmons, Barker and Biffo held on to lifelines as they watched him and waited for orders to furl, reef, or set the sails, loosen that sheet, or whatever else Mr Kingston ordered. Waves breaking over the bow of the smack cascaded over them and would have swept them away had they not been holding onto the lifelines. Us apprentices sheltered in the fo'castle until we were called for. We were all in an indescribable state of painful fear and excitement. All the time Mr Kingston was shouting instructions to Mr Simmons and the others, of which I couldn't understand a word. It was all double-dutch to me!

'Hold fast lads... hold fast, you'sell beat this bugger yet,' he bellowed into the wind.

We could hardly hear him over the sounds of the crashing waves and the howling wind. No matter that we couldn't hear what he was shouting we knew he was roaring words of encouragement to keep our spirits up...

I can picture him still, holding on to the tiller with every ounce of strength he possessed. Every muscle and sinew in his arms, legs, back and shoulders must have been crying out for relief. Many a fisherman had been lost in storms because a big wave had hit the rudder, causing the tiller arm to pitch the man holding it into the sea. If the tiller came out of your grasp, the smack would turn and be at the mercy of the waves and wind. It would be doomed!

As though he was carved out of English Oak, Mr Kingston stood steadfast, uncompromising, unyielding and fighting for our lives. It was a battle between him and the storm. Much of the time he was swearing and cursing at the wind, or calling for God to give him strength. Watching him made me admire his fortitude and determination. I swore that if I ever owned a smack, or sailed as skipper, he would be my role model...

Several times during the height of the storm, as the *Mary-Ann* pitched and rolled and was hit by big waves, someone lost their footing and slid across the deck. It was only through providence and good luck that they managed to take hold of something as they slid, or had been grasped by a crew mate, that saved them from going overboard and the certainty of being drowned. Men and boat were taking a battering, but the *Mary-Ann* held fast. She was a tough old lady...

Throughout the storm, Robbo and John, the more experienced apprentices, went about their tasks with the minimum of fuss or regard for their own safety. It was dangerous work, as Robbo found out when the smack rolled while they were taking in the big jib. The sail bellied out and lifted him level with the top of the bulwarks. Fortunately for him the sea was kind, the smack rolled and he was able to slip out of the sail and back on to the deck and grab a hold of something, otherwise he would have been pitched into the sea. Like many apprentices of that time, he could not swim. Not that you would be able to survive in the raging sea…

Watching the experienced hands doing whatever the sea and storm asked of them was inspirational and encouraged me. If they were frightened, they didn't show it, they were courageous men. Unlike, poor old Nobby who was shaking and looked about ready to burst into tears. Clearly, he was terrified, but was trying his best not to get agitated… For once, Barney had little to say. Tight lipped and grim faced, just like the rest of us he just got on with whatever he was asked to do… You may not believe this, children… once the storm was upon us, I was surprised at how calm and composed I was…

Before the storm hit us, I was as nervous as the other boys. Why I was so calm in the midst of that howling wind and rain, I don't know. Perhaps it was my faith in the Lord. But, I knew then that I was destined to a life at sea. I found the experience with the storm quite exhilarating…

For nearly seven hours, we fought that storm, all the time not knowing who would emerge the victor. It was nearly eleven o'clock at night before it started to blow itself out. We had prevailed and we were safe, for now. Finally Mr Kingston started to relax. Including time while we were fishing, he had manned the tiller and given the orders for over fourteen hours. He must be totally exhausted I remember thinking.

'Well done lads… well done all of you'se… I think we've won that one.' He shouted to us, grinning from ear to ear.

We looked around at each other and smiled. Even misery guts Barker managed to crack a smile.

'Aye, we did Henry… we did that,' Mr Simmons, who was also smiling broadly, shouted back to Mr Kingston.

'Well done Master Kingston… That's seamanship that is,' Barker said. '…Real seamanship.'

At that moment, we could see from the look on Mr Simmons face and Albert Barker's genuine compliments that, we had come through something rather special.

'Now tell me you didn't enjoy that, lads,' Mr Kingston yelled to us apprentices.

'It was a rough one alright,' John replied.

Barney and I were too numb to answer. With a sort of half smile, we just nodded our head.

'...Take the lads below, George... get them something to eat... that's enough for one day, we'll start fishing again in the morning.'

'Yes sir, I'll do that.' He replied. '...Look lively lads before the master changes his mind.'

'...Mr Simmons told us to go down the companion ladder and put on dry clothes from our sea-bag, if we had any. Before taking to our hammocks, we ate some cheese, hardtack and had a cup of sweet tea. Because of the storm, no one had eaten since early afternoon. I'd forgotten how hungry and thirsty I was...

After silently giving thanks to the Lord for our deliverance, I soon fell asleep. Even Barney managed to get into his hammock at the first time of asking.

'Well now Jake... I'm not so sure I want another twelve hours like we've just had anytime soon,' Barney said, or something that sounded like that.

'...Goodnight, Jake.'

I may not have heard him clearly, I was already falling asleep.'

'Just after sunlight, at about five o'clock the next morning we were roused from our hammocks, had a cup of tea in the cabin and then went up on deck. The sea was running a moderate swell and although the sky was cloudy, plenty of blue could be seen. Other than slight damage to bulwarks, stanchions, one broken spar and rips to the jib sails on the smack, there was no other evidence of the foul weather of only a few hours earlier. Even though the *Mary-Ann* had suffered damage and repairs would need to be made, it was not enough to make us return to port. We could still fish. With Mr

Simmons at the tiller, and Mr Kingston on deck giving the orders, before we resumed our hand-line fishing, every one pitched in and we made whatever repairs we could to the broken spar, sheets and sails and, anything else that had been damaged in the tempest. Unlike many other smacks, the *Mary-Ann* was in fairly good shape…

Jacob paused for moment. He took a deep breath, sighed and looked at his daughter and then the children before continuing. His mood had suddenly changed. Sarah-Eliza could see from the sad and sombre expression on his face that what he was going to tell them next still caused him pain and anguish.

'…Through good luck and God's will, we had survived the storm… unlike many other poor souls who now sleep beneath the sea… Those that have no grave to mark their passing, and only the Lord Almighty knowing where they lie,' Jacob said. His voice was wavering with emotion.

'…Fishermen's lives and vulnerable sailing smacks were always at the mercy of the violent gales which raged in the North Sea and southern part of the Arctic Ocean… Although we got snippets of information, from other smacks we happened upon, we didn't really know the full devastating consequence of the storm until we returned to Grimsby several weeks later… The storm proved to be disastrous to the port. The fishing smacks had suffered severely… Very few of them that were at sea during the gales had escaped without damage…

Altogether thirty seven vessels were listed as suffering damage such as: loss of masts, small boats, sails, gear, boom, anchors and chains. The smack *Trent* lost her skipper. He was washed overboard while manning the tiller. A fifteen year old boy was washed overboard from the smack *Peggy* and, the cod smack *Favourite*, sunk with the loss of all nine hands… They're just the ones I can recall,' Jacob said sadly.

'In total, about forty men and boys were lost and many smacks damaged or destroyed in the gale from which I, at the age of thirteen, had prevailed. The number of fishermen that were lost may well have been many, many more because accurate records of losses were not kept at that time.'

The children were quiet. Sarah-Eliza could feel the tears welling up in her eyes.

'Oh Father... how awfully sad!'

'Yes my dear, how terribly sad... a cruel price was paid and over the years to come would continue to be paid to harvest the bounty of the sea,' Jacob said rather solemnly.

Jacob stopped talking and deep in thought looked out of the window. He was thinking. Nobody spoke. The children looked at each other and then their mother. Almost imperceptibly she put a finger up to her mouth and whispered shush. They all sat there in silence.

'I thought the mood on the *Mary-Ann* the morning after the storm was strange,' said Jacob who was still staring out of the window. He turned to face the children.

'...Mr Kingston, George Simmons, Barker and Biffo, went about their work as though nothing untoward had happened. They all seemed rather blasé about the danger they had faced and being so close to meeting their God. Other than discussing the damage, there was no talk of the storm's ferocity. Clearly it was an occupational hazard... If only to themselves, they must have given thanks for their salvation. I thought... We young apprentices were openly more thankful that God had seen fit to spare us...

'Sweet Jesus...that was frightening,' said Barney. '...at times, I thought I would be having breakfast with 'Old Nick' himself this fine morning.'

'What makes you think he'd be wanting your company,' joked John.

'For sure... a fine and dandy Irish lad is welcome anywhere, John,' Barney replied.

'I was really scared witless... nearly cacked my strides,' big Robbo admitted. 'Especially when the jib sail got a hold of me... What about you Jake... how did you feel?'

Not wanting to be seen as being overly calm about the storm, I replied,

'Oh... I was too busy being really scared to be frightened.'

Realising the absurdity of what I had just said, we all started laughing. Even nervous Nobby was more relaxed and laughing with us.

'C'mon lads, no time for joking, we've got plenty of work to do,' Mr Simmons said good-naturedly.

'The next few weeks passed quite quickly. Out on the vast expanse of the North Sea and the Northern waters, without a timepiece, it is easy to lose all concept of time. The rising and setting of the sun and the waxing and waning of the moon are your only guides. Before too long I had no idea what the date was, or even what day of the week it was. The further north we went, the hours of daylight got shorter and confused me even more... About a week or so after the storm, I knew it was my thirteenth birthday. I couldn't say for definite which day because I'd lost track of the days. I told no one, not even Barney. They all thought I was fourteen when I signed on, so I wasn't about to tell them I was only thirteen...

Each day, under the guidance of Mr Simmons and sometimes Albert Barker, we were given different jobs to do. We were learning how to fish and sail the smack. Even though he had bragged to Mr Kingston when we signed on, we soon discovered that Barney was no cook. The best thing he ever made was halibut head soup and, even that was foul. But when you are hungry you will eat almost anything... Barney chopped up some halibut heads, including the eyes, teeth and tongue, added potatoes and onions and cooked until it was so soft that we could eat the bones and all. He then added broken biscuits to the dish...

'It really was ghastly and, that was the best thing he made,' Jacob said laughing at the look of disgust on his daughter and grandchildren's faces.

'That sounds absolutely revolting, father,' said Sarah-Eliza.

'It was... but like I said, when you are hungry... and if there's nothing else... you'll eat almost anything,' Jacob replied.

'I wouldn't... I'd leave it,' said Gabriel. 'Wouldn't I mother?'

'So would I,' said Grace.

'If you were hungry enough you'd eat it… You would,' said Daniel, which set the children off bickering.

Jacob smiled at the children. 'Hush now… Stop this arguing or I won't continue.'

'…Old Barney was no fool… after two or three more disasters, much to his delight, Mr Kingston asked nervous Nobby to be the cook. Even with all its dangers, like me, Barney loved working on the open deck of a fishing smack… and, I liked having him there, working alongside of me…'

'For us, life on board the smack settled into the regular pattern of work, eat and sleep. The weather varied between being calm and stormy, but nothing was as ferocious as the 'big blow'. As we moved into the start of winter, our heads were occasionally under the snow squalls, frequent rain and drenching waves. Our feet were often in icy slush, which, even when the skies are kind, at all times overlays the deck…

On the smacks we were butchers as well as fishermen. Once the fish had been hauled in, seated in the slush of the deck, our knives were never idle. The cod fish were killed by being gutted alive. We gutted and gutted and were drenched as we worked. As the 'putting down' proceeded, the quagmire of blood and filth, in which we worked rose ever higher and higher. Our oilskins and clothes became covered in the slime and ooze from gutting the fish. We really were the dirtiest of men. Always the wettest and, in winter, the coldest… Our hands were often wounded, our fingers gashed and torn, so there was suffering always… Amongst all this filth, slime and ooze, strong bonds were often formed with your crew mates. Unfortunately, as I have already told you, unspeakable cruelty and brutality was also sometimes allowed to happen… For Barney and me, it was a bond that would last our lifetime… He really was my best friend and was never found wanting…

One day, in the middle of cleaning the deck after putting the fish down, he came over to me. It had been a fine day. We stood in silence and looked out over the sea as the sun was setting. Half of the sun had already dropped below the horizon causing the sun's rays to shine through the surface of the water making it shimmer like a golden haze.

'Tis a beautiful sight, Barney… is it not?' I said.

'Well now… it is that,' he said and put his arm around my shoulder.

'Jake my boy… for sure it was a most fortunate day for Finbar McHugh when you darted into that alleyway to avoid the crusher.'

'That's what I think too,' I replied and joked. '…I saved you from a life of crime.'

'We'll make a fine pair of fishermen, Barney… and, one day we'll have our own smacks.'

'That we will… Rawlings and McHugh… smack owners… For sure it's got a nice ring to it,' Barney said enthusiastically.

'As we stood in silence watching the setting sun, Barney kept his arm draped around my shoulder. Quite suddenly, our moment of innocent bonding and peace was broken by the swoosh of a ropes end that Albert Barker laid across Barney's back… With a yelp of pain and surprise, Barney spun round. His eyes flashed with an anger that I rarely saw in him.

'What 'as you just roped me for… ya miserable old git' Barney asked. He was furious.

'As well as being an Irish bog idiot… I can see you're a bit of a margery… Is this your nancy-doxie?' Barker sneered looking at me.

I didn't have a clue what he meant. But, Barney did.

'No, Barker… you're a fool and a foul mouthed idiot… Jake is my best friend… someone I would trust my life with,' Barney said defiantly.

'…For sure, no one will ever say that of you… will they… you're a lonely friendless old fart.' Barney glared at Barker, his eyes showing an inner fury.

Because he knew it was true, Barney's comment hurt Barker and made him even angrier.

'AAGH!' he roared as he raised his arm meaning to strike Barney again with the rope.

I quickly stepped forward to place myself between them, but didn't need to. Biffo had come up behind Barker and caught hold of his arm, preventing the blow from being struck.

'Calm down Albert... what on earth's the matter with you?' Biffo asked. '...why the rope... the boys haven't done anything wrong.'

Still holding Barker's arm, Biffo said to us,

'Go on lads... go about your work.'

'What is your problem Barker... why is you so hard on them boys?' Biffo asked.

'They're a pair of lazy miss-nancies,' Barker said contemptuously.

'No they're not... you daft old sod... they're just two young friends who happen to look out for each other,' Biffo replied before adding,

'...Now, unless they're really doing wrong, you leave 'em be... or you'll have me to answer to,' Biffo warned him.

As we returned to our work, Biffo, who was a bigger more powerful man than Albert Barker, let go of his arm. He wasn't going to argue with Biffo. Still glaring at us with his eyes full of spite and malice, he went back to what he was doing before he had decided to use the rope-end. Biffo walked over to Barney and me.

'I don't know why, but that old scrote don't like you boys any... Does he?'

'No Biffo... he doesn't and we don't know why... Thanks for helping,' I replied.

'Yes, thanks Biffo... I swore that after being whipped in the S'uthell Workhouse, nobody would ever put a lash on me again... For sure that old bastard has once too often,' Barney said.

Clearly still upset, he added '...He won't ever do it again... and, before God I swear he may live to regret what he has just done.'

'Come on Barney... let's get on with our work,' said I.

'Just watch how you go lads... you've made a real enemy there.' Biffo advised.

'For sure… misery guts 'as made an enemy of me... One day, one day…' Barney muttered, leaving the last sentence uncompleted, as we went back to work.

We were grateful to Biffo that he had seen fit to protect us. Mr Kingston was down below in the galley and didn't see what happened. But, Mr Simmons who was on the tiller did. He had watched the incident and would have intervened if Biffo had not. Biffo looked across at Mr Simmons. They nodded to each other, they were like minded…

'Other than that incident, the days soon passed and were fairly uneventful. We got on with learning how to fish and sail the smack. Throughout the trip, all of us apprentices watched out for each other. We took care to be forever mindful of Albert Barker's moods, especially when he was instructing us… and made sure we didn't do anything to anger him and warrant the ropes end. After living with Thaddeus Stone and his beatings for all those years, I wasn't frightened of Barker… For the last rope-ending, Barney hated him with a passion...

Fortunately, for the remainder of that trip, Barker left us alone. Biffo didn't have to come to our aid again except on one occasion when I lost my footing while hauling in my hand line and nearly went over the side into the icy water… Having got the hang of hand lining, I'd been fishing well and was catching plenty of cod and the odd halibut. Although the deck was being washed by the occasional wave which splashed over the bulwark, it still became slippery underfoot from the slime of the fish. I was leaning too far over the bulwark with my face not far from the water.

When the *Mary-Ann* rolled, I lost the grip on my hand line, my feet slipped backwards and I was about to vanish over the side into the 'ogging. If Biffo, who was working next to me, hadn't gotten hold of the back of my oilskin I would have gone overboard and been drowned…'

'Better you stay this side of the bulwark, young Shrimp,' he said.

'Thank you Biffo,' said I struggling to catch my breath and spit out the mouthful of sea water I'd taken in when my face hit the water.

'…You've just saved my life.' I think I said to him.

'Ok Shrimp… you can buy me a couple of ales when we're back in port… and we'll call it squits,' he said with a smile.

Jacob laughed, 'My life was valued at a couple of pints of ale.'

He turned to carry on with his work. Remarkably, nothing more was said about the incident… Biffo had saved my life and then acted as though incidences like that was a daily occurrence…'

'Blimey,' said Daniel, looking amazed. 'Flipping eck!'

'Had it not been for Biffo Barnes, father… none of us would have been here,' Sarah-Eliza said. '…he saved your life and you can't even remember his proper name… that's dreadful.'

'I know dear… but that's what old age does to you!' Jacob replied with a huge grin on his face.

'…shall I carry on… before I forget what else I was going to tell you?' he asked mischievously.

'Father… Don't be a tease… please carry on,' said Sarah-Eliza.

'Yes please grandad,' said Gabriel.

'…Each day, Mr Kingston sailed the smack further north until we were fishing the waters just a few miles south of Iceland. By then, we had stopped hand lining and were fishing with long lines, which had to be towed out and hauled in using the smack's row-boat… That was very dangerous… I hated doing it.'

'Why did you hate it grandad?' Gabriel asked.

'Many boys lost their life rowing the boat out as far as two miles from their smack… I was lucky,' Jacob replied. 'Unfortunately, others were not.'

Jacob paused to think.

'I'll tell you some more about that danger in a moment…'

'The fish we caught were salted or iced immediately they were gutted. Once we had a full cargo, it was taken into the Shetland Islands and sold. There Mr Kingston would obtain fresh water, bait and more supplies before returning the *Mary-Ann* to the fishing grounds...'

'The smack only carried about two week's supply of water in barrels... putting into a port regularly was essential...' Jacob explained.

'Just as Mr Kingston promised we were reasonably well-fed, that much is true, except for the few occasions that Barney cooked. Getting plenty of sleep was a different matter... Sometimes we would get just two hours sleep out of twenty-four. When the fish were plentiful, we hauled the lines every few hours, getting no sleep at all, often for two consecutive days and nights... To the eyes it seemed like a pleasant life, and perhaps it was for anyone who loves to watch the sunlight on the land and sea, the unending and marvellous movement and surprises of the waves. But only to the eyes was it pleasant, but not, as Barney and I found out, to our hands, arms and legs, fishing toughened you up.... Despite the discomfort, I loved it...

We fished those northern waters for over two months until Mr Kingston decided it was time for us to be homeward bound. All the way home we fished, icing fish along the way. As we got closer, the best of the last catch made before we returned to Grimsby, was put in a special purpose built well in the middle of the *Mary-Ann*... The well was an integral part of the vessel, designed in such a way that fresh sea water could flow through a series of small holes. The cod fish we put into the well would stay alive, be in good condition and fetch a better price on the market...

Finally, after nearly three months at sea, at the Smeaton Lighthouse, Mr Kingston turned the smack to starboard and we sailed back up the River Humber. The Dock Tower was such a welcoming sight. We were home again. Only, other than the *Mary-Ann*, we had no home to return to. Barney and I had left Grimsby as two naïve innocent boys and whilst we were not yet fisherman, we now knew what it meant to be one... Fishing was to be our lives for the next fifty or so years. But, after that first trip, once we were safely in port we needed to find somewhere to stay before we went to sea again.'

'Why... why couldn't you stay on the *Mary-Ann*, grandad?' asked Daniel.

'No Daniel, that was not possible... Mr Kingston made it clear, when we signed our papers, that in port we had to fend for ourselves until we put to sea again.' Jacob replied. '...this was not unusual... and in hindsight, as you will see Barney and I benefitted from it.'

'But, before we could do that, our fish had to be sold and, we needed to be paid our first wages... We were lucky, others were not so fortunate.'

'...For some apprentices, not only did they have a hard time at sea, but also when they were home ashore... Lads from Grimsby would, of course, go home to their homes and families... The lads who came from the workhouses and orphanages had no family to return to. Unless they stayed with the master, which some did, they had to fend for themselves and find appropriate lodgings... Sadly, not all were appropriate. There were always unscrupulous people, like thieves, pickpockets and dollymops, in the mean streets of the dockland area who would take advantage of the apprentice boy's innocence and naivety...'

Jacob paused for a moment and sighed.

'Also, what most people don't know is that, if their apprenticeship was cancelled and they were deemed *'not suitable for sea'*, as some boys were, they couldn't return to the orphanage from which they had come. The orphanages had done with them. They were turned out onto the streets... often never to be heard of again. Some of these unfortunate lads were as young as fourteen. Can you imagine that, being all alone, homeless, penniless, friendless and frightened?'

'There's little wonder then that some boys took to crime and ended up in prison,' Jacob said as he slowly shook his head.

'...all because someone at the orphanage, or the workhouse had arranged for them to be apprenticed, which got the lad off their hands... It was so very wrong and made me very angry!'

Chapter 10

Learning To Be Streetwise In Dockland

'Shortly after five o'clock on the fifteenth of November 1865, on the evening tide, we sailed back into Grimsby. The *Mary-Ann* was tied up alongside the pontoon and was made ready to off-load the fish for the next day's early morning market. It was just over eleven weeks since we had left the port and, twelve weeks after I had killed Thaddeus Stone, whom I had completely forgotten about.

Children, I don't really expect you to fully understand this, but there is something about the sea and its many moods, which can change in an instant that binds men together to survive its wrath and stay alive. Although I was only thirteen, your age Daniel, I had stood shoulder to shoulder with men more than thrice my age and, stared death and devastation in the face and survived…

As much as I had missed my mama, those eleven weeks at sea had been the happiest time for me in many years. Although I was still a boy, I had seen and done things that changed my life forever. I can remember thinking there was so much I couldn't wait to tell my mama when I saw her again. Sadly, I wasn't to know until four years later that, just two weeks after I had safely returned from my first trip to sea, my mama died in prison and was buried in an unmarked grave… For my future, my mama had sacrificed herself…'

Jacob's voice nearly broke with the emotion of what he had just said. He stopped talking and for the moment was deep in thought. He held his hands in his lap. There was no fiddling with his pipe. He sat quite still - looking out of the window, his eyes were moist and he was struggling to contain the tears. Nobody spoke. Sarah-Eliza had never seen her father like this before. Jacob took a deep breath, swallowed hard and managed to regain his composure. He carried on with the story and soon had the humour back in his voice. Sarah-Eliza and the children relaxed.

'…We were allowed to sleep on board the *Mary-Ann* that night until about four o'clock in the morning when we roused and, without having any breakfast, started to unload the fish. Working by candle light in the fish room and paraffin lamps on the deck, our fish was unloaded onto the pontoon for the market. After three months on a smack that was forever moving about, it felt strange being on firm land again. You don't realise how quickly and sub-consciously your body compensates for the smack's movement. That's what I meant when I said about getting your sea legs…

'Look at all that fish Jake, 'said Mr Simmons. '…let's hope it sells well enough to be able to pay you some wages.'

Mr Simmons winked at Albert Barker, whom, although I didn't like him and he didn't like us, I had learned to respect as a fisherman. Barney was not so forgiving!

'What do you mean, Mr Simmons... you may be able to pay us some wages,' I asked.

'…If it's a poor market and we don't get much for the fish, we can't pay you... besides you still owe Mr Kingston for all the gear he got for you from Charlie Banks's store, before we sailed.'

'…He'll take back the money for that... afore any money goes in your pocket.' Mr Simmons explained.

'That won't do at all... Mr Simmons,' I said, rather concerned and unsure whether he was having a joke with me or not.

Barney piped up. 'Well now... how can you work for eleven weeks in some of the worst parts of God's holy creation and end up with no dosh in yer pocket... That's an Irish riddle for sure.'

'How can I make my fortune this way?'

'It happens all the time Barney... the cost of the trip has to be paid before the crew gets paid.' Mr Simmons replied.

'Don't worry lads... Mr Kingston knows what he's doing... We got a good money for the fish we sold in Shetland and it should be a good market today... you'll be getting wages,' Mr Simmons reassured us.

'Well that's alright then... I'm happy about that.' Barney replied and put his back into off-loading the fish. Mr Simmons looked at Barney, chuckled and shook his head as he walked away...

All along the pontoon quayside, smacks were being unloaded by hand by the crews of the smacks and shore based lumpers. Everywhere you looked, baskets of fish were being laid out... Just like it had been, all those weeks before when we wondered around in amazement, the pontoon was the busiest, noisiest, smelly place... Men were shouting, boxes and baskets of fish were dropped onto the floor, dozens of gulls were shrieking and crying and occasionally swooping down to try and take a smaller fish from the open baskets. It was chaotic. I don't really know why, but as cold and noisy as it was, I loved it. It was so very different from Calthorpe...

At six o'clock, the fish market sale began. Our fish sold well. Mr Simmons wandered over to where Barney and I were stood mesmerised watching the sales proceed. We couldn't tell who'd bought what, or what price they had paid. I couldn't understand a word of what the auctioneer, who was selling the fish, was saying. Everything was happening so fast. It seemed like a blur.

'You'll be getting wages when we settle up later this morning lads,' Mr Simmons told us.

'We've done well... Henry Kingston knows his fish and the market... He's a canny old bugger.'

'Come to see him about eleven o'clock... all should be sorted by then.'

In high spirits and as instructed, we went to see Mr Kingston, who had our wages already worked out.

'Right now lads... let me see. Thar's due eleven weeks wages at four shillings and sixpence a week... So that makes two pounds, nine shillings and sixpence. Agreed?'

Barney couldn't do multiplication of numbers and I didn't work it out, so I just said yes, agreed.

'For your sea gear, that I paid Charlie Banks, you owe me one pound, eleven shillings and three-pence... Are you'se happy with that?'

Again we just nodded and said yes.

'Well... that leaves you with eighteen shillings and three pence wages each... Are you'se happy with that?' he asked.

It didn't seem very much for eleven weeks of hard and dangerous work. It was just a little more than the fifteen shillings my mama had given me. Although, we knew he wasn't cheating us, our faces betrayed our disappointment... We still said agreed. At least it was wages. Mr Kingston looked at us and waited a moment. He smiled and leant back in his chair before saying,

'I'll tell you what lads; you've done well this trip... As I'm impressed with the both of you... not that I like your cooking Barney, I'll give you an extra five bob each.'

'What do you say to that?' he asked.

'Yes Sir... that'll be right fine and dandy and much appreciated,' said Barney.

'Thank you Mr Kingston,' said I.

'There you go then lads... one pound, three shillings and three-pence each.'

He counted the money out and gave it to us.

'...Mind how you spend it now, thar's many temptations ashore,' he cautioned. '...and, thar's many a bludget and dippers who will try to take it from you.'

'Thank you sir... we'll be careful,' Barney replied. 'I'll look after young Jake here.'

'Mind you do Barney... it's tough out there.' Mr Kingston said.

'...and you Jake... keep your eye on this daft Irish lad too.' He added good-naturedly.

'Yes sir... I will,' I replied and laughed.

We were all in fine humour...'

Although some masters and skippers discouraged it, many apprentices and younger crew members would squander their hard earned cash on drink, music halls and prostitutes [dollymops]. If an apprentice, or young fishermen, could find no amusement in their lodgings during the evenings, they would go out to seek some other means of entertainment. It was inevitable that the older boys would frequent music halls and public houses. It could hardly have been expected, that young men, such as the older apprentices, should have been restrained from going into such places.

This was the squalid dockland quarter of the town. Life was cheap and all manner of vice was prevalent. Dark secrets could be hidden in the dank and dingy streets at night. It was an area of rough ale-houses, the bawdy, double-entendré world of the early music halls and stage door Johnnies, to the drabs out on the streets selling themselves for a penny.

All too frequently, lads as young as fourteen years of age could, without difficulty, get served with as much beer as they wanted. As if they were not vulnerable enough on the streets, being drunk made them more so. Fisher-boys were not hard to distinguish and, had they wished to do so, the owners of the various public houses and music halls could easily have refused admission to any of the very young apprentices. But, they had money in their pockets and were an easy target in a very predatory neighbourhood. Without parent or friend to watch over them, many became ready prey to the large underclass of society who lived on debauchery and vice.

Jacob continued with his story.

'…Right now, you'se lads have got to find somewhere to stay… we'll not be sailing again until the morning tide a week next Saturday.' Mr Kingston said.

'…'ere, I've written the address of Molly Cocking… she's a fisherman's widow, who takes in lodgers… go and see 'er and say I sent you… If she's room, she'll take you in and, she'll wash your gear for you.'

'Well now… no point in giving the address to me… Jake's the scholar,' said Barney.

I took the piece of paper and put it in my pocket. We turned to leave when Barney asked,

'What times will the tide be when we sail?'

171

'That my lads, is for you'se to find out… start thinking like fishermen,' Mr Kingston replied. '…the *Mary-Ann* will be all baited and ready to go… don't let me down by stopping the ship.'

'No sir we won't,' said I.

'Don't forget that next time,' said Mr Kingston. '…You'll not have to pay me for the sea gear, so most of the wages will go into yer pockets.'

That brought a smile to our faces.

'Thank you sir,' we both said and picking up our sea-bags, we left the *Mary-Ann* to go and find the lodgings.

'…You'se take real care now lads,' he shouted after us.

'Yes sir… we will,' I shouted back.

Quite excited, with our first wages and the money we each had left from mama's fifteen shillings, we both had nearly two pounds in our pockets. With our sea-bag on our shoulders and a spring in our step, we set off down Fish Dock Road to leave the docks and go into Grimsby.

'What's a bludget, Barney?' I asked.

'Well now… I don't really know… but I'm sure we'll find out soon enough.' he replied.

'It didn't take us too long to find the address that Mr Kingston gave us. Orwell Street, where Mrs Cocking lived, was close to the entrance to the dock. Although, it was mainly houses, just a couple of shops and the *Lord Raglan* ale-house, which became a favourite of mine, it was quite a busy street. People were going about their business and some were just standing on the street corner talking. With our sea-bag on our shoulder, Barney and I didn't look out of place. We didn't attract much attention as we looked for Mrs Cocking's house...

From the outside, her house appeared to be well kept. Better than most in the street. The paintwork on the front door and window frames was in good order and the windows were clean and dressed with colourful curtains. The doorstep had been regularly stoned. Barney and I looked at each other...

'Well now… this seems to be ok,' he said looking around. '…Standing 'ere on the pavement scratching our bum, ain't gonna get us a bed for the night.'

'No… it won't,' said I, as I walked up to and knocked hard on the door.

Hearing a noise from inside the house, we stepped further back on the pavement. Molly Cocking opened the door. Her appearance at first startled us. She wasn't at all what we expected. Mrs Cocking was a very large, red faced, formidable looking middle aged lady and was wearing a voluminous black dress with a white apron. Her greying hair was tied up in a bun and she had a clay pipe clenched tightly in her mouth making her look quite stern. Before saying a word, she looked us up and down.

Taking the pipe from her mouth, which softened her expression a little, Mrs Cocking blew out the smoke from the burning tobacco. We could then see that, except for a single tooth on her lower jaw, she was toothless. We stood there open mouthed, trying not to laugh.

'Yes... what can I do for you lads,' she asked rather abruptly '…Come on speak up... I haven't got all day.'

'Are you Molly Cocking?' Barney asked.

'What if I am… what's it got to do with you?' she replied, still looking us up and down.

'…and, it's Mrs Cocking to you.'

'Mrs Cocking, erm… Mr Kingston sent us,' I said rather timidly.

'…He thought you might be able to give us lodgings… till we're ready to sail again.'

'He did now, did he… so, you're two of Henry's likely lads are you?'

'Yes missus… we're off the *Mary-Ann*.' Barney replied and added, '…not sailing again until a week next Saturday… and for sure, we need some fine lodgings.'

'I suppose you've both got some manky gear to be washed as well,' Mrs Cocking said.

'Yes Mrs we have… it is rather dirty and smelly,' I said.

'Oh… no different from normal then,' she replied.

'…Mr Kingston's lads you say,'

She stared hard at us, before breaking into a sort of smile that, with her single tooth, made her look more comical than intimidating.

'Well you'd better come in then... and wipe your mucky boots on the mat,' she barked.

'...And, just so you know... I don't give anything... it'll cost each of you two shillings and sixpence a week.'

With exaggerated effort, we both wiped our boots on the mat and stepped inside. And, like a pair of ducklings waddling behind their mother we followed Mrs Cocking into the house and down the hallway into the large kitchen, where the smell of good food cooking on the range had us almost drooling. It was three months since I had last smelled anything as good as that.

Barney and I looked at each other and grinned... This would suit us just fine.

'Molly Cocking was a widow. She had lost her fisherman husband seven years before in 1858, when he was sailing as the third hand on the *Mary-Ann*, under Mr Kingston. During a heavy sea, James Cocking had been washed overboard. At first he managed to save himself by making a grab at the rail when the smack lurched. But, before he could be hauled back on board, another wave struck him, loosened his grip and pulled him away from the smack. His crew mates watched helplessly as he struggled in the water, pleading for God's help as he drifted further away. The sea took him...

While all losses at sea are tragic, what made James Cocking's particularly so, is that the *Mary-Ann* was only twenty five miles away from the mouth of the River Humber. It was on its way back home and would have been safely in port just a few hours later. Mr Kingston had the most difficult of tasks for smack owners to perform. He had to tell Molly how her husband had been lost and that nothing could be done to save him. It had all happened so quickly...

I later learned that Henry Kingston bought the house in Orwell Street and although he would always own it, she would live there and run it as a lodging house for the rest of her life.

He had made sure that Mrs Cocking had a home and an income. That was typical of him…

'Mr Kingston seemed to be a very kind and caring man, father,' Sarah-Eliza said.

'He was dear… he was a very kind, compassionate God fearing man,' Jacob replied.

'…Back in Brixham where he came from, his father and youngest brother were both Methodist preachers… Henry Kingston had the same values as them…if only all smack owners had been like him.'

Jacob sighed before adding,

'Sadly they weren't… many regarded the young boys merely as a cheap means for taking fish and turned a blind eye to the cruelties that were being inflicted upon them.'

'…The lodging house was larger than most of the others in the street. It had three bedrooms. One, Mrs Cocking shared with her sixteen year old daughter Ethel, the only child left living at home. The other two bedrooms and the front room were for the lodgers. She never took more than six lodgers or had less than four. I worked it out that if she charged them all two shillings and sixpence per week she would have an annual income of nearly forty pounds. Mr Kingston had made sure she was well provided for…

Molly Cocking's appearance belied her true nature. Her bark was far worse than her bite as she really was a good natured person. Only, her intimidating size, the clay pipe in her mouth and the single tooth in her head made her look fearsome. Also, she had adopted the ghastly habit of chewing tobacco, which was one of the reasons why she had lost so many teeth. But in truth she was a likeable friendly person…

'Right… put your sea-bags down there lads… We'll sort your stinking washing out in a minute,' she ordered. 'Don't suppose you've eaten much today yet… have you?'

'No, Mrs,' I quickly replied. '…We only had a cup of tea, before we unloaded the fish for this morning's market.'

'That's typical of Henry on market day… nothing else matters but selling his fish,' she said.

'For sure… I'm right starvin,' said Barney.

Mrs Cocking looked at Barney

'What's that accent boy… where are ya from?'

'I'm a fine Irish lad from County Down… God's own wonderful country,' Barney said proudly.

'Oh… Are you now?' Mrs Cocking said and with a smile added, '…and what do I call a fine gentleman like you?'

'I'm Barney… Barney McHugh.'

'And you… little un, what do they call you?' she asked.

'Jacob Rawlings… but, most people call me Jake,' I replied.

'Right… for now you can both call me Mrs Cocking.'

'…Come on Jake… and you, Barney, sit down at that table, I'll get you something to eat.' Mrs Cocking said.

'…We'll sort the lodge money out later… If you're Henry's lads, I'll trust ya.'

'We didn't need asking twice. For the first time in months, we had a meal at a table and ate the most wonderful stew, dumplings and freshly baked bread. This was what we could smell when we came into the kitchen… Savouring each delicious mouthful I said to Barney,

'I think we'll do right well here… Don't you?'

Barney wasn't listening. He was staring, open mouthed at Ethel Cocking who had just come into the kitchen… She had been up the stairs changing the bedding. Ethel could see Barney looking at her and smiled demurely at him.

'Barney… shut your mouth… You look like a gaping codfish,' said I. 'Barney,' I said again, and gave him a nudge.

'Well now, Jake… she's a prim looking star gazer… That's for sure.' He whispered, obviously captivated by Ethel.

'There ya go again… she's a what?' I asked.

'Jake… don't you know nothing?' Barney quietly replied. 'I can see I'm gonna have to edumacate you.' He laughed.

'What!' I asked.

'She's a good looking girl… is what I mean… I wonder who she is.'

Although, we were whispering, Mrs Cocking heard every word.

'She's my daughter, Ethel,' she said firmly. '…Don't you boys start getting any ideas now.'

'…Room and board is all that you'll get here.'

'Yes Mrs,' said I.

'For sure… we'll behave like the gentlemen we are,' Barney said.

Undeterred, he introduced himself.

'…Ethel Cocking, I'm Barney McHugh and I'm very pleased to make your acquaintance,' he said.

He looked directly at her. Blushing slightly, Ethel held Barney's gaze and smiled back and said,

'Hello Barney… pleased to meet you too.'

She ignored me completely.

'Right now lads… these are my house rules,' Mrs Cocking said as she gave her daughter a disapproving look.

Barney wasn't really listening. He was smitten.

'…You'll share the double bed in the front bedroom, it'll have clean sheets once a week and there's a wash stand and jerry pot in there… There's also some drawers in the room for your clothes, but don't leave any money in there. Keep it with you, or better still put some in a bank…The privy is out in the backyard… If you're out there having a cack, sing, hum or make some other noise that we can hear…Ya don't want me or Ethel walking in on you… Do ya?' She laughed and Ethel blushed.

'Breakfast will be at eight o'clock, here in the kitchen. After you've eaten, you must leave the lodgings by ten o'clock… I can't have you loafing about and under my feet all day… If the weather's bad, you can sit in the parlour, as long as you don't make a nuisance of yourself… Dinner is at six o'clock and, if you go out of an evening…Try not to stay out after eleven o'clock…I don't lock the door, but will hear you if you're coming in late… Don't make a habit of it.'

'...Is that understood?' Mrs Cocking asked and without waiting for an answer added,

'If you take a drink… try not to come in too drunk… Cos, if you throw up, you'll clean it up… have I made myself clear?'

'Yes Mrs Cocking,' I replied.

'Barney... are you'se listening? She asked sternly, knowing full well that he had been distracted.

'Yes Mrs Cocking... that's fine with me.'

'Final bit of advice lads... You need to buy yourself some decent strides and shirts for wearing here... I don't want the house and furniture stinking of fish...You can leave them with me when you're at sea, they'll be safe.'

'Yes Mrs Cocking, we'll do that,' said I.

'We'll be proper dandies... you'll see,' said Barney.

'Don't forget dinner is at six o'clock... if you're late, you get none,' she said.

'Right off you go then... leave your sea-bags, Ethel and I will sort out your washing.'

Seeing the look of horror on our faces as Barney and I looked at each other, she cackled out loud.

'Yours won't be the first lot of dirty and soiled under-garments I've had to sort through and wash... Off you go now,' she said still laughing.

'Well now... you haven't seen mine yet,' said Barney.

'Or mine,' said I.

'Oh... I'm sure we'll manage,' said Mrs Cocking.

She stopped laughing.

'...Mind what you're doing out there boys. Keep a tight grip on your poke and your money and, watch out for each other.'

I noticed that, in a motherly concerned way, she had referred to us as boys...

'Barney and I set off to find the shops to buy some fresh clothes and then, to explore the town, such as it was. It wasn't too long before we realised that, back in the 1860s, there wasn't that much for a young man to do during the day and, parts of Grimsby were not the pleasantest of places...Taking care and keeping our wits about us, we walked around for a few hours getting to know the town and especially the dockland area of the East Marsh...

It was a whole new and far dirtier world to what I was used to and had grown up in. In the dockland, every cobbled street was made up of small shops, houses and a mixture of small businesses such as carters, coal merchants and marine stores dealers, all crowded together, existing by side by side. Not many of the houses had running water…What water they needed had to be drawn from communal hand pumps that were situated in the streets and courtyards. Even in the sunlight, the area looked pretty grim… On nearly every corner, it seemed, there was a pub or an ale-house… Little wonder then that so many took to drink. It was their escape from the pits of despair, which I came to understand, was how many saw their pitiful life…

From almost every chimney dark smoke, from the coal fires within, belched and hung heavy in the November air and assailed our nostrils. For nearly three months, the only smells Barney and I had come into contact with were the ozone of the sea, fish and sweaty men.

On the steps outside their humble houses, groups of women sat talking. Many, like Mrs Cocking, were smoking clay pipes. They watched us with suspicious eyes as we walked past. We were strangers in their street. Barefooted and meagrely dressed children were also sat on the steps, loitering about, or playing in the streets... The children really were rag-a-muffins.

Strung across many of the streets and in the courtyards were clothes lines laden with washing, which we had to duck under, or risk being throttled. *'Oi… watch what ya doing…ya rag-arses you… I've just washed them there clothes'*, we were scolded by one old harridan when we happened to accidently touch the washing as we ducked under the clothes line.

'Rag-arse is it… we'll soon see about that,' Barney mumbled to me.

'Sorry Mrs,' I shouted back quite politely.

'Looking at the shite stains on those long johns… you ain't made a good job of washing them.' Barney shouted back at her.

Chuckling, we swiftly carried on down the street…

We saw and ignored old soldiers, some of whom were wearing the ragged remains of a once proud uniform and, were hanging about outside the ale-houses. Several had limbs missing.

'Spare a penny for an old soldier, young gentlemen', they would beg. *'...I lost my leg with the Light Brigade at Balaclava'.* Or somewhere similar would often be claimed.

About to give one man a penny, Barney stopped me and said quietly,

'Jake, never get your money or your poke out in the street... If you want to give him a penny, fiddle around in your pocket till you can feel one... but, don't let anyone see what you're doing... bring the penny out on its own...if you must.'

'I took Barney's advice and chose not to, on that occasion,' said Jacob.

'We also ignored the begging old crones and the enticements that were shouted for us to go into buildings and houses of ill-repute...Barney kept turning round to check that we weren't being followed. When the sun was behind us, he kept looking at our shadows on the ground...

'The sun'll let us know if anyone's coming up behind,' he said.

'We didn't want to find out what a bludget was so soon... Barney was far more street wise than me...I was learning how to survive in a rough and mean dockland. I swear I turned my head too much to look back that I ended up with a crick in my neck...'

Jacob laughed.

'Even though, horses and carts were trundling down the street, stray dogs fighting and scavenging and, people were going about their business, it was all so very, very different from Lincoln and Calthorpe... It looked, smelled and felt different... There was an air of menace about the streets...but, strangely enough I found it really exciting...'

'Children, the town that you know is nothing like the Grimsby, Barney and I found when we first arrived. We were shocked and horrified at some of the things we saw...'

'Although, it's not very pleasant... I think it is important for you to know what the dockland area was really like,' said Jacob.

'...After all, I lived there for many years... I haven't always lived here in this nice big house.' Jacob explained with a beaming smile...

'Victorian Grimsby, like many other towns, was notable for a wide range of social contrasts. Great wealth and extreme poverty lived side by side because the slum housing, of the working classes and the fishermen, were often not much more than a stone's throw from the larger elegant houses of the rich merchants, businessmen and the smack owners...

The dockland area of the East Marsh was mainly tightly packed back-to-back working-class houses with communal box privies. In some courtyards, the privies faced the front of the houses close to the doors of the living rooms... Water closets and toilets, which you are familiar with, were a luxury still a long way off in the future. The stench from the communal privies, especially in the summer, was appalling...

Many people went hungry, especially as they found they could not afford the rents that were being charged. Often, to make ends meet, they rented out space in their room to one or more lodgers who paid between two-pence and four-pence a day for a bed for the night. Consequently, there was intolerable overcrowding and appalling conditions for the people who lived there. Within all this stench and squalor, malnourished children running around barefooted and raggedly dressed, was a common enough sight...

As well as poverty, overcrowding and poor sanitation, the courtyards and alleyways became notorious as an area frequented by the dollymops and their clientele. [Although, Jacob could recall that dollymops' clients were often 'accommodated', day and night, standing up against the walls of the houses and passageways in full view of anyone passing by, which became known as, a *'tup-penny upright',* he kept those thoughts to himself]... It was almost as though the East Marsh liked being dirty and degraded...a god forsaken den of vice and misery. Inevitably, in areas such as these, robbery, muggings, drunkenness, disorderly conduct and extreme violence thrived and were commonplace...

181

Worst of all... Barney and I walked down one street that had a tidal ditch running through it... We gazed in horror at the drains and sewers emptying their filthy contents into this ditch. We also saw a whole tier of door-less privies in the open road, common to men and women built over it and, we heard bucket after bucket of filth splash into it...'

'Oh Father, no... that's appalling,' Sarah-Eliza said. Her face showing the revulsion of what she was thinking. '...How those poor people had to live.'

'Yes dear... it was dreadful and, it would be many years before their lot improved... Sadly for some, it never did.' Jacob replied, sorrowfully shaking his head.

'...Don't forget, Barney and I lived and socialised in this area for quite some time.'

'Did you really grandad?' asked Grace. 'Was it horrible...I mean really horrible?'

'Yes, my precious...we did and it wasn't very nice,' Jacob said looking at his beloved grand-daughter.

'Barney and I never ever forgot that some of these poor wretched people needed a lot of help...'

Chapter 11

Child Slaves, Absconding and Prison!

'As we wandered around on that first day, we thought that the narrow cobbled streets seemed to be quite crowded. We later discovered this was normal... In fact, it was getting worse, because nearly every day, more and more people were arriving in the town looking for work and somewhere to live... Inevitably, most of the new arrivals ended up in the already overcrowded dockland area...

During the day, many people, especially those with no work to attend to, stood around talking on street corners, with their hands in their pockets and jackets buttoned up tight and shoulders hunched against the November cold weather... Even though it was only early afternoon, drunks were already emerging from the pubs... Around the courtyards and back streets, the dollymops were looking to make some easy money from the drunks, or anyone else they could interest. Several tried to entice Barney and me into the alleyways or their house...'

'What's a dollymop, grandad?' asked Daniel.

'Yes, grandad... what is it? Gabriel, following Daniel's lead asked.

This was the question Jacob had been waiting for. He felt sure that Daniel knew what a dollymop was and only asked the question to be mischievous. Gabriel would have no idea. Sarah-Eliza, with a very quizzical expression and a half smile, looked across at her father. How was he going to explain this she was thinking?

'Erm... erm... a dollymop is a wicked lady, who would try to get you off the street and out of sight... so she could rob your money from you,' Jacob blustered an explanation.

'…Yes, that's what she is… Pay them no more mind.'

Jacob wanted to move on. Sarah-Eliza smiled with supressed relish at her father's discomfort.

'…In the nicer dockland areas and other parts of the town, there were a few coffee houses where people sat huddled together, talking and smoking their pipes… Coffee houses had become quite fashionable at that time, for those that could afford it… There were no parks or pleasant open spaces. The main source of entertainment in the dockland area, especially at night came from the music hall and the smoke filled, candle lit, spit and sawdust pubs and ale-houses….

Just like most fishermen and the many apprentices whom Barney and I became friends with, this is where we would always meet up… Several of us gathered together talking about the smacks we sailed on and the people we sailed with. As short as I was in those first few months, I had no trouble getting served ale and hard liquor such as rum…'

'Yes, before you ask, Daniel… I was your age and, I had started smoking a pipe and drinking strong ale… That wouldn't be allowed now… but, it was all very different in those days.'

'Didn't it make you ill, father?' Sarah-Eliza asked.

'Yes dear, at first it did… but I persevered and got used to it,' Jacob replied with a smile.

'We soon found out, which pubs were safest for us to frequent and those to be avoided because they were too violent or, full of low life, who would steal anything from anyone. By spending time in the pubs and through the experiences of the friends we made, we came to know how other apprentices had fared and, what happened to those apprentices who absconded…'

'Absconding, children… is when an apprentice runs away and 'stops the ship' from sailing,' said Jacob before adding, 'For young boys – fishing was a hard life and very frightening during rough and stormy weather. Many, many apprentices could take no more and ran away. Some, like young Brewer, took more drastic action and committed suicide by jumping over the side of the vessel and drowning… Through listening

184

to other fishermen and apprentices, we discovered who the brutal and sadistic task masters were… Not all masters were as caring as Henry Kingston,'

'For a brief moment, just so that you understand the whole story I'm telling you, I need to digress…'

'What's to digress?' Grace asked Gabriel, who shrugged his shoulders and shook his head.

Jacob ignored the question and carried on talking.

'Although many apprentices were the victims of assaults and cruel ill-treatment, the perpetrators were not always the skipper or the smack owners. It wasn't uncommon for the some of the youngest lads to be beaten and bullied by the third hand, the deckhands, or even the older apprentices…Invariably, whenever apprentices got together, over a pint or two, stories were shared…

Occasionally, too much beer led to some experiences being exaggerated. But, most I believed to be true. *'I had my head held under the water in the sole tub'*, said one boy. *'I was burnt on the arm by a hot poker from the fire'*, said another. *'I was punched, throttled and frequently hit with a knotted ropes-end'*, a third lad said… Those were some of the milder assaults… some assaults, as you now know from the fate of Frederick Brewer, were far, far worse…

'Why didn't you complain?' I asked on more than one occasion.

'Because we're apprentices and orphans, no one will believe us… they won't listen, they own us,' was the frequent reply…

For many boys, life at sea was child slavery as one lad, aged sixteen, told me and Barney… He was due to leave for Iceland, the smack was already baited up, but after the previous trip he had had enough and couldn't face any more of the conditions in which he was forced to work and, the beatings he had taken. Not the first time, in fact, it was the third, he hid… When found, he was brought before the magistrates, who we used to call the 'beak', and was found guilty of absconding and 'stopping the ship' and was sent to Lincoln prison for a month…'

'Magistrates were not very forgiving in those days,' said Jacob.

'Aren't you a 'beak', Grandad?' Gabriel asked and looked at Daniel for confirmation.

'Hush, Gabriel… let grandad continue,' Sarah-Eliza said to Gabriel.

'DANIEL! Pay attention.'

'Thank you dear,' said Jacob.

'…Along with nine other prisoners they were shackled in twos and threes, taken to the railway station, and put into carriages, arriving at Lincoln in mid-afternoon. They looked a sorry sight… Heavily chained together they were frog marched through the busiest part of the High Street for more than a mile, past the passageway where Barney and I met, to their destination at Lincoln Castle…

Inside his cell, which had a concrete floor, was a wooden boarded bed and bed roll. There was a little shelf for a Bible or prayer book and a small table, a stool, a chamber pot and wash bowl, all made of tin. Throughout his stay in prison, he made mail bags… The governor, chaplain and warders considered him and the others as pigs, not human beings… Despite all this, he thought prison was better than being at sea. I later found out that this boy absconded once more and vanished into the streets, never to be seen or heard of again…

Regrettably, it wasn't uncommon for apprentices who were treated so atrociously by their masters and others to repeatedly run away. Even though they knew full well that when caught, they would probably be sent to prison for as long as ten weeks… Many seemed to prefer the very harsh treatment in prison to that of going to sea, and often absconded several times…

Over the years, there were literally thousands of cases brought before the magistrates… At that time and for many years thereafter, their worships were, *'determined to put down all subordination of this kind'*. I was told… during a five year period in the 1870s approximately eleven hundred apprentices were sent to Lincoln jail for absconding… It is worth remembering that many magistrates actually had a financial stake in the fishing trade… So they were not always impartial...

Although so many apprentices were sent to prison, I can still remember some of the stories we were told… Joseph Garlick, who Barney and I became good friends with, was an old offender. He absconded three times and was committed to prison with hard labour for two months… Surprisingly he finished his apprenticeship and became a good fisherman…but, the sea eventually took him...'

Thinking of the loss of an old friend, Jacob paused momentarily and briefly stopped talking. He sighed and slowly shook his head.

'Joseph was only three years older than me… God bless him,' Jacob said sadly.

'…He was sailing as the Mate on the smack *Zephyr*, when it sank with the loss of all hands after being swamped by gigantic waves during the great storm of March 1883.'

After a moment's reflection, his face brightened at the thought of what he was going to tell them next. He smiled at the children.

'Another absconder, William Weathers, I remember because of his name. We knick-named him, 'Windy Willy' though some called him, 'Wet Willy'.

At this the boys burst into fits of the giggles. Seeing them laugh, so did Jacob.

'Alright now… that's enough of that,' said Sarah-Eliza reproachfully.

'Father, don't encourage them… they're mischievous enough without your help… thank you.'

'Ok dear… I'm sorry.'

'William Weathers was only fifteen when he was charged by his master with absconding. Having repeatedly offended in this respect he was sent to prison to be kept at hard labour for three months… His time in prison, and the hard labour of turning the crank up to a thousand times a day, nearly broke him… After his release and his return to sea, we lost contact, so I've no idea what became of him... It is likely that he either absconded again and was never caught or, was lost at sea…

As much as I loved fishing and being at sea, listening and talking to other fishermen taught Barney and me that, much needed to be changed to improve apprentice's welfare... We both agreed that if we became smack owners or masters, there would be no cruelty and rope-ending on our vessels. None of our apprentices, if we had any, would have a need to abscond... They would be recruited fairly and would be released if unsuitable... Barney and I were agreed on who our role model would be...'

Again Jacob paused. He needed to collect his thoughts, so he began to empty the ashes from his pipe and refill it with fresh tobacco. As he did, he looked at his daughter and down at his grandchildren. His genial face was a picture of happiness and contentment. Despite the certainty of knowing what the future will now bring, Jacob knew he had been blessed. Drawing deeply, he savoured the fresh tobacco and wasn't going to be rushed. For the moment, the children were patient. When he was ready, he started again.

'Right, let me see now,' he said.

'On that first day in town, we managed to keep out of trouble and returned to Mrs Cocking's lodging house in time for dinner...I had bought myself a cheap pocket watch and thought about buying a snazzy waistcoat so I could wear the watch on a chain across my belly, in the manner of the successful merchants and smack owners I had seen that morning at the fish market. Barney dissuaded me from doing so.

'Jake, my boy... you do that in an area like this and for sure... you'll have it taken from you before you've walked a hundred feet down the street,' he said.

'Are you sure?' I asked naively.

'Well now... I'm not only sure, I know so... a flimp or dipper will have it off you without you even knowing,' he replied earnestly.

'Or, Sweet Jesus forbid... you'll be mugged with a cudgel, by a bludget, and you'll lose your watch and anything else of value you have in your pockets,'

Barney had already figured out what a bludget was. Although he was uneducated and couldn't read and write, he had a street wisdom about him that kept us safe and out of trouble. I was glad to have him as a friend.

'Oh, I didn't think, did I, what shall I do, Barney?' I asked rather pathetically.

'No worries, Jake my boy… just keep it in your pocket… Don't get it out when there are people around you.' He replied.

'…The secret to staying safe on streets like this…is to look as poor and destitute as them… Don't let them see that you've got anything worth filching.'

'Thanks Barney, that's another lesson learned… I'm real glad, that I met you,' said I. '…we're gonna do well together, aren't we?'

'Well now, that's for sure, Jake my boy.'

'…Come on, let's go into this pub 'ere, and see if they'll serve us a beer.' He said. 'We've got time for a glass before we need to be back at old snaggle tooth's for dinner.'

Chuckling, or maybe with false bravado, we went into the pub… I was nervous. The pub was quite dark and it took a while for our eyes to adjust to the changing light. Barney asked for two glasses of porter... I'd no idea what porter was…

'Despite only being five foot tall and, even though the barman looked me up and down, once he saw the money we put on the bar, we got served without any trouble at all… Barney advised keeping ourselves to ourselves until we had sussed out what was what… With our mugs of beer in hand we went and sat in a corner and watched all that was happening…Barney seemed more at home than me. I'd never been in a pub before and, if truth be known I didn't really like the taste of beer… But, I eventually got used to it,' Jacob chuckled.

'The dimly lit pub was noisy, smoky and busy and the smell of stale body odour was everywhere. A fire was roaring in the grate… there were no carpets on the stone floor, just sawdust scattered about… All the men seemed to be shabbily dressed in a similar manner; boots, course trousers, heavy cotton shirts and waistcoats. Some were wearing rather tatty old frockcoats, others a shorter jacket. Several were wearing billycock hats. Most had big whiskers, moustaches and beards...A few of the men were playing cards, others dominoes, some were just sat talking. Although some men held short stubby wooden pipes, many were smoking clay pipes, which were still being used at that time...

In the background, someone was trying, without much success, to scratch out a tune on an old fiddle, causing several other drinkers to bellow at him,

'Shut that bleeding racket up...sounds like a cat's being strangled,' shouted one.

Undeterred, he ignored the abuse and just carried on playing, or should I say trying to play...

Wherever we looked there were animated conversations and even the occasional disagreements... While we were there an argument started close by us. With raised voices and fists being banged on the table, two men, who were both drunk, quickly jumped to their feet. One was quicker than the other. He punched his antagonist senseless to the ground shouting,

'You'se leave my woman be, she's not for the likes of you...ya foisty weasel.'

'...If you touch her again and I'll bloody well kill you next time.'

'Oi, Oi... that's enough of that, Fred... calm down now, or you'll be feeling this,' the barman shouted.

He had come from behind the bar and was holding a short heavy cudgel, which I later learned was knick-named the persuader.

'...Go on, help your brother to get up... and both of you get out and go home,' he said to the one still standing.

'GO ON... help him up now.' The barman ordered.

'You'se can come back in tomorrow... when you're sober... Not before.' He said banging the persuader on the bar.

The ruckus was over as quickly as it started. Throughout the whole of the bad tempered flare-up, many of the others in the pub, hardly took any notice, fights were nearly a daily occurrence in dock land pubs. I was amazed. Barney was less impressed. He had seen it all before at the camps where the

Irish navvies had lived and worked... For me it was one new experience after another...

It was fascinating to sit there watching the drunks, dippers and dollymops. Drunks I'd seen before, dippers never… I saw hands going into the pockets of coats that were hung on chairs. With one portly old gentleman, while he was distracted with the game of dominoes he was playing, a hand went into the pocket of the frock coat he was wearing… Dollymops were wandering around looking for likely pickings…a pair even wandered over to talk to us. They were soon sent packing by some choice words, which I won't repeat, from Barney. I learnt much during that hour we spent in *The Crooked Billet*…

Once we were back at Mrs Cocking's and, after we'd changed into the clean trousers we had bought, dinner was on the table… Meat pie, potatoes, vegetables and thick gravy… It was a veritable feast that went down really well, especially as it was followed by plum duff pudding… As much as Barney loved the dinner, he couldn't take his eyes off of Ethel as she busied herself helping her mother serve the meal…

'What do you think, Jake?' he whispered to me. '…Isn't she pretty… do you think she's got a fella?'

'I don't know, Barney… shush or she'll hear you,' I said.

'I know… for sure I think I want her to hear,' Barney whispered again.

'Yes… but her mother will hear as well… Best fill that gaping mouth of yours with your dinner before it gets cold,' said I.

We both laughed and carried on eating.

Dining with us, during that first stay at the lodgings were three others. One, an apprentice and two other lads, who were now deckies, having recently completed their apprenticeship… It's far too long ago for me to remember their names, but I do recall that they were good company… On a couple of nights, we all went out for a drink together… There was safety in numbers!

The days we had ashore soon passed and before long we had to be back on the *Mary-Ann*. Although I was sorry to leave the lodgings, which had been most comfortable and agreeable,

I was looking forward to going back to sea. Picking up our sea-bags, with all our nice clean fishing clothes in them, we said our good-byes to Mrs Cocking and Ethel.

'You've been two good lads... no trouble at all,' Mrs Cocking said. 'I've taken quite a shine to you both.'

'Henry has chosen well again... I'll always find room for you boys when you need a bed.'

'Thank you Mrs Cocking... that will be very kind of you,' I replied.

'I will be pleased to come back here if we can.'

Barney's face was beaming. He was looking at Ethel, who seemed to be just as happy as he was.

'Well now Mrs Cocking... for sure this has been the most wonderful place to stay... I'll be right pleased to come back to stay with you again when we are next in dock,' Barney said effusively.

'You can stop your Irish blathering right now... we both know why you want to come back here...don't we?' Mrs Cocking said smiling and looking at her daughter.

Both Ethel and Barney blushed... and, smiled warmly at each other.

About a month before Christmas in 1865, Barney and I walked back down the Fish Dock Road to re-join the *Mary-Ann* for our second trip. Mr Kingston and George Simmons were pleased to see us both.

'Glad you're back aboard lads... How did you'se fare at Mrs Cocking's...did she look after you?' Mr Kingston asked.

'She did that Sir, made us right welcome... she did,' I replied.

'For sure...it was a great drum... and, the scran was wonderful,' Barney said in his strange way of describing things.

'I don't suppose either of you noticed the daughter... did you lads,' Mr Kingston suggested as he winked at Mr Simmons.

'Not at all... I don't think we took much notice...'

'I'm sure you didn't, Barney,' Mr Kingston replied and started laughing.

'Come on lads, there's work to be done… we sail in two hours,' he said.

'Come with me lads,' Mr Simmons said. '…Let's get your gear stowed below.'

We went down the companion way into the communal cabin. With the exception of Albert Barker, Biffo and the other apprentice lads were pleased to see us... Barker, who stank of stale beer, just glared, especially at Barney…

'I'll be keeping my eye on you… ya Fenian bastard,' Barker snarled.

'Aye Barker…you better make sure you do… cos for sure, I'll be watching you,' said Barney equally venomously.

'I can remember thinking, there's going to be trouble ahead. We stowed our sea-bags and went back on deck to get on with the work we were given by Mr Simmons. Within two hours and on the morning tide, the *Mary-Ann* was through the lock gates and sailing down the River Humber heading for the open sea and the distant northern waters. Only this time, Barney and I weren't novices... we knew what to expect out there on that great expanse of water… Especially now that it was the winter…'

'Let's stop there and have a break and a sandwich for lunch shall we,' said Jacob.

Sarah-Eliza and the children had been so engrossed with the story that Jacob was telling, despite briefly stopping in the mid-morning, so that they could get a drink and a biscuit, no one had noticed the hours slipping by. They all rose to make their way to the kitchen. The children raced out of the room and down the hallway.

Sarah-Eliza hung back and out of the children's earshot said,

'Father, wait a minute… can I ask you something?'

'Yes dear of course you can… is there something troubling you?' Jacob replied.

He could see from the expression on her face that she was concerned about something.

'Why are you telling us this story of your life now?' she asked earnestly.

'Why is it so important for us to know...? You've never talked to us like this before, and in so much detail?'

'...And, I can see that some of the memories are upsetting you, father.' Sarah-Eliza added.

Jacob hesitated before replying. 'Erm... It is important... because I want you... no, I need you and the children to understand and appreciate the hard life and the sacrifices that were made by so many,' Jacob replied quite firmly. He looked his daughter in the eye and held her gaze before adding,

'...Sacrifices which have helped you and your children to live the very comfortable lifestyle that you have had and enjoyed.'

Sarah-Eliza, felt a little uncomfortable. Her father's piercing gaze and the manner in which he had just spoken, had unnerved her. She nodded her head and before replying she looked closely back at him, hoping his face may betray what she felt sure was being hidden.

'Yes father, I can understand and I do appreciate that... but why tell it now and in such graphic detail?' she earnestly asked again.

'Because it's time, my dear... It's time for you and the children to know the whole true story,' Jacob said.

'...Come along, I'm hungry... Let's go and get our sandwiches.'

The conversation was over. Following her father out of the room, she knew that was the only answer she was going to get for now.

Still Sarah-Eliza was troubled... something was not quite right, but she didn't know what.

Chapter 12

Albert Barker Picks On Barney!

After their late lunch of cold meat and pickle sandwiches, cake and a cup of tea, Jacob, the children and Sarah-Eliza returned to the sitting room. Walking down the hallway, Jacob gave a noticeable shiver. It was getting quite chilly outside and a cold draft could be felt throughout the house. That's the problem with these big old houses, they take a lot of heating, Jacob thought. Once they were back in the sitting room, the children sat waiting patiently on the rug, while Sarah-Eliza, placed more coals on the fire and, poked at it until the flames started roaring again. With the door shut and the heavy curtains partially drawn, the room soon became warm and cheery. Jacob lit his pipe and waited for Sarah-Eliza to sit down before he began talking again.

'We sailed off towards the northern waters and fished for over eleven weeks with long lines. And, just as we did before on the previous trip, we would put into Shetland, sell the fish we had caught and take on fresh water and supplies. This voyage was remarkable only in as much that, besides an on-going spat between Barney and Barker, nothing remarkable happened… Yes, we had bad weather and we had to fish in awful and atrocious conditions, but that was fishing and the life we had chosen… If we didn't fish, we didn't get paid… we couldn't make a run to port every time the sea got a bit rough or the weather changed for the worse…

Fishing was a hard and perilous life. In those early days, when I was starting out, fishing smacks under sail had to rely heavily on the wind and weather conditions and the skill of the smack's master…The *Mary-Ann* was a tough little old lady, but she was only sixty feet in length and weighed just forty-two tons. So she did get tossed about quite a bit... Within twenty or so years, smacks would be double in size and weight and, when the steam driven trawlers came, they would increase considerably in size again... But, like I said, the *Mary-Ann* was a grand old girl and, it and Mr Kingston, gave me the start in life that would lead to mine and Barney's fortune...

The ill feeling between Barney and Barker persisted throughout the trip... but Barker never again attempted to rope end Barney... He confined his animosity to just a continuous stream of insults and abuse. For some reason, which we never found out, he really didn't like the Irish. He gave Barney the worst, dirtiest and, whenever he could, the most dangerous jobs. Mr Simmons kept a close eye on the pair of them. He always made sure that Barney was never left alone on deck at night with Barker. But, he could only protect him so much... This was still a working fishing vessel...

Whilst picking on Barney, Barker left me alone... I was most concerned for my friend, but really had no need to be. Barney was made of stern stuff, he had an inner strength and could give as good as he got when it came to insults... It would take more than Barker had to break him.

Unfortunately though, poor old Barney was often the one Barker chose, along with Robbo or John, to row the smack's small boat out to haul in the long lines... This was a dangerous and arduous task and one made no easier by the attendant danger of being in a small boat in a sea whose mood and propensity for violence could change in an instant. Barker knew it was by no means uncommon for a smack's boat to be unable to regain its parent vessel, due to either a sudden change in the weather or fog... The sea and the weather were and always would be the masters...

Just a few months before we started fishing, the smack *Repulse*, docked short of four hands. The four apprentice boys were out in two small boats hauling in the lines when a snow squall hid them from sight and afterwards they could not be found. Fortunately for two of them, they were picked up by another smack and landed at Shetland. The two other boys were not so fortunate, they were never found... Neither were two boys from the smack *Valiant*...when their work was completed from hauling in their fishing lines, the boys found that their vessel was nowhere to be seen. They couldn't see it, nor could the master of the *Valiant* see them... Sadly, they too were never found...

'Can you imagine how terrified those poor boys must have been?' said Jacob.

'...Drifting all alone in that great expanse of angry and unforgiving sea... knowing that the chances of them being found were slim.'

The children shook their heads and Sarah-Eliza mumbled to herself, 'Those poor boys!'

'Albert Barker was probably hoping that the same fate would befall Barney and what's more Barney knew that.' Jacob added.

'One day, in foul weather and with the sea running a deep swell, Barker sent Robbo and Barney out to haul the lines in. Concentrating on what they had to do and getting on with the job, they momentarily lost sight of the *Mary-Ann*. They didn't panic. They chose to row to where they thought the smack would be. It was getting darker...If they were still adrift by the time night fell their salvation would be in God's hands. It was only by pure providence and good fortune that two hours or so later, they spotted the smack's mast-head light and managed to row the boat back to the *Mary-Ann* and a relieved Mr Kingston and most of the crew...

'Never, was I happier or more relieved to see my old friend,' said Jacob.

'Permission to come aboard, Sir,' Barney jokily shouted to Mr Kingston as the boat came alongside the *Mary-Ann*.

Although he had been frightened and was angry, Barney wasn't going to give Barker the pleasure of letting him know he had been scared.

'Aye lads... Get your'sell aboard,' Mr Kingston shouted back. 'Thought you'se had deserted!'

He smiled, clearly happy to have his lads safely back.

'Albert Barker said nothing... He just glowered as the boat, Barney and Robbo were brought back on board the smack,' said Jacob.

'Once he was safely on board, outwardly, Barney made little of the incidence and went about his work securing the boat, but inside he was seething mass of anger... He glared intensely at Barker. One day there would be a reckoning, he was thinking...'

'For sure... I swear that filthy grub worm is hoping that the sea'll take me,' Barney said to me later that evening, when Barker was below deck and couldn't hear us talking.

'Well now... that piece of dog-shite doesn't know Finbar McHugh,' he added quite furiously. '...I'll see to him before he sees to me... You see if I don't.'

Barney was really angry. His face was redder than normal and he was breathing heavily.

'Davy Jones may well be having a visitor before too long, but it won't be Finbar McHugh... that's for sure.'

Barney had a rope-end in his hand, which he kept slapping hard onto the bulwark. From the moment I met him, this was only the third time I'd heard him use his proper Irish name. Never before had I seen him so infuriated and agitated.

'Barney... Don't talk or even think of revenge like that... no good will come of it... Believe me I know,' I said to him.

'...You can't let Mr Kingston or Mr Simmons hear you making those threats... they'll turn you off the *Mary-Ann* and may even need to tell the police... What will Ethel think then if you get banged up by the rozzers?'

It was my turn to be wise. At least in the subject of revenge I had some experience... It felt like the right thing to say...

'What do you know of these matters, Jake?' Barney asked.

He was calming down a little.

'Believe me Barney...there's plenty that I know and could tell you,' I said.

I also wondered whether this was the moment for him to hear the truth about Thaddeus Stone. But, I decided against it. Barney had enough on his mind without worrying about me.

For a brief moment nothing was said. He then looked me in the eye and smiled.

'Jake… for sure, you are right… I'll not let that miserable old fart get to me again,' he said while holding my gaze.

'…and, when you're ready… you can tell me what you know… Can't you?'

I could tell by the way Barney was looking at me that he knew I had a hidden secret.

'Yes… yes… Barney… I'll do just that.' I replied. 'You just keep away from misery guts.'

'Other than that one incident, as I have already told you, the trip was quite unremarkable. We all got on with our work of catching fish. Barney kept out of Barker's way as much as was possible on a small smack... not that there are many places you could go. I did notice though that Barney wasn't picked on as much to row out the smack's boat. The task was shared out evenly among all the apprentices, and the deck-hands… Even Barker, on a couple of occasions, rowed the small boat out.

After eleven and half weeks, on a fine day in the early spring of 1866, we returned to Grimsby with a hold full of prime fish, which sold well on the pontoon market… And, just as the previous trip, after the morning's market we went to settle up with Mr Kingston. Mr Simmons was already there talking to him.

'Come on in lads… your money's already for you.' Mr Simmons said.

'…Only, this time lads, you'se has got no sea gear to pay for… You'll be pleased to know.'

That brought a smile to our faces.

'Here you are lads… three pounds six shillings and three pence each, plus twelve shillings and seven pence from the liver money,' said Mr Kingston.

'…That makes three pound eighteen shillings and tenpence each.'

I couldn't help it but I said, 'Gosh… thank you sir.'

'Much appreciated, Mr Kingston,' said Barney.

'You've earned it... you've both done well again lads... Mr Simmons and me think we'll make good fishermen of you yet,' he said with a broad smile across his face.

'Get ya gear then... off you go and see if Mrs Cocking's got room for you,' Mr Kingston said.

Mischievously, he added before bursting into laughter.

'She may be full up...eh Barney! That'll be a real shame... won't it.'

'Henry... Don't tease the lad,' said Mr Simmons.

Both Barney and I knew what they were joking about... the lovely Ethel. Barney blushed and I stood there grinning.

'Right lads... we're sailing next Friday on the early morning tide... So we'll see you then. Don't be late,' Mr Simmons said.

'Just a moment before you go,' said Mr Kingston.

'Albert Barker won't be sailing with us again... Even if he is a good fisherman he's not the sort I want on my vessels... I've paid him off.'

Then Mr Kingston looked directly at me.

'That was real good advice you gave, young Jake,' he said before adding. '...Aren't you glad you didn't do anything foolish, Barney?'

'Yes Sir... for sure that I am,' Barney replied, surprised by what Mr Kingston had just said.

Henry Kingston looked hard at Barney then nodded his head and smiled... I too was surprised by what I had just heard and so I kept quiet.

'Right... off you go now lads' Mr Kingston said.

'...And, take care to keep out of Barker's way, he's not a happy man at the moment.'

'Yes, Sir... we will,' I replied.

'Oh yes, one more thing... Barney, when you'se comes back for the next trip... George and I are going to do something about your reading and writing,' said Mr Kingston.

'Thank you, Sir... that'll be real fine and dandy,' said Barney.

'But, you've got a hard job of your hands, if you'se think you can make a scholar of me.'

We all laughed.

'See you next Friday lads,' said Mr Simmons.

'Thank you Mr Kingston… Mr Simmons.' I said.

'Thank you'se both,' said Barney.

We picked up our sea bags, shouted cheerio and headed down Fish Dock Road in high spirits and with a pocketful of cash.

'How did they know Barney?' I asked. '…They must have heard us talking.'

'Well now Jake… I'm sure I don't know… Let's just say the good Lord moves in mysterious ways.'

Barney couldn't get to Orwell Street and Mrs Cocking's house fast enough. He was almost running…

'This time Barney knocked. Mrs Cocking opened the door and seemed quite genuinely pleased to see us. Taking the ever present pipe out of her mouth she said,

'Hello boys… I've been expecting you back… Henry Kingston called to see me late last night, just after you docked,'

'Hello Mrs Cocking,' we both said.

'Well… come on in then… Don't stand there dawdling.'

'Thank you Mrs,' said I.

Barney said nothing. Without being told to, we wiped our boots on the mat and stepped into the hallway down which drifted the familiar smell of good food that was cooking in the kitchen. Barney was straining his neck to look past Mrs Cocking. She smiled that ridiculous one toothed smile…

'ETHEL,' she shouted. '…Get you'sell down here we've got visitors.'

We could hear sound of footsteps in the bedroom above us before Ethel came running down the stairs and stopped in the hallway. She was a little breathless.

'Hello Barney,' she said excitedly as she tried to push back her hair, which was falling over her face that was already going crimson.

'Hello Ethel, how are you this fine day?' said Barney who was doing his best to look all nonchalant and not overly keen.

'I'm keeping fine Barney… and how are you?' Ethel replied as she held eye contact with him.

'Well now… as of this moment, I'm tolerably well,' Barney replied smiling back at Ethel.

'Lord, give me strength!' said Mrs Cocking raising her eyes upward in an exaggerated manner. '…Will ya listen to them both?'

'Ooh, I'm well… how are you… la, la, di, da, da,' Mrs Cocking mocked them. She waved her hands about in an effete manner, which made me laugh.

'Barney you'se can stop your Irish blarney,' she said good-naturedly. '…and Ethel, say hello to young Jake,'

'Oh yes… hello, Jake… Are you well?' Ethel asked half-heartedly and hardly taking her eyes of Barney.

'I'm fine thank you Ethel,' I replied, but she wasn't really listening.

Mrs Cocking put her pipe, which was unlit, back into her mouth and with a huge grin on her face, she shook her head.

'I don't know,' she exclaimed to no one in particular.

'Come on lads… let's get you sorted…put your sea-bags over there,'

'…have you'se eaten yet?'

'That children, was how we started the second of the many times, over the next few years, we stayed with Molly Cocking and her daughter Ethel… She always had room for us, because Mr Kingston arranged it. Our bed space would be let out while we were at sea, but Mrs Cocking always knew to within a couple of days or so, when the *Mary-Ann* would be back in port, so she made sure the room was free… Mr Kingston really was our benefactor in more ways than one and we never ever let him down…'

'Were Barney and Ethel sweethearts?' Grace asked suddenly, interrupting Jacob.

Daniel and Gabriel just huffed at Grace's question. They weren't interested in such matters.

'Now, now boys,' said Jacob.

'Yes… they became sweethearts, Grace… And, they did eventually get married but not until nearly seven years later when both Barney and I had finished our apprenticeships… I was the best man at the wedding.'

'Were you grandad?' asked Grace.

'He's just said he was,' Daniel said tetchily and tutted.

'That's enough of that, Daniel,' said Sarah-Eliza. '…and who is HE?'

'Sorry mother… sorry grandad,' he apologised.

'Ok… now, let me carry on,' said Jacob frowning at Daniel.

'Henry Kingston was a very private man who let few people get close to him. At first, other than knowing that he came from Brixham and was a practising Methodist, we knew very little about him. During the times we stayed with Mrs Cocking, once she knew she could trust us, she told us about the private side of his life… Not that she was gossiping, she held him in far too much regard for that. We already knew that Henry Kingston was one of the kindest most caring people we ever met. He looked after the health and welfare of his fishermen and never underpaid or sorely used anyone who worked for him. Sadly though, he was dealt some intolerably cruel blows in his own private life...

Shortly after buying the *Mary-Ann* and, because he had a business that could support a wife and family, he married his childhood sweetheart… Rebecca, I believe she was called. They planned for a family from the moment they were wed. Although Rebecca had no problem in becoming pregnant, she was never able to give birth to a child that survived. Her first child, a son, was still born at full term. Rebecca miscarried her second child at seven months and then a third at five months. Her fourth child was also still born…

'Oh no… my God… how tragic,' said Sarah-Eliza. '…How could life be so cruel to such caring people?'

Sarah-Eliza had also given birth to a still born child, before she had had Daniel. She was remembering her own pain and heartbreak.

'Sadly dear, far worse was to come,' said Jacob. 'Fate dealt them a particularly cruel blow.'

'After the death of her fourth child and a break of nearly two years, Rebecca fell pregnant again... As soon as Henry Kingston knew that she was with child, he organised the best medical care he could afford for her... She spent most of the pregnancy in bed, being looked after and cared for and, not allowed to do anything that may harm the child she was carrying. After a long and difficult period of labour she was safely delivered of a baby boy... The extent of their joy was unimaginable... They couldn't have been happier...

Unfortunately, Henry Kingston's faith in the Lord Almighty was severely tested by what followed next... A month after the confinement, their new born son took ill and died from diarrhoea and sickness... Rebecca, who was still weak and had not recovered completely from the birth collapsed and refused to believe that the child had died. She launched into frequent bouts of hysteria and quite quickly started to lose her mind; talking gibberish and accusing people of taking her baby away from her, which of course was nonsense... Very quickly she became simple-minded...

Henry did all that he could although he knew that he was losing her. Within a few months, on the advice of several doctors, Rebecca was taken and incarcerated in St John's Lunatic Asylum in Lincoln... He loved his wife dearly, but she had become an imbecile and was a danger to herself... She died just two years before we started sailing on the *Mary-Ann*. Other than his brother Charles, who was unmarried, Henry Kingston had no other family in Grimsby... George Simmons was the closest thing to a son that he had... We also later learned that he spent much of his wealth helping those less fortunate than himself...

'While we were in port after that second trip, I decided to tell Barney the truth about how Thaddeus Stone had met his death and, my belief that the police were still looking for me... I just waited for the right moment... It was a lovely clear day, although there was a bit of a nip in the air. We had taken a walk around the docks and were sat on the quayside, throwing stones into the water playing ducks and drakes as we watched the brigs and barques being loaded and unloaded… Nobody was within fifty yards of us, so it was safe to talk…

'Barney, there's something I've been waiting to tell you,' I said.

'What's that then, Jake?' he said. He turned to face me.

'…Is this about, the plenty that you know and could tell me… Eh?'

Barney was so shrewd. Though illiterate, he was no idiot. But, sometimes acted like one.

'Yes… yes, it's just that, Barney,' I said. 'How did you guess?'

Barney, listened intently as I told him the whole sequence of events of that terrible night; Thaddeus dying at my hand, mama making me leave home in the dead of night, Aunt Eliza looking after my half-brother and sisters… and, yes I was on the run from the crushers when I met him… Bizarrely, Barney was impressed…

'I knew it… For sure, I knew you were hiding something when we spoke in Lincoln… You're not a good liar…I don't suppose you've had much practice have you?' Barney said.

Before I could answer, he carried on talking.

'Well now, Jake my boy… there's certainly another side to you… Bloody 'ell,' he said.

'…What else could you have done? He was killing your mama.'

'I know… that's what I think. I could have knocked him senseless I suppose… but no, I really wanted to kill him,' I said angrily.

'Alright, Jake… easy now… How are you going to get news to your mother that you're faring well in the care of Barney McHugh Esq, a gentleman from the beautiful Emerald Isle?'

We both laughed at that, which put me at my ease. Barney really had a way with him.

'I've got to write to my Aunt Eliza, but not before four years have passed,' I replied.

'Why wait four years?' Barney asked.

'I don't know… but that's what mama said… I think,' I said.

'For sure… that'll pass soon enough… Look how quickly the last seven months has gone.' said Barney.

'Jake, thanks for telling me… I appreciate your trust in me,' he added very sincerely.

'You're my best friend Barney… whom I'll always trust,' said I.

'Well now, best friend, Jake… that's enough of this depressing talk,' he said. 'Come on, trust me to find us a decent ale-house, I'm gagging for a beer… Spitting feathers 'ere.'

'And so the years passed. Just as Barney said, the weeks, months and years seemed to fly by as we settled into the regular routine and life of a distant water long-line fisherman. We would be away at sea on the *Mary-Ann* for ten or eleven weeks at a time and then home in dock, staying with Mrs Cocking and Ethel for between ten to fourteen days… Every trip, once we had settled up, just as Mrs Cocking had advised us to do, both Barney and I put some money into the bank accounts we had each opened… I was determined that one day, I… no we, would buy a smack of our own. But first we had to become fishermen and we could have had no better teachers than Henry Kingston and George Simmons…

We were also growing up and like most young men, who had money in their pocket, we would spend a lot of time in the pubs and music hall… looking for a good time. They were the main sources of entertainment in those days… Yes, we sometimes got drunk and ended up in a fracas or scuffle… In the main we managed to stay out of serious trouble, although one night, when I was only sixteen I was mugged…

'Well, I say mugged… because I wasn't hurt, robbed is perhaps a more accurate description.'

'Why what happened, father?' asked Sarah-Eliza.

'It was my fault… I'd gone to one of the pubs on my own, hoping to meet up with someone, or anyone I knew. Barney wasn't with me… he was courting Ethel, in the front parlour at the lodgings. There was nobody I really knew in the first pub, so after finishing my beer, looking for company, I moved onto a second, and then a third and so on… Consequently, I got so drunk that, I could hardly stand… Even to this day, all I can remember is someone, a dollymop perhaps, saying something like, '*come along young gentleman, you've had quite enough beer… I'll help you back to your lodgings*'.

She never took me to the lodgings. I must have collapsed in the street, because that's where I woke up. My cheap timepiece was gone, the money I had in my pocket was gone, but what annoyed me most, my brand new boots, which I'd only bought that day, were also gone… and, I'd been sick all down my trousers… People were walking past me as though it was an everyday sight to see a drunk lying in the gutter...

'Oh father, that's terrible… at least you wasn't hurt.'

'No, only my pride was hurt… but I'd learnt a valuable lesson about how vulnerable a young lad is when wondering around alone and drunk in dockland,' said Jacob. 'Once, they knew that I was unhurt, both Barney and Mrs Cocking found the incident highly amusing…'

'About a year after we met him, Biffo Barnes, transferred to Mr Kingston's other smack the *Mary-Jane*. We were sorry to see him go… he was a good sort. If we met him in any of the pubs, we would always spend time chatting to him over a glass or two of beer. He became a very good friend. The apprentice, nervous Nobby, try as hard as he did, never made it as a fisherman… Reluctantly, Mr Kingston had to annul his indentures and cancel his apprenticeship. Nobby returned to his parents and agricultural labouring in Lincolnshire…

John and Robbo, the two older apprentices, stayed with the *Mary-Ann* for some years and later became its deck hands… In those early trips, to make up the crew numbers, Mr Kingston took on a third hand to replace Albert Barker, another apprentice and later a deck hand to replace Biffo… We became a happy vessel and all worked well together…

Misery guts Barker on the other hand, we heard from friends in the pubs, started to drink more heavily and bore a real grudge against Barney. He was going around saying, to anyone who would listen, that Barney had him spragged and thrown off the *Mary-Ann* without a good testimony, which was not true at all. But that was what Barker chose to believe. He would get his revenge he promised...especially when in drink. Regrettably, we would have more problems with Barker in the years ahead...

With each passing day at sea, Barney and I became more experienced at both fishing and sailing the *Mary-Ann* and just like Mr Kingston and Mr Simmons we came to love that smack. We were also becoming men. Barney, who was two years older than me, but thought it was only one year, grew into a powerfully built man... Not overly tall, about five feet eight inches, which was about the norm, but deep chested and broad shouldered... I was slow to grow, so the Shrimp nickname was apt. But, by the time I was sixteen going on seventeen, I'd shot up to nearly six feet and was much taller than Barney, only he was twice as wide as me...

Jacob chuckled.

'I looked like a pipe cleaner, all long and skinny, and Barney looked like the pipe, short and stubby,' Jacob was really laughing out loud now.

'What are you laughing at now, grandad?' asked Daniel.

He couldn't see what was so funny for his grandad to laugh at.

'Well Daniel... it's because I grew so quickly that, for a year or so, it seemed every time I got back in dock, I had to buy new best trousers, because the last pair I'd bought were now half-mast.'

'Although, a couple of times Mrs Cocking did try to lengthen them...I was forever buying new strides,' said Jacob roaring with laughter.

The children didn't find it as amusing as he did. But, they couldn't see the image that was in his mind's eye; a skinny lad with trousers halfway up to his knees. After a short while, Jacob stopped laughing. The expression on his face changed and he became serious again.

'Four months after my real seventeenth birthday, with Barney's prompting, in January 1870, I decided it was time to write to Aunt Eliza and get news to my mama about how well I was faring... I wanted to let her know where I was and what I was doing and, what my plans for the future were. I was hopeful that, if it was safe to do so, mama and perhaps my half-sisters and brother could visit me in Grimsby... It was the right time to write...

It was just a few days after Christmas in 1869, when we docked from the last trip before I wrote to Aunt Eliza. Mr Kingston surprised us all. He gave us extended time ashore while the *Mary-Ann* was being converted from a cod-man into a trawler. He had decided that it would be more profitable for the smack to make short trips, ten days or so, to trawl for fish in the Dogger Bank and Silver Pitt area of the North Sea, rather than the ten or eleven week trips long-lining in the far off waters off Iceland and the Faroe Islands... As we were going to be in dock for longer than normal, I had the time to send a letter to Calthorpe and to get a reply before we went back to sea. The conversion of the *Mary-Ann* from a cod-man into a trawler suited Barney. He certainly liked the idea of being back in port much more frequently...'

Jacob stopped talking and slowly rose from his seat and walked over to the walnut bureau at the side of the room. From one of the draws, he took out a yellowing piece of paper. He returned and sat down in his chair. His face was quite sombre as he unfolded it.

'What's that, father?' Sarah-Eliza asked with concern.

Looking at the expression on his face, she could see he was deep in thought.

'This, my dear daughter and children...is the very letter which I wrote on the 3rd January 1870, to your great-great Aunt Eliza,' Jacob replied solemnly.

He unfolded the letter and began to read out loud...

> *My dearest Aunt Eliza,*
> *I trust I find you and my mama keeping well and in good spirits as we celebrate the start of this New Year. Let us hope, God willing, that it is a good year for us all and I can see you both again soon. I have fared very well since leaving Calthorpe. I am seventeen now*

and have been a fisherman in Grimsby these past four years. Grimsby is a far different place to what I was used to. I have made the most wonderful friend in Barney McHugh and my master Henry Kingston treats me kindly and ensures that I am well provided for. I am enjoying the life that fate has chosen for me. One day, I will own a fishing smack. Please tell mama that, just as she said, I am making something of myself and I hope she will be very proud of me.

I have missed my mama, you and my sisters and brother so much and cannot wait for the time when we can all be safely together again. The thought of which sustains me when I am low in spirits. I look forward to hearing from you and mama soon. It is safe for you to write to me at this address where I lodge when not at sea. I will not be returning to sea for twelve more days yet.

I remain your devoted nephew.
Jacob

The children were quiet, Sarah-Eliza was weeping gently and Jacob's eyes were very moist. Jacob gently folded the letter up and for the moment put it on a small table which was near his chair. He picked up his pipe and leant back in his chair.

'Did your Aunt Eliza reply?' Daniel quietly asked.

'Yes, Daniel, she did... Within three days I received a letter, which I have since lost, saying she had much to tell me that couldn't be put in a letter and, was coming by train to Grimsby, with the two eldest of my sisters, Hannah and Harriett.'

'I was so excited at this news,' said Jacob.

'After four years...I was going to hear from my mama again... Or so I thought.'

Part Three

Chapter 13

Aunt Eliza Reveals the Truth

'Two days later, dressed in our Sunday best clothes and our boots polished, Barney and I went to the town station to meet them coming off the train,' Jacob said.

'...As I waited for the train to arrive, I realised that I was actually nervous.'

I walked about, first with my hands in my pockets and then with them out. Several times I looked at the new watch I had bought after the other had been stolen.

'Are you'se alright, Jake?' Barney asked watching me pace up and down. '...You'll wear that watch out, the times you've looked at it.'

'Not really Barney... I'm really bricking it... This is the first time I've seen any of my family since the night I killed Thaddeus.' I replied.

'...I don't know what happened and what was said after I ran away.'

'Jake, they're your family... they wouldn't be coming all this way to see you if things weren't alright,' Barney said.

'No, I don't suppose they would... Would they?' I replied, still not convinced.

Looking directly at Barney and feeling quite emotional I can remember saying.

'...I really want to hear about my mama and how she managed to square it with the peelers.'

'Relax, Jake... For sure you'll be fine...and they'll be pleased to see you... I'm sure your mother will have made things right with the crushers,' Barney said reassuringly.

Before I could reply, the engine's shrill whistle could be heard.

'It's here... they're here!' I said excitedly to Barney

'Easy, Jake... take it easy, you'll be fine,'

'We heard the train long before we saw it. Then from round the bend in the track it came into view. With steam hissing from the engine and smoke belching from the smoke stack, the train approached the station and with a squeal of brakes came to a halt... With much banging and clattering, the carriage's doors were being flung open and a teeming mass of people emerged... I looked up and down the platform, searching for faces I could recognise among the many people that were leaving the train. There they were... I saw them emerging from a second class carriage. Rushing down the platform, with Barney trailing in my wake, I ran towards them...

'AUNT ELIZA... Aunt Eliza,' I shouted excitedly.

Hearing her name, Aunt Eliza looked up and looked around. The voice she could hear calling her name was unfamiliar and she couldn't see anyone she recognised.

With Barney panting behind me, I stopped in front of them. Our breathless appearance startled Hannah and Harriett.

'Aunt Eliza... it's me Jacob... Don't you recognise me?' I said.

'Jacob... Jacob,' she said as she looked me up and down. '...Is it really you?'

The last time Eliza and the two girls had seen me, I was not quite thirteen years old and a lad, barely five feet tall. Stood before them now was a deep voiced, seventeen year old strapping young man, a little over six feet tall. Aunt Eliza looked no different from how I had always known her.

'Jacob... oh Jacob,' she said bringing a handkerchief up to her mouth and starting to weep.

'Let me look at you now,' she said. 'I can hardly recognise you... You have the look of your father.'

Hearing that I had the look of my father, William, pleased me. After a moment's pause, still looking closely at me, Aunt Eliza held out her arms,

'Come here, Jacob... give your Aunt Eliza a great big hug,' she said.

I embraced my Aunt so firmly that I almost lifted her off her feet. We both had tears in our eyes. Finally letting me go, Eliza stepped back but still held my hand.

'Jacob, these are your sisters, Hannah and Harriett,' she said. 'Say hello.'

I had hardly noticed them, but recognised them when I looked at them. They had grown into very attractive young women.

'Hello Hannah... hello Harriett... How are you both?' I asked.

'We are both well brother Jacob', said Hannah, who was the least shy of the two.

Poor old Barney, who had been completely forgotten about, made a coughing sound and cleared his throat. Aunt Eliza and the two girls turned round to face him.

'You must be Jacob's best friend,' Aunt Eliza said.

'Well now... that I am... Barney McHugh...and very pleased to make your acquaintance, Aunt Eliza,' Barney said.

'... And you too sister Hannah and sister Harriett.' he added, pouring on the charm like thick treacle as he shook their hands.

The girls smiled back at him and started giggling.

'Aunt Eliza and my sisters had planned to stay for a couple of nights at the newly opened hotel, which was situated close by the station. Barney and I picked up their cases and happily we set off to make the short walk. With her arm linked through mine, I walked ahead with Aunt Eliza. Other than general pleasantries, we said very little...

Barney dawdled along behind, with Hannah and Harriett. Unlike Aunt Eliza and me, he was animated, entertaining and making them laugh. He really could charm the hind legs of a donkey, I thought. My nervousness had gone. I was thrilled at seeing my aunt after all those years and had so many questions I needed answering. As we approached the hotel entrance, I could wait no longer.

'How's my mama, Aunt Eliza... is she keeping well?' I asked. '...Has she sent any word or letter for me?'

'I really can't wait to see her again and to hear her news,' I said happily.

'Aunt Eliza stopped walking and turned to face me. She looked me in the eye and took hold of my hand. I can remember to this day how sad and downcast her expression suddenly became. The cheeriness in her face was gone. She looked troubled and was hesitating before speaking… I could sense that something was not quite right… Barney, who had also noticed the unexpected change in Aunt Eliza's demeanour, was no longer playing the fool and joking with my sisters. They had stopped talking and were stood a few feet away from us. Still my aunt hesitated before replying...

'Aunt Eliza, what's the matter… what's wrong?' I asked anxiously.

'Jacob… Oh Jacob, my dear boy… there's something that I have come to tell you,' she replied her voice choking with emotion.

'But, not out here on the street,' Aunt Eliza added.

'I couldn't understand why she had started crying again, but would soon find out… In January 1870, four months after my seventeenth birthday, in the privacy of their hotel room, Aunt Eliza told me what had happened to my mama after I had fled…and that, I was not, and never had been, a fugitive from the law… So my dearest grand-children, I was told that my mother, your great-grandmother, had effectively sacrificed her life for my future and, was buried in an unmarked grave inside the prison walls… And, there was no memorial or gravestone to remind anyone of her passing...

'Barney, and my sisters who already knew the story, had sat in silence listening intently to Aunt Eliza. Seeing that I had become upset, Barney spoke,

'For the love of sweet Jesus, Jake my friend… you're a free man… No more worrying about the crushers…' he said gently. This was not the time for brash Irish humour or platitudes.

'Barney's absolutely right, Jacob,' said Aunt Eliza.

'…It was all that your mother ever wanted… for you to have the chance in life to make something of yourself, which she and your father William never had…'

With tears streaming down my face, I stood there in silence, unbelieving and bewildered by what I had been told. Barney, being the true friend that he was tried to ease my pain.

'Jake…your wonderful mama made sure that you were free to go wherever and do whatever you want… Mine just ran away and left me,' he said.

Aunt Eliza nodded her head in agreement of what Barney had just said, before saying, 'Jacob, you have a family… a brother and sisters in Calthorpe, who love you and can now be part of your life again… And, you will always have me,' she said before giving me a big hug.

'I'm sure you'll not let your mother down.'

'Pacing around my Aunt-Eliza's hotel room, I was deeply distressed and struggled to deal with what I had been told. *'I'm sure that you'll not let your mother down'*, my Aunt Eliza had said. It was all very difficult for me to take in and accept that my dear mama had only lived for a few weeks after I had left home. And, had she not been pregnant with my sister Charlotte, she would have been hung for the murder of Thaddeus Stone… Just the thought of my beautiful mama hanging from the gallows with her neck snapped broke my heart and made me almost hysterical. There were so many questions, for which I wouldn't get the answers I wanted to hear, I needed to ask...

Why didn't they believe her I asked my aunt? Stone had beaten and abused her for so many years… he was vile and evil… is there no justice in this world… did nobody speak up for her? Would they really have hung her? Whatever my Aunt Eliza replied, I didn't really hear. I was too distraught. With sad and sombre faces, Barney, and my sisters who were crying, sat in silence…

When I started to calm down and cease my sobbing, Aunt Eliza asked me to sit down. She got out of her chair and walked over to me and gently put a reassuring hand on my shoulder.

'Jacob, believe me... we did all that we could,' she said. '...Your family, Charlotte Kite and the priest from St Joseph's all spoke for her... But to no avail.'

'We never stopped trying, Jacob,' Aunt Eliza said tenderly. She paused before adding.

'I have something for you from your mother.'

I looked up. From her purse, my aunt took out an unopened letter...

'Jacob... the last time I saw your mother, which was just two days before she died she gave me this letter for you,' Aunt Eliza said gently.

'You have a letter from mama for me?' I asked

'Yes Jacob, I have,' she replied, trying to hold back her tears.

'I was instructed to give it to you only if she died in prison... Your mother was still hopeful that, if someone came forward to testify about the bare-knuckle fight, she may be released,' said Aunt Eliza.

'...Even though we all knew it was most unlikely... it was a forlorn hope that she clung on to.'

'With trembling hands, I took the letter from Aunt Eliza,' said Jacob.

Jacob took the dog-eared letter out of his pocket. He had read it many times since being given it on that sad day in January 1870. It had become a source of inspiration and comfort to him during the dark days when he was in low spirits.

'Is that the letter grandad?' asked Daniel.

'Yes, it is,' Jacob replied. '...this is what my mama, your beautiful great grandmother, wrote to me nearly sixty years ago...'

The children looked at their grandfather in subdued silence.

Sarah-Eliza, her face a picture of sadness and concern, sat with her hands in her lap holding a screwed up handkerchief, ready for the tears, which she felt sure would come when her father read out the letter.

Jacob cleared his throat and with his voice cracking with emotion began to read.

'My dearest son, Jacob,

If you are reading this letter I know that more than four years will have past and you are now a grown young man. Aunt Eliza will have told you that I am dead and have been buried inside these prison walls and you will not find any marker as to where I am buried. This was not what I expected when we planned for you to leave home. Quite wrongly, I thought I'd be believed that I'd acted in self-defence and after being acquitted would be able to arrange for you to return home. Obviously, this was not to be – God must have other plans. Don't worry about me. I take great comfort that in death I will be re-united with your beloved father, William, whom I loved so much. Together we made you.

Jacob, losing my life will not have been in vain, if you make something of yours. The fact that you have survived for over four years shows that you have determination and a will to succeed. You were not quite thirteen years old, when all alone you set off in the dead of night to seek your fortune. I am so very proud that you have made it on your own so far – not a day has gone by when I didn't think of you. It broke my heart to watch your back vanish down the road but, that's what we had to do. Whatever you now do in life, whatever you achieve and whatever you become will be the only marker that I want.

Jacob, you are what you believe you are– you just defended your mother when she was being killed. Make no mistake Thaddeus would have killed me that terrible night.

You are not a murderer!

I have made a small provision for you, which Aunt Eliza will explain. Be successful Jacob, make William and I proud of you and the name Rawlings. Until the

day that God wills we should meet again, William and
I will be watching you from heaven and holding you in
our embrace.
   Your ever loving mother
   Sarah Rawlings
   November 1865

Jacob stopped talking. Twice he faltered as he read the letter. Sarah-Eliza and Grace were sobbing. Daniel and Gabriel, were both red-eyed and doing their best not to cry.

'Father, that's so sad… I am beginning to understand how you feel,' said Sarah-Eliza between sobs. '…without my grandmother doing what she did… you wouldn't have come to Grimsby and met my mother… me and the children wouldn't have happened.'

'No, none of what I have told you would have occurred.' said Jacob.

'Besides you and the children, I wouldn't have met Barney and, the 'Rawlings and McHugh Steam Fishing Company' would never have come about. This is one of the main reasons I need you all to know and understand the foundations on which your inheritance and lifestyle has been built…

'Aunt Eliza explained that my mama had left me £120, some of which she had saved and kept hidden from Thaddeus Stone. The greater part she'd inherited when her father Nathaniel had died. She had also left me her bible, which brought her so much comfort in the days when she was being abused and during the dreadful time she spent in prison. I was also left a silver cross, which had been her mothers. Most importantly, my mama left me with a something far more important than money or bibles. I became driven, single-minded and resolute in my determination that she didn't die in vain. Her sacrifice gave me the strength of mind and character to become someone. But, as I will explain in a minute, if I hadn't had the support of Barney and Henry Kingston, it would have all been so very different…

My aunt and my sisters stayed in Grimsby for a couple of days. I was able to spend time with them and ask questions and get to know more about my family and what had happened in the four and a half years since I left Calthorpe. They were my only link to my dear mama. Promising to visit Calthorpe whenever I could, I took them to the station and saw them off on their return journey. We hugged each other. Aunt Eliza broke into tears as she held me. *'Take care Jacob, remember we are your family who love you'*, she said to me. As I waved them off, in my heart, I knew that that part of my life was over and I wouldn't be returning to Calthorpe any time soon. There were too many bad memories there. I also felt terribly alone...

It would be another week before we returned to sea. The work on converting the *Mary-Ann* from a cod-man to a trawler had taken longer than expected. Barney took the opportunity, the extended time ashore had given us, to spend more time with Ethel, with whom he was totally besotted. I saw little of him. Consequently, I spent much of that week on my own... mainly in the ale-houses. There was nothing else to do! Wallowing in self-pity and wandering from pub to pub, I would sit alone drinking more ale than I could cope with. [Jacob could also remember when he wasn't alone – on more than one occasion, he took some comfort from the dollymops. But that wasn't for telling to his daughter and grandchildren].

Frequently, I was so drunk that I got into scuffles with other drunks who offended me. More often than not, the offence was in my mind rather than what really happened... The more I drank to blot out the images and sadness of my mama dying in prison, the darker my mood and behaviour became. Even though she hadn't, I couldn't get the picture out of my mind of mama hanging from the gallows for something that I had done. I felt so much guilt that it didn't take much to bring the awful image to mind and send me into a rage. Mercifully, God took her in childbirth and she didn't have her neck snapped by the hangman's rope...

The thought of my mama being hung got me into a fight, which ultimately brought me to my senses... It all started innocently enough. But, at the time, I didn't see it that way...I had been drinking for most of the day and was in the *Freeman Arms* pub. I was drunk and unsteady on my feet. As I staggered to the bar, I accidently, but quite strongly, bumped into a group of men causing some to spill ale out of their glasses.

'Oi, ya clumsy bugger... Watch what you're doing you've spilled me beer,' one annoyed man said.

I ignored him and pushed my way past to get to the bar.

'Hang about lad... what you gonna do about my spilled ale?' he said as he got hold of my shoulder and pulled me back.

'Get your bloody hands off me... What's that you said about hanging about?' I said angrily and stared at him.

'What... are you deaf as well as drunk?' He replied. The tone of his voice had changed into one of aggression.

'Leave him be... he's pissed' his friend said. 'Don't start any trouble!'

'Hang about... there won't be any trouble if he says sorry and buys me another ale,' he said rather cockily.

He'd too had had a good drink and most of his front was drink fuelled bravado.

'What about it lad... another pint for me and one for Ernie here whose ale you also spilled.'

I now realise that he used the expression 'hang about' as a figure of speech and no insult was intended, but with the distress I was feeling at the thought of my mama hanging, this is not what I heard and I was not in a mood for standing any nonsense...

'What... you've a snowflakes chance in hell of getting any ale from me,' I said to him.

All the anger I felt was welling up inside of me. Though he was older, I was larger, stronger and probably much fitter. That's what fishing did for you. The drink in me talked!

'Now back off old man... before I spill your blood as well as your ale,' I threatened him.

The tension and hostility of the situation had cleared my head a little. People who were stood around us in the bar stopped talking and stepped back, clearing a space. They knew that a fight was about to start. As they stood looking at us, the silence in the room was deafening and added to the tension!

The aggressive man knew that he had to do something to save face. He had picked an argument and was now in a fight that he didn't expect to happen... He had bitten off more than he could chew. Not sure what to do next, he looked about him. He looked at his friends and then at me. I could tell by the changed expression on his face and how his eyes were darting from side to side that he was not so confident and cocksure now... But, to save face he had to do something. Clumsily he threw the first punch, which I easily deflected before knocking him to the ground with two quick punches of my own.

'That's it... that's it lad... It's over, he's down, now leave him be,' his friend said firmly.

'Ok... that's fine with me... Pick him up... Just advise him to keep his loud mouth shut in future,' I said, whilst standing over his fallen friend.

'I stepped back and turned to face the bar. Suddenly I heard someone shout *'lookout'*. He had risen to his feet and had lifted a heavy beer bottle from a table, which he was going to bring down on the back of my head. Turning quickly, I managed to avoid being knocked senseless and punched him several times until he fell to the floor unconscious and bleeding from his mouth and nose...

This was the most aggressive I'd ever been, or ever would be, to anyone in my life. Even the fights we had with other crews when our long-lines had accidently been cut, were not as vicious as this. All the anger and hurt I felt about my mama's death, was now evident on this total stranger's battered and bleeding face...'

Sarah-Eliza and the children stared at Jacob in stunned silence at what he had told them.

'As I stood there looking at his prone body, the door of the pub burst open and two constables came rushing in... A barmaid had run outside and shouted for the constables, who happened to be nearby. Although my antagonist threw the first punch, after asking a few questions of others in the bar, the constables arrested me and I was taken to the local jail. Apparently, my opponent was a well-known and well liked local merchant... I was in deep trouble...

'Were you charged with assault father?' Sarah- Eliza asked.

Before Jacob could answer the boys, who were impressed with this part of the story, spoke.

'You really biffed him... didn't you grandad,' said Gabriel in boyish admiration.

'Yes... bash,' said Daniel throwing a mock punch at nobody in particular.

'BOYS...that's enough of that talk... fighting is not clever,' Sarah- Eliza admonished them. 'Father, were you charged by the police?' she asked again.

'Sorry dear... I had to tell that part of the story so that you would all understand how I felt... and, perhaps appreciate more what happened next,' Jacob said.

'Boys, your mother is right, fighting when you don't have to is not clever... and, even if you have to, it's still best to be avoided if you can.'

'Was I charged... well yes and no,' said Jacob. 'Initially, help for my predicament came from a most unlikely source.'

'A young girl, probably a dollymop, whom I only knew by sight from visiting the bars and had spoken to just a couple of times, witnessed what happened. When the constables took me way, for some reason, to this day I don't know why, perhaps she held a grudge against my antagonist, ran to the Orwell Street lodgings to look for Barney. Fortunately for me, Barney was there and when he heard what had taken place, he left Ethel and went to find Mr Kingston who, when found, also stopped what he was doing... Together they came to the police station...

As they made their way there, Barney told him what the girl witnessed and that I had just received the news that my mother had died. Barney suggested [it] may explain why I was behaving in the manner that I was. He said nothing to Mr Kingston of the circumstances leading up to my mother's death... Barney really was a good friend...

At the police station, Mr Kingston, who was well known as a successful smack owner, businessman and employer spoke up for me. He was listened to. I'd been charged with affray and

223

assault and was locked in a cell... According to what Barney told me later, Mr Kingston pleaded my case saying, I was his apprentice and was not a violent person and what had happened was totally out of character...

He told the police sergeant I had just heard the bad news about my mother and was distressed and thought that the man I assaulted was making fun of me... He also pointed out that although he came off worse, there are several witnesses who saw the man throw the first punch and then attempting to brain me with a beer bottle... my reaction was self-defence. When Mr Kingston suggested that he would press for my opponent to also be charged, the police sergeant's attitude changed. He decided enough was enough and released me without charge and the slate would be wiped completely clean. There would be no record of the incident...

If Mr Kingston had not been successful in getting the charge dropped, I would have been brought before the magistrates, fined, and probably have had to spend a few days in jail, which for me, although inconvenient would not have been too bad. It would however, have inconvenienced Mr Kingston being short a crew member. My absence may have stopped the *Mary-Ann* from sailing. Fortunately, with a reprimand from the police sergeant, but a clean record, I was released into Mr Kingston's care...

A few years later, I realised just how fortunate I was for Mr Kingston's intervention. If I had been brought before the bench, fined and had a criminal police record, I could not have become a Freeman of Grimsby when I married your grandmother. And, without being a Freeman, I could never have become a magistrate in my later life... It was something else that I had to thank my benefactor for. I was also grateful to the girl, whoever she was and, for Barney's swift response to go and find Mr Kingston...

As we left the police station, Mr Kingston turned to face me.

'Jake, I'm not impressed with you'se at all... This is not how I expect my apprentices to behave... brawling in dockland pubs... Go home to the lodgings, sleep off the drink and come and see me at my office at ten o'clock sharp in the morning,' he said.

The tone of his voice left me in no doubt that he was very angry.

'Barney, you had better also come with Jake tomorrow morning... at this moment right now lads, I'm thinking about cancelling your indentures Jake... I'll need some persuading not to... I don't like violence... I never have,' Mr Kingston said.

'You need to learn...actions always have consequences,' he added.

Without saying good-bye he walked away and left us on the steps of the police station. He was angry.

'Do you think he really means it Barney?' I asked.

'For sure... I'm not sure,' Barney replied. 'What a mess you've got yourself into when I wasn't there to look out for you... but, Jake my boy, we'll sort it... whatever the outcome.'

'The next morning at precisely ten o'clock, after a night of broken troubled sleep, I nervously knocked on the door of Mr Kingston's office to hear my fate. Hoping that my appearance may have some influence on whatever decision was reached I had taken the trouble to dress well in my Sunday best and polished my boots...Barney had taken some trouble to smarten up. But as usual he looked as he always did – not quite the finished article...

Sarah-Eliza smiled and the children giggled.

'On the walk to the office, we had talked about what I would do if my indenture was cancelled. As always, Barney tried to reassure me...

'Jake, it won't be cancelled if you tell Mr Kingston the whole story... For sure he's a good Christian man...he'll understand.'

'I can't tell him that I killed Thaddeus... other than my family Barney, you're the only one who knows what really happened,' I said rather fretfully.

'Jake, you must tell him...let him know... He won't go to the police,' Barney replied. 'He needs to know why you acted as you did.'

'Still undecided about what I was going to say, we arrived at Mr Kingston's office and I knocked on the door. '*Come in Jake*', I heard him shout. In trepidation, I opened the door and Barney and I stepped into the office. I didn't realise it at the time, but the outcome of this meeting would shape my fate and future just as much as the decision to flee from Calthorpe over four years before had. Mr Kingston looked relaxed sat behind a desk. He was trying not to look too imposing. George Simmons was stood just to one side of him…

'Come on in lads…don't be nervous, I'm not going to eat you'se,' Mr Kingston said.

Clearly his anger of the previous day had abated somewhat. Trying to ease our fears, George Simmons smiled and gestured for us to come closer.

'Ok Jake… what's this all about? …You're not a fighting man… this is not like you,' Mr Kingston said. 'Why did you get into that trouble?'

I hesitated before replying, still unsure what to say.

'Jake, I can't decide what to do if you don't tell me why you behaved so out of character,' said Mr Kingston.

Still I hesitated.

'Jake, you've got to help us to make a decision as to whether we keep you as an apprentice,' George Simmons said.

'For God's sake Jake, tell 'em,' Barney pleaded. 'Tell Mr Kingston what happened.'

'Erm… I… I thought he was taking the mickey out of me cos I was drunk,' I mumbled a reply.

'What!' Mr Simmons exclaimed. 'You seriously assaulted a total stranger because he was taking the mickey out of you?'

'Yes sir… I did,' I replied looking at Barney and shaking my head.

Barney stared back at me, not quite believing what I had said and, my negative gesture.

'You really expect me to believe that Jake…is that all you'se is going to say?' said Mr Kingston.

'Yes sir… it is,' I replied.

'If that is all you'se have to say in your defence… I'll have no option but to cancel your indentures… You understand that don't you?' Mr Kingston added.

'He will, Jake… if you leave him no choice,' Mr Simmons stressed.

'No sir! Please don't do that,' pleaded Barney.

'Jake, for Christ sake tell 'em about your mother,' Barney said to me quite angrily.

Surprised by his outburst, George Simmons looked at me and then Mr Kingston.

'Jake, I know from Barney that you were upset because you'd just had news of your mother dying,' said Mr Kingston gently.

'Help me to help you if I can.'

Still I hesitated. Barney turned to face me and looked directly into my eyes and in earnest said,

'Jake, you're my best friend… the best any man could wish for... and I know that you trust me, but for sure…if you won't tell Mr Kingston the whole story of your circumstances, I will…'

'I really will.' Barney stressed.

All eyes were now on me as I stood there making up my mind whether to confide in them or not. I looked at Barney and after a short while nodded OK.

'Erm… Mr Kingston… Mr Simmons, if I tell you my story and you still decide to release me, I thank you now for the four exciting and wonderful years, I have enjoyed working for you... You have both been an inspiration to me,' I said and then added.

'If you decide to keep me… I will have taken you into my confidence and you will be the last persons that will ever hear this story from me.'

Mr Kingston looked me in the eyes and then across at George Simmons. They nodded their head in agreement.

'In that case… I will tell you the whole sorry story,' I said.

'I've a feeling that this is going to take some time Henry,' said Mr Simmons, who had gone over and locked the door.

'We don't want to be disturbed do we…? Shall we all sit down?'

After a hesitant start, I told them my story, beginning with how my father had died; Thaddeus Stone's brutal assaults and the beating of my mother, the still birth he caused and how he frequently beat me. They listened intently without commenting. I told them of Stone's campaign of hatred against Tom Kite and poor old Hector who was poisoned and that Stone callously murdered Tom in cold blood…

When I came to the night I killed Thaddeus, I faltered. Barney looked at me and mouthed encouragement, *'go on tell 'em what happened'*. Still listening intently, both Mr Kingston and Mr Simmons now had furrowed brows and stern expressions as they concentrated on every word I said. I told them about the bareknuckle fight and why I hit Thaddeus with his cudgel. And then I explained my mama's plan for me to flee Calthorpe and how I met Barney and journeyed to Grimsby. They were surprised that I was not quite thirteen when I signed on the *Mary-Ann*. Finally, I told them about Aunt Eliza's visit and how I found out the fate of my mama… I then let them read my mama's letter.

I stopped talking. For a while everyone sat in silence while first Mr Kingston and then Mr Simmons with solemn faces read what mama had written. Eventually Mr Kingston took off his pince-nez glasses, rose from his chair and came and stood in front of me and handed the letter back.

'Jake, that is an appalling sad story… is all of it true… did your mother suffer those beatings and the still birth… did Mr Stone die just as you are telling me?' he said.

'Look at me… I'll know if you'se is lying.'

Yes sir, every word is true… that's what really happened,' I replied.

Mr Kingston paced the room and thought for a moment. Finally he stopped and faced me.

'Well then Jake, your mother is right… you'se is not a murderer,' he said. '…You'se was defending your mother, which I would expect any man in the same circumstances to do.'

'I was sir… she was screaming in pain… it was more than I could stand,' I said.

I started to become upset. Barney and Mr Simmons look across at me… I could see they were concerned.

'Now, now lad…don't upset yourself… I've decided that I can help you to forget the past and put it behind you by keeping you on as an apprentice and securing your future… Just as your mother wanted… Do you agree with that George?' asked Mr Kingston.

'Yes Henry I do,' Mr Simmons replied with a broad smile.

'For sure… I do too,' said Barney as he jumped to his feet and came over to me and shook my hand.

Barney's comments lightened the mood and everyone grinned.

'Tell me young Jake, what are your plans for the future… Have you any ideas for how you will honour your mother and father and make them proud of you'se?' asked Mr Kingston.

'Yes Sir, I have,' I replied. '…With my mama's small legacy and money that I have saved… one day, when we are ready, Barney and I will own a smack.'

'I've been saving my money too,' said Barney feeling a little left out.

'Yes that's right... Barney and I will find the money to buy a smack… We've already decided that our company will be called the Rawlings and McHugh Fishing Company,' I told Mr Kingston.

'Well, well, well… that sounds like a good plan… and, it would be a fitting tribute to your mother,' said Mr Kingston. '…What do you think George?'

'Well now… as Barney here would say… for sure it's a fitting tribute to Mrs Rawlings,' Mr Simmons replied.

The mood in the room was now much lighter. Mr Kingston then stunned us all with what he suggested next,

'Lads… as you know, I have no children of my own… Mr Simmons here is as close to a son as I'll ever get… but I've taken quite a liking to you two scallywags.'

'You work hard and you are quick learners… I'll make a bond with you,' he said.

'...first you finish your apprenticeship with me... erm... Jake, we'll have to think about your age... just twelve years old when you started... eh... harrumph!'

He smiled and then winked at me.

'Right lads... learn all you can from Mr Simmons and me,' he added. '...Then when you think you've learned all you need to know... I'll arrange for you to spend some time with my brother on the *Mary-Jane* and on other fishing vessels of friends of mine so you can learn some more.'

'...Become competent skippers and save your money... When the time is right, I'll help you buy the first Rawlings and McHugh fishing smack... I'll advise you what to buy and as a loan, I will make up any shortfall in the money you need to buy the vessel.'

'What do you reckon, George?' he asked. 'Have I taken leave of my senses?'

'No Henry...you haven't. I think it's a splendid idea... that way the fishing industry gets two more fair and honest skippers...The Lord knows how much we need them,' Mr Simmons replied.

'That's what I thought George... Ok lads... what do you'se say to that?' He asked.

Barney and I were momentarily stunned into silence. Finally Barney spoke. My head was in a whirl. I was still trying to fully understand what had just been said.

'Well now... that's a proper Irish riddle for sure,' said Barney.

'...Young Jake here came into this office thinking his indentures were going to be cancelled... only now we're walking out with a potential future business partner.'

Barney shook his head and rubbed his chin before saying,

'...the Lord certainly moves in mysterious ways... Thank you very much sir.'

'Thank you'se Barney,' said Mr Kingston. '...But, long before then Barney, I hope you will have made an honest woman of young Ethel Cocking.'

We all laughed and Barney blushed.

'Now then Jake... what do you have to say?' Mr Kingston asked me.

'Thank you sir, that's wonderful... it really gives me and Barney something to strive for,' I said and added.

'We'll work hard for you and learn from Mr Simmons... how long do you think it will take to be competent enough to safely skipper a smack?'

'About ten years,' he replied. 'Don't worry, you'll still be a young man...after all, you'se started young,' Mr Kingston said before winking again at me.

'Off you go now lads... Don't forget we sail in two days,' he said.

We all shook hands. As Barney and I and walked to the door, I heard Mr Kingston say,

'Jake, believe she is watching you... and you won't let her down again.'

'Yes Sir, I believe she is... and I won't let her down,' I replied.

Chapter 14

The Dream Starts to Become a Reality

Jacob leant back in his chair, looked at his family sat around him and smiled at them. He drew contentedly on his pipe before continuing. Sarah-Eliza and the children waited eagerly to hear what he was going to tell them next, even though some parts of what they had been told so far were distressing and upsetting. Sarah-Eliza, in particular, was seeing a side to her father she had never seen before. This gentle man, who she loved, had killed someone and had frequently brawled in dockland pubs. It all seemed surreal. All through her life, she had only ever known her father as a successful man, a pillar of society and not the man whose story she was hearing.

Although Jacob had taken most of the weekend to tell his story they were all fascinated in hearing the truth of how he had lived his life and the people who played such a big part in helping to shape his fate and fortune. Sarah-Eliza thought she was beginning to understand what her father wanted her to know. Still she wondered why and why now. Why was it so important for her to know such details now?

Jacob took his pipe out of his mouth and continued with his story.

'Although it would be several more years before we were able to buy our first smack, in reality on that January morning in 1870 in Henry Kingston's office, what eventually became the Rawlings and McHugh Steam Fishing Company stopped being a boyish dream and became the goal we were striving to achieve. But, before we could even think about being a smack owner, Barney and I still had so much to learn. There were many more dangers to be faced and adventures and experiences to be had… Above all, we both had much to thank Mr Kingston, and George Simmons for…

'Mr Kingston really was your benefactor... wasn't he father?' said Sarah-Eliza.

Gabriel and Grace had no idea what a benefactor was. They didn't ask and it wasn't explained.

'Yes dear he was... to Barney and me, he was almost the father we didn't have,' Jacob said. '...There was so much to be admired about Mr Kingston and also Mr Simmons.'

'I trusted them both completely... from that day until this weekend nobody else, including your mother, was told the full story of what had happened,' said Jacob.

'My mother... never knew the truth about what had happened,' Sarah-Eliza asked rather surprised.

'No dear... she didn't.' Jacob said as he shook his head.

'You never told her... you must have lied!' Sarah-Eliza exclaimed.

'What did you tell her... how did you explain your mama's death?' she asked.

'Now you listen to me my dear,' Jacob said firmly, '...There was nothing to be gained by your mother knowing that I had killed Thaddeus Stone... nothing at all... The truth about that part of my life had to stay hidden.'

'...We stuck to the story that mama had killed Stone in self-defence and she had died in childbirth in prison while waiting to go on trial... and, most probably would have been acquitted when her case was eventually heard,' Jacob explained.

He was angry and Sarah-Eliza could see that he was.

'...I couldn't sully my mother's memory and tell my wife that my precious mama was a convicted murderer and had been sentenced to hang for something she hadn't done... could I... could I?' Jacob said assertively.

'Well...could I?' he asked as he stared at his daughter.

His kindly face had gone red and a vein stood out on his temple.

Sarah- Eliza could see from his changed expression and tone of voice that her father had become very annoyed by her questioning him and his judgement. She wasn't used to seeing him so angry. She knew she had touched a raw nerve. The children, who could also sense their grandad's irritation, were unsure what to say. So they said nothing.

They sat quietly waiting.

'No father... I don't suppose you could,' said Sarah-Eliza contritely. 'Erm...I'm...I'm sorry I questioned you... Please continue with the story.'

For a moment Jacob said nothing. He just looked at Sarah-Eliza and then his expression softened. Finally, he smiled at her like the loving father he was. He didn't like to be angry with her. She smiled back at him and the mood relaxed.

'Ok dear...enough said,' Jacob replied.

Purposely, he took his time to fill his pipe and light it. His anger was subsiding as rapidly as it had risen. After being satisfied that his pipe was burning brightly, he blew a smoke ring, grinned at the children and resumed his telling of the story.

'I've already told you that the *Mary-Ann* was converted into a trawler. In the early days after its conversion, Mr Kingston operated it as an individual unit, or in a pair with its sister smack, the *Mary-Jane*, which had also been converted into a trawler and was still skippered by Mr Kingston's brother, Charles. At first we mainly fished the areas of the North Sea known as the Dogger Bank and the Silver Pitt. In a fine season, we sometimes fished off of the Dutch coast. The average duration of our voyages was eight to ten days. This suited Barney just fine, because he got to see Ethel more frequently...

Though he was courting her, after my fight in the *Freemans Arms*, he didn't like me going out on my own and always tried to include me whenever they went anywhere. I don't think Ethel minded too much, but I had the good sense to occasionally decline their offer... They needed some time on their own. Even so, Barney and I still managed to spend some time ashore together having a few beers and talking of our plans for the future...

We quickly discovered that fishing on a trawling smack was a new experience from long lining. Hauling the trawl aboard a smack that was pitching and rolling was the most dangerous severe work and in this all hands took their share. Sadly, over the years, many, many fishermen were lost overboard during the haul... It was not widely known outside of fishing families, that in the 1870s, before proper accurate records were kept, more than six hundred fishermen were lost at sea, mainly from falling overboard or, being washed overboard. And, in just a two year period from 1880 to 1882, once accurate records had begun to be kept, nearly two hundred Grimsby fishermen lost their lives of which, more than half were less than twenty-one years old...

'Many of those unfortunate wretches were just fourteen or fifteen years old,' said Jacob forlornly.

'That's appalling father... those poor boys and men,' said Sarah-Eliza as she looked at her own children.

'Yes dear... it was appalling... sadly in the years that followed, far worse was still to come,' Jacob replied.

'...this is exactly what I want you and the children to appreciate... I want you to value what you have had and, will have in the future. '

'A terrible, terrible price was paid for the comfortable lifestyle that us and, many like us, have enjoyed.' Jacob said sorrowfully and shaking his head.

He paused, sucked on his pipe and then quoted from the bible.

'Jesus said to his disciples, *'I will make you fishers of men,'*

'...Well the Lord God certainly was an excellent fisherman... he regularly cast his net and took many, many good men.' Jacob said sadly.

Jacob had again become misty eyed. In his mind's eye, he was reliving every piece of bad news of catastrophe and disaster that made its way back to the port. Sarah-Eliza and the children knew him well enough to realise at that moment it was better for them to say nothing, so they sat in silence. Especially as he had been so angry only a short while before.

Sarah-Eliza looked with concern at her father. She could see that telling this story was proving to be very emotional and hard for him. Probably more than he had expected. He seemed to have visibly aged over the weekend. It was as though reliving all that had happened was draining the life force from him.

Eventually, when he was ready, Jacob cleared his throat and continued with his story.

'When the fish were plentiful, we hauled the nets every three or four hours and would get very little sleep often for two days at a time. Once the fish had been brought on board and the trawl shot away again. We had to gut the fish and pack them away in the fish room and make the deck ready for the next haul. It didn't leave much time for sleep... I can clearly remember the strained faces and the haunting weary, weary eyes that I have seen around the cabin table on a trawler. Fishing certainly hardened you...

As hard work as it was, I don't think that a sight more wonderful can be seen than when at the midnight haul, the great net rose out of the sea under the white glare of the acetylene or paraffin lamps...The sea all around you is black and the trawl bag is all white. It is like a bag full of pearls... the water streams out of it. Under the glare of the lamps it looks like a cascade of precious jewels. Being hauled by the derrick, the bag rises from the sea and is swung round over the deck. The cod-end knot is undone and it opens and there pours down a torrent of liquid mother-of-pearl, which floods the deck, a shimmering, quivering agitated mass...'

Regularly drawing on his pipe, his eyes twinkling and using his voice for affect, Jacob was story telling again in the manner that he had done so many times before in the dockland pubs. He really enjoyed embellishing a yarn. Looking intently at the children he carried on.

'When you looked closer, at first the mass seems to be all eyes staring back at you. After a while you discern weird forms and faces, the catfish with its human like head and the devilish apparition of the monk. The moving mass before you divides and separates for you to see; the heaving of the halibut, the leaping of the haddock and cod, the gliding of the shark like dog-fish, and the flapping of the flatfish... In addition to the fish, there would also be star-fish, sea urchins, crabs and if you were lucky a decent lobster or two. All around the smack, huge swarms of sea-birds would be flying, shrieking and crying and looking for the easy pickings of the smaller fish that would go back into the sea. On the deck, those quivering masses of marine life that we butchered and packed away were like living gold. They paid our wages and brought great wealth to the smack owners, the merchants and the town...'

Jacob paused and his expression changed yet again.

'For this wealth, a cruel price in human terms was being paid... Yes children, I know I am repeating myself... but, it's important that I do,' Jacob stressed.

'During the 1870s, as the industry began to grow, the smack owners began to appreciate the advantages to be gained from operating their vessels in fleets. Some larger companies owned enough vessels to operate their own fleets, and did so. Smaller owners tended to combine their resources to make a fleet of associated owners, which is what Mr Kingston decided to do...

When fleeting, each smack transferred its catch to a fast steam carrier while still at sea. The carrier would then convey the fish to port, leaving the smack on the grounds to continue fishing. The advantage of this system was that instead of dozens of vessels returning to port independently and spending time unprofitably travelling between the fishing grounds and the dock, only a relatively few vessels sailed to and fro while the remainder fished...

Although this suited the smack owners, it had its disadvantages as far as the crews were concerned. Fleeting meant smacks would remain at sea for much longer periods... In the summer season, a voyage of a trawling smack could be extended to eight, ten or even twelve weeks. Although the crew could earn more, fleeting didn't really suit many, particularly the family men and our Barney. It was a long time to be away from family and loved ones without putting ashore...

At least when we were long lining, we would get a break from the fishing when we put into Shetland and other ports... Not only did we have to work longer periods without shore leave we had to work harder... and, because we were remaining on the grounds, we didn't get to enjoy the relatively slack periods that occurred when sailing between the fishing grounds and the port... Perhaps more significantly, fleeting meant we were exposed to additional dangers...

When we were fleeting, the catch had to be conveyed in boxes to the carrier from the *Mary-Ann* by means of the ship's row boat. In heavy and violent seas this was extremely dangerous, especially as several smacks would be sailing close to each other and the steam carrier. More often than not, the perilous journey to transfer the fish from smack to carrier was generally rowed by the apprentices... As you might expect, being in a small wooden row boat in treacherous seas amongst the fleet of smacks, accidents could happen and did. Hundreds of men and boys were drowned as a result of collisions occurring during the transfer of catches from smacks to the carrier...

'Did you hear that Daniel?' asked Jacob. 'Hundreds of men and boys drowned as a result of collisions.'

'Yes grandad...I did hear... I was listening,' said Daniel.

'Good,' said Jacob, '... it's important that you did.'

Jacob stopped talking. His hands were held limply in his lap. He wasn't looking at the children, or his daughter. With a forlorn expression on his face, he stared into the flames of the fire burning cheerfully in the grate. Without raising his head and still looking into the fire, Jacob said,

'I've never told you this before... when I was nineteen, Barney and I nearly drowned as we were transferring the boxed fish to the steam carrier...'

Surprised at what he had just said, Sarah-Eliza and the children stared at him in open mouthed attention. Jacob deliberately waited for a moment and in a voice, which at first faltered, he continued.

'It was a bitterly cold winter's day and the sea was running a fairly deep swell... The *Mary-Ann,* along with the *Mary-*

Jane, was fishing in a fleet about one hundred and fifty miles from the River Humber. Mr Kingston sent Barney, me and the third hand, a twenty-three year old lad called Harry Riley, in the row boat to convey the fish to the carrier, which was about four hundred yards away. *'You'se take care now lads'*, he had shouted as we pulled away from the *Mary-Ann*...While we were rowing to the carrier, our boat was run into by the smack *Northward* and cut clean in two, pitching the three of us and our boxes of fish into the icy cold water. Shouting for help, Barney and I were quickly rescued by the crew of the *Northward*. For a short while before I was rescued and pulled onto the *Northward*, I managed to hold on to Harry and keep his head above the water... But, once I'd let go and before they could get a hold of him, Harry, crying out for his mother to help him, succumbed to the cold water and slipped beneath the waves.'

Jacob looked up and said,

'Harry Riley was not just the third hand, he was our friend with whom Barney and I had often had a drink.'

Jacob briefly paused and then said,

'He drowned right before my very eyes and there was nothing... nothing at all I could do about it.'

Sarah-Eliza gasped. The children were stunned by what Jacob had just told them. She looked across at them and quickly raising her finger to her lips whispered *'shush'* and, gestured for them to be quiet. She did not want the children asking questions. Jacob hadn't noticed what she'd done. For what seemed a long-time, but in truth wasn't, it just seemed it, everyone sat in silence. Clearly upset again, Jacob sat rigidly still. He was deep in thought. Finally, Sarah-Eliza spoke.

'Father, let's have a break... you've been talking for a long time.'

She could see that recollecting and reliving his memories and the past was upsetting him. Perhaps more than he had anticipated. Jacob didn't move or speak. The children looked at their mother. She shook her head, indicating for them to remain quiet. Sarah-Eliza was worried.

'Father,' she said gently, '...shall we stop now?'

Still Jacob did not move or speak. He looked tired and weary. Although he was in his seventies, he suddenly looked much older!

'Father,' she said, only a little louder this time. '...I think we should stop now.'

Jacob stirred. He looked at Sarah-Eliza.

'What did you say dear?' he asked.

'I think... perhaps this is the time to stop,' Sarah-Eliza said.

'No, no, no... I cannot stop now,' Jacob replied. 'I've come this far... I've got to finish what I need to tell you and the children.'

Before Sarah-Eliza could reply, Jacob added.

'...I may not get another chance to talk to you all together like this.'

Sarah-Eliza was concerned and alarmed, not only by what her father had said, but the urgency in his voice. She decided not to press her concerns in front of the children. That would come later when the children were in bed.

'Ok father... have it your way,' she conceded, '...At least let's have a cup of tea before you carry on with the story.'

Jacob agreed and they all rose from their seats and made their way into the kitchen. The children ran ahead, they knew where the biscuit barrel was.

After they had had their tea and were refreshed, they all returned to the cosiness and warmth of the fireside in the sitting room so Jacob could resume his story. As she watched her father rise unsteadily to his feet, Sarah-Eliza was convinced that there was something he wasn't telling her. She meant to find out what.

Although, he seemed brighter and more relaxed after taking the break for tea, Sarah-Eliza was still anxious about his welfare. During this weekend, whilst he was telling the story, she had witnessed aspects of her father's behaviour and changing emotions, which she had never seen before. This was so unlike him. She wanted answers! When they were all settled, Jacob continued with the story.

'Barney and I were safely conveyed back to the *Mary-Ann* following the accident... When Mr Kingston heard the fate of

Harry Riley and how he had drowned, just an arm's grasp away from safety, he gave thanks to the Lord for our deliverance and was very upset that a fine lad like Harry had been taken. Although all fishermen accepted that it was an occupational hazard that we had to face every day, it was no less a sad and sorrowful occasion when the sea took someone.

Mr Kingston said to me,

'Jake... don't blame yourself... you'se did what you could for Harry... It was the Lord's will that Harry be taken,'

'For sure Jake... what more could you have done... you held on to him as long as you could,' said Barney.

Although I knew they were both right, it didn't make me feel any better. Harry had drowned just a few feet away from me...

Mr Kingston cared as much for his men as he did about making money from fishing... Some, Barney and me included, would argue more so. We knew, from talking to other apprentices, that Mr Kingston was paying us more wages than most of the other smack owners would have done. The *Mary-Ann* had been on the fishing grounds for about five weeks and we were having a successful trip until then... plenty of fish had been caught. Mr Kingston decided to cut the trip short and take the *Mary-Ann* back to port. Harry Riley's widowed mother needed to be told what had happened to her son. And, it was only right and proper that he was the one to tell her and not someone off the *Northward* or the steam carrier, or any of the smacks that were fishing the grounds at that time of the accident... Mr Kingston gave George Simmons, who was standing close by, the order to make the *Mary-Ann* ready for the journey home...

'That's enough George... let's take her home,'

'Ok Henry,' Mr Simmons replied.

'C'mon lads... look lively, we're homeward bound,' he shouted to the crew.

'Mr Kingston lived, breathed and practiced his strong Christian beliefs in everything that he did. We later learned that he made a small financial provision for old mother Riley, just as he had done for Molly Cocking when she was widowed.

As well as how to be a good fisherman, from   Henry Kingston, Barney and I learned the importance of being a decent human being. He was as much a philanthropist as he was a businessman... and that the two could go together. Other than Barney, never a better man have I met. All that I did and, all that I became was based on Henry Kingston...

After the *Northward* accident, the years passed quickly and comparatively uneventfully... Barney and I completed our apprenticeships. Because he was allegedly a year older, Barney finished his apprenticeship and had his indentures signed off a year ahead of me. Also, under the guidance of Mr Kingston, George Simmons and occasionally with my help, Barney had started to learn how to read and write. His school book was a bible, which he took to quoting from. Although it was a slow process, he was getting there...

With regard to my apprenticeship, Mr Kingston and I decided it would be better if I continued, for his records, to be one year older than I really was. And, that I had started my apprenticeship a week before my fourteenth birthday and not my thirteenth. It would mean that I still served a full seven years before my indenture was signed off... which is what I did. I was twenty-seven and just about to get married before I finally corrected my age...

Even though Barney and I were now experienced fishermen and had started sailing as deckhands we still had much to learn. It is worth remembering that when we were learning, early trawlers had none of the technology and equipment which would come later and help the skippers have a successful trip. There was no wireless, radar, gyro or electricity. It was hand steering, magnetic compasses, paraffin lamps, candles for the fish room and before the smacks had derricks, everything was all handled by the crew... A successful trip depended on the skill and experience of the smack's master or skipper... Apart from having an ability to sail a smack in all weathers and knowing how to find and catch the fish, there were so many other things we had to learn if we were ever going to buy and operate our own smack...and, make the Rawlings and McHugh Fishing Company a reality...

If you are employed as a fisherman, there is only so much that you need to know and be able to do to earn your wages. Many other aspects of life on board a fishing vessel didn't concern you. Others had to worry about them. But, as the smack owner and an employer of fishermen you are responsible for everything... In addition to the skill of choosing and employing the right fishermen to crew the vessel, other important things such as how to maintain and keep the smack in seaworthy condition and, how to provision and equip the vessel for each voyage... understanding what is needed, where to get it from and the best way to pay for it, all have to be thought about. To be able to viably operate a smack as a successful and profitable business requires its own set of skills. And in Mr Kingston, Barney and I had the ideal teacher and mentor...'

Jacob stopped talking, drew on his pipe and exhaled the smoke before he started to chuckle.

'Barney... dear old Barney,' he said while still chuckling. '...He did make me laugh and I do miss him,'

'Why, what did he do that's made you laugh now grandad?' asked Daniel.

'Yes father, what have you remembered?' asked Sarah-Eliza. It pleased her to see her father more relaxed than he was earlier.

'Oh... It was nothing in particular...he just had such a zest for life and was so comical in his way of talking... I don't think he always appreciated how funny he really was... he was just Barney,' said Jacob.

'You must have remembered something to make you chuckle,' said Sarah-Eliza as she smiled at her father.

'Well yes OK, I did... but you may not find it so funny... At the time it tickled me and still does now,' replied Jacob.

'We were in one of the dockland pubs having a drink with Mr Kingston and George Simmons, who we could call George, now that we were no longer apprentices... Mr Kingston had been explaining to us how to set up a company and the need for proper accounts and book-keeping. It wasn't just a case of buying a smack and setting sail into the sunset hoping to make your fortune...

As Mr Kingston talked, I could see from the quizzical expression on his face that, Barney was struggling to understand all the detail and intricacies of what we were being told about being a smack owner. It amused me to watch him and his forever changing expressions. Although he listened intently and tried hard... he really couldn't grasp what was only basic book-keeping. Finally, totally exasperated he interrupted and said,

'Mr Kingston, Sir...for sure...I'm sorry to say it, but what you're explaining makes less sense to me than sweet Jesus's Sermon on the Mount.'

George and I looked aghast at Barney, hoping Mr Kingston wouldn't take offence. He stopped talking and for a brief moment looked at Barney before breaking into a loud belly laugh. Why Barney had initially made the comparison with Christ's sermon, I had no idea, other than he had used the bible to learn how to read...

'That's me told...eh, George,' Mr Kingston said

'Did you not understand what the Sermon on the Mount was about?' asked Mr Kingston.

'No Sir...I did not...no offence meant to our Lord, but only an Irishman would ask all those people to come and hear him speak and then only have enough fish and bread for dinner for a few,' Barney said before adding.

'For sure, what you're saying... I understand even less,'

George and I laughed, and nearly choked spluttering our beer everywhere. Mr Kingston didn't know what to say so he slapped his thigh and laughed loudly.

'I'll say this... you'se 'as got a right way with you Barney McHugh,' Mr Kingston said

We all sat laughing. Finally Barney said,

'Well now... Jake my man... I'll tell you what we'll do...this is how Rawlings and McHugh are gonna operate... I'll sail the smack, find and catch the fish and put them on the deck... You can then count them, species by species and put the numbers in the book... What do you say to that?'

With that we all burst into such loud laughter that we attracted the attention of most people who were in the bar. Barney winked at me. It was a very happy time.

For Barney and me, the 1870s turned out to be an important and eventful decade. After completing our apprenticeships, Mr Kingston ensured we learnt our craft and got as much experience as possible. He and George worked us hard and were very demanding... but we didn't mind... It was all serving a purpose. To get the feel of and become competent at sailing and handling other vessels, Mr Kingston arranged for us to sail as deck-hands and later as third hands on other smacks. Some of which he owned and some that were owned by friends of his. At the beginning of the decade, in addition to the *Mary-Ann* and the *Mary-Jane*, Mr Kingston owned two other smacks. By 1879 he would own nine smacks...

When we moved to another smack, sometimes Barney and I sailed together, sometimes we did not. The first time we sailed on different smacks, it was the strangest feeling. From the very first day that I met him, eight years earlier in 1865, we had not spent a single day apart. We had watched each other's backs and looked out for each other. He was my protective shadow and I was his. Mr Kingston, quite wisely, reasoned that we needed to develop our abilities and be independent of each other, because, if we were to become successful smack owners there would be times in the future when this would be necessary. At first it felt like my right arm was missing...

'You take care and fare well...brother, Jake,' Barney said to me that morning on the North Wall when we both went to board different smacks.

'You too...brother Barney,' I replied. 'May the good lord watch over and protect us.'

We looked at each other, nodded and shook hands before we made our way to the smacks...

During the early years of the development and growth of the fishing industry, it was entirely unhampered by official rules and regulations. Not only was there no proper regulation and safeguards for the apprentices, no certificate of any kind was required from skippers in charge of smacks and there was no compulsory inspection of the vessels as to their sea-worthiness. It was often the case that a crew could be sent to sea in an unseaworthy smack in the charge of an incompetent skipper...

It wasn't until the early 1880s that regulation of the industry required that skippers and mates should be given some form of licence. And that no fishing boat shall go to sea unless the skipper was the holder of a certificate of competency... Although, at that time, we had no certificate of competency, Barney and I were being taught all that we needed to know by the best men... We became excellent sailors and fishermen and, we learned the importance of being decent caring men...'

Jacob paused and looked at his daughter and grandchildren and smiled benignly at them.

'It wasn't all hard work... we did have time for the nicer things in life,' Jacob said. '...or else you wouldn't be here... would you now?'

'About a year after I completed my apprenticeship, with me as the best man, Barney finally married Ethel Cocking at St Andrew's Church. Mr Kingston, George Simmons and many of our friends, who were in dock at the time, came to the church and to the *Coach and Horses* pub for the celebration drinks. As you can imagine, with anything that Barney was involved with, it was an enjoyable and lively affair... Cheerful fiddle music was being played, plenty of ale was being drunk and everyone was having a good time. That is until, late in the afternoon when a figure from the past, Albert Barker, staggered into the pub and went to the bar. He was drunk...

In a slurred almost incoherent voice, he gruffly ordered his ale and went and sat in a dark corner. At first Barney didn't notice him, but Mr Kingston and I did. Sitting alone, he looked around taking in all that was going on. As he slowly drank his ale, Barker never took his eyes of Barney and Ethel. He finished his pint, got out of his seat and unsteadily walked to the bar to order another glass. That's when Barney saw him...

Leaving Ethel, he walked over. Mr Kingston and I rose from our seats in anticipation. I can remember thinking, there's going to be trouble...

'Hello Mr Barker,' said Barney as he extended his hand. 'It's my wedding day... will you take a drink with me... can we forget the past, shake hands and let there be good humour between us this fine day.'

Barker, swaying slightly, faced Barney and glared at him.

'What? You...you must be joking,' Barker snarled. '...Why should I shake hands and drink with you... ya Fenian bastard... you had me spragged.'

'No I didn't,' replied Barney, surprised by the venom in Barker's slurred voice after so many years. '...I didn't have anything to do with you leaving the *Mary-Ann*... That was all your own doing.'

'Yes you did... you and your miss-nancy friend over there,' Barker replied gesturing towards me.

Swaying and unsteady on his feet Barker spat out his hateful spite. He had spittle on his lips and his breath reeked of stale beer and tobacco. He stunk. Barney took a step back.

'...and even if you didn't... why should I raise a glass to an Irish piece of shit that has defiled yet another sweet English girl.'

'Will she see those stripes on your back tonight... or has she already added some of her own to them?' he said.

Barker really hated Barney and the Irish... why, we never ever found out.

'You evil foul mouthed bastard... for sure you're a stench in the nostrils of honest and decent men.' Barney snarled back.

He had gone red in the face and was very angry.

'For that insult... I should thump you, ya lousy turd... but it's my wedding day so I'll not,' said Barney glaring hard at Barker, before suddenly adding,

'The 'ell I won't.'

With that he punched Barker to the ground.

The music stopped, Mr Kingston and I rushed over and stepped between them.

'Barney... that's enough,' I said. 'Don't let him spoil yours and Ethel's special day.

'Jake... Mr Kingston... did you hear what the miserable git just said about Ethel?' said Barney, who was still very angry.

'Yes...yes I did Barney... he's a drunken low-life, so let it go... and calm down,' was my reply.

'Jake's right Barney... calm down now and get back over to that lovely new wife of yours... you've a wedding to celebrate,' said Mr Kingston.

'Yes sir... for sure I will,' Barney replied and turned towards a distressed Ethel, who with her mother's arm around her had watched Barney thump Barker. She had never seen him so angry before.

Mr Kingston helped Barker, who was not too badly hurt, to get to his feet and led him towards the door.

'Shame on you Albert Barker for spoiling the lad's wedding... best you'se leave now,' said Mr Kingston.

'...Just so that you'se knows... the lad had nothing to do with me letting you go... you brought that on yourself for being too handy with the rope end... I did warn you!'

Barker didn't really take any notice of what Mr Kingston had said. He stopped walking and looked back at Barney.

'This ain't over yet... ya Irish bog bastard,' he shouted.

'No Barker it's not,' Barney shouted back.

'... but for your sake, you'd better hope that it is...or for sure one day soon, you'll get what's coming to you,' Barney threatened.

Mr Kingston took Barker outside and then returned to the celebrations. Barker never came back in to the pub. Barney consoled Ethel and before too long, he had regained his cheerfulness and the music started to be played again. Leaving Ethel with her mother, he came over and put his arm around my shoulder.

'Well now Jake,' he said to me. 'It can't be a proper Irish wedding without a punch up can it.'

'I don't know Barney... first one I've been to,' I said jokingly.

Everyone, even Mr Kingston who hated violence, laughed at what Barney had said...

Although he had made a joke of it, I could tell that Barney was still angry at the vulgar comment Barker had made about Ethel. There would be a day of reckoning...

Chapter 15

Drink and the Scourge of the Coopers

'After the wedding, until they found a place of their own, Barney and Ethel continued to live at the lodging house. Only this time Barney shared a bed with Ethel and not with me. I shared another bedroom with just two lodgers. Mrs Cocking had a small room to herself. She was in her fifties now and hadn't been keeping the best of health of late. It suited her to not have so many lodgers to look after. Barney became a major source of income to the house. Not that he minded. This was the first proper family home he had ever lived in. And, he had his best friend sharing it with him... It was a very happy home.

It wasn't too long before they started a family. Just over a year after the wedding, Ethel had a son, whom they called James. He was the first of the eight children, three boys and five girls, she and Barney had together... Although, Barney and I were not really brothers, I looked upon his children as my nephews and nieces and your cousins Sarah-Eliza. I was so pleased when he asked me to be James's god father.

'Jake my friend... when are you going to find yourself a nice girl and get married,' Barney asked me at James's christening party.

'How do you know I've not already,' I replied with a laugh.

'Well now... I think you would have told me,' said Barney. 'For sure I know you well enough.'

That's true enough,' I replied. 'When I do Barney... you'll be the first to know.'

'...Besides, how will I know if I've found the right one without your seal of approval?' I said.

'I'll be happy to give it, Jake my man... better not be too long about it though... A bachelor's life, like old misery guts Barker, is not for you.'

'No! That's for sure,' I replied.

Every so often I lapsed into Barney speak... we both laughed.

I chose not to tell him about Eleanor Jewitt, a very attractive young woman I had seen when I took our money to the bank, because there was nothing really to tell. One day I would pluck up the courage to speak to her... Then I may have something to tell Barney, but not before...

'That's enough about weddings and babies for now,' said Jacob. '...there is more that I need to tell you about the perils of being a fisherman.'

'Will you tell us about your wedding, grandad?' asked Grace, who had enjoyed hearing about Barney's.

Jacob smiled at Grace.

'Yes dear, I will do, because that is also important... but all in good time,' said Jacob.

He drew on his pipe and made them wait before he carried on. He was a master story teller!

'Fishing was and still is a very hard life, fraught with danger and the potential for disaster... The more Barney and I learned and the more experienced we became, we soon realised that the fortunes of fishermen was down to fate and providence... You could do the same things, day after day, in the same weather conditions and be fine... But, if god wills it, on another day, it could be your last day on Earth,' said Jacob.

'Even though you may not want to hear what I am going to tell you next, I think you should. It is important that people remember... remembering our past, children, can add value to our futures,' Jacob said earnestly.

'Memories are like gold... so very valuable, because they shape our thinking.'

Jacob paused and looked intently at the children and then at his daughter. He spoke slowly.

'In the twenty years between Barney's baby James being born and your tenth birthday Sarah-Eliza, one thousand, two hundred and eighty seven fishermen sailing from this port were lost at sea,' Jacob said.

'...Can you imagine that many people... do you understand that number... Gabriel...Grace?' Jacob asked.

Even though they nodded their head in agreement, he wasn't sure that the two younger children really understood the magnitude of what he had said. Again Jacob drew on his pipe and gave them a moment to think before he continued to tell the story...

'There are those who would argue that, there was an equal danger and the potential for loss of life in many of the industries that were helping to make and shape this wonderful country of ours... Industries that made Great Britain great! Although the mills, the mines, the factories, ship building and construction industries all had more than their fair share of fatalities, in the days of the wooden smacks, until the steam propelled iron hulled trawlers came along, fishing took a devastating toll of men and boys... and even then although the fatalities were reduced, they were still higher than all the other industries'

'I don't want to keep repeating myself talking about the tragic losses... so, I'll not say anything else on that matter right now,' said Jacob.

'...Although there is something else regarding good men being lost at sea that I will have to tell you later.'

'For the smack owners, darker more difficult days were drawing near... Not all the dangers that we fishermen had to face and endure were naturally occurring. Heavy seas and foul weather we expected and learned to cope with. Unfortunately, some of the worst and most dangerous situations for the smacks and men were man-made... Because of the continuous daily hazards and dangers of fishing, sadly, many fishermen turned to strong drink to help them cope while at sea... But, not on Mr Kingston's smacks, I hasten to add...

Greed and the willingness of some men to exploit the weaknesses of others, led many fishermen into disaster and ruin... More often than not, what started as just a drop of alcohol would become a binge drinking session with shocking

252

results... Drink wasn't the answer to their problems,' Jacob said.

'It was the problem!'

'Time and again crews were drunk to a man. Frequently even the skipper was so drunk that he was unable to take control of his vessel...'

'That's unbelievable, father,' said Sarah-Eliza.

'Where did they get the drink from grandad,' asked Daniel.

'Some, they took on board the smack themselves,' Jacob replied.

'...but most came from Dutch and German traders who were quick to exploit the situation and, feed the fishermen's craving...'

'The 'Coopers', as they became known, were smacks fitted out purely for the sale of spirits and tobacco. They sold or, if money was not available, bartered vast amounts of alcohol to the English fishing fleet... Not only did these coopering boats lead to the bartering of ships' stores and gear for cheap grog, they encouraged theft and dishonesty, which helped bring about the demoralization of the hands... and some of the skippers. Consequently, coopering led directly to unnecessary risk and loss of life... They were floating grog shops of the worst description, and were under no control whatever...'

'Obviously, this caused great concern to the smack owners. Drunkenness took a dreadful toll on both men and the vessels... There were cases of men falling overboard and drowning as a result of drinking bouts... Unbelievably, sometimes because the entire crew was so drunk, an apprentice boy, with little or no seagoing experience would have to take control of the vessel... This immoral bartering system brought ruin to many skippers and their crews... In reality, the coopers were really no better than pirates...'

Jacob looked at the children. For dramatic effect, he leant forward towards them and changed the tone of his voice.

'You may find this hard to believe, children... the evil of bartering grew so much that in the worst days of the coopers it wasn't unknown for a skipper, in order to satisfy his craving for drink, to barter away all his gear and even, in extreme cases, the smack itself,' said Jacob.

'Well now, what do you think about that?' he asked as he leant back in his chair.

'What? I cannot believe that,' Sarah-Eliza exclaimed. 'You're exaggerating the story a little bit now, aren't you father?'

'I mean... just for drink they bartered away a smack and equipment that wasn't theirs,' she added.

'No dear, I'm not... although I wish that I was,' Jacob replied.

'The concerns of the smack owners were taken up at government level... Communications on how to deal with the coopering problem passed between her Majesty's government, Queen Victoria, was our monarch at the time and, the governments of the foreign countries who were keen to stop this nefarious traffic... Although most of these coopers sailed under foreign flags... It grieves me to say this, but evidence emerged, which showed that some coopers sailed under the British flag and, took their stores on board in British ports...

'Eventually coopering was brought under control... but not before much equipment had been bartered, many men had been ruined and many lives unnecessarily lost,' Jacob explained.

'What's bartered mean?' asked Grace who was trying hard to understand.

'Swopsies,' said Daniel smugly. '...don't you know anything?'

Jacob frowned at Daniel.

'Don't be so clever, Daniel, it doesn't become you... Grace is only nine and asked a perfectly good question,' Jacob said.

Daniel dropped his head and looked down at his feet and mumbled a half-hearted, 'sorry!'

'So you should be, Daniel,' Jacob replied tersely before continuing.

'Drink drove many fishermen to commit awful crimes. Extreme brutality was common place, few victims dared to complain... even those who did were often not listened to... In the days of the sailing smacks foul deeds could be and were so easily concealed... Many dreadful offences, some I've already told you about, were committed for which no punishment could be imposed, because the perpetrators were not known... Hearsay evidence suggested that in drink, some skippers subjected their apprentices to cruelty bordering on the insane... When the boys took their complaint to the police, it was they who were hauled before the magistrates and often jailed for desertion and absconding...'

'What? That's terrible father... how was it allowed to continue?'

'Yes it was terrible,' said Jacob. '...that was why Barney and I became so passionate about the issue... and determined to see it stopped.'

'Was it stopped, grandad,' asked Daniel.

He wanted to get back into his grandad's good books again.

'Yes, Daniel, eventually... but it was a long time before it stopped altogether.' Jacob replied.

'Occasionally some crime would come to light, which would be dealt with by a magistrate or, in more serious cases a judge and jury... These cases gave the public a brief insight into the lives of fishermen and, told of heroes, villains and the victims of the early fishing fleet... Men and boys courted death as part of their everyday working lives. One, in which drink, sadly played a major and often tragic, role... It was coopering and drink that eventually led to the ultimate downfall of Albert Barker... which I'm going to tell you about in a moment...'

Jacob sat upright and with his hands on his knees and with a cheery smiling face looked at the children.

'...But, before I spend more time talking about old misery guts, I want to tell you a nice part of this story... I want to tell you about how I met your grandmother, Eleanor Jewitt...' he said.

Grace smiled back at her grandad and then at her mother. She was interested again!

'I first saw your grandmother when I opened the savings accounts at the bank for Barney and me, soon after we first started fishing. She was in the bank, holding hands with a tall heavily whiskered well-dressed gentleman, whom I later learned was her father and the manager of the bank. Other than finding her pig-tails amusing, because I thought they looked ridiculous, I took little notice of her... Why should I? I was only thirteen and she was twelve. She didn't notice me at all...

I didn't see her again for a several more years... In fact, I had nearly finished my apprenticeship when I next saw her and really took notice for the first time... Gone were the pig-tails, which I would have loved to have pulled when we were young. She had turned into a beautiful young woman... with flawless skin, hair the colour of ripened corn and blue eyes. Your grandmother was very, very attractive. She was, what Barney would have called, a head-turner...'

Jacob stopped talking and had a wistful far-away look on his face. He was reliving that special moment when he knew who he wanted for his wife. He smiled wryly at Sarah-Eliza, sighed and continued to talk. She instinctively knew what he had just been thinking. She smiled back and nodded her head. Not a word needed to be said between them.

'Although Eleanor wasn't officially working at the bank, she was frequently there helping out... After all her father was the manager. When I had concluded my business, without making it too obvious, I would often just look at her... I could find no reason or excuse to talk to her, no matter how much I wanted too... If she wasn't there when I did my banking, I'd often hang about outside hoping she would turn up and I could get a glimpse of her. More often than not, on most days I went away disappointed...'

Jacob laughed out loud.

'I was totally infatuated,' he said.

Two or three more years passed and although I tried to catch her eye and smile at her whenever I could, not a single word passed between us. Although, I was pleased though when she smiled back at me and occasionally held my gaze. So, when Barney asked me at James's christening, *'when was I going to find a young woman to marry,'* I already had, but didn't have a clue as to how I could let her know that I was

256

interested in her... Fish, big or small, foul weather and heavy seas I could deal with. But, when it came to women, I was hopelessly gauche and naïve... She must have thought I was an imbecile who, every so often, came into the bank and stood grinning at her...'

'Oh father! ...Were you really that hopeless?' asked Sarah-Eliza, who had started to laugh.

'Yes dear, sadly I was,' said Jacob. '...I was inept and ill-at-ease in the presence of refined young ladies... Not that I had met many at that stage of my life.'

Sarah-Eliza gently laughed at the thought of her father being awkward and clumsy. She had never thought about it before. To her, he was always the epitome of a professional gentle businessman. At this stage the boys had lost some of their interest and looked bored.

'How did you manage to sort it out father?' said Sarah-Eliza, '...you must have done, or we wouldn't be here.'

Daniel yawned.

'Well now!' Jacob said sounding like Barney. '...I didn't...Eleanor did... She spoke first.'

'What?' asked Sarah-Eliza, '...we are here because my mother spoke to you first.'

'Yes dear, she did... it was quite by accident really,' said Jacob.

'One day, I was going into the bank as she came rushing out, not looking where she was going... She caught me off balance and collided into me... knocking me over onto the seat of my pants and dropping her handbag at the same time...'

The children laughed at the thought of their grandad being knocked over onto his backside.

'Embarrassed and red-faced, I got to my feet and before I could say anything she spoke,'

'After three years, this is a fine way to start a conversation, Jacob Rawlings,' she said.

I was taken aback... It never occurred to me that she would know my name, or that she wanted to talk to me.

'Oh, I'm so sorry, Miss Jewitt are you ok,' I asked in a nervous squeaky voice.

'Yes I am fine, Mr Rawlings... Aren't you going to pick it up for me,' she said looking at her handbag.

'Yes...yes... of course,' I replied as I bent to recover the handbag.

I had never felt so clumsy in all my life and Eleanor could sense it. She smiled at me and took the initiative.

'You look badly shaken Mr Rawlings... I'm just going to that tea-shop across the road, would you like to accompany me and take some tea?' she said. '...That is, if you don't think me too forward and bold in asking you.'

'No, no Miss Jewitt...it will be my honour to escort you to the tea-shop,' I said rather stiffly.

'Come on then,' she said smiling at me. 'And, Mr Rawlings, don't be so formal.'

With that she put her hand on my arm and led me across the road. Once we were in the tea-shop I relaxed and enjoyed her company and she did mine. We made each other laugh and although proprieties were observed, we were not formal and uncomfortable with each other... She called me Jacob and I called her Eleanor but, when others were around us, it was Mr Rawlings and Miss Jewitt... I knew that morning this was the woman I wanted to marry... For a few years, from a distance, I had admired her. Sitting with her, eating cake and drinking tea, I realised that I was in love with her... but, it would be quite a while before I told her...'

'That my dear daughter was how, at the real age of twenty-three and, ten years after I had left Calthorpe, I met your mother...who became your grandmother, children.' Jacob said smiling broadly.

'...After that first meeting, Eleanor and I would often meet in the tea-shop, or go for a walk through the nicer parts of the town or along the sea-front... I told her about my life and the plans that Barney and I had for the future as smack owners... I also told Barney and Ethel, who was now pregnant with their second child, about Eleanor, they were delighted for me. Barney recommended marriage...'

'One beautiful sunny morning, several months after we first went to the tea-shop, as we were out walking, Eleanor stopped, turned to face me and asked,

'Do you really care for me Jacob?'

'Yes...yes I really do,' I replied.

'I wanted to tell her more, but was unsure how to do it,' Jacob said. 'I was uncomfortable and not very good in these circumstances...'

'I mean do you really, really care for me?' Eleanor asked looking me in the eyes. '...You never tell me you do,'

She looked so lovely. I couldn't help myself.

'Eleanor...I love you,' I blurted out. 'I...I truly, truly love you.'

'Oh Jacob... Jacob, that's wonderful, because I love you too,' she replied before throwing her arms around me and kissing me on the lips.

I was surprised and flustered. We were stood in the middle of the street. It was so improper for her to kiss me in the full view of strangers. She didn't care. Her face was a picture of happiness. Seeing my reaction she laughed and said,

'Oh...don't be so stuffy Jacob...no one knows who we are.'

Just as she said that, a man who was walking down the street, smiled and winked at me as he passed by. I smiled back, secretly pleased.

When Eleanor kissed me, that was the moment when we realised we would get married, but first I had to formally meet her parents. As I was sailing the next morning, meeting her mother and father had to wait until the next time I was in dock. Happily we continued with our walk. For a while very little was said between us. We were elated that what we had each been feeling for some time was now out in the open and all that needed to be said had been said...

Although I was nervous when, several weeks later, I walked up to her house in a nice part of the town and knocked on the door, I needn't have been. Mr and Mrs Jewitt were very hospitable, kind and made me most welcome. Seeing that I was uncomfortable as we took tea, they did their best to put me at my ease...'

Jacob noticed that the two boys were not really interested in hearing this part of the story...

'I won't bore you with too many details of that first meeting with Grandma Eleanor's parents except to say, Mr Jewitt was impressed with my plans to become a smack owner... Although marriage was not mentioned on that occasion, we all knew that was what would happen; I think he liked the idea of Eleanor planning to marry a smack owner and not just an employed fisherman...

Mr Jewitt, Samuel to his friends, was not only a bank manager; he was a Freeman of the Borough and also a magistrate. Whoever married his daughter would be entitled to become a Freeman if they weren't already one by birth-right. Social status was important to him... Mr Jewitt, being a magistrate, would later prove to be very helpful to a friend of mine...

'I can see from your banking and savings Jacob that you are thrifty and serious about becoming a smack owner... When you, and your friend Barney, are ready, if need be come and see me and let's see if the bank can help,' said Mr Jewitt.

'Yes sir, thank you... we will,' I replied.

Jacob chuckled. Even if the children were getting bored, he was enjoying telling this part of the story. They would just have to be patient and wait.

'I really don't know why I was surprised that Mr Jewitt had taken the trouble to look at my banking details. After all, I was courting his daughter and like all fathers he wanted the best for her and, had to be sure that whoever she married could provide for her...

It was two more years before Grandma Eleanor and I got married and, at least another year after that before Barney and I were in a position to become smack owners. Before then we still had more to learn and our money needed to be saved. And, there was another incident with old misery guts Barker that had to be dealt with...

'About twelve years after the trip when he first laid the rope's end across Barney's back, Albert Barker, was sailing as the mate on another company's smack... One night in *The*

Crooked Billet, we were talking to a fourteen year old apprentice boy from the workhouse named James Bratton. We had befriended him because he looked so frightened and vulnerable. He told Barney and me about how he had been frequently punished by Barker…especially when Barker was drunk. It seems that in the years since we had sailed with him, Barker had become more brutal and excessive in his handling of the young apprentices... He really was a very lonely old man and drink, which fuelled his extreme behaviour, was his refuge from the reality of the lonely life he had.

Besides being beaten in various ways, many bruises and scars from being rope-ended were still visible on Bratton's body. He had also been compelled to eat 'slithers', a filthy jelly like substance, which causes a stinging pain if it comes into contact with the skin… Barker also forced him to eat lice and fish guts and held his head down in a bucket of filthy water, before he was thrown overboard, fully dressed with sea boots on and towed behind the vessel. Barker was allegedly drunk at the time, from grog supplied by the Dutch and German Coopers who, as I have already told you, were the scourge of the fishing fleet.

'The miserable old git did what?' Barney asked angrily. '…Did he really do all that?'

Barney had never forgotten or forgiven Barker for the rope-ending he had received from Barker all those years before, or for the foul insults he made about Ethel at their wedding.

'Yes, and more,' Bratton replied nervously.

'Have you made a complaint to the rozzers?' Barney asked.

'No, I haven't…they wouldn't believe me… Would they?' said Bratton.

'For sure they will… The miserable old git is still at it…he needs to be stopped.' Barney said.

He was quite agitated.

'What do you think, Jake?' he asked me.

'I agree, Barney… Now then, Bratton, were there any witnesses?' I asked. '…Think now!'

'Yes there was… but will they help?' Bratton asked. 'I don't want to become known as a stoolie, or sent back to the workhouse.'

'They will… we'll talk to them and you won't be a stoolie.' Barney told him. '…This sort of thing 'as got to be stopped... For sure we'll help you.'

'Are you sure it will be alright?' Bratton asked again.

'Yes it will... Jake and I will come with you to the Bridewell,' said Barney.

'Through prompting and being encouraged by Barney and me, Bratton went to the police station and made a formal complaint against Barker... I did something else... I went to see Mr Jewitt in his capacity as a magistrate.

He listened intently as I told him how Grimsby was developing a justly deserved reputation for the cruelty to lads at sea. He was appalled at the stories and incidents I told him about, such as the fate of Frederick Brewer at John Grice's hands and the uncaring attitude of some of the smack owners...'

'Mr Jewitt... it's a hard enough life, without the sadistic behaviour of people like Barker and Grice,' I said.

'Jacob... is all that you are telling me really true... No exaggeration or embellishments?' he asked.

'Yes sir... every word is true,' I replied.

'...Believe me, I could take up much of your valuable time telling you all that I have seen and heard these past years that I have been a fisherman.'

'The lads need to be safe in the knowledge that if they complain or report such cruelty, they will be believed and taken seriously by the police and their worships the magistrates.'

'Then it must be stopped... What do you want me to do, Jacob?' Mr Jewitt asked.

'Use your influence... just make sure young Bratton gets a fair hearing is all I ask,' I said.

'Ok I'll see what I can do,' Mr Jewitt replied.

'...Thank you for coming to see me and telling me the appalling truth about what sometimes happens out there.'

He paused and looked at me before saying,

'Jacob, you've got a wise head on those young shoulders... You should go far!'

'Thank you Mr Jewitt... I appreciate that,' I replied, genuinely pleased by what he had said.

'I'm lucky... I've got a good teacher in Henry Kingston,' I added.

'I can see that,' Mr Jewitt replied.

'Albert Barker was brought before the magistrates and accused of the ill- treatment and assault of James Bratton... He was found guilty and was sentenced to three months imprisonment with hard labour in Hull Gaol... Although Mr Jewitt wasn't on the bench, he was sat in court listening to the case. Hearing the magistrates pass sentence, he smiled and looked over at me and Barney who were there to support Bratton... I smiled back and nodded my acknowledgement and thanks...

'Yes! ...How do you like them apples...ya miserable sadistic git?' Barney shouted as Barker was taken down.

As he left the dock to begin his prison sentence, Albert Barker turned and glared his hatred at Barney. His eyes were so full of malice and an unspoken promise that this wasn't the end of the matter. Not that Barney needed to worry. Barker never ever rope-ended anyone, or even sailed again. The daily hard work of walking the tread-mill in the gaol proved too much for him and his body that had been addled by drink over many years. He had a fatal heart attack and was buried in the gaol... Not a single soul mourned his passing...

'That's sad father,' said Sarah-Eliza. '...Everyone should have someone to mourn for them.'

'Yes... I suppose it is,' Jacob replied. '...but Barker brought it on himself.'

'As you sow... So you shall reap... Isn't that true children?' Jacob asked.

Unsure what to say the children just nodded and mumbled, 'yes grandad.'

'What happened to James Bratton father?' Sarah-Eliza asked.

263

'He fared well... Mr Kingston took over his indentures and he sailed with us.'

Jacob paused and thought for a moment before he carried on talking.

'I regret to say, sadly, not all magistrates would have convicted Barker. At that time, regrettably, many owners, merchants and even magistrates, especially those that had a financial investment in the smacks and trawlers, actually turned a blind eye or, were in denial regarding these alleged hardships and ill-treatment the apprentice boys faced... Unfortunately for some lads, even after the reforms and regulations, which would soon be forthcoming, the attitude of denial prevailed for many more years to come...'

Jacob sighed loudly and drew heavily on his pipe.

'To explain this, I need to briefly jump ahead a few years,' Jacob said.

'Nearly twenty years later in the late 1890s, shortly after I became a magistrate, I was having a rigorous discussion, though some would say argument, at my club with some local businessmen and other magistrates. When asked about his understanding regarding the ill-treatment and brutalising of apprentices, another local magistrate, whose name I will not tell you because we regularly see him and his family in church on Sundays, denied that it happened. He argued that often, the alleged incidents were exaggerated by a few trouble causers... He also contended *'there were no real cases of hardship'*, but accepted there were rare cases of *'hard discipline'*, when mates and third-hands had, quite rightly he said, beaten boys with rope ends.

When pressed and asked if there was great mortality among the fisher-lads, he bridled and huffed and puffed before replying,

'Poppycock... absolute nonsense... we have the finest sea going boats on the coast and our boys are not afraid of going to sea.'

'Never have I met a more deluded or misinformed magistrate... I was determined that if such cases came before me when I was on the bench... they would get a fair and just

264

hearing... Fortunately, not all magistrates held the same draconian blinkered opinions... And, there were also others within the fishing industry that held more progressive views,' Jacob said assertively.

'About the time of Barker's incarceration the Board of Trade directed that an inquiry be held into the apprenticeship system to address numerous complaints and criticism about the system. Two commissioners were appointed and instructed to confine their inquiries to Grimsby. Along with many others, smack owners, merchants and some apprentices, both Mr Kingston and George Simmons, who held strong views on the subject, were requested to speak to the commissioners... I wanted to be part of the enquiry, but was never called... Nevertheless, I aired my voice and opinions and championed the rights of apprentices often enough in the years to come...

After the enquiry, although the commissioner's report was favourable in broad principle to the apprenticeship system, it was also very critical...It stressed that the condition of the apprentices was far from satisfactory, due mainly to the lack of proper monitored training and supervision. Specific recommendations were made... one of which was implemented almost immediately. The Port Superintendent would record, *'...all assignments, cancellations, and terminations of indentures...'* And, would also keep details of the character and complaints relating to apprentices...

Not before time, the industry was becoming regulated... These records were started in 1880, a year after Grandma Eleanor and I got married, which I will tell you about in a moment... The entries recorded when the boy signed his indenture and gave details concerning his, name, age, where he came from, length of apprenticeship to be served, master and where he was to live... Important additional details were added to the records when the Superintendent interviewed the boy during the period of his apprenticeship and as reports of the boy's activities and progress were received... At long last, the apprentice boys had a voice and would be listened to...' Jacob said with passion.

'Although my memory is not what it was... I know for a fact that, in the first decade after the records began over three thousand three hundred apprentices signed indentures, of these: more than a thousand absconded, about twelve hundred completed their apprenticeship and nearly nine hundred indentures were annulled... Sadly, during this decade, over two hundred boys died...'

'Can you believe that... over two hundred boys were killed?' Jacob asked.

'No father I cannot... It's amazing that you remember so much detail,' said Sarah-Eliza.

'Disturbing numbers like that you don't ever forget!' Jacob said rather bluntly.

'...also by that time, Barney and I were sailing as mates and under Mr Kingston's guidance, we had each made short trawling trips as the skipper... and, we became smack owners later that same year, which I will tell you about in a moment, so we needed to understand and operate within the new regulations... Especially if we wanted to employ apprentices,' Jacob explained.

'Perhaps more importantly... Barney and I cared a great deal about apprentices' welfare and did all we could, whenever we could to improve their lot,' Jacob explained.

'Oh, of course... I think I now understand, why you are telling this story in the manner that you are.' Sarah-Eliza replied.

'I'm pleased that you do Sarah-Eliza... your understanding will be very important to you in the future.' Jacob said looking directly at her.

What a strange thing for her father to say, Sarah-Eliza thought... That was another question she needed to ask!

Jacob could see that the children, especially Gabriel and Grace were becoming restless and a little bored. Too much detail he thought... but at least his daughter knew what he wanted her to know and just as importantly Daniel was still paying attention.

'Let's forget about all these nasty and unpleasant things for a moment while I tell you about your grandmother's and my wedding,' said Jacob, grinning from ear to ear.

'Yes please do, grandad,' said Grace. She had become interested again.

Both Daniel and Gabriel sighed. 'Oh bother!' one of the boys muttered.

Chapter 16

It Was a Very Good Year

'Fourteen years after I left home, in August 1879, in front of our families and friends, Eleanor Jewitt and I married in the parish church of St James. It was bright and sunny day, which added to the cheerful atmosphere in the church. Eleanor was a vision of loveliness. Standing there, with Barney next to me as my best man, I felt so proud, as I watched her walk down the aisle with her father towards me. The church was full and all eyes were on her...

'Isn't she a picture, Barney,' I said.

'Well now...that she is Jake... Ethel and I are so pleased for you brother.'

'We've come a long ways together... haven't we?' said I.

'That we have, Jake... that we surely have,' Barney replied looking me in the eye.

It was a good job Eleanor was drawing closer, because Barney and I had become misty eyed... It wouldn't have taken much for us to start crying with the emotion of the moment and our treasured memories of the journey we had made together...

Mr Jewitt, being a well-known and relatively wealthy professional man and magistrate wanted a large wedding with as many of his friends and business contacts there as possible. Aunt Eliza and two of my mama's sisters and their husbands, who I've not really talked about, came over from Calthorpe for the wedding. As did all my half-sisters and brother, including Charlotte, who by then was a young women and I'd never ever met her... They were all staying at the hotel next to the station, which was only a stone's throw from St James church...

After my Aunt Eliza and my sisters Hannah and Harriett, had come to Grimsby with the bad news about my mama, nine years earlier, I never returned to Calthorpe although I promised them that I would... There were far too many bad memories there. I had kept in contact with Aunt Eliza by letter but, that was it... My wedding was the first and would be the only time I ever spent with all my siblings together... although, at the time we didn't know it...

'Oh Jacob... She is so beautiful,' Aunt Eliza tearfully said to me after the ceremony.

'Your mother would have been so proud of you and what you've become,'

'Thank you Aunt... I'm sure she would... I do believe she is watching me now...that's how I cope with losing her,' I said, trying hard not to become upset.

'She is Jacob... she is... keep believing,' Aunt Eliza said before embracing me in a tearful hug.

Letting me go but still holding my hand she said,

'William is watching you too... he was a good man, Jacob... It's a pity you didn't know him... he would have also been so proud of you.'

'Yes Aunt... I'm sure he would,' I replied.

'Go on... go and greet your guests and don't worry about soppy old me... I'll be alright.' She said with a forced smile.

'Thank you Aunt,' I said and kissed her on the cheek.

Mr Kingston, his brother Charles, with whom I had also sailed, George Simmons and Biffo Barnes and many other friends that we had made since we got here, all came to the wedding. Ethel, who was pregnant with her third child, came along with their eldest son James, who by then was five years old. Although Mrs Cocking's health was causing concern and she was unsteady on her feet, she made the effort and came dressed in her Sunday best and wearing an outrageous hat... Quite what Mr and Mrs Jewitt made of her and her one toothed smile is anyone's guess.

Ethel had forbidden her from smoking her pipe, *'Mother you leave that pipe at home... we can't have you shaming Jake...can we?'* Barney later told me what Ethel had said. I was glad that Molly was there... I was very fond of her. After Barney had married Ethel, she said it was time we started calling her Molly...

'Following the ceremony, the wedding feast was held in the banqueting suite of the hotel where my family was staying... It was a grand affair...silver service and uniformed waiters and waitresses. Mr Jewitt meant to impress his guests. Everyone seemed to be having a good time... Mr Kingston, who was seated next to Aunt Eliza, was keeping her entertained... almost to the point of flirting with her... I did notice that he also spent some time deep in conversation with my new father-in-law, which I assumed was business related. But, with Aunt Eliza, he was attentive, animated and laughed a lot as did she...

As we were mingling with the guests after the meal, Barney walked over with two glasses of ale. One he gave to me. Without a word, we touched glasses and toasted each other. After taking a sip from his glass he said,

'Jake my man... I do believe Mr Kingston might be planning to soon be your Uncle Henry.'

We both laughed, he didn't need to explain further.

'I think you're right... he does seem interested and Aunt Eliza is certainly encouraging him.' I replied. '...that wouldn't be a bad thing for them both would it?'

'No it wouldn't...but let's not get ahead of ourselves... We've this wedding breakfast to finish first,' said Barney laughing.

With that, we touched our glasses together again and, toasted each other's health only this time we spoke,

'Good health and good fortune to you and Eleanor, Jake.'

'...Same to you and Ethel, Barney!' I replied.

In fifty years I never ever tired of Barney's company or his humour...

'The celebrations went on until late in the evening... With the cheers and good humoured banter from our guests ringing in our ears, Eleanor and I took our leave and climbed the stairs to spend our wedding night in the bridal suite of the hotel. The next morning, we sheepishly breakfasted with my aunt and sisters and brother. I do believe that Eleanor blushed when my sisters giggled as we entered the dining room... After breakfast, Eleanor and I caught the train and went to Lincoln for a couple of days for a short honeymoon. This time I wanted to look round and enjoy the city, without having to keep looking over my shoulders for the crushers, as Barney would call them... Mr Kingston had arranged to call on my aunt later that morning to show her around the docks...'

Jacob chuckled. 'It was another very happy time.'

'When Eleanor and I returned from Lincoln, we went to live in our first home. It was a small but comfortable two up two down terraced house, not far from the town centre and not quite in the East Marsh. It was an agreeable area in which to live. Eleanor's father, who asked me to call him Samuel, provided the deposit as a wedding present and arranged for me to take a mortgage through his bank for the balance... Over the next few years, Samuel would provide invaluable advice and support as we bettered our circumstances and were financially able to move to a larger house... Nonetheless, our first house was a very welcoming place to come home to... Once the door was shut behind us, that little house became our sanctuary where we could escape from the madness of the world around us...

'Grandma Eleanor soon became pregnant and, less than a year after we married, although she had a difficult time, was safely delivered of a beautiful baby boy... your Uncle William. We named him after my father. In fact, we named him after both our fathers. His full name was William Samuel Rawlings...'

The children, especially Grace and Gabriel looked at each other rather bemused. *'Uncle William'* they said to each other with quizzical unknowing expressions on their faces...

'Who is he?' Gabriel whispered to Grace.

'I don't know,' Grace replied shrugging her shoulders.

Jacob looked first at Sarah-Eliza and ever so slightly shook his head. She understood why! And then looking at the children he explained,

271

'William was your mother's brother... The only son I ever had,'

'...and a fine young man he was...but.....'

The rest of the sentence was left unsaid. Some memories were still distressing. However, sooner or later the children would need to be told. After a brief pause, initially with false enthusiasm, Jacob looked up, smiled at the children and carried on talking.

'1880 would turn out to be a good year for Barney and me... Besides Grandma Eleanor giving birth to William, in the early Spring, Ethel and Barney had their third child... a second son, who they named Joshua in honour of my brother who had died when only a week old. *'I like that name Jake'*, Barney said. Grandma Eleanor was godmother to Joshua. William's god parents were Barney and Ethel. His christening provided another opportunity for Aunt Eliza to come over to Grimsby. Two of my sisters... only this time I cannot remember who, also came across with her. Grandma Eleanor and I noticed that Aunt Eliza seemed especially pleased to see Henry Kingston at William's baptism... We wondered why! It turned out that they had been exchanging letters since our wedding the year before...'

'Why did they write to each other?' asked Daniel.

This time it was him and not his younger siblings who was being naïve.

'Oh, I think I'll let your mother explain that later,' Jacob replied breaking into laughter.

'Thank you father... I really appreciate that,' Sarah-Eliza said in mock annoyance.

Jacob smiled again.

'Shortly after William was born, I had the honour to become a Freeman of the Borough of Grimsby,' said Jacob. Again the children looked at each other unsure what their grandad was talking about.

'What's a freeman grandad?' asked Daniel. '...isn't everyone except the prisoners in gaol free?'

Jacob chuckled at that.

'No, no...It's not that sort of free, Daniel... It's a very old and ancient tradition that is only granted to some special people... under certain circumstances.' Jacob explained.

'...It's important that you understand, because when the time is right, both you and Gabriel will also have the opportunity to become freemen.'

Even though they didn't have a clue what it meant to be a freeman, Daniel and Gabriel beamed with boyish delight.

'What about me?' Grace asked petulantly, feeling a little left out.

'No Grace... because you are a girl, you cannot become a freeman... But, when you get married, your husband will be able to become a freeman,' said Jacob.

'...so you will benefit just the same as your brothers.'

Although Grace smiled at that, Jacob thought he better make it clear what he was talking about.

'Freemen of Grimsby are descended from, or whose wives or daughters are descended from, Freemen of the ancient Borough of Grimsby. Through ancient custom, the freemen benefit financially from the freemen's estate, which is the land within the Borough of Grimsby that had been vested in the freemen by King Edward III, over six hundred years ago in the middle-ages...'

'Wow...crikey!' said a very impressed Daniel. He looked at Gabriel and Grace. They all smiled.

Jacob continued. 'Women were not able to become freemen in their own right... But being the daughter of a freeman, which you are Grace, their husbands could become a freeman after they married. This is what I did...Grandma Eleanor's father, Mr Jewitt, was a freeman. So I became a freeman by marrying the daughter of a freeman...this enabled me to participate in the financial and other benefits that had been granted to the freemen all those years ago by the old King...'

'Do you understand what I am saying?' asked Jacob.

The children nodded their heads.

'In the olden days... the life of a freeman was one of public duty and responsibility. Freemen were the only citizens

273

allowed to vote in elections and, the only ones who could occupy positions of authority within the local government or hold public office... Each Freeman was required to swear an Oath of Allegiance... being a freeman was a very serious business indeed. All municipal duties were carried out by freemen. The mayor, common councilmen, aldermen, constables the bailiff and magistrates were all freemen...In reality and practice, the freemen were running the town and, the Freemen's Court provided all the local government the town needed. People who were not freemen could not vote and therefore could not hold Borough office...

It's all changed quite a bit now... it's not the same anymore... but it is still important and an honour to be a freeman...'

Jacob laughed, which made the children smile.

'...As well as being able to vote and the added benefit of not having to pay the tolls within the borough...freemen had ancient pasturing rights for all their livestock... Not that we have any sheep or cattle to pasture any more... but, if we had instead of our flea bitten cat, Mr Tom......'

Jacob laughed again heartily. Sarah-Eliza and the children laughed with him.

'Only the freemen had the right of education for their children at the Corporation Grammar Schools for boys and girls, which opened in the 1860s. Your mother and Uncle William went to different schools from Barney's children... I was a freeman and Barney was not, although he was very impressed that I was...'

Jacob paused before adding in a more serious tone of voice,

'Now then... If I had been charged, after that rowdy fracas in the *Freeman's Arms*, I would have had a criminal record and could never have become a freeman and or a magistrate...and, your mother and you children wouldn't have gone to the Grammar School...

'We have all benefitted greatly and, you children will continue to benefit by being a freeman, long after I am gone.

So, we have much to thank Barney and Mr Kingston for their action on that day...' Jacob said.

'Yes... a great deal.'

'Don't talk about you being gone Father... I don't like it,' said Sarah-Eliza.

Ignoring his daughter's comment and drawing on his pipe, As he had done a couple of times before, Jacob waited for a moment to let what he had just told them to sink in before he continued.

'Later that same year, Barney and I were ready and able to take the next step on the journey to making our fortunes,' Jacob said.

'1880 was a very good year... one day, among many good days in that year, particularly so!'

'I can remember it so very well...it was bitterly cold. Near horizontal sleet chilled the marrow of your bones when Barney and I stood on the North Wall and took possession of the very first fishing vessel that we owned. Not that we really noticed the cold... a life at sea hardens you to the extremes of weather. Our life's journey together, which had begun fifteen years earlier as we hid in a dirty alleyway in Lincoln, had brought us to this point. Not only were we now experienced fishermen, we owned our first smack. Together, for £405 and another £50 for fitting out, we had bought the smack *Serendipity*, which had been built in 1856 in Gravesend...

My best friend was now my business partner... As we stood in that freezing cold, admiring the smack we looked at each other, smiled and shook hands.'

'Well now Jake, aren't we a pair? ...your mammy and papa would be so proud of what you have become,' said Barney. '...You've not let her down.'

'Aye, that she would Barney... she'd have been right proud of you too... Just like Aunt Eliza said, you're part of my family now,' I said.

'You really are my brother in every sense of the word.'

'Do you really think so Jake... is that how you see me?' Barney asked earnestly.

He was more than a little choked with emotion at hearing what I had said.

'Well now Barney my lad… for sure you're my brother… be Jesus, I've spent more than half my life with you,' I replied in the worst imitation of Barney's accent that you will ever hear.

The children laughed at their grandad.

'…Don't you go getting all sentimental on me Barney McHugh… we're business men now,' I added.

With that, without feeling any embarrassment because people who were working, or sheltering from the cold, nearby may be watching, we stopped shaking hands and embraced each other firmly. Not another word was ever said on the matter…

Although it was a day for celebrations it was also a day for remembering how it had all been made possible… '

'During the heyday of the sailing smack, before the increase in iron steam propelled trawlers, it had been quite common for a skipper with a small amount of capital to buy a smack with a heavy mortgage and to 'work out' the vessel until the debt to the mortgagee was paid. In the early 1880s, the more modern sailing smacks with steam capstans, stores and nets cost from £1200 to £1500 to be ready for sea… The practice of 'working out' the purchase of a new smack entailed a high degree of risk. Very few skippers had much start-up capital and therefore had to borrow the greater part of the purchase price of their smack. They would have a big debt that needed to be repaid… Consequently a bad season, or even a single poor voyage, would sometimes be sufficient to cause the mortgagee to repossess the vessel if the owner defaulted in the repayment of the loan, forcing the unfortunate owner into bankruptcy…

'Do you understand what I am saying?' asked Jacob.

'Yes,' said Daniel quite firmly.

'I think so,' said Gabriel.

Grace shook her head. 'No Grandad, I don't.'

'Ok Grace... Let's say I borrowed three-pence off you to buy a new jig-saw puzzle and didn't pay you the money back...What would you do?' Jacob gently asked her.

'I'd take the jig-saw off you and keep it for myself,' she replied.

'Exactly, Grace... that's what I am talking about... The person who lent the money taking back the item that the money has been used to buy,' Jacob said cheerily.

'...Only, instead of pennies, I am talking about much larger sums of money and instead of jig-saws I am talking about fishing smacks... now do you see?

Grace smiled and nodded her head and then looked across at her mother, who smiled back at her.

'As with all businesses that have a high risk the rewards could also be great. A skipper who bought a vessel on a mortgage could either become a bankrupt or, he would succeed in paying for his vessel. And, in time, that vessel may even become the first in quite a large fleet of smacks...

Although a new sailing smack cost well over a thousand pounds it was always possible for ambitious men, which Barney and I were, to purchase a good seaworthy vessel relatively cheaply. Especially when the sailing smacks started to become obsolete... In a remarkably short period of time, steam trawlers made the sailing yawls and ketches out-of-date. As a result, obsolete sailing vessels and equipment commanded very low prices... Within just a matter of months a smack owner could find that the resale value of their new sailing smack had dwindled away to a fraction of what they paid for it...

If you started out initially with an old smack, it was always possible for a skipper or owner to progress to buying bigger and newer smacks until they was in a position to purchase one directly from the builder's yard... As several smack owners did… And, that, my dears, was exactly what Barney and I intended to do… At a total price of £455, the *Serendipity,* which we renamed and registered as *Sarah Rawlings* was bought from a mortgagee who had foreclosed on an owner for defaulting with his repayments... However, one fishing vessel was never going to be enough for us.

'The *Sarah Rawlings* was the first of a fleet of Rawlings and McHugh vessels... and is how your inheritance, the Rawlings and McHugh Steam Fishing Company, was started,' said Jacob.

'How did you find the £455 you needed to buy the first smack father?' asked Sarah-Eliza.

'Although Barney and I had both been saving money almost from the day we had started fishing... We added the £120 plus the interest that it had earned, which your grandmother had left me to our savings. It still wasn't quite enough to buy the *Serendipity* and provision her for the first voyage before we started catching fish and earning money. Just as he had promised all those years before, the remainder came from Henry Kingston,' Jacob replied.

Deep in thought, Jacob paused again for a moment and sucked on his pipe. He sighed before adding,

'Although she had been dead for fifteen years and lay in an unmarked prison grave... my mama, through her legacy, was still helping to shape and provide for my future.'

'It was a really very proud day for Barney and me, when our smack the *Sarah Rawlings,* (the renamed *Serendipity*), left the lock gates and headed down the River Humber towards the sea for the first time. Until we bought a second smack, which was our intention, Barney and I had decided to sail the *Sarah Rawlings* as joint masters. There was no problem about who was in charge. We never ever contradicted or competed with each other, although if truth be known, I have to admit, Barney was a far better sailor than me. In all our life together we never once had a proper argument...

To be able to provision and supply the *Sarah Rawlings*, for each voyage, with Mr Kingston's help and advice, in addition to the stores for which we had to pay cash, we set up credit accounts with the ice company, marine stores and ships chandlers, like Charlie Banks's. This was where we had been kitted out before our first voyage on the *Mary-Ann* all those years before. Mr Kingston vouched for our good name and integrity. He even offered to underwrite any default in payment we may make. He trusted us not to, and we never ever let him down...

'Mr Kingston really was good to you and Uncle Barney... wasn't he grandad?'

'Yes Gabriel... he was very good to us,' Jacob replied. '...He treated us kindly and generously... he was the type of man we would all do well to copy.'

'When I look back at my life I realise that, from the moment I walked away from the cottage in Calthorpe until now I have been very, very lucky. Besides Barney, who is the best, I have made some wonderful friends, who have helped me on my way. And, I have also survived some extremely dangerous situations and circumstances in which I found myself...when others did not and perished... This is why... I suppose, I became determined to help others less fortunate than me...'

'As I have got older and become more contemplative, I really do believe that was the purpose the Lord God had planned for me.' Jacob said. '...to help others wherever I could.'

Jacob paused for a second or two and drew on his pipe, he was thinking again.

'Enough of that maudlin talk... let's get back to the story of the first voyage of the *Sarah Rawlings*... shall we?' he asked.

'Barney and I had a hand-picked crew that we could trust. It included experienced fishermen and apprentices with whom we had become friends over the years. James Bratton, you might remember who misery guts Barker had beaten, completed his apprenticeship with Mr Kingston and then sailed with us as a deckhand on that first voyage... I cannot begin to tell you the deep joy we felt as we sailed, with Barney on the tiller and I stood beside him, towards the fishing grounds...

The *Sarah Rawlings* sailed well and through the creaking of its timbers and sounds of the sails and riggings it had a different voice from the *Mary-Ann*. I imagined it was my mama talking to me and promising to take care of us whenever danger threatened...'

'Does that sound daft?' Jacob asked and without waiting for an answer added.

'...Although it was a cold day with a biting wind, the spray hitting our faces was invigorating and intoxicating. Barney and I couldn't have been happier...'

Jacob's face was so cheerful and his eyes bright as he recalled and enjoyed the memory of the special day that Rawlings and McHugh became a fishing company. Sarah-Eliza looked at him with pride and delight. She really loved her father, seeing him smiling and happy, brought her real contentment.

'We fished the Dogger bank for about ten days before we returned to port. The weather had been kind to us and was normal for a November... a few blustery winds and some heavy swell, but nothing too bad. Although the sea always should be respected, we hadn't had to fight or ride out any severe storms, which allowed us to concentrate on fishing and earning money. We found and caught plenty of fish. Not an overly exceptional amount, but still a good series of hauls of quality fish nevertheless. If the market was favourable we would show a profit... In the manner of Mr Kingston, after the last haul, Barney said,

'Let's take her home Jake.'

'Aye, let's do that Barney my man,' I replied feeling so happy and fulfilled.

'Taking it in turns on the tiller, Barney and I brought the *Sarah Rawlings* back to the mouth of the River Humber and back home to our families. The familiar landmark of the old Smeaton lighthouse that had guided us for years would soon be replaced by the Spurn lighthouse, which is still there today. We couldn't wait to get home to our wives and children, but first there was the little matter of unloading the fish onto the pontoon and hoping that it would sell well...

Off-loading the fish from the smack, Barney worked like a dervish and seemed to have the strength and stamina of ten men... I suppose that's only natural when it's the first time you are putting your own fish onto the market...We were anxious and excited at the same time... We needn't have worried.

Again lady luck seemed to be on our side. Not a lot of fish had been landed for that morning's market, so what was landed sold for a price higher than normal. Ours sold well and after paying the costs of our stores and provisions, we actually made a profit...

'Well now Jake... has ya done the sums, have we made any dosh,' he asked earnestly.

'Yes Barney, that we have,' I said.

'Even though Barney's reading and writing had got much better, he was still not so good with the numbers and arithmetic and left that side of the business to me...'

'...After paying for stores and the men's wages we have quite a decent amount of cash left over for putting in the bank.'

I cannot recall exactly how much it was, but I do remember I was trying hard to contain my excitement and be calm and matter of fact about it... I also remember, dear old Barney wasn't so reticent about showing his delight when I told him how much.

'HOW much?!' he asked again, not quite believing what I had told him.

'Be Jesus... for sure we are on our way to becoming rich men... aren't we Jake?' he said in a booming voice and patting me on the back with the big ham fisted hands that he had.

'That we are, Barney... that we are.' I said equally delighted, but not quite as noisily.

'I wasn't going to be a kill joy and dampen his enthusiasm but, I was already thinking that we may not catch as many fish each trip and, the market may not always be so favourable... This later proved to be the case... because that was the pattern of fishing. Good trips, bad trips and indifferent trips... Over the years we had them all...

Barney and I worked hard and we worked our crews hard without taking unnecessary risks. Although we had some bad trips in those early days, generally we did well. Well enough, in fact, to be able to buy our second smack, the *Unity*, another repossessed vessel, less than two years after taking the *Sarah Rawlings* on its first trip... We had no debt left on the *Sarah Rawlings* and only needed a small mortgage for the new smack, which I arranged with my father-in-law, Samuel Jewitt...

Other than the *Sarah Rawlings*, which we agreed would always be called that, Barney and I had decided to name all of our new vessels the RAM vessels after our initials. That was Barney's idea... he had seen the word ram in the bible and thought how much it looked like the combined initials of our surnames, R & M. Over a beer, we came up with the name and decided to register the *Unity* as the *Kingston Ram*. Mr Kingston was delighted when we told him, *'thank you'se lads'*, he said, *'I really appreciate that'*...

Barney and I agreed, initially I would sail the *Sarah-Rawlings* and he would sail the *Kingston Ram*, which was a newer and slightly larger smack. And, for a while, the two smacks would leave and enter the port together and fish close by each other. That decision, along with the fact that you, Sarah-Eliza, was about to be born, proved to be a decision that possibly saved both our lives...

'What are you saying father...I don't understand how me being born could have saved yours and Uncle Barney's life.' Sarah-Eliza exclaimed, rather surprised.

'You've never ever told me anything like that before... Mind you there's much that I have heard this weekend that you have never said before,' she added, a little bit disconcerted.

'Yes dear...don't chide me... There has been much that I have told you,' Jacob replied.

'And, there is still more that I need to tell you...be patient with me... It's all for a purpose... you'll soon see.'

'Sorry, I don't mean to chide you father... but, I have some questions that I need answering later when the children are in bed,' said Sarah-Eliza.

'Ok dear... that's fine, but can I carry on now?'

Sarah- Eliza nodded her agreement.

'Unlike Barney's wife, Ethel, who comfortably carried and safely delivered all her eight babies, your mother did not have the easiest of pregnancies when she carried your brother William and then you... She was often very sick and the last few weeks on both occasions were particularly difficult for her... Consequently, I decided, if only for my own peace of mind, that I wanted to be in dock, and at home by her side, when the time came for you to be born. Barney agreed and was happy to be at home for a little longer than we normally would be...

At that time, we were still taking the *Sarah Rawlings* and the *Kingston Ram* out together and our fishing trips were only lasting between eight to ten days... So, it was quite easy for us to plan a schedule of voyages and to work out when to be in dock so we didn't lose too much time away from the fishing grounds...

Although we had planned to be home, it was fate or perhaps God's will that, your Uncle Barney and I were in dock when your mother's time came... Being ashore, we were spared from the greatest disaster that befell the fishing fleets and claimed so many...'

Chapter 17

Happiness and Despair Make Strange Bed-Fellows

Sarah-Eliza and the children, who were sat listening in silence, wondered what their grandad was going to say next. Once he'd stopped fiddling with his pipe, which had gone out, they would soon find out. Jacob shuffled in his seat and made himself comfortable once more. He was thinking and biding his time before starting again. After listening to him for most of the weekend, Sarah-Eliza realised what he was doing. She instinctively knew that what he was going to tell them next wouldn't be the happiest part of the story. Just as their patience was wearing thin, Jacob finally spoke.

'It was late in the afternoon of Monday 5th March 1883, when your mother went into labour. We didn't know at that time, whilst she was struggling to give birth to you, the British Isles would be swept by a violent gale from east north east during Monday night and early Tuesday morning. It was the worst storm to hit the east coast of Britain for over one hundred years. Numerous disasters occurred to shipping, not just the fishing boats, brigs, barques anything that was out there was caught up in it. There was a terrible loss of life... the poor unfortunate souls...'

Jacob paused and slowly drew on his pipe, which he had refilled and lit. Sarah-Eliza and the children were listening with engrossed attention. He was taking his time. These were particularly painful memories.

'...The day had started off well enough. It was early spring and was quite mild. The sky was bright and the daffodils and crocuses, which were in full bloom in our garden, were a pleasant sight to see. Your mother had been sat out in the garden admiring the flowers and resting, when she went into labour. She was quickly conveyed inside, taken to bed and the mid-wife sent for. As her labour progressed into the evening, almost out of nowhere, the lovely spring weather dramatically changed. What at first were just blustery winds within a short space of time became a raging gale...

From the safety of our house, we could hear the wind howling and damage being done to properties all around us... Slates were being blown off the roofs and chimney pots were falling to the ground. Much, much worse than the bad weather we had yesterday when I first started this story. As bad as it was in town, we had no real idea of the chaos and tragedy that was occurring out at sea and along the coast line...

At first, I wasn't interested in the weather and the howling wind, my beautiful Eleanor labouring to deliver you, and screaming out loudly in pain was all that mattered to me... Little did I know that as your mother laboured for several hours trying to bring you into this world, many men and boys were in peril and were fighting for their lives out there on a raging sea...

The Great Storm, as it became known, had quickly turned into the severest of gales. Blinding snowstorms at intervals were adding more danger to the violence of the wind and waves. The gale, which raged with the greatest severity all along the east coast, from the north of Scotland right down to the Kent coast was taking a heavy toll on ships and men. Vessels that had made it back to the River Humber estuary were not always safe. Several smacks were blown ashore onto the beach a few miles down from the lock gates. Even the smacks and ships that were already safely tied up in port were taking a battering... Some lost parts of their masts and rigging...

When badly damaged smacks and ships started to limp back into port, the news of the unfolding disaster quickly spread around town. Rather than wait at home not knowing, several smack owners, many men, wives and girl-friends hurriedly made their way to the docks. Not that they could do anything. For them being at the dock waiting on the quayside was the only place to be. Braving the ferocious weather and in agitated concern they stood around, sheltering wherever they could, hoping to hear some good news about their smacks or, their friends and loved ones. Hysterics, rumours and half-truths abounded...

Slowly, as the night progressed and more and more damaged smacks managed to return to port, news would come in. With each new arrival, I really should say survivors, people, especially wives and girlfriends, would clamour noisily around the smacks shouting question after question at the smack's tired and battered crew. Have you seen the 'Westward-Ho', or the 'Blighty' or, the names of many other smacks? They were distressed people and desperate for some news. Any news! It was the not knowing that was the worst part...

Sometimes, news would come in about a smack that was lost only to be contradicted later by someone else saying it had made it to safety. With no radio communications, like we have now, the only information came from what people saw, or thought they had seen. Not all of it was reliable. In the chaos of the darkness, the raging gale, howling wind and the snowstorms, no one was really sure what was happening, except everyone knew it was bad and many men were dying out there...'

Jacob paused. No one spoke. They all sat patiently waiting for him to continue.

'The first I really learnt of the growing tragedy was when Barney came rushing to my house. His face was very grim. After enquiring about Eleanor, who he could hear still struggling to deliver you, and asking if it would help if Ethel came over, Barney said to me,

'Jake, it's not good... it's far worse than that there big blow when we started out... I think many smacks and men are going to be lost.'

'Is it really that bad?' I asked only half-heartedly, I'm sorry to say.

I was more concerned about Eleanor being safely delivered of her child than the smacks at that point.

'JAKE, it's as bad as it gets,' he said gravely and louder.

I was still only half-listening. Eleanor's wailing and screams, which could be heard all through the house, really had my attention and were cutting me to the bone.

'Jake...Jake, listen to me... the *Mary-Ann* and the *Mary-Jane* are out there,' Barney said as he got hold of my arm.

'What? ...oh no, Mr Kingston.........,'

What I was going to say next was cut short because, at that very moment, Eleanor gave out one last shrill cry and then we could hear you crying. My darling daughter, you were born at the very instant I learned that Henry Kingston was out there in that maelstrom fighting for his life and the lives of his crew...'

Jacob paused and sighed before drawing on his pipe. The sadness in his eyes was evident to all.

'The next day and in the days that immediately followed, more reliable information started to come to light. It took quite a while to be able to see the full picture of the disaster, because we didn't know which smacks had been lost and which had made it to safety in any one of the ports and harbours along the east coast. Eventually the local newspaper published as near as correct a list as it could. Fourteen smacks had been lost, I can't remember all the names, but there on the list was the *Mary-Ann* and the *Mary-Jane...*

No one knows what happened to the *Mary-Jane,* it just vanished. The *Mary-Ann* was last seen off Flamborough Head trying to make it to port. Henry Kingston was at the tiller, bawling into the wind to encourage his crew, when it was swamped by a huge wave and taken down. According to witnesses there was nothing that could have been done to save them. It was as if the sea just opened up a great cavernous mouth and swallowed them whole...

'Henry Kingston, George Simmons, Biffo Barnes; all good men were taken by the sea that night,' Jacob said sadly and shaking his head.

'I had lost my benefactor, my mentor and my friends.'

'Do you know... never once did I get to call him Henry... he was always Mr Kingston,' said Jacob sorrowfully.

Tears were now streaming down Jacob's weather-beaten face. Hearing how Henry Kingston had died and seeing her father so distressed, Sarah-Eliza had started weeping, as did Grace. The boys were trying hard to hide their sniffles. To stifle his tears, Jacob took a handkerchief from his pocket and blew his nose, dabbed his eyes and slowly regained his composure before carrying on.

'When I wrote and told my Aunt Eliza what had happened, from the tone and nature of her reply, I could tell she was heartbroken. She never ever found love, nor visited Grimsby again...

Within five to six weeks, the full magnitude of the storm became known. Grimsby lost fourteen smacks and ninety six men and boys, which left thirty-four widows and sixty-seven orphaned children under 14. Many of the fisher lads were the entire support of mothers who were already widowed. The tragedy cast a gloom over the whole town. People and traders donated £1,000 to a fund, which was set up to help the families of those who had been lost...'

Jacob stopped talking and leant forwards towards the children.

'As a good Christian, I shouldn't say this, or even feel this, but there was some justice in the storm,' he said.

'God didn't just take the best... Evil John Grice, who you may remember was the reason the apprentice Frederick Brewer committed suicide, was washed over board and lost...'

'He died screaming and terrified!' said Jacob. '...Isn't that poetic justice?'

The children and even Sarah-Eliza nodded their heads in agreement.

Jacob leant back in his chair and waited a moment.

'Grimsby was not alone in suffering the tragedy. The port of Hull suffered even worse. They lost thirty-two smacks, over two hundred fishermen with sixty-five widows and more than two hundred orphans and many aged parents. Through local response, over £3,300 was collected but it was not enough to meet the needs of the families... There had been no such disaster in human terms in living memory...'

'As I told you earlier, figures like that you don't forget,' Jacob stressed.

Soon the full extent of all the losses of each port all along the east coast became known. In a letter from the Lord Mayor of London, who had met with Mayors of Hull, Grimsby and Colchester, plus representatives from Scarborough, Yarmouth, Lowestoft and several other ports appealing for a national relief fund to be set up, he wrote: *'The statements made to me by that deputation were of a very distressing character being to the effect that in one gale alone no less than 982 men and boys were drowned'*.

'Can you imagine that, Sarah-Eliza... Nearly one thousand people became a statistic the night you were born,' Jacob said passionately but not meaning to hurt her.

He was still very upset, as was Sarah-Eliza, who really didn't want to know what she had just been told. It wasn't a fair thing to say. This terrible connection would now stay with her for the rest of her life... Given the manner in which her father had been telling the story, she felt sure that was exactly what he wanted.

'Although there were only one or two funerals, because very few bodies were actually found, a memorial service for the lost fishermen was held at the parish church of St James... Many hundreds of people, relatives, smack owners, merchants and local citizens attended to pay their respects,' Jacob said sombrely.

'It was one of the darkest and most despondent periods in the history of the town... For me, other than when I heard about my mama's death, it was the saddest time of my life and there was nothing that I or any mortal man could have done about it... It was God's will.'

Jacob stopped talking, sighed and sat looking at the flames from the fire dancing in the grate. Patiently and in silence, the children and their mother waited.

'About two months after the disaster, Barney, Molly Cocking and I were asked to go to the office of Alex Browne and Son, a local solicitor, for the reading of Mr Kingston's will. It was a meeting that changed all our lives forever. Mr Browne opened his office door... he looked exactly like I had imagined he would. Small, narrow shouldered and walked with a slight stoop. He was going bald and had a pair of rimless glasses perched upon a quite large hooked nose. He had a friendly welcoming manner and greeted us cordially.'

'Come in Mrs Cocking... gentlemen,' he said.

We went into his office, my father-in-law Samuel Jewitt was already there. It turned out that, at my wedding, he had agreed to act as an executor of Mr Kingston's will. I later found out why Mr Kingston had asked him to do so... We all shook hands and I greeted my father-in-law.

'Please take a seat,' said Mr Browne, gesturing to the chairs that were already positioned in front of his desk.

'I understand that you all know Mr Jewitt, who is here in his capacity as an executor of Mr Kingston's will,' said Mr Browne in a deceptively deep voice for a small man.

'Yes we do,' said I.

Barney didn't speak, but nodded an acknowledgement to Mr Jewitt and Mr Browne.

'It is a sad day indeed... Mr Kingston was a well-liked and respected man throughout the town,' said Mr Browne.

'Yes he was, Mr Browne...very well-liked,' I replied.

'Mrs Cocking sniffled but didn't speak. She was nervous. She kept looking around and seemed very ill-at-ease in Mr Browne's office. Barney, who was never the most comfortable in those types of surroundings, didn't say anything either. The loss of Mr Kingston had hit him hard. *It's like losing my father all over again... only worse. Mr Kingston looked after me and gave me a chance'.* Barney said to me when we found out that he had perished... I recall saying much the same thing back to him...

'We both openly shed tears,' said Jacob.

'It was a typical solicitor's office. There were papers everywhere. Some were in rolls tied up with red ribbons, others just piles of lose paper. Many were covered in dust... it was what I would describe as organised chaos. Seated behind his huge leather topped desk, which had a handsome ram's horn and silver inkwell as its centrepiece, Mr Browne had an array of papers in front of him. He looked up and at us over the top of his glasses...'

'Mrs Cocking ...gentlemen, this is the last will and testament of Henry Obadiah Kingston, dated 29th August 1879,' Mr Browne said rather theatrically and proceeded to read it to us...

I won't bore you with all the legal details and jargon... but, Mr Kingston had made provisions in his will that had a profound effect on the rest of our lives...

To Molly Cocking, he left the house in Orwell Street, with the instruction that on her death, ownership would revert to Barney and Ethel. So that she no longer needed to take in lodgers, Molly would benefit from an annual income of £40 per year from his estate for the remainder of her life. *'At this time of her life, she should be able to smoke her pipe in peace without having to worry about washing fishermen's soiled and smelly underwear'.* That made us all smile...

'What Mr Browne explained next shocked us to the core... We were left speechless,' said Jacob.

'In addition to a very special provision, which I will explain in a moment, Mr Kingston had instructed the executors of his estate to organise its distribution in this manner... A sum of £2500, plus a few personal items, would go to his brother, the Methodist Preacher, in Brixham. With regard to the ownership of the Kingston fishing fleet, his offices and his interests in the merchants with whom he had invested, would be shared on a seventy/thirty percent basis, between his brother Charles Kingston and George Simmons... Within his thirty percent, George Simmons would receive two of the smacks, *'In the expectation that you will thrive and prosper in the Christian manner that you rightly deserve'.* Mr Kingston had written...

Mr Browne continued reading.

'Barney and I were to receive from the estate, *'the sum of £2000 for the specific growth and development of the Rawlings and McHugh Fishing Company',* Mr Kingston had stipulated. If that sum of money had been all we were to receive, Barney and I would have still been delighted and extremely grateful... But, Mr Browne had more surprises in store for us...

Being the thoroughly prepared man that he was, Henry Kingston had also considered the situation whereby his brother Charles may die before him. In that case, and if George Simmons was still alive, he would receive sixty-five percent of the estate and thirty-five percent would go to Barney and me. *'Jacob Rawlings and Finbar McHugh, being of the same disposition as George Simmons, will make ideal partners to help him carry on the company in the same god-fearing manner that has been my guide and stay,'* said Mr Browne as he carefully explained Mr Kingston's wishes...

We were dumfounded... Barney and I looked at each in stunned amazement. Molly Cocking had been too shocked to speak from the moment she heard that she had inherited a house and an income. She never said another word all the while we were in Mr Browne's office...

That was not the end of it, as we found out when Mr Browne carried on explaining the will...

'Gentlemen, as Henry Kingston, Charles Kingston and George Simmons all perished in that terrible storm, Mr Jewitt and I, in our capacity as executors have concluded that other than the specific named provisions, there are only two major beneficiaries of Mr Kingston's fishing interests... that is, Jacob Rawlings and Finbar McHugh,' said Mr Browne.

'...And, as both Charles Kingston and George Simmons died intestate and are both unmarried, as executors we can only distribute the estate as we think Mr Kingston intended.' Mr Browne explained.

'What's intestate Mr Browne?' asked Barney.

'It means without making a will, Mr McHugh... so you and Mr Rawlings, other than the provisions I have already outlined are the sole beneficiaries,' he replied.

'What! What are you saying Mr Browne?' I asked, not quite believing what I had just heard. '...Barney and I are to inherit nearly all of Mr Kingston's estate?'

'Yes Mr Rawlings, that's just about the long and short of it,' he said.

'You will receive, all his smacks, offices and everything connected to his fishing business. Mr Jewitt is holding at his bank, details of how Mr Kingston invested in local merchants, ice providers and other businesses, these will all revert to your company, the Rawlings and McHugh Fishing Company... In addition, you will receive the insurance money for the smacks, *Mary-Ann* and the *Mary-Jane*, which were sadly lost...'

Barney sat open-mouthed, too shocked to say anything. It took a lot to stop Barney from talking!

'Congratulations gentlemen, you have just become wealthy men,' Mr Browne said.

He came from behind his desk and walked over to shake our hands, as did Samuel Jewitt. It didn't seem right that our good fortune was provided by the tragic misfortune of others...

'Mr Browne gave us a moment to take in what we had just been told before he continued. Over the next couple of weeks, Mr Jewitt and I will take care of everything...the transfers of ownership, new registrations and all other legal matters... You will have very little to do in respect of these provisions in Mr Kingston's will... There is however, another major requirement of the will that, Mr Kingston intended you both to become involved with...'

'If you choose not to, the other aspects of your good fortune, which I have already outlined, will not be withdrawn... When we were drawing up his will, Henry Kingston said to me, *'I know my boys, they won't let me down,'* said Mr Browne.

'What is it, Mr Browne?' I asked. 'What does Mr Kingston want us to do?'

'Mr Kingston had plans to be a 'philanthropist', that's my word not his, in every sense of the meaning of the word.' said Mr Browne.

'He has set up a trust fund and wanted to involve both of you in identifying how the fund should be used. *'There is something that I have seen in both of you that gladdens my heart and encourages me to think that you will support me in this endeavour',* he had written in his will,' Mr Browne explained.

'...Gentlemen... Mr Kingston, has transferred a rather large sum of money to a special account at Mr Jewitt's bank, which is to be used for the singular purpose of setting up a charitable trust fund to help fishermen and their families when in dire circumstances... There is over £25,000 on deposit at the bank.'

'What... how much did you say?' I asked. '...that's a fortune!'

'Yes it is Mr Rawlings... Mr Kingston had very specific purposes that he wanted the money to be used for,' replied Mr Browne.

'There's still more that you need to know,' said Mr Browne. '...To ensure that the trust fund remains viable and active, the Kingston fishing interests, irrespective of whoever has ownership, will contribute annually, for the next twenty-five years an additional sum, which they will determine but, it will never be less than £4000 per year... Mr Kingston has instructed.'

'Jake... Barney,' said Samuel Jewitt, who had mainly been sat quiet while Mr Browne read the will.

'...When I spoke with Henry at the wedding, he told me of his plans to set up this trust fund and how he felt both of you had the right qualities to act as trustees...'

'I totally agree with him,' Samuel said. '...You are fair and compassionate men who care about the lives and conditions of fishermen and their families and, want to improve their lot... Put quite simply, that was what Henry Kingston wanted too.'

' ...As you are now the owners of the Kingston Fishing Company, and are required to make an annual financial contribution to the trust fund... it makes sense that you act as trustees to help direct how the fund can best be used,' said Samuel.

For a moment, I sat in silence. Then Barney spoke.

'For sure... I'm no scholar, Samuel... How can I be one of these trustee things... I've only just learned to read and write,' he said.

'You can Barney, because you care about people... You don't need to be a scholar...you recognise hardship and injustice when you see it... Just give us your opinions... that's all you'll have to do,' Samuel earnestly replied. And, then added,

'You can talk...can't you?' He asked mischievously.

'With that, with the exception of Mr Browne who didn't know what the joke was, we all burst out laughing...

After talking through who the other trustees would be and how the Kingston Trust Fund, which is what we decided to call it, would work and, arranging to return the next time we were in dock, Barney, Molly and I left Mr Browne's office... As we walked away, our heads were in a whirl. There was so much to take in... Molly was delighted that she would no longer have to wash fishermen's clothes and make meals for people she often didn't like...'

'I'll sit on my step, smoke my pipe and watch the world and his dog go by,' she said cackling away to herself.

'You do that mammy... Ethel and I will occasionally sit with you,' said Barney smiling at his mother-in-law, of whom he was very fond...

It all worked out very well for Molly. Being able to relax and not having to work hard to survive was very agreeable. Her health improved and she lived for many more years until gently passing away in her sleep at the age of seventy-six...

'We all talked excitedly about what had happened. Barney and I couldn't believe our good fortune... If we had not walked down onto the North Wall at that particular time on that first day in Grimsby, seventeen years before, most probably, we would never have met Mr Kingston and sailed on the *Mary-Ann*. How different our lives would have been, if we had had the misfortune to sign on to a smack under a sadistic skipper like evil John Grice...

'Well now, that was fate,' said Barney when I shared my thoughts with him.

'No Barney... I believe that was my mama willing it for me,' I replied.

Barney could see that I was serious.

'Perhaps it was Jake... it would be really nice to believe that.' Barney said.

'Aye... that it would Barney,' I replied.

From the moment we left Mr Browne's office, our lives had irretrievably changed forever...'

Sarah-Eliza, who had been listening intently to her father, was about to find out that soon her life would irrevocably change too.

Chapter 18

Things Will Never Be The Same Again!

Sarah-Eliza had grown up knowing about the inheritance and had always been aware of the Kingston Trust Fund. Now she knew all the events leading up to it being established and why and how her father and Uncle Barney had become involved. She also understood why it was so important to them and why they cared so passionately about the good work that it did. As she listened to her father, his motive for telling the story in the manner that he had was becoming clearer. Although, she thought she now understood what this weekend had been all about, there were still some missing pieces of the mental jigsaw she was completing in her mind.

Jacob looked tired...telling this true story, with its raw emotions and painful memories, had exhausted him. But, he knew that it had to be done. Soon he would tell Sarah-Eliza the real reason why. He could see that the children were flagging and were also starting to look tired. As he didn't have much more to tell them, he decided to press on.

'Children, you have all been very patient. Over many hours this weekend, I have told you about some good men, some wicked men and many tragedies of fishermen and apprentice boys being lost at sea... I needed you to know how important it is that we don't forget all the suffering and the trials and tribulations that made Grimsby the town that it became,' said Jacob.

'You do understand that don't you?' Jacob asked.

The children nodded their heads in agreement.

'If I don't tell you... who else will...eh?' said Jacob smiling at them.

'...Most of what I am going to tell you now your mother already knows... So this part of my story is mainly for your benefit...'

'The *Sarah Rawlings* and the *Kingston Ram* became part of a larger fleet when we took over Mr Kingston's vessels. Out of respect for him, we didn't immediately change their names and re-register them as a RAM vessel. That would come later. The years passed quickly... Barney and I worked hard, both as fishermen and also as champions of the rights of fishermen and apprentices. We supported the Port Superintendent, the newly opened Fisher-Lads Institute and within the Guilds of Trawler Owners and Merchants, we frequently argued for proper monitored and supervised training for the boys. Just as we had learned from Henry Kingston, we also tried to lead by example...

Before long, we had gained a reputation similar to that which he enjoyed... We were considered to be fair and generous employers who didn't sorely use or abuse their crews... As our reputation grew, it wasn't difficult to sign up good men... We prospered and so did our crews... They earned a fair wage and were treated well. Henry Kingston once said, *'You catch more flies with honey than you do with vinegar!'* That was exactly how Barney and I ran our company... no rope-ending and no brutality... Even though, elsewhere in the industry it still happened...

The harder we worked, the more our company prospered and the better Grandmother Eleanor, your mother and Uncle William could live. Before too long, we were able to move into this lovely big house in one of the best parts of the town. And, we had Barney and Ethel living just round the corner... Our life could not have been better.

Over the years, Barney and Ethel had five more babies. Unfortunately, after your mother gave birth to you, Sarah-Eliza, she was unable to have any more children... That didn't matter at all. We were a very happy home with you and William... Your mother and I adored you both and we were very contented.'

Looking at the children, Jacob said,

'Barney's children were almost like brothers and sisters to your mother and Uncle William... They often came to visit and regularly stayed over... Both families always spent Christmas and holidays together...'

'This house regularly echoed with the wonderful sound of the children laughing, playing and running around,' Jacob said wistfully. '...If only my dear mama could have seen it.'

Jacob paused briefly.

'I really liked Barney's eldest boy James. Just like his father, he had a way and a sense of humour with him. Being five years older than his brother Joshua and our William, in one respect, he was a little bit like you, Daniel... aloof.' Jacob said, winking at Sarah-Eliza, who smiled.

'I'm not aloof grandad,' Daniel protested.

'Oh yes... you can be,' Jacob replied.

'What's a loof, grandad?' asked Grace. '...Do you know what a loof is Gabriel?'

Jacob and Sarah-Eliza laughed. Before any more could be said on the subject of Daniel being aloof, Gabriel ignored Grace's question and asked.

'Grandad... what happened to Uncle William... where is he?'

Slightly startled by this interruption, Sarah-Eliza looked with concern at her father...she knew that even after all these years talking about William could still upset him. And, with the range of raw emotions he'd been through over the past couple of days, she was sure it would do so again.

'Patience Gabriel... Please don't rush me... I will tell you about your Uncle William in a moment,' Jacob said gently. 'But first, let me finish telling you about James.'

'James, being the eldest of our children, was the first to show any interest in fishing and going to sea... He couldn't wait until he was old enough to be properly apprenticed... Barney insisted that he complete his schooling first.

'Well now... you don't want to be a unedumacated numpty like me,' Barney said to him.

'I don't know dad... for sure, you've not done too badly,' James replied.

That amused Barney...

'At the age of fifteen, when William and Joshua were only ten years old, James went to sea with his father for a couple of trips. Just like Barney, he loved it... the sea excited him. He decided quite early on that fishing would be his life... He was his father's son and took to sailing and fishing as easily as a duck takes to water...

Once we were certain that James had what it takes to become a fisherman, Barney and I thought it would be better for him, if he learned his skills on another of our trawlers and not with his father... so we apprenticed him to one of our best skippers, Arnold Wainwright, on the *Yorkshire Ram*... He did exceptionally well and learned very quickly... He did not disappoint his father. In later years, James would become one of the youngest skippers sailing out of the port... and he would serve with distinction in the Royal Navy during the Great War...

With the continuing success that all our hard work brought us, Barney and I became owners of quite a large group of companies of which the Rawlings and McHugh Fishing Company was just one. With guidance and help from Samuel Jewitt, we'd managed to build up most of the business interests that Mr Kingston had bequeathed to us... Although, there were some that, after taking Samuel's advice, we decided to move away from. In addition to the fishing we also became successful fish merchants in our own right...

On the catching side, as the years passed, we started to replace our sail rigged wooden smacks with iron hulled steam trawlers, which we were in a financial position to commission the shipyards to build. As more steam trawlers came to the port, not just our vessels... the casualty rate and numbers of ships lost at sea dropped quite sharply. Steamers, as we used to call them, could cope better with the ferocity of the sea better than wooden smacks... Nevertheless, fishing was and still is a very dangerous business... Not only were we able to build up a fleet of the latest up-to-date steam trawlers... we also employed the best professional skippers that we could find who held full certificates of competency...

'Did you still go out to sea grandad?' asked Daniel.

'Yes, Daniel... for many years I did,' Jacob replied. '...I stopped skippering and going out on a regular basis with the boats about 1898.'

'...That was thirty-three years after I had first set foot on the *Mary-Ann*!'

'Barney and I agreed, because of the increasing size of the company and the range of business interests we now had... even though Samuel Jewitt was advising us and we had reliable and honest people working for the company, they needed to be directed by someone on shore, which was me... He still sailed regularly though... Dear old Barney never ever lost his love of fishing and being out on the open sea.' Jacob added.

'The confines of an office is not for me, Jake,' Barney said. '...you're the scholar.'

'Remember... we agreed, I'll catch the fish and you do the numbers.'

We laughed and smiled at each other.

'Ok Barney my man, have it your way,' I replied to him. '...but, only on the understanding that as you get older...you'll spend more time ashore... Fishing is not a game for old men anymore!'

'For Christ sake, Jake... I'm only forty-eight,' said Barney. '...For sure I've twenty more years or so left in me yet.'

'Sorry Barney, you just look older... my mistake,' I said '...Ethel must be working you too hard,' I replied and winked at him.

'Well now, that's for sure,' Barney said and we both fell about laughing.

Jacob stopped talking. His head dropped and he looked down at his feet. Sarah-Eliza could see by the far-away solemn expression on his face, he was lost in thought and painful memories.

'Father, are you going to tell the children about William?' asked Sarah-Eliza. The tone of her voice gave away the concern she was feeling.

'Yes dear... in a moment,' Jacob said quite abruptly without looking up.

Eventually he raised his head and looked at the children, Gabriel in particular.

'Gabriel... you asked me what happened to your Uncle William... As much as it hurts me to do so I'm going to tell you,' Jacob said.

'...Although, as your mother knows, I have not spoken of this for many years... you all have a right to know what happened to William.'

'Your Uncle William and Barney's second son, Joshua, were nearly the same age and even though they went to different schools became best friends. They couldn't wait to get home from their schools and go out to play... Just like Barney and me, they were inseparable and regularly got up to boyish mischief. When they were fifteen and had finished their schooling, neither of them was a brilliant scholar, both tried going to sea... but, didn't take to it. Fishing was not the life for them... They wanted something else. They wanted adventure and to travel, William had told me... We were foolish enough to let them.'

'It was the worse decision, Barney and I ever made.' Jacob said forlornly.

'...Because I was financially able to... I indulged William. I also lived, more in hope than expectation, that he would get it out of his system and return home to learn how to run the business. If not at sea, but on the shore side of things... Barney thought much the same about Joshua...

Sadly, it wasn't to be...

In 1897, at the age of seventeen, William and Joshua left home with our reluctant blessing... We thought they would journey around England in stages and maybe go into Northern Europe... France, Germany and places like that. Grandma Eleanor, Barney, Ethel and I saw them off at the train station. After much hugging, tears from their mothers and them promising to write... we waved them off as the train, which still fascinated me even after all the years, pulled out of the station... They had plenty of money in their pockets and decent clothes on their back and in their luggage...'

'We didn't know that we would never see or speak to either of them again,' Jacob said.

His voice almost broke with the emotion and rawness of his memories. He stopped talking and took a moment to compose himself and collect his thoughts.

'Ironically, the boys only got as far as Lincoln where, as you know, Barney and I had met thirty-two years earlier... We don't know why or how they were persuaded, but William and Joshua joined the British Army. The Lincolnshire Regiment, to be precise... It wasn't long, thereafter before they got their craving for adventure and travel satisfied...'

Jacob faltered again and his voice wavered. He was taking his time, speaking slowly and picking his words very carefully. There were no dramatics or exaggerated gestures.

'The first that Barney and I knew about what they had done was when we received a very brief letter informing us they were with the 1st Battalion Lincolnshire Regiment. And, they had embarked with the British Army for the Sudan in Africa...'

'Golly... that's exciting isn't it Gabriel,' said Daniel insensitively.

Jacob ignored Daniel's comment and put his pipe in his mouth and drew deeply. He needed it. The taste of tobacco had a calming effect. Sarah-Eliza frowned at her son.

'In the Sudan, William and Joshua took part in the Battle of Omdurman in 1898. It was a one-sided battle, in which modern machine guns dominated and resulted in the slaughter of the Mahdist forces... Only forty seven British soldiers were killed but, more than ten thousand Mahdist were killed and thirteen thousand injured. William and Joshua, mine and Barney's innocent boys just eighteen years old, took part in that awful butchery and slaughter... and, undoubtedly would have killed fellow human beings...

William sent me a letter from Khartoum. You would think that how he described the Battle of Omdurman, *'as good sport, with some top class fellows'*, he was on a local pheasant shoot.

I couldn't believe what he had written. I was so angry with him and what I read that I threw the letter onto the fire... although I instantly regretted doing so it was too late to recover it. That was the last thing I ever received from my only son...'

Jacob was becoming red faced, breathing heavy and agitated, but he continued.

'That wasn't enough for those two foolish boys... While still in Africa, they transferred to the 2nd Battalion Lincolnshire Regiment and travelled with the army to South Africa and became involved in the Boer War. This was their undoing...

In many ways, the Boer War was different from other wars where two armies would face each other on a chosen ground and fire away... the Boers adopted guerrilla tactics. One day while out on patrol, William, Joshua and about twelve other soldiers and a junior officer were ambushed by the Boers. According to the 'official' report made available later, the patrol was trapped in a gulley and had to shelter from murderous crossfire from the Boers who were hidden in the rocks above them and trying to pick them off one by one...

It soon became clear to the officer leading the patrol that they couldn't stay there trapped in the sweltering African heat. He needed to somehow get word to the main body of the regiment who were only about three miles away... William and Joshua, being the youngest and probably the fastest runners, volunteered to try and break through the Boers' cordon and bring the help the patrol badly needed...'

Although Jacob's voice was now breaking and he was getting upset, he carried on slowly talking.

'Crouching low and trying to keep their heads down they ran together and were cut down in a hail of bullets before they had gone fifty yards. Though mortally wounded, William and Joshua didn't die instantly. Like the good friends they were, they helped each other to reach shelter behind a large rock. They were isolated... no one from the patrol could get to them and they couldn't move. Propped up against the rock in the searing African heat and with no water, they held each other's hand, talked and tried to reassure each other that they were going to be alright and slowly died...

They needn't have died... Only ninety minutes after their brave but foolish run, the Boers withdrew because a larger body of soldiers, who had heard the shots being fired, were fast approaching...

'Just ninety bloody minutes,' Jacob said vehemently, shaking his head. '...William, Joshua and three other soldiers were the only fatalities of the Boers' ambush.'

'They were later buried side by side near Ladysmith...'

The children were very subdued and Jacob had started sobbing, but he chose to carry on.

'It was nearly four months after the ambush before Barney and I received news about what had happened. Grandma Eleanor became hysterical and struggled at first to cope with the loss of William... For quite a while she just gave up and lost interest in everything. Ethel seemed to be made of stronger stuff and was able to cope much sooner. The fact that in addition to Barney, she had two other sons and five daughters who were strong support, I believe, helped Ethel to come to terms with the tragedy...

At first, it was a very difficult time for your Grandma Eleanor she only had me and your mother, who was only fifteen, for support. And, I was at work most of the day. Just when I thought I was going lose her to a never-ending pit of despair and melancholy, it was her father, your great-grandfather, who by then was an old man, who came up with the idea that helped bring her back.

'Jacob, she's spending far too much time alone in this big old house,' he said to me. '...Loneliness and not having anything to do or anyone else to think about is fuelling her depression.'

'...Eleanor needs something to do that will occupy her mind and give her something else to concentrate on.'

'What have you got in mind, Samuel?' I asked.

'The Kingston Trust Fund, Jacob... the trust fund... Let's make her a trustee or an administrator and give her something to do that has real responsibilities,' he suggested.

'...Make her think of others.'

Samuel knew his daughter...it was a perfect idea. After discussing it with Barney... that's exactly what we did. Grandma Eleanor was a little reluctant and unsure at first and needed persuading...eventually, she agreed to try. Once she got over her nervousness and uncertainty, and with a little cajoling and support, Grandma Eleanor became very single-minded about the Kingston Trust Fund and the practical and financial help it provided for others... In fact, she became very fervent and passionate about its purpose.

'Jacob... I didn't realise how vacuous and empty my life was... Living in comfort with money to spend whenever I wanted to,' she said to me over dinner one evening.

'...Working with the trust, has opened my eyes to the misery and hopelessness, which is the daily life of so many others.'

Not only did the trust fund become a major focus of her daily life....she was encouraged to help other benevolent funds and charities... Grandma Eleanor, thanks to her father's suggestion, had a purpose, which along with her strong Christian faith sustained her for the rest of her life... The wonderful reputation and respect that your grandmother earned in the town, was as a direct consequence of her having to find a way to deal with the tragic loss of our son William... So, some good came out of his needless and senseless death...'

Although she knew what had happened to William and her mother's way of dealing with it, Sarah-Eliza was gently weeping at hearing her father tell the children this part of the story. She thought perhaps it was time to finish the story telling.

'Father, it's nearly the children's bed-time and we haven't eaten yet. Shall we stop now?'

'No, no...I want to finish now... There's not much more I need to tell.' Jacob replied. 'Just give me a moment to get my breath back.'

'A few months after we learnt of William and Joshua's death at the suggestion of my father-in-law, I was proposed and accepted as a Magistrate...'

'The bench needs people like you, I've told you before that you've a good head on your shoulders,' Samuel said one evening when he, and your great-grandmother, joined Eleanor and me for dinner.

'...We need new blood and radical new ideas about justice ...There's too many old and blinkered views that will not serve the town, or the country, well in this next century... The ways of the world are rapidly changing.'

'So my dear children, I became a magistrate in 1899 and have been one ever since... I was only forty-six years old...one of the youngest magistrates in the county,' Jacob said proudly.

Being a magistrate meant that, even on an irregular basis, I couldn't go out with our boats as much as I had been doing... Nevertheless, it suited me to become a magistrate, especially as many 'fishing' related cases were still coming before the bench and, I had first-hand experience of life on a fishing vessel... I understood the issues, not like some of the misinformed magistrates that I have already told you about... It also complemented the work Barney and I and then Grandma Eleanor were doing with the Kingston Trust Fund...because we would be seeing at first hand the wretched manner in which some people had to live...

Everyone knows that the town grew and prospered through the fishing industry. Many people, like Barney and me, were lucky enough to make great fortunes. But for some, which included many of our crew members, life ashore though different, was just as hard for them as it was at sea...The conditions that some fishermen and their families had to live in during the latter part of the nineteenth century were often appalling... Squalid, poorly built, back to back houses with inadequate sanitation and overcrowding. Is there any wonder that the infant mortality rate among fishing families was so high.

In fact, the conditions were so bad that, the town on several occasions had to deal with outbreaks of Cholera... A Cholera outbreak, in 1893, which centred on the dockland area, where Barney and I lived and socialised when we first came here, killed two hundred and forty six people... Living, if you could call it that, in this wretched manner, was there any wonder that crime was so rife.

'I bet they didn't teach you that at school... eh!' Jacob asked.

The children shook their heads.

'No I didn't think they would,' said Jacob.

He was getting too serious again so he sucked on his pipe to give him thinking time.

'I've nearly finished, I just need to tell you about your dear old Uncle Barney,' Jacob said.

'All our energies went into making Rawlings and McHugh Steamship Fishing Company, one of the finest operating out of the port. And, that's precisely what Barney and I succeeded in doing. The port was getting busier and busier and we grew stronger and larger... But, we never ever forgot that the crews were vital to our success and they needed fairness, justness and protection....

'In the early 1900s, politically, Europe was becoming unstable and by the time that the dark clouds of the Great War, where your daddy was killed, were looming on the horizon, we had twenty-four trawlers in our fleet. The original *Sarah Rawlings* and the *Kingston Ram* were long gone but, both had been replaced with modern steam trawlers and re-registered with the same names... Those two special names would always link our future to our past...'

In the early 1900s an Admiral, Lord Charles Beresford, recommended in the event of a war, that to free up warships for other duties, steam fishing trawlers should be used in the role of minesweepers and a new rank, Skipper Royal Navy Reserve, to be introduced for the trawler skippers... Once it was inevitable that war was imminent, in 1914, approximately eight hundred trawlers from the River Humber fishing fleets were requisitioned for minesweeping and anti-submarine duties... Sixteen Rawlings and McHugh trawlers were among those requisitioned. During the four years of that terrible, terrible war... we lost nine vessels and their crews, to enemy action... Of the eight hundred trawlers that were requisitioned, nearly a half, were lost in the conflict...

Only one quarter of the Grimsby fleet, mainly the older early steamers, remained on fishing duties. Parts of the North Sea fishing grounds were placed out of bounds due to the dangers of enemy surface naval vessels and mines... By continuing to go to sea in those dangerous days, our fishermen helped to keep the country supplied with first class food source... Many decorations for gallantry and courage were earned by them... Unfortunately for some fisherman, even after the war was over, and fishing resumed, danger was still ever present from the hundreds of German mines that had not been cleared from the North Sea. Often, with fatal consequences, vessels would hit a mine, or one would get caught in the trawling nets and gear...

Barney decided he had been ashore too long and would go out for one last trip with his son James who was the skipper on the *Nottingham Ram*, one of our larger trawlers... James had served with distinction as a Skipper Royal Naval Reserve on the *Nottingham Ram*, after it had been requisitioned and converted into a mine sweeper. Now, almost exactly a year after the war had ended, we had it back again as a trawler...

'Oh no!' said Daniel. He had a good idea what was coming next.

'What's the matter?' said Gabriel as he looked at Daniel.

'Hush boys... let grandad continue,' Sarah-Eliza said with a look of disapproval.

Jacob thanked her and carried on telling the story.

'Well Jake... being ashore all this time has been an absolute bugger... I thought my feet were going to grow roots,' Barney said to me.

'So, I'm gonna go out with James... got to make sure the boy still knows how to fish,' he joked.

'Oh...I'm sure he does... he's one of the best we've got,' I replied. '...And, he is his father's son alright.'

'We said cheerio and Barney set off to walk from our office to board the *Nottingham Ram*...

That was the very last time that I spoke to Barney. From my office window, I could see him stood on the bridge of the *Nottingham Ram* waving to me as the vessel made its way across the fish docks and towards the lock gates. And then it was out into the river and gone...

It was last seen heading east north east towards the fishing grounds. After many worrying days without contact, the *Nottingham Ram* was posted as missing and believed sank after hitting a German mine, thirty miles east of Spurn point between the 8th and 14th November 1919... No one could be sure where and when. No remains of the crew, or any wreckage from the vessel, were ever found...

Barney, my best friend for well over fifty years, was sixty nine when he died... Blown to smithereens, just like his father had been all those years ago when Barney was just a lad...

'He should never have been on that bloody vessel at his age,' Jacob said quite vehemently.

He was now very upset and had started to sob quite strongly. The last hour, talking about William and then about Barney had been particularly difficult for him.

'The foolish, foolish man... but, then again that was Barney,' said Jacob sadly.

'No matter... I will see him, my mama, Eleanor and William again,' said Jacob. 'My time will come soon enough.'

'Stop that... that's enough of that sort of talk now father,' Sarah-Eliza said.

Jacob didn't answer her. He sat quietly weeping. The children didn't know what to do or say, so said nothing. They were shocked and surprised at what their grandad had told them. And, they were upset at seeing him upset. For a moment everyone sat in silence. Finally, Sarah-Eliza decided that was enough story-telling for one day.

'Come along children, time for bed,' Sarah Eliza said rising quickly to her feet to get the children moving.

'But mother... we haven't eaten yet,' wittered Gabriel.

'I'm starving,' said Daniel.

'Go on get up to bed and I'll bring you all a sandwich and some hot milk, you can have them in your bed,' Sarah-Eliza said to them.

The children were slow to move.

'COME ON, get a move on!' She said, starting to raise her voice.

'And some cake,' suggested Daniel.

'Yes Daniel, there'll be some cake... NOW off you go, get up those stairs.' Sarah-Eliza said. '...And, say goodnight to grandad.'

One by one, the children went over and gave their grandad a hug and a kiss before saying goodnight and leaving the room to go up to bed.

'Love you grandad,' said Grace as she gave him a big hug.

'Thank you... I love you too my little petal,' Jacob replied.

Once they'd all left the room, Sarah-Eliza said,

'Father, I want to know what's going on... you and I, are going to have a little talk once I've taken the supper up to the children.'

Jacob nodded his agreement and sighed,

'Yes dear... I think it's about time that we did.'

Jacob had stopped weeping. He slowly filled his pipe and lit it and savoured the fresh tobacco. Leaning back in his chair and looking around the room he thought this isn't going to be easy. So many good times had been had in this room in front of this fire. Children's parties, Christmas parties, birthdays, the room represented a library of happy memories from an emotional but mainly contented and fulfilled life. Soon it would all end...

It wasn't long before Sarah-Eliza returned to the room and pulled up a chair to sit closer to her father. She looked him in the eye and asked,

'What's that matter father? ...I know there's something you're not telling me.'

Sarah-Eliza took hold of his hand.

'Whatever it is... I want to help... I am your daughter and who better to help you than me,' she said, almost pleading with him.

'Yes dear... I know, and a better daughter I couldn't have wished for,' Jacob said.

He was now holding both her hands in his.

'You can't help me... in fact, my dear, nobody can.'

'Why father, why can't I or anybody help?' she asked

'Because I'm dying, my precious... I haven't got very long to live,' Jacob said as softly and gently as he could.

For a moment, Sarah-Eliza sat silent, too stunned to speak. This was not what she had expected. Then she reacted as a much loved only child would. She became nearly hysterical. Question after question tumbled out, one after the other.

'What... what do you mean you're dying... who says you are?' she asked tearfully.

'You can't be dying... you look so well.'

'How do you know father... how do you know?' she asked. Her face showed her anguish and fear. She sobbed pitifully.

'Father ...are you sure?'

'I am certain dear... When I went to London two weeks ago, you thought I'd gone to Billingsgate on business. I hadn't... I had actually gone to see two specialists in Harley Street. They both agreed with the diagnosis I've been given at my doctors and, the results from the tests I've been having at the hospital here,' Jacob said.

'I had to make absolutely certain of the diagnosis before telling you... Sarah-Eliza, I have advanced pancreatic cancer.'

'Oh no, no, no,' she wailed. 'Can't you see someone else?' she asked.

'My dear, don't you think I haven't tried... There's nothing that can be done about it,' said Jacob. '...No matter how much money you have!'

'Oh no... How long have you got father?' Sarah-Eliza asked.

'Six weeks... two months at the most, if I'm lucky,' Jacob replied.

Sarah-Eliza started to weep and wail more strongly.

'Oh Lord no, no, no,' she cried again. 'Are you in pain?'

'No...Not really... more discomfort at the moment, but the pain will certainly come... then we'll find the strength to deal with it when it does... eh!' Jacob said trying to be cheery.

Jacob slowly rose from his chair. He put his arms around her and warmly embraced his daughter. They stood in silence as Sarah-Eliza sobbed on his shoulder.

'Come on now dear,' he said softly. '...No matter how bad the news... from that moment my mama set me on the road, I've had a good and long life.'

'...Now, we have to face up to some hard facts and be ready to deal with them,' he said as he sat down again.

'This is the real reason for me telling you and the children the complete truthful story and in the manner that I have,' said Jacob.

'Sarah-Eliza, you need to listen to me... and listen to me very carefully,'

'With Barney and James gone and Daniel still only a minor... There are going to be major demands put upon you and tough decisions will have to be made... I had hoped to be around a while longer until Daniel was old enough and sensible enough to take over the running of the business...'

'That was not to be... God obviously has other ideas,' Jacob said.

'In addition to continuing the work with the Kingston Trust Fund, which you took on when your mother died two years ago... From the two families, you alone will have to run all the other businesses after I am gone... There is no one else!

I have instructed my solicitor, whom I trust completely, that you will take sole charge of the Rawlings and McHugh companies. He and others, whom I also trust, will advise and guide you, but the final decisions, will rest with you... You know about the companies and have spent enough time with me in the office to know what is expected of you... You probably know more about the businesses than you think... That is why I wanted you and, to a lesser extent Daniel, to appreciate the heartbreak and hardship on which the company has been founded... And, I wanted you both to know the values that were important to Barney and me as we made the company what it is... You will now have to effectively steer the rudder until Daniel has completed his university education and is ready to join you in running the business... Barney's children will all be fine about this.

When Barney's will was read, he made good his promise to pay back a hundred times or more, the seven shillings and three-pence I gave him that day when we were on the road to Grimsby. Other than the good living which he provided for his daughters and I have honoured ever since he died six years ago, Barney signed over all his shares and interests in Rawlings and McHugh to me... I am the sole owner of the company. And, in my will, the companies have all been left to you in trust for your children...

Our solicitor will advise you on that and the living that Barney's children will continue to receive from the company. Barney's youngest son Donal works for the business. Unfortunately, he is not the brightest of men, so will not advance any more than the general labouring job that he has now. He is a simple soul but, seems content enough with what he is doing. I need you to watch out and protect him... After all he is a McHugh... dear old Barney's boy...'

'Come on now, no more tears... I know this has come as a shock to you... but, there's nothing I can do about that.' Jacob said gently. '...We just have to get on with it.'

'Sarah – Eliza, I have complete confidence and faith in you and I will be here to help you for a few more weeks yet...You have the spirit of your grandmother Sarah in you... I expect you, and eventually Daniel, to take the company forward and that the names Rawlings and McHugh will continue to be something we can all be proud off...

My mama and daddy William, dear old Barney, Mr Kingston and me will all be watching and guiding you both in the years ahead... I know you won't let us down...'

Just eleven weeks later, in the early spring of 1926, Jacob Rawlings gently passed away in his sleep. He was seventy-three years old.